BLACK FLAG

DAVID RICCIARDI

BERKLEY
New York

BERKLEY
An imprint of Penguin Random House LLC
penguinrandomhouse.com

Copyright © 2020 by David Ricciardi
Excerpt from *Shadow Target* copyright © 2021 by David Ricciardi
Penguin Random House supports copyright. Copyright fuels creativity, encourages
diverse voices, promotes free speech, and creates a vibrant culture. Thank you for buying
an authorized edition of this book and for complying with copyright laws by not
reproducing, scanning, or distributing any part of it in any form without permission.
You are supporting writers and allowing Penguin Random House to continue to
publish books for every reader.

BERKLEY and the BERKLEY & B colophon are registered trademarks of
Penguin Random House LLC.

ISBN: 9781984804679

Berkley hardcover edition / May 2020
Berkley premium edition / February 2021

Printed in the United States of America
1 3 5 7 9 10 8 6 4 2

Cover art: *helicopter* © by Janne Vaittinen / Alamy Stock Photo
Cover design by Pete Garceau

PRAISE FOR DAVID RICCIARDI

"Ricciardi's exciting third Jake Keller thriller . . . .build[s] to a final, head-snapping twist. Ricciardi has hit his stride with this outing."
—*Publishers Weekly*

"Once again David Ricciardi will have you turning pages as fast as you can in this imaginative, well-plotted, highly-plausible riveting tale. And then with the ending he'll hit you with a surprise you never saw coming."
—*The Washington Times*

"Fast, relentless, and superbly plotted, *Black Flag* is Ricciardi at his best, and the sky is the limit for this series moving forward. Fans of Tom Clancy and Mark Greaney will especially want to give this one a go."
—The Real Book Spy

"Fans of the first two Keller novels will certainly want to read this one, and action-adventure readers who haven't yet met Jake should seize this opportunity." —*Booklist*

"Starts with a bang and then gets better and better. . . . One of the best thrillers you'll read this year."
—#1 *New York Times* bestselling author Lee Child

"[A] blazing thriller with relentless pace and impressive detail . . . that will keep readers flipping pages to the end."
—Mark Greaney, #1 *New York Times* bestselling author of *Relentless*

Berkley titles by David Ricciardi

WARNING LIGHT
ROGUE STRIKE
BLACK FLAG

To Henry and Claudia, my inspiration for the second half.

In the era of square-rigged sailing ships, a black flag was flown by pirates to warn other vessels that an attack was imminent, but mercy would be shown if the crew surrendered without a fight. However, if the target refused to comply, the pirates would then hoist a red flag. The "bloody flag," as it was known, was a signal that no mercy would be shown and no quarter would be given.

CHARACTER LIST

Badeed ("Shark Food"), Hawiye clan warlord

Cawar ("One Eye"), largest arms dealer in Africa, Isaaq clan

Clap, CIA Special Activities Center, Ground Branch team leader

Peter Clements, CIA, associate deputy director, intelligence

Farida, director of the Hawiye clinic

Gadhka Cas ("Red Beard"), boss of the Bakaara Market

Ted Graves, CIA Special Activities Center, chief

Jake Keller, CIA Special Activities Center, paramilitary operations officer

Masaska ("Snake"), disfigured Darood enforcer

Nacay ("Detestable"), son of Yaxaas

John Pickens, CIA, operations officer

Robleh, Hawiye clan elder, owner of Caafi water company

Athena Romanos, Greek shipowner (daughter)

Giánnis Romanos, Greek shipowner (father)

Steve, major, U.S. Army Special Forces

Saahid and Mahad, in INTERPOL's Global Maritime Piracy Database

Yaxaas ("Crocodile"), Darood clan warlord

IT WAS A bad week for peace on earth.

Born the scion of a Greek shipping dynasty, the young man was said to have seawater running through his veins, but he cared not for the wheeling and dealing of the industry or the megayachts and private jets that came with it. His relationship with his family was strong, but its enormous wealth brought him neither pride nor shame—it simply did not define his existence. When he graduated from high school and the time came for him to choose between college and the family business, he decided instead—as he would for the rest of his life—to chart his own course.

The young man ventured 1,400 miles northwest, to the Dutch port city of Rotterdam, where he found work as an ordinary seaman at a competing line. He signed on under an alias—eager to prove to himself that he had earned his position—and was soon scraping paint, cleaning heads, and scrubbing decks. He worked hard, learned quickly, and moved rapidly through the ranks on everything from

150-foot tramp freighters to 1,200-foot oil tankers. Soon there wasn't a crewman's job aboard any ship, anywhere, that he couldn't handle.

So he left the industry.

But he wasn't finished.

He was just getting started.

The young man moved to Belgium and attended maritime college, where he spent four years studying navigation, load handling, and engineering before returning to the sea as a ship's officer.

Strikingly handsome, with a square jaw and wavy dark hair, his resemblance to his father grew as he aged until, by his late twenties, even strangers would comment on the similarity. Once he'd attained the rank of ship's master, he resumed using the family name. No one he'd served with would dispute that he knew his ships and the sea as well as anyone who'd ever commanded a merchant vessel.

In short order he was hired by the largest shipping company in the world to drive supertankers across the seas, taking 1,400-foot-long behemoths through storms that would frighten a statue and across oceans so vast that the crew would often go days without sighting another ship.

But as the years passed and the ships became more automated, the crews became smaller and satellite telemetry made him feel less like a master and commander and more like a bus driver. By the time he was in his late thirties, he'd moved back to his family's shipping line, where he could once again manage the voyage and not simply optimize fuel consumption based on computer models and satellite predictions of weather and current.

WITH ASIA TO his north and Africa to his south, Captain Romanos was at the helm of the 860-foot M/V *Lindos* as it steamed east through the turquoise waters of the Gulf of Aden.

Sixty feet wide and with walls of glass, the oil tanker's bridge offered a spectacular 360-degree view of the world as the sun fell through scattered clouds and disappeared below the horizon. The ship's officers watched the sky and sea meld into blackness, interrupted only by the stars above and their reflections on the water below. Though they'd seen it happen a thousand times before, its mystical beauty never failed to reinforce their calling to the sea.

It was five past midnight when the captain prepared to retire to his stateroom and turn the bridge over to his second-in-command. Romanos was halfway to the door when the navigator spoke up.

"I've never seen that before," he said, mostly to himself.

The captain stopped short.

The navigator and most of the other officers had come with him from the larger shipping company where they'd worked together for nearly a decade. They'd become like brothers, spending more time with one another than they did with their own families, and they'd learned to trust one another's judgment and anticipate one another's thoughts. Together they'd survived typhoons, been boarded by unfriendly navies, and had more barroom fistfights than anyone could count.

As far as the captain was concerned, the navigator had seen everything.

Romanos turned around.

"All three radars are full of static," said the navigator. "Lost the GPS too."

"Radio?" said the captain, nodding toward the single-sideband.

The communications officer turned up the volume.

"Nothing but noise. Same with the VHF."

The captain looked at the chief engineer. "It could be electrical interference, but—"

The doors on both sides of the bridge burst open.

Six men in black and gray uniforms stormed in, three on each side, with rifles snugged in tight against their shoulders.

For as long as anyone could remember, ships' crews had been instructed to cooperate when boarded. They would be threatened, they might even be abused, but their value as hostages decreased by 100 percent if they were dead. It had been the same with the airlines. Pilots had been told to appease hijackers because most were looking only to make political statements or maybe catch a ride to a forbidden destination. More often than not, all of the hostages were released safe and sound.

Cooperate and live. It had worked for most of modern history.

But piracy was experiencing its 9/11 moment.

The captain faced the gunman closest to him. The tall

man's blue eyes locked on like a hawk tracking its prey, but the captain stared right back.

"What do you—"

The pirate fired three rounds into his heart.

Captain Romanos was dead before he hit the ground.

TWO DAYS LATER, and a thousand miles to the north, a security guard met three trucks covered in dust from their long journey through the desert. The guard escorted the small convoy through the seaport's high-security gate to a darkened warehouse and parked outside by the door while the trucks drove inside.

A lieutenant colonel from Iran's Revolutionary Guards stepped down from the lead vehicle and began issuing orders to the forklift operator who'd been collecting overtime for the past four hours, waiting for the trucks to arrive. The lift operator had just finished unloading a dozen crates of rifles and rocket-propelled grenades from the first truck and was on his way to the second truck when two soldiers grabbed the warehouse's metal doors and slid them shut in the security guard's face.

Four soldiers climbed into the truck bed. Though it was midsummer in the Persian Gulf, the men shivered as they raised the plastic case by its handles. Roughly the size of a footlocker, the case wasn't heavy, but the men moved it slowly and deliberately as they lowered it from the truck and placed it inside a slightly larger wooden crate.

Another soldier packed the empty space with blocks of dry ice and placed the wooden lid on top. A bead of sweat formed on his brow as the colonel handed him a hammer and a dozen nails. The soldier had seen the biohazard symbols painted on the plastic container and had no desire to disturb whatever was inside, but the colonel's stare was unyielding. The soldier carefully aligned the hammer and tapped each nail into place with the minimum amount of force required to complete the task.

An hour after they'd arrived, the three trucks emerged from the warehouse and were escorted back to the main gate by the guard who'd been waiting outside. The entire operation had been shrouded in secrecy, from the civilian trucks to the late hour, and the guard's name had been deleted from the roster—with explicit instructions from his supervisor to forget everything he'd seen.

The guard turned in the keys for his pickup and went to the employee locker room to change out of his uniform. He sat on a worn wooden bench and rubbed his eyes. It had been a long day and his shift was finally over. But he still had a phone call to make before his work was finished.

ONE

SIX MONTHS LATER . . .

JAKE KELLER FELT the blade of the machete against his throat.

The Somalis had gotten the jump on them.

"We're with the United Nations," Jake said in English. "We're here to help."

"You want to help? You give us money," said Dameer. The nickname meant "donkey," and he bared his teeth as he burst out laughing. His henchmen laughed too, as if he'd said the funniest thing they'd ever heard.

Dameer slammed his fist down on the table and the laughter stopped. His eyes were bulging and bloodshot.

"Pay us!"

He folded his arms across his chest while two of his cohorts brandished AK-47s. They were even more doped up than their leader.

"We just want to talk," Jake said calmly. He'd been in worse spots before.

The Middle East, Europe, North Africa. Trouble had followed Jake like a hungry dog for the last two years—ever since he'd gone into the field for CIA.

"No money, no talk," said Dameer.

Jake could smell the rancid breath of the man holding the knife to his throat.

"Maybe we take you hostage," Dameer said. "Then UN pay us!"

He put his hands on the table. He was missing two fingers on his left hand. They looked as if they'd been cauterized with a rusty piece of iron. Punishment for something, no doubt.

"We'll pay for protection," said Pickens. "We just need to know who we're paying."

Dameer glared at him. Though Pickens was black, he looked nothing like the wiry Somalis. He'd been an outside linebacker at Northwestern University before joining the Agency. Beads of sweat glistened on his thick biceps and shaved head. He was built like an oak tree.

"Money, now!" Dameer shouted, slamming his fist against the table.

Pickens retrieved four fifty-dollar bills from his pocket and placed them on the table. Each one was a month's wages for an honest Somali.

But there wasn't an honest Somali in sight.

Dameer scooped up the cash and stuffed it in his pocket.

"More money, *gaal*." It meant "infidel" in Somali, but the locals used it for any foreigner.

"There will be a lot of money," Jake said, "once we talk to your boss."

"You pay me," said Dameer. "Then you go to Kitadra."

It was the pirate capital of the world.

With no prospects on land, young Somali men with nothing to lose had taken to the sea to kidnap their way to riches, but aggressive countermeasures by ships' crews and the world's navies ensured that by 2015, the era of the Somali pirates was dead.

But it had made a comeback.

A new type of piracy had emerged in the last six months, and it was far more profitable and far more lethal than the old one. With each attack, twenty men disappeared and twenty million dollars' worth of stolen cargo vanished— neither the crew nor the ships were ever seen again.

And it was a lot of money—enough to exert enormous influence over the broken nation of Somalia. It backed private armies and bribed corrupt politicians. It supported terrorism and funded human trafficking. For the country's citizens, it meant a lifetime of living in fear: extortion, rape, murder.

The new wave of piracy was about to put the struggling country down for good.

And Jake and Pickens had been ordered to stop it.

"Who do you work for?" Jake asked.

Dameer said something in Arabic to his accomplices.

Jake didn't know the Somali dialect well, but he understood enough of what Dameer had said to know what was coming next.

And it wasn't good.

Pickens spoke Arabic and Somali, but he stuck to English around the locals. He learned a lot more when they thought he didn't understand.

Like now.

It was going to be four-on-two. Dameer and the man with the machete, plus the two men with the Kalashnikovs, but they were so doped up that they probably couldn't hit the air in front of them. The biggest risk from those idiots was a ricochet.

But it was a real risk.

The small room was made of concrete with a corrugated steel roof. Each bullet would have a couple of chances to find a target and if the gunmen went full Somali-style— rifle held at the waist and trigger held down until the gun was empty—there was a better-than-even chance that no one on either side would walk out alive.

The two Americans made eye contact. Pickens nodded almost imperceptibly.

Jake snapped his head back, shattering the nose of the man with the machete, then grabbed the hand with the knife and pushed the blade away.

The man staggered backward with tears in his eyes and blood streaming down his face.

Jake turned and punched him in the throat, then kneed him in the groin. The Somali crumpled to the ground, out of the fight.

Dameer stepped out from behind the table and squared off against Pickens. The Somali was tall and lanky, with a sweat-stained shirt, crazy eyes, and a knife of his own. It was rusty and dull, except for the edge, which was shiny and sharp.

Pickens brought his forearms up to protect his face and chest, like a boxer.

Old school.

The Somali waved the knife back and forth like he was trying to sell it. He took half a step forward.

Pickens faked right, then rotated his two-hundred-forty-pound body and launched a left into Dameer's face. The blow lifted the man off his feet and hurled him into the back wall.

His sandals were still on the floor where he'd been standing.

It was a hell of a punch.

But the goons with the AK-47s had finally discovered that something was amiss. They were shouting and yelling and gesturing wildly—and pointing their rifles at Pickens.

TWO

THE TWO MEN with the Kalashnikovs were shaking.
It might have been from the drugs, or maybe
they were nervous, but Jake wasn't looking to make
a diagnosis.

He was trying to keep his partner alive.

"Drop the weapons!" he shouted.

He had a 9mm pistol up and was shifting his aim between the two gunmen, making sure they each had a chance to look straight into the muzzle before he switched targets.

They could shoot Pickens, but it would cost them their lives.

It should have been an easy decision, even in a drug-induced haze, but the gunmen didn't react.

Jake yelled again, this time in Arabic, and the men literally dropped their rifles onto the concrete floor.

Pickens scooped up the weapons and the two Americans backed through the door to a beige Daihatsu hatchback—a car so generic that it was like a third-world cloak of invisibility. With Pickens behind the wheel, they quickly disappeared into the low-rise streets of Mogadishu. Voted "the most dangerous city in the world" for twenty years running, it was a place where machine gunfire punctuated conversations and truck bombs ended them.

Though the thugs who'd tried to ambush them probably couldn't walk a straight line, much less tail them through city streets, the two CIA officers didn't take any chances. Pickens drove a full surveillance detection route over the narrow roads. The routes were designed not only to spot a tail but to do so without making it obvious, because acting like a trained intelligence operative was the surest way to confirm that someone was a trained intelligence operative.

Pickens spotted an accident blocking the road ahead and turned down a narrow side street to avoid a potential ambush. Lined on both sides with crumbling stucco buildings, it was impossible to tell where the blown sand ended and the cracked pavement began. He steered carefully around a man sleeping in the shade of a parked car and back onto a larger road where the two men could relax— somewhat.

"I've never seen a man knocked out of his shoes before," Jake said.

Pickens grinned.

"The key," he said, "is to rotate your hips and follow through on the swing."

Jake checked the side-view mirror. "Too bad those idiots didn't know anything."

It was the third meeting they'd had in the four days since Jake had arrived, and each one had nearly cost him his life.

"We've got to start somewhere," said Pickens.

John Pickens had been with the Agency for twenty years and working the Mogadishu account for the last eight. It was a medium-sized CIA station, but most of his fellow officers in the Directorate of Operations were working with their counterparts in the Somali National Intelligence and Security Agency or deployed in Counterterrorism Center teams. The CTC pursuit teams were the sexier side of CIA and, for the past twenty years, counterterrorism had been the fast track to advancement.

Pickens was in a career backwater.

"Everyone knows you're understaffed here, John, but this is a new threat and we need a new response. Seven tankers have disappeared without a single distress call or ransom demand."

Pickens snaked around the site of a recent IED attack. Two days prior, al-Shabaab terrorists had daisy-chained together half a dozen 122mm Russian artillery shells and detonated them in the back of a delivery truck. One hundred forty-six people had died. The air still smelled of diesel fuel and gunpowder, burnt plastic and seared flesh. An African Union soldier was in the blast pit, searching the twisted chassis for a vehicle identification number while children played nearby on piles of concrete rubble that had been their homes just forty-eight hours earlier.

"I told Ted this should be a joint op with the FBI," Jake said, "and he told me to shut up and find out who's in charge of the pirates."

"Is that what Black Flag is about?" Pickens looked over. "Is Graves looking to put people in the ground?"

Ted Graves was chief of the Agency's Special Activities Center. The paramilitary officers under his command operated in the field with little oversight and were known for using their considerable autonomy wisely and ethically.

The same could not be said for their boss.

"Phase one is to identify who's behind it," Jake said. "I'm guessing phase two is rolling him up, but Ted hasn't shared his long-term strategy with me."

Pickens laughed and fist-bumped his new partner. "With you or with anyone, brother. I'm just trying to figure out why the Seventh Floor brass suddenly care. Piracy has been a way of life down here for twenty years."

"It's about oil."

Pickens shrugged. "Always is."

"But not the way it used to be," Jake said. "Now that the U.S. isn't importing as much from the Middle East, we're reducing the military presence we've had there for the past fifty years."

"The 'Pivot to Asia'?"

"Exactly. Our forces are moving east to deal with national and regional threats, but whoever is stealing these oil tankers is clearing close to twenty million dollars each time they sell the cargo on the black market. That kind of money can fund terror networks and weapons of mass destruction."

Pickens turned down a side street. "Then why aren't the pirates ransoming the crews? That's where they used to make their money."

"Anonymity," Jake said. "Headquarters doesn't have a clue who is behind this: not an email, not a text message, nothing. You start making ransom demands and you leave a trail. Whoever is behind the hijackings understands operational security. This isn't six-skinnies-in-a-skiff anymore. We're up against professionals with training and resources, probably ex-military."

Pickens scowled. "I don't know, Jake. We take out this pirate and somebody will take his place before the body is cold. There's no rule of law down here. People have gotten used to taking what they can today because they might not be alive tomorrow."

"Economic opportunity is the long-term solution, but that's never going to happen unless we find the pirate leader and put him out of business."

The two men were stopped behind a line of cars and Pickens was tapping his hand against the steering wheel. Jake couldn't tell if the anxiety was from the traffic, the narrow escape, or something else.

"I'm on board with the mission," said Pickens eventually, "because that's my job, but Somalia is a lost cause."

THREE

JAKE AND PICKENS drove past Villa Somalia. Built by Italian colonialists, the whitewashed Art Deco building was the official residence of the Somali president, but with the country embroiled in a civil war since 1991, the villa changed tenants like a hot-sheet motel. The current government had been in place for less than a year, and though it didn't control much territory outside Mogadishu, the new president took his personal security very seriously. He'd paid a lot of bribes and made a great many promises to secure his election, and he wasn't going to waste the opportunity to grow rich off it. Armored personnel carriers staked out the compound's corners and drop-down Delta barriers blocked the entrance.

Just a week earlier, the surrounding neighborhood had been evacuated and sealed when security forces were alerted to a smoking vehicle on a nearby street. A military demolition team had examined the stolen delivery truck and found it packed with thousands of pounds of home-made explosives—and a faulty detonator. Traffic in the neighborhood had been frozen for the better part of a day while the bomb was defused.

Four blocks east of Villa Somalia was the safe house Pickens had been using for the past twenty-six months. It was close enough to the villa to benefit from the additional security but far enough away that it wouldn't become bug-splat the next time someone tried to kill the president.

Like many private homes in the area, the quarter-acre property was surrounded by a high concrete wall. The small house had a pale yellow exterior and a red roof. Aside from a few pockmarks from a decade-old mortar attack, it would have looked at home anywhere in the tropics.

Pickens opened the sliding steel gate with a remote control. He kept a variety of cars, trucks, and motorbikes on the property. They were rotated often, swept regularly for tracking devices, and rented through shell corporations set up by the Agency—with the collision-damage waivers fully paid up.

Jake and Pickens walked across the small courtyard under a cloudless blue sky that had dropped less than an inch of rain on the country in the last two years. The two men entered the house and spent an hour reviewing what had gone right, and what had gone wrong, during their meeting with Dameer. They'd had several similar encounters and were still no closer to identifying who was behind the resurgence of piracy.

Jake had just suggested a change in strategy when the buzzer rang for the front gate. A live video feed popped up on Pickens's cell phone of a lone man standing on the street. Lean, relaxed, with a medium-brown complexion and an untucked shirt, he looked like half the men in Somalia.

Pickens buzzed him through the gate and led him through the front door.

"I'm Steve," he said as he shook hands with Jake.

"Steve is a major in Army Special Forces," said Pickens. "His team is here killing terrorists."

"Our mission," Steve clarified, "is to improve border security, allow the rule of law to take hold, and give the democratically elected Somali National Government a chance to save the country."

"That's a tall order," Jake said. "How are you going about it?"

"By killing terrorists," Steve deadpanned. "Over the past six months we've started using their tactics against them: disruptive attacks, destroying their infrastructure, and killing high- and low-value targets to show them that no one is safe. It's already hurting operations and recruitment."

The three men stood in the small kitchen as Steve opened a manila folder and spread half a dozen photos across the counter. The images were from various U.S. manned and unmanned intelligence, surveillance, and reconnaissance assets that routinely overflew much of the country. CIA may have been the nation's lead intelligence gathering agency, but the U.S. military had exponentially more assets in the Horn of Africa.

"Six days ago," Steve said, "the Port of Kismaayo was hit with staggered, vehicle-borne IEDs, followed by mortars and heavy machine gunfire. The Air Force deployed a

U-28 surveillance aircraft on an overhead collection mission after the attack and spotted this three-vehicle convoy just north of the city." He pointed to an ultra-high-resolution image of an anchor and crossed rifles on the side of one of the trucks. "These are four-ton Leyland trucks, clearly marked as Kenya Defence Forces, but we talked to the KDF after the fact and they didn't have any assets in the area."

"Where did the trucks go?" Pickens asked.

"We don't know," Steve said. "The U-28 saw the KDF markings and moved on. We dialed up a couple Predators once we realized the trucks were fakes, but the aircraft didn't find anything noteworthy except two facilities along the Jubba River: one outside the town of Jilib, and one in Dujuma."

He pointed to two images on the counter.

"Either of those mean anything to you?" he asked Pickens.

The CIA officer studied the photographs. He might have been stuck in a dead-end job, but his eight years in-country had made him a go-to resource for many of the U.S. agencies and military units that were operating in Somalia.

"The place outside Jilib used to be a commercial farm," Pickens said, "but the Jubba River is fed by rainfall from the Mendebo Mountains, and they haven't seen so much as a drop in two years. The river dried up and that region turned to dust. I'm guessing the place near Dujuma was a livestock ranch, but those animals are long-since dead and the ranch is probably abandoned."

"Well, that's fan-fucking-tastic," said Steve. "We'll keep looking, but keep your ear to the ground. We've picked up some chatter that one of the warlords is running a camp somewhere out there, but we haven't been able to locate it."

"Do the warlords operate in the open?" Jake asked.

"Like they own the place," said Pickens. "They have motorcades and regular tables at the local restaurants. They provide security and dispense justice. The government here is so corrupt that the warlords have taken over the job."

"But you wouldn't confuse them with civil servants," Steve said as he walked to the door. "They're the most ruthless men you'll ever encounter. They fund terrorists, bribe politicians, and use private militias to extort and control the population. Fortunately, they've been keeping one another in check through a constant war of attrition. The real disaster for the Somali people would be if one of the warlords was able to take out his competition—then the whole country would collapse into a dictatorship."

FOUR

THE HORN OF Africa.

For more than a millennium, its two thousand miles of coastline had attracted Roman, Chinese, and Indian merchants and turned it into a vibrant hub on the Silk Road trading route. Yet it wasn't until a heavy Arab migration in the seventh century AD that Somalia would acquire the culture that would define it for the next 1,400 years. The country had taken its name from Samaale, an émigré from the Arabian Peninsula, and 95 percent of its population belonged to one of the six clans descended from him and his brother.

The nation became a successful blend of traditional clan and moderate Islamic values, but like Yemen to its north, Somalia's strategic location and vibrant food and livestock production attracted unwanted outside attention. European and African nations competed for control of the area for hundreds of years, using military force to impose their will on the Somali people—until the middle of the twentieth century, when the foreigners abandoned their empire-building and left the Horn.

What should have been a golden opportunity swiftly turned into a disaster. The Somali people were finally free, but with an ineffective government and an economy in shambles, their nation was in a state of crisis. The former colonial powers continued to harvest the rich fishing grounds off the nation's coast with commercial fishing boats while the Somalis could barely put to sea a fleet of small skiffs with handmade nets. The balance of the country's citizens were agro-pastoralists—raising crops and livestock—and barely eking out a sustenance living because of years of dry weather.

In this land of strong clans and weak government, the tattered economy created a power vacuum that attracted those with the might to impose their will. It was a pattern that would repeat itself many times over in the nation's tragic history—most notably in 1969, when General Siad Barre declared himself president in a coup. He ruled with brute force, marginalizing the clans until he too was eventually overthrown in 1991.

The country fell into civil war.

There was no law, no order, no government services.

Foreign governments sent peacekeeping forces but most of those left after a few years, judging the mission to not be worth the cost. Between 300,000 and 500,000 Somalis died. Over a million lost their homes and livelihoods.

The clans resumed their roles as the primary administrative authorities in Somalia, enforcing justice, brokering deals, and taxing the population. Many clan leaders grew corrupt, using their clan's cash flow to amass personal fortunes. Soon they were building armies and fighting one another.

They'd become warlords.

Nothing was off-limits in their quest for money and power: extortion, drug smuggling, human trafficking. The civilian population of Somalia was caught in the middle of the warlords' frequent conflicts and routinely subject to brutality and deprivation.

The warlords fought in the streets of Mogadishu, and they fought in the countryside. The constant battles came at an enormous cost to the population. Those lacking the ruthlessness necessary to gain and retain power were eventually killed or relegated to administrative positions within their own clans.

It was a power struggle that raged for decades, claiming victim after victim, until the struggle to be the next dictator of Somalia had come down to two men.

THE ONE THEY called Badeed had been one of the earliest Somali pirates.

Hungry and made homeless by the civil war, he'd been thirteen years old when he rowed out to a pleasure yacht anchored off the beach. He climbed aboard at night, while the British couple who owned it were asleep, and robbed them in their berth at knifepoint—relieving them of three hundred pounds, a few radios, and a Swiss watch. By the time he hauled his boat back onto the beach, the victims had already raised anchor and begun to sail away.

It was a seminal moment for the young boy.

There would be no consequences.

He sold the swag and used the proceeds to buy an old pistol and a smoky outboard engine. He gathered friends and robbed more boats. The group soon acquired rifles and began boarding commercial ships. When the ships stopped anchoring near land, Badeed bought a second engine, slightly larger than the first, for his eighteen-foot wooden skiff. Soon he was attacking targets that were fifteen miles offshore and under way, steering the mismatched outboards by their tiller handles while his cohorts fired Kalashnikovs at the ships' crews until they stopped their vessels.

It was during the eighth of these offshore boardings that he'd acquired his nickname. Most Somali men had them—unflattering monikers that highlighted some unfortunate physical characteristic. He'd been scrambling up a wooden extension ladder, halfway up the side of a ship with a rifle slung over his shoulder, when a wave rolled under the skiff and knocked the ladder out from under him.

He wasn't in the water more than a minute when a shortfin mako shark took a bite out of his leg.

From then on, he was known as *Libaax Badeed baa Cunay*. It meant "The One the Shark Has Eaten," but everyone called him Badeed.

Though the attack left him forever scarred and with a limp, its timing was fortuitous. Badeed used his convalescent time to think about his business, and he quickly realized that the five to ten thousand dollars that he was making from stealing portable electronics and the crews' personal possessions were never going to make him rich. He started running his pirate gang from shore, using the proceeds from each mission to fund three more.

Soon his crews were launching high-speed skiffs from eighty-foot motherships and using rocket-propelled grenades to attack armed and fast-moving ships. But Badeed's teams were no longer robbing the ships' crews; the pirates were bringing them back to shore, to his hometown of Kitadra, a Hawiye clan stronghold.

With white sand beaches, turquoise waters, and palm trees overhanging the ocean, the tropical beach community would have made a popular port of call for cruise ships, but the men Badeed brought to Kitadra were far from tourists. They were hostages. Ransom payments were demanded from shipowners, insurance companies, family members, and anyone else who had an interest in the survival of the captives. Some of the men were held for weeks and some were held for years. Many died waiting for money that never came.

But it made Badeed a millionaire many times over.

He became chief elder of the Hawiye clan.

And he raised an army.

With the unemployment rate in Somalia above 50 percent, thousands of Hawiye clansmen joined up for little more than a meal, a gun, and a mat on which to sleep. From former military officers to boys too young to shave, Badeed's fighting force took shape. He struck at the hearts of his rivals, quickly defeating all of the other warlords.

Except one.

* * *

LIKE MOST SOMALIS, Yaxaas was tall and lean, and his shoes were covered with dust from the dirt streets, but unlike most Somalis, his shoes were made from crocodile skin, and he owned the streets.

His father had been a high official in Siad Barre's regime but had resisted Barre's growing embrace of Islamic socialism. He didn't approve of the socialists' flawed economic policies, their fundamentalist religious beliefs, or their overbearing Soviet masters.

He was executed soon after they took power.

On the day he learned of his father's death, the boy's mother revealed that his former nanny, a Bantu slave girl who'd been sold to his grandfather many years earlier, was his natural mother. The boy was cast out—no longer welcome in the family home.

He was nine years old.

The filthy alleys of Mogadishu were far from the socialist workers' paradise envisioned by Barre, and the boy was soon reduced to fighting stray dogs for scraps of fetid garbage.

He'd been living on the streets for three years when a Darood warlord known as Madowbe saw him wrestle a snarling mongrel to the ground and snatch a discarded chicken carcass from its mouth. Madowbe stopped his Cadillac sedan and his two bodyguards hauled the boy into the back seat. The warlord took one look at the boy's chipped and crooked teeth, and from that day forward, he was known as *Yaxaas*.

It meant "crocodile."

The warlord's men spent a year training the boy to be an enforcer. He was sent to a jungle camp where he learned to fight and to kill. He learned well. Using his bare hands to end a man's life elicited no more emotion from the thirteen-year-old than changing his shirt.

The warlord realized that the boy's mind was even tougher and more capable than his body. Yaxaas was given a job collecting protection money from local businesses. His production was exceptional. Shopkeepers and restaurateurs who'd resisted for years quickly submitted—or they found their loved ones kidnapped, tortured, and eventually killed.

Yaxaas climbed swiftly up the clan hierarchy. He spent several years bribing public officials, extorting foreign aid workers, and leading the clan militia. It was a productive and profitable time for the young man. He'd found his calling in the warlord's organization.

Until the warlord got in his way.

Madowbe had sensed the younger man's ambition and worked to keep his protégé in check, but in a quiet moment alone, Yaxaas beat his mentor with his fists and didn't stop until long past the moment of death, until the warlord's face was unrecognizable.

And Yaxaas became the new Darood warlord.

He gained power and wealth rapidly, and though he'd always resented his nickname, he made it his own. He bought crocodile shoes, crocodile belts, and even a pair of crocodile-skin cowboy boots.

Six years later, he bought a real crocodile.

Fourteen feet long and eleven hundred pounds, with skin like cobblestones and teeth like icicles, the Nile was the largest species of freshwater croc in the world—an apex predator.

And Yaxaas kept it outside his office.

The warlord's compound filled an entire block in the Yaaqshiid District in eastern Mogadishu and he'd acquired it several years earlier when a missile launched at Ethiopian peacekeepers had slammed into the residential area. The blast destroyed several small homes, killing six and wounding eleven more. Yaxaas evicted the survivors and had the land bulldozed.

From the outside, the cinder-block building looked like a warehouse that one might find in any urban area: surrounded by a high perimeter wall topped with barbed wire, a sturdy steel gate, and several vehicles. But the large courtyard in the center of the square building looked as if it belonged in a Mediterranean palazzo. It held a lush garden with a pond, a dozen different species of ferns, hundreds of Giant Protea flowers.

And the crocodile.

Little Yaxaas.

FIVE

THOUGH IT WAS small by Western standards, Pickens's CIA safe house was luxurious for Mogadishu. It had two bedrooms with air conditioning units built into the wall, a combined kitchen and family room, tiled floors, and working plumbing. But as it was in most buildings with concrete walls, cellular coverage inside the safe house was terrible, and Pickens had gone outside to make a call on his mobile phone.

Jake was sitting on his bed. He'd just finished typing a cable to headquarters on his laptop and was looking forward to indulging in one of the house's greatest luxuries—a shower just after the water truck had just made its weekly delivery.

Between the drought and the civil war, most of the city had no public water supply. The only way for homes to get fresh water was by delivery—usually from a truck, but nearly as often from a donkey cart with a plastic tank on it. But in either case, home delivery was expensive, and most of the city's poorer residents were forced to carry water by hand from neighborhood wells.

Jake's first few days in-country had been so hectic that

he'd been living out of his duffel bag and washed little more than his face. A real shower with real water pressure had passed the point of luxury and now become a necessity. He hauled his duffel out of the closet and accidentally dragged away a brightly colored woven mat that had been covering the closet floor.

Underneath it was a trapdoor.

Jake tugged at the recessed handle, but it didn't budge.

"I wouldn't do that if I were you." Pickens was standing behind him.

"Didn't mean to pry, just curious."

"You'd be a lousy field officer if you weren't."

Pickens moved some clothes out of the way to reveal a digital keypad. He entered an eight-digit code.

"Try it now," he said.

Jake lifted the trapdoor easily. Below it was a stairway.

"You're not cleared for this," Pickens said, "but we're partners now, so no secrets."

The two men had saved each other's lives—it had forged a bond.

Pickens fist-bumped Jake and flipped a light switch at the bottom of the stairs.

"Holy shit," Jake muttered.

"The program serves a dual purpose," Pickens said. "It takes this stuff off the streets and redistributes most of it to our African partners in the war on terror."

Jake walked farther into the cavernous room. Stacked floor-to-ceiling were wooden crates and plastic containers with identifying marks stenciled on their sides: rifles, pistols, ammunition. He looked to the right and spotted the raw materials for IEDs: crates of explosives and artillery shells. He looked to the left: RPGs, Russian land mines, and large, olive green crates with Chinese characters on them.

"Are those—"

"FN-6 shoulder-fired missiles," said Pickens. "Designed to target low-flying aircraft. The Chinese sold them to the Saudis, who gave them to the Syrian rebels, who sold them in North Africa to generate some cash. Over here are a couple of crates of PE8—British plastic explosives—that just showed up one day at a shop in Mogadishu. It's serious stuff, and I'd never seen it in the Horn of Africa, so I bought every last block."

Pickens opened the top crate, revealing dozens of two-kilogram packs.

"Like I said, I buy some of it just to take it out of circulation. Once it ends up on the dark web or in the crypto-bazaars, we lose it forever."

"How long have you been at this?"

Pickens laughed. "Since the CIA was called the OSS."

Jake wandered through the basement in amazement. "Did you always dream of being an arms dealer?"

"The only arms I dealt were these." Pickens flexed his biceps. "I wanted to play in the NFL."

He was quiet for a few seconds. His lighthearted mood disappeared.

"And I did it . . . I walked onto the New York Jets after college, added another twenty pounds of muscle, and suited up for the kickoff return in the first game of the season. Tore my hamstring halfway down the field and got cut that night. My pro football career lasted one play."

"Sorry, John. That must have been tough."

"It was a good lesson. My parents raised me to believe that if I worked hard enough, I could have anything I wanted, but that's not how life works."

"Not always, but you're serving your country, helping to stop a civil war, and keeping weapons out of the hands of warlords. That's a job worth doing."

"Maybe, but it doesn't pay much, and my wife divorced me when I skipped my first rotation back to the States. Now I see my kids three or four days a year. The job has cost me a lot."

Jake understood the sacrifice better than most. Born Zac Miller, he'd been chased across two continents, shot, and nearly killed on his first field mission for the Agency. The political fallout had forced him to fake his death, change his name, and abandon the only woman he'd ever loved.

And it got worse from there.

He derived a great deal of satisfaction from what he did—the mission to protect those who couldn't protect themselves was what drove him forward when it would have been so easy to quit—but the toll on his mind and body was enormous.

Only a handful of people knew the real story, and Pickens wasn't cleared for any of it.

"Sorry, brother," said Jake.

"I'm cool with it, but I've learned that you've got to do what you can, when you can, because you never know when your time is up."

Jake examined a crate of AK-47s lying open against the wall. On the side was stenciled *SO XDS*.

"What does that mean?" he said.

"Somali Army issue. Somebody raided an armory outside town, sold them to a dealer, and the next day you could buy one in the Bakaara Market for seven hundred bucks. That's the scale of the problem we're dealing with down here. Someone literally stole the army's guns."

Jake kept walking. Along the back wall was a bench press, a gun safe, and a concrete ramp to a set of Bilco doors that had to be opened from the inside.

"And all you have protecting this is that trapdoor in my closet?" Jake asked.

Pickens gestured to the ceiling. Evenly spaced around the room were two dozen blocks of C4 plastic explosive that were connected by bundles of explosive detonating cord that ran to an alarm panel.

"You wire that yourself?" Jake asked.

"With a safe-separation timer, a collapsible circuit, and everything." Pickens grinned. "I've become something of an expert in the field."

"It would turn this place into a volcano."

Pickens nodded. "If you hear the alarm, it's probably too late."

"Do the sellers of all this stuff know you're Agency?"

"Hell no." Pickens laughed. "And I'll be doing this long after you're gone, so I'll need to maintain cover while you're here. I won't be able to go to every meeting with you."

Jake nodded as he walked around the basement. "I just can't get my head around all the weapons," he said. "How many arms dealers are there in Somalia?"

"Too many to count," said Pickens, "but most of the serious stuff is handled by a dude named Cawar."

SIX

THE NICKNAME MEANT "one eye."

He'd lost the other one to an American bullet during the Battle of Mogadishu in 1993, but unlike most men who'd lost an eye, Cawar didn't wear a patch or dark glasses.

It was just sewn shut.

And by the looks of it, by someone with no prior experience in the field.

HE'D GOTTEN HIS start soon after the Barre regime was deposed and Somalia fell into civil war. Frustrated with the near-anarchy, conservative Muslim elements in the southern part of the country had formed what came to be known as the Islamic Courts Union. Its original goal had been relatively narrow in scope—to provide a judicial system that transcended the clans, in this case, a system based on Islamic sharia law.

But like most bureaucracies, the ICU continually sought

to expand its mandate and soon attempted to regulate all aspects of Somali life, by force, if necessary. By 2006, the ICU controlled most of the country from the southern border with Kenya up to the capital city of Mogadishu.

What passed for a government at the time and its Ethiopian allies advanced on the city, but Somalia was already in a massive humanitarian crisis, and retaking Mogadishu would have been costly in treasure and in lives. The government forces feared that an invasion would turn the city's densely packed streets into rivers of blood.

So they laid siege to it.

Overextended across the country, weakened by a string of defeats, and facing a patient foe, the ICU appealed to the nation's clan leaders to broker a deal. The clans whose power had once offended the Union now became its only salvation. The ICU sheiks approached Cawar—already a respected elder of the powerful Isaaq clan—and negotiated the surrender of the ICU's armored vehicles, small arms, and heavy weapons. It was a massive collection of armaments, enough to deter two national armies from invading the capital city, but the clan took control of the weapons without incident. The ICU sheiks resigned their positions, the fighters melted into the population, and the government troops retook the city.

And Cawar became the largest arms dealer in Africa.

Government officials, Islamic radicals, other clan leaders, and the nation's warlords all sought his support, but Cawar remained steadfastly neutral. He sold weapons and ammunition to anyone who could pay, never tipping the scales too far to one side lest the conflict come to an end. War wasn't just good for business. It was his business.

Cawar reinvested the proceeds from his initial windfall and cultivated fresh sources of new weapons from black markets on three continents. He became immensely rich, but worked out of a dingy warehouse in the northern Shi-bis district halfway between the Damanyo government military camp and the local soccer stadium. It was outside his traditional clan stronghold in the Hodan district, and surrounded by squalid private homes, a truck dealership, and the Islamic University.

But Cawar had chosen the location carefully, intent to show that he was a friend to the government, the people, the warlords, and the religious.

An equal-opportunity merchant of death.

SEVEN

THE MAN WAS on his knees, pleading for his life.

They always did.

It was pathetic.

The forty-six-foot fishing boat rolled a few degrees as a small swell passed underneath her. The calm winds and a cloudless blue sky would have been ideal weather had it not been the same, every day, for the past two years. The sun had been relentless: scorching fields, killing livestock, and starving the population.

It was the same offshore.

Hot, still, oppressive.

It was time to finish this thing.

"Two things can drown you," Badeed said to his captive, quoting an old Somali proverb, "too many enemies and too much water. Unfortunately for you, you have both."

The warlord nodded to his henchmen.

One of them kicked the prisoner in the back, sending him face-first onto the deck, and bound his wrists behind his back. The man was in tears, explaining that he had a family, that he would come up with the money, if only the warlord would let him live.

But the time for that had passed.

One of the crew rolled an empty fifty-five-gallon drum across the deck and poked a few holes in it with a screwdriver and a hammer, although the barrel was so old and rusty that he hardly needed the hammer.

The prisoner was spewing gibberish now—alternately threatening and cajoling his captors. Two deckhands yanked him to his feet and stuffed him in the drum. Another one dumped an eleven-inch brown rat into the barrel before clamping on the lid.

The rat shrieked its displeasure.

So did the man.

Cries for mercy echoed from inside the barrel as the two largest deckhands lifted it from the deck and balanced it on the ship's gunwale.

Badeed gave the signal. It was a subtle gesture, no more than a flick of the chin, but two seconds after the warlord did it, the barrel tumbled into the ocean. Water seeped through the holes while the man thrashed inside, desperately trying to escape.

The rat attacked, fighting for the rapidly shrinking space inside the barrel that still had air. Squeals and screams floated over the water as the drum drifted away.

Blood seeped into the ocean.

The waters off the coast of Somalia were excellent fishing grounds and dense with marine life, and the deckhands traditionally made bets on whether the sharks would come before or after the prisoner drowned. The predators usually investigated the barrel with their snouts and their teeth until they found a spot where the rusted metal was soft. Then, like a can of tuna fish, they'd tear open the metal and feast on the meat inside.

The irony was not lost on the warlord.

But no bets were made today. The crew was eight miles from shore, the heat was stifling, and Badeed had an important lunch meeting. The barrel had just dipped below the surface when they fired up the engines and headed for the dock.

EIGHT

T HE TWO MEN had met for lunch for nearly a decade. Though families and careers and the other complexities of life often caused their outings to be rescheduled, they were never canceled, for the meetings were more than social gatherings. They were matters of life and death.

Despite a thatched roof providing shelter from the sun, and two overhead fans stirring the otherwise still air, the open-air restaurant was mostly empty. The thirteen armed guards stationed along the dead-end road might have had something to do with it, but no one complained, because Badeed owned not only the restaurant but the town as well.

"You have done wonderful things for your hometown," said Cawar.

Badeed might have dismissed the compliment as an attempt to curry favor were it not true. The warlord had provided Kitadra with not only security but a medical clinic, a school, and a new mosque. He had done the same for the Hawiye areas of Mogadishu. In the absence of an effective central government, the clan leaders had stepped into the void.

For a reasonable fee, obviously.

"I am sorry I was delayed," Badeed said. "I had some business to attend to."

The two men raised their glasses of sweet chai tea. The conversation meandered like a winding river, touching on family and friends, who'd been born and who had died, and of course, the drought, and how to best profit from it. One of Badeed's associates had become fabulously wealthy after wresting Mogadishu's bottled water concession from a Darood clan rival.

The two men shared plates of stewed camel meat and roasted goat.

"Business has been challenging of late," began the arms dealer. "So many AMISOM and U.S. forces are here that what used to be simple is now complex and what used to be highly profitable is now much less so. Were it not for a single large client, my business would be down significantly from last year."

Badeed looked at his lunch guest and waited.

The arms dealer looked around to ensure no one was in earshot. They were mostly alone in the restaurant, but the dramatic gesture had the desired effect—Badeed leaned forward to hear better.

"Yaxaas has been arming to the teeth," said Cawar.

Badeed scowled at the mention of his nemesis. Yaxaas had demanded protection money from him in the early years of Badeed's ascendancy, and the two warlords were now the dominant powers in Somalia—evenly matched after nearly a decade of armed conflict. The country would belong to whoever was able to defeat the other.

"What's the old crocodile up to?"

"I do not know his plan," said the arms dealer, "but I can feel his ambition."

"He is like a shadow," said Badeed dismissively. "In the morning he is turned in one direction, and in the evening, the opposite. I have seen this before."

"Not like this. He is spending every last shilling on arms and men."

"Then do me a favor, old friend—for every weapon he buys, you must sell me two."

NINE

YAXAAS STOOD IN the bedroom adjoining his office. A Bantu girl lay naked on the bed next to him, rubbing her wrists where the handcuffs had dug into her skin.

Though Mogadishu was barely a hundred miles north of the equator, the room was pleasant with a ceiling fan turning slowly overhead and the French doors open to the courtyard.

A white goat stood among the flora, eyeing the pond. It took a step forward, poking its head through a cluster of ferns. The water was twenty feet away.

The goat walked to the pond's edge, took a sip, then raised its head in alarm. Its eyes, with horizontal slits for pupils, could see almost three hundred degrees around its body—and they'd sensed motion.

But it was only a gust of wind rustling the plants.

The goat lowered its head and resumed drinking.

The fourteen-foot-long crocodile exploded forward, closing the distance in less than a second. The goat turned to run, but the prehistoric predator clamped its teeth around the goat's rear leg. The croc's jaws were the most powerful force in the mammalian world, exerting almost 3,500 pounds of pressure per square inch. The goat wasn't getting away.

Little Yaxaas dragged it backward into the pond, and the goat's plaintive bleating stopped as the croc took it to the bottom.

The warlord smiled and finished getting dressed.

Yaxaas walked downstairs and out of the building. A security guard carrying a Kalashnikov unlocked the gate as the warlord approached. Other guards were already out on the street, patrolling the perimeter.

The dogs were on their feet, waiting. One was missing a leg, another an eye. All had scars on their necks and haunches. They were wild, feral animals, snarling and nipping at one another as the warlord approached.

He took a basket from one of the guards and tossed chunks of goat, cow, camel, and chicken to the street, letting the dogs determine who would eat and who would not. In ten minutes, they'd eaten more meat than the average Somali family would consume in a month, or maybe a year.

A few beggar children were out as well, watching with dirty faces and bare feet, but Yaxaas had nothing for them but scorn.

He knelt down and let the dogs lick his hands. Maybe it was gratitude, or maybe the animals were just lapping up juices left over from the meat he'd thrown, but the warlord didn't care. He scratched the last mutt behind the ears for a few seconds and headed inside past his guards.

His only son was waiting for him.

Born thirty-two years earlier to a mother who'd disappeared a few months after his birth, he had inherited many of her physical qualities—he was taller and more muscular than Yaxaas—but his personality had undoubtedly come from his father.

He was known as Nacay. The nickname meant "detestable" and it had not been given in jest. Even Yaxaas had blanched at some of the things his son had done. Where the father was calculating and dispassionate in the application of violence, Nacay was capricious and often viewed it as a form of entertainment. He reveled in the suffering of others, taking an almost erotic pleasure in watching someone—be it man, woman, or child—beg for their lives.

"Cawar is waiting in your office," he said.

The warlord grunted and father and son went inside to join the arms dealer. Adorning the walls of Yaxaas's office were African tools of war from the last ten thousand years: iron axe heads, copper spear tips, and dozens of knives and daggers. It was an impressive collection, worthy of a museum—or a slaughterhouse.

Cawar rose from a rattan sofa and greeted his host. He gave Yaxaas a three-foot-long Ngulu sword. Its question-mark-shaped blade was designed to catch and sever a man's neck.

"I will find a place of honor for it."

"I am sorry for arriving unannounced," said the arms dealer, "but if I hadn't, I believe that you would wish I had."

"All is forgiven. We have been friends for many years and survived many trials together."

Cawar smiled. "Like the Ethiopians?"

Yaxaas snorted and slowly shook his head.

The arms dealer turned to face Nacay. "It was many years ago, when your father was still working for Madowbe and I had not yet acquired my trading business. We were driving an old truck on a dirt trail at night, with no muffler and no lights, when we were suddenly blinded. There were so many spotlights, headlights, and searchlights that I thought we had driven straight into the sun. We were surrounded by Ethiopian security forces."

"There must have been fifty of them!" added Yaxaas. "All yelling and pointing weapons at us. We stepped out of the truck with our hands up when their officer approached and demanded to know what we were up to."

"I told him we were delivering vegetables," Cawar admitted sheepishly.

"We had no bananas, no cucumbers, absolutely nothing to support the fiction. Old Cyclops here couldn't even remember what kind of vegetables we were supposed to be carrying when the soldier asked him."

"The officer opened the back of the truck and there was nothing there. We told him we'd sold everything and were on our way home, but he didn't budge, so Cawar offered him twenty U.S. dollars. He took it but still didn't move, so Cawar gave him another twenty."

"I saw him shift on his feet," Cawar said, "so I knew we had him. I gave him a handful of Ethiopian notes, probably worth another five dollars, and told him it was all we had. The soldier waved us on, and we made it home a day and a half later, none the worse for wear."

"They were looking for poachers," said the arms dealer.

"And we had a quarter of a million dollars hidden in the truck's spare tire!" said Yaxaas. "That army officer could have been rich."

The three men were still laughing when the young girl knocked on the door and entered. Cawar examined every curve of her body as she poured three glasses of tea through a strainer and walked out of the room.

"Tell me what's bothering you," Yaxaas said.

"It was told to me in confidence . . ."

The warlord looked sideways at his old friend.

"Out with it," said Yaxaas. "You can take her home with you to salve your conscience."

Cawar's leering eyes shifted to the warlord. "It's Badeed. He's amassing men and weapons . . . far more than he needs for defense."

"So what does he have planned?"

"Forgive me for being blunt, but these skirmishes in Mogadishu have weakened you both."

"So he's re-arming?"

"It's more than that . . ."

Yaxaas gave his old friend another look.

"He thinks you're weak," said Cawar. "He senses an opportunity to consolidate power once and for all."

"Then he's stupider than I thought. Whatever he's buying, I'll buy double."

TEN

I T WAS JUST after midnight when the twelve pirates split up.

Eight stayed aft and four went forward, led by a tall man with piercing blue eyes.

Though the *DoubleDown* was technically a *Suezmax*-class ship, anyone outside the shipping industry would have called it a supertanker. Nine hundred feet long and one hundred sixty feet wide, the ship steamed through the Arabian Sea at eighteen knots as she ferried a million barrels of jet fuel from a refinery in Mangaluru, India, to the Mediterranean Sea.

Clad in gray and black camouflage, the four pirates advanced in the shadows of several large cargo transfer pipes that ran the length of the ship. By the time they reached the foredeck, they were seven hundred feet from the superstructure and invisible to the crewmen standing watch on the bridge.

There were two former French marines facing forward, watching the sea and crewing a mounted machine gun.

They were part of the ship's vessel protection detail. The armed detachments had been effective against the first-generation pirates who'd assaulted ships using extension ladders and AK-47s, but the group of men that had snuck aboard the *DoubleDown* was nothing like first-generation pirates—they were a tier-one special operations team specializing in noncompliant boardings—and short of a military force, they had no equal.

They advanced slowly, silently.

Maritime assault boots. Knees bent slightly. Rifles at high ready.

From twenty yards away, the pirates lined up on the two vessel protection marines and fired a suppressed round into the back of each man's head in case he was wearing body armor.

"Bow clear," said the lead pirate over his radio.

"Bow clear, roger," came the reply from the mission commander.

The breacher in the team of eight pirates used a Halligan tool to pry open a metal door at the base of the superstructure and the eight men poured inside. There was a staircase ahead and a few utility rooms to the sides, but no sign of the ship's crew. Two pirates held the space while the others returned outside and divided their force once again. Three went to port and three to starboard.

The pirates had practiced the takedown so many times that they knew how many steps it was between each turn, every blind spot, and every area that presented a risk of fratricide.

They reached the port and starboard exterior staircases

and climbed five flights. The next level up on the T-shaped superstructure held two metal catwalks. Known as bridge wings, they were outdoor extensions of the bridge that allowed the ship's officers to walk the full width of the ship from eighty feet above the deck.

The teams crouched along the catwalks until they reached the doors to the bridge. One of the pirates from the port-side team peeked inside. It was a massive room— seventy feet wide and eighteen feet deep. Except for the dim red lighting, it looked more like a high-rise office building than a ship. There were leather chairs, a dozen computer monitors, and six men standing watch.

The *DoubleDown*'s chief mate was discussing the ship's malfunctioning electronics with the chief engineer. The two men speculated that only a generator malfunction, or maybe a massive solar flare, could have caused everything to crash simultaneously.

"Could be an electromagnetic pulse," suggested one of the other officers.

Each was hesitant to voice what he really thought.

The chief mate had spent sixteen years as a merchant marine officer, mostly on tankers plying the Indian Ocean and the Mediterranean Sea. He was no stranger to the threat of piracy. He'd been at sea during its heyday in the Gulf of Aden, and it was not something one forgot— stories of ships' crews being held at gunpoint off the Horn of Africa for months or even years, living in fear and filth until distant insurance companies and faceless shipowners could agree on ransom payments for the safe return of the ship, crew, and cargo.

The chief mate had also heard stories about a recent spate of disappearances. Bermuda Triangle–type theories had emerged about an area of the Indian Ocean with rogue waves that were uniquely dangerous to tankers, but the mate had as much faith in those theories as the ones he'd heard as a child about mermaids and sea monsters.

He raised the crew radio. *"Vessel protection detachment, check in."*

He repeated the instruction, but the handheld radios were full of static too.

All eyes in the bridge were upon him as he lowered the handset.

"Everyone into the citadel. Now."

Like a good leader, he said it with a calmness he did not feel.

Like a safe room in a home, a citadel aboard ship was an armored room from which the crew could radio for help, control the ship, and wait in safety for naval forces to dispatch the pirates. Most citadels were in the superstructure. It was close to the bridge, fresh air, and radio and satellite antennas.

The chief mate activated the silent alarm next. It would have broadcast a distress signal from the ship's satellite communications equipment and its radios, indicating a possible pirate incident, except that the communications gear was still a garbled mess—which left the opposite of a silent alarm as his only remaining option. He flipped up a plastic cover and pressed a large red button.

The general alarm.

The ship's massive horn began to sound: seven short

blasts, followed by a long one. Everyone within miles could hear it, including the pirates.

Outside, on the starboard bridge wing, a pirate checked the door handle. It was unlocked.

"Starboard, green," he said over his radio.

The team on the port side did the same with the same result.

"Port, green."

"Execute, execute!" came the order.

The pirates burst into the bridge.

Four men were standing in the middle of the room.

Two of them froze at the sight of the camouflaged gunmen and died where they stood, while a third crewman dove behind a bank of instruments. A pirate put three rounds into the man's back and made sure that he never got up again.

The chief mate was standing at the helm, watching a pile of bodies form at his feet.

"Please don't harm the others," he said. "I'll—"

He joined the pile.

Seven seconds after the door opened, the bridge was silent and the smell of gunpowder hung in the air.

The point man from the port-side team shut off the general alarm.

"I spotted six crew in here before the breach," he said. "We only killed four."

"Two squirters off the bridge," the team leader said into his radio headset. *"Starboard bridge team coming down."*

The three pirates hustled through the open doorway

after the escaped crewmen. A few seconds later they heard several bursts of gunfire.

"*The two squirters are down,*" said another pirate. "*We located the citadel—accommodations tower, echo deck, port side.*"

The invaders had killed the six men on watch in the bridge, plus three others who'd made it to the saferoom, but a *Suezmax* usually sailed with at least twenty crew, plus the vessel protection detachment.

The pirates coursed through the ship, methodically dispatching the others. Men were shot as they approached the citadel, in the control rooms, and in their berths.

No quarter was given.

Not a man was left alive.

ELEVEN

JAKE WAS STILL on eastern U.S. time and working on his laptop when Pickens woke up. The big man strolled into the kitchen wearing gym shorts and a double-extra-large T-shirt that was still a size too small. Though he hadn't played football in twenty-three years, there wasn't an ounce of fat on his two-hundred-forty-pound frame.

"Do you have mobile phone numbers for the contacts we've met?" Jake said.

"Most of them," Pickens said as he poured himself a cup of tea. "What's up?"

"I want to do some target discovery—maybe use contact chaining or voice intercepts to get us to the pirate leader—basic SIGINT analytics."

"'*SIGINT analytics*'?" Pickens said derisively.

Jake stopped typing and looked up.

"It means 'signals intelligence.' Didn't you intercept Morse code when you were in the OSS? This is the same idea, just for this century . . ."

Pickens laughed. "Fine, wiseass, but human sources are where the real intel is."

He returned from his bedroom a few minutes later holding a sheet of paper with half a dozen phone numbers on it. His mood was decidedly cool as Jake started entering them into the computer.

"Look, John, I know we need to work our way up, but these street thugs don't fit the profile of our pirates."

"What profile is that?"

"Funny hats, parrots, maybe a few eye patches."

"Peg legs?"

"Maybe," said Jake. "I'll run it by headquarters. In the meantime, we should be looking for skilled operators."

"Skilled operators don't advertise."

Jake sent the encrypted request back to headquarters.

"I agree, but we need to use every resource available. It's just you and me on this one."

"Which is another mystery," Pickens said as he scratched the stubble on his chin. "I figured Graves would've sent a team down here."

"Ted doesn't like to leave a big footprint."

"He's a paranoid sonofabitch, isn't he?"

"His view is that with your contacts, and my technical skills, we should be able to find out who's running the show."

"And his ass is less exposed if we end up dead." Pickens pointed at the laptop. "I need to grab a workout. How long till the nerds get back to you?"

"That depends on how hard it is to access the local phone company's records."

* * *

IT TOOK NINETY minutes.

Pickens was still lifting weights in the basement when the data came back.

A regional network exploitation team working with the NSA's Tailored Access Operations group had delivered exactly what Jake requested. He cross-referenced the mobile phone records against the dates of recent pirate attacks and discovered that each phone had been onshore and actively used during the attacks. He did the same with the commonly called numbers for each of the phones and arrived at the same conclusion.

Not a single man they'd met with was involved in the pirate attacks.

Jake stared blankly at the screen, hoping for a pattern to emerge from the data.

And then he started typing.

Furiously.

TWELVE

KITADRA.

Dameer had mentioned the small coastal town moments before Pickens had knocked him out of his sandals. While the drugged-up, would-be kidnapper's word wasn't worth much, the coastal town loomed large in piracy lore, having been the original, and the most successful, pirate haven throughout the first generation of piracy. If street thugs were still talking about it like a city of gold, it was probably worth checking out. Pickens had arranged a meeting to get a read on the current situation.

Kitadra was two hours north, and Jake kept the accelerator close to the floor as they drove through Mogadishu. The narrow city streets were packed with a mishmash of two-, three-, and four-wheeled vehicles, all vying for the same space at the same time.

Right-of-way was decided by testosterone and kinetic energy.

The driving changed once they left the city and headed north on the "highway," two lanes of broken pavement surrounded by acres of sand and an occasional stand of bent gum trees. They passed petroleum tankers, water trucks, and freight haulers. Cars and trucks coming from the opposite direction thought nothing of forcing other vehicles to the shoulder to complete a pass without slowing down.

The international media often wrote about the low value ascribed to human life in Somalia, and it was hard to fully comprehend, but a couple hours on the road proved it with mathematical precision. Lives were risked for the most insignificant advantage. Vehicle-to-vehicle gunfire was common. Burned-out wrecks littered the roadside.

Hell is nothing to fear when you're already there.

Occasionally a group of vehicles would pass by at high speed. In the middle was usually an armored Land Cruiser or Range Rover with tinted windows. Two pickup trucks full of gunmen seemed to be the standard escort for a warlord or a high government official—from the average Somali's point of view, the difference was negligible.

The nation was facing its third famine in two decades. Starvation and illness ravaged the population despite foreign assistance that ran over $1 billion per year. Most of the aid was food, some of it was cash, and maybe 10 percent of it actually made it to the people in need. The rest was diverted to pay for armored SUVs and pickup trucks full of gunmen.

The warlords and government officials called it a tax.

The people called it extortion.

THERE WAS NO "Welcome to Kitadra" sign at the edge of town, just sand and scrub, a few palm trees, and a dozen dilapidated homes. No bigger than ten-by-fifteen-foot rooms, the shanties had discarded cardboard covering holes in tin roofs, woven mats hanging over doorways, and rain barrels as their only source of water. With earth-moving equipment scarce and expensive, the residents had built their homes on the flattest land available, leaving them strewn about at odd angles and distances.

Jake and Pickens arrived two hours early for their meeting to scout the area and assess security. Jake unbuckled his seat belt so it would be easier to reach the Glock 19 pistol holstered inside his waistband and the curved karambit knife sheathed under his shirt. Pickens did the same, although he could have concealed a machine gun without most people noticing.

The standard of living seemed to improve as they reached the center of town. A busy market square held twenty or thirty people haggling over prices for clothing and food. Across the street was an elegant mosque with whitewashed walls and a robin's egg blue roof made from handmade tiles. Up a side street was a large building with a light green roof and fake shutters painted onto its cream-colored walls.

"That's the Exchange," said Pickens, pointing at the cream-colored building. "It was pirate central during the first go-around. The locals contributed anything that could be used in an attack: money, weapons, boats, themselves. It was all valued and assigned a share of any payout. Probably ten percent of the deals hit, and ransom payments took a long time to negotiate and collect, but those that paid out, paid big. Some investors made a hundred times their original investment."

"Like venture capital for criminals," Jake said.

He kept driving. They passed more homes and a few commercial buildings until they reached the outskirts of town.

"Call it," Jake said.

"We should be safe as long as we lay low."

"Works for me."

Jake pulled a U-turn across the road, forcing two cars in the oncoming lane to slam on their brakes and swerve around him.

"You're assimilating nicely," said Pickens. He checked his watch. The drive through town had taken all of five minutes. "We've still got two hours. Let's grab some lunch."

The sedan attracted a few glances but little more as they crept down a dusty side street that dead-ended at a wide sand beach. As far as the eye could see, the ocean was calm and the sky was clear as the sun continued its remorseless assault.

There were additional private homes by the beach, but they were modern and multi-story, with late-model cars and trucks parked in their driveways. On the right, surrounded by dozens of banana trees, was an outdoor restaurant. Parked outside were several tricked-out SUVs and an old pickup truck with no windshield and three mounted machine guns, one for the front seat passenger and two on pintles in the back. A group of men was standing nearby chewing qat and talking among themselves. A few had rifles slung over their shoulders.

"Are you familiar with the term 'recon by fire'?" asked Pickens.

"That's not exactly laying low. I'm the only white man within a hundred miles."

"That's some racist shit right there," Pickens said with a grin, "but I'm going to let it slide this one time. Let's do this . . ."

Jake wondered if that was really such a good idea, but the big man was already out of the car and past the armed men on his way into the restaurant.

Jake cursed, press-checked his pistol, and did the same.

The beachfront café was a collection of simple tables with a dirt floor and a palm-frond roof, but the air smelled of roasted goat and stewed camel meat—expensive delicacies in the famine-wrought country.

Jake sat facing the road and Pickens watched the rear as a waiter approached their table. Pickens ordered in English.

"What you want, gaal?" the waiter asked Jake.

Jake ordered the *baasto*. It was a popular dish and a window into Somalia's past—pasta from the Italian occupation seasoned with spices from the Silk Road era.

"Not baasto. Why you here?" the waiter asked, choosing not to tiptoe around the issue of Jake's race.

"We're with the UN High Commissioner for Refugees," said Pickens, and they had the credentials to prove it, although the UNHCR staff might be surprised to learn it.

The waiter walked away.

"I think he likes you," said Pickens.

"He raises a good point," Jake said. "Why *are* we here, exactly?"

Pickens leaned across the table. "There's money here, Jake. A lot of it. The market square was packed with people buying actual food in a country that's starving, this restaurant is almost full, and some of those SUVs outside would cost $100,000 back in the States. That's more than most Somali families will earn in a lifetime. There's only one way people can earn that kind of cash in this country, especially in a small coastal town. We're getting close."

The food took forever to come out, which was odd because it appeared to be precooked, in large bowls, within plain sight of the table. Other parties arrived and were quickly served. The waiter passed by Jake and Pickens several times but said nothing. The restaurant filled up and became noisy.

"The waiter is setting us up," Jake said.

"We've still got ninety minutes to kill before the meet."

"Let's spend it somewhere else."

The two Americans slipped out of the restaurant and returned to their car. Pickens took the wheel and drove through town, constantly checking his mirrors for a tail. A handful of people were walking to and from the market with pushcarts and baskets, but the two Americans were clean. They soon found themselves in front of the cream-colored building with the green roof. It was empty.

"Let's check it out," said Jake.

Pickens frowned.

"C'mon, John. Maybe you're right about Kitadra. Consider this background for our investigation."

"All right," said Pickens, "but just for the record, this is going to end poorly."

THIRTEEN

THEY PARKED NEXT to a rusty car that looked as if it hadn't moved in decades.

Jake stepped out of the Daihatsu hatchback. He was deeply tanned, and wearing long pants and a long-sleeve shirt, but everyone on the street was staring at the white man before his first foot hit the ground.

Like many buildings in tropical Somalia, the cream-colored Exchange had no windows or doors, just a wide entrance in front and window-sized openings on the other three walls. The interior was a single open room, maybe fifty feet by thirty feet, with a dusting of windblown sand over its tile floor and a raised dais on the far side. Affixed to the walls were relics from past pirate missions. The provenance of each had been inscribed on the wall next to it, but the Somali script was faded and illegible.

Pickens walked between a ship's bell and a porthole window with a bullet hole in it, while Jake wandered to the back and stepped onto the dais. There were two window-sized openings on the far wall. Hung above them was a weather-beaten ladder that was missing a leg. The soft wood had been bleached white by years of exposure to salt spray and the sun.

Jake wondered how many pirates had climbed its rungs over the years and how many seafarers had died because of it. Though the building had the feel of a museum, Somali pirates had killed and tortured countless men, funded criminal and terrorist organizations, and perpetuated the civil war that had destroyed their country.

Jake was curious, but he wasn't an admirer.

"Hey, Pick, can you read this?" he said.

The inscription under the ladder was in better condition than the others. The big man joined Jake on the dais and grimaced.

"It's something about the building being a gift of Allah's will, the broken ladder, and a lion."

"No offense," Jake said, "but I think you might need to go back to language training."

"I don't know the dialect," Pickens protested with a laugh. "Let's head back to town and see what shakes loose."

Jake looked to the street. "Whatever it is, it's about to start shaking."

A Mitsubishi SUV with two-tone paint and a cracked windshield skidded to a halt in front of the building. Four men climbed out. They were dressed in frayed pants, faded shirts, and well-worn sandals. One wore a safari jacket and a pair of knockoff Ray-Bans. All were brandishing weapons.

While kidnapping for ransom wasn't as popular as it

had been in the heyday of the pirates, grabbing a couple of foreigners off the streets of Kitadra was about as easy as it got. Soft targets, hard currency, and no consequences whatsoever.

"John, out the windows!"

Jake took two steps and vaulted through one of the openings in the back wall. Chips of concrete flew as one of the gunmen opened up with his Kalashnikov and stitched a line of bullet holes in the wall where Jake's head had been a few seconds earlier.

Pickens landed on his feet next to Jake. He and Jake drew their weapons and started running.

The neighborhood was a maze of footpaths and small houses. Jake sprinted down the nearest path with Pickens right behind. The two CIA officers nearly collided with a group of children playing in the sand before darting through a cluster of one-room shacks made from discarded building materials and plastic tarps.

A burst of gunfire rattled through the neighborhood. The gunmen weren't far behind.

The Americans turned down another footpath, between a pair of cinder-block homes and two old men sitting in plastic chairs. At the end was a small palm grove.

Jake stole a look over his shoulder. The Somalis were thirty yards back. Jake and Pickens made a series of random turns through another group of shanties until the alley opened onto a dusty patch of open ground.

Half a dozen young boys were playing soccer with a ball made from discarded duct tape when one of the Somalis fired a burst from his rifle, narrowly missing the boys. Jake turned down another alley to keep them out of the line of fire and the Americans piled on the speed, banging out a five-minute-mile pace through the tiny residential neighborhood. Though Pickens was nearly fifteen years older, he was right on his partner's heels. They ran down another dirt path, looking for a place to hide or a car to steal, but there were too many people and almost no cars.

The ground opened up at the end of the path.

They'd reached the edge of town.

The land was flat and empty for miles.

Another burst of automatic weapon fire ripped through the air behind them while the Mitsubishi SUV appeared from a side street and blocked their escape.

The Americans were going to have to resolve the threat.

Jake ducked inside a darkened shed and motioned Pickens into an open doorway. It placed them in an L formation where they could cover two approaches and concentrate their fire.

Jake took a deep breath and exhaled slowly, trying to slow his breathing and his heart rate. He listened to his surroundings, isolating the different sounds: the breeze rustling the trees, the children playing nearby, the Mitsubishi's engine shutting down.

The Somalis were being patient. Time was on their side.

Jake needed to go on the offensive. He lobbed his cell phone twenty feet away into a cluster of scrub brush. Thirty seconds later, the timer he'd set started ringing.

There were footsteps . . . running . . . stopping . . . then advancing slowly as the phone continued to ring.

Two of the Somalis rounded a corner with their rifles

up. They glanced in Jake's direction, but he remained invisible inside the darkened shed. The gunmen fanned out, one on each side of the small alley, and turned toward the sound of the phone.

Jake fired twice and dropped the first Somali to his knees, then switched his aim and put three shots into the second man just as he was turning around. He crumpled in a pile of arms and legs. The first man was still on his knees, holding his rifle, and screaming in pain.

Jake fired again.

The screaming stopped.

The timer was still ringing, but it wasn't fooling anyone anymore.

Jake caught a glimpse of a third gunman and raised his pistol, but the man disappeared before he could take the shot.

A panicked woman burst from one of the nearby shanties and ran in front of Jake's muzzle with two children in her arms.

He took a deep breath. There were too many innocent bystanders around.

A minute later he heard a muffled, one-sided conversation. It was another one of the Somalis, on his mobile phone, coordinating a counterattack.

Smart.

It wasn't a quality Jake appreciated in an adversary.

He dashed across the alley into the abandoned shanty, pushing aside the hanging carpet that was its door and ducking under some laundry drying on a clothesline inside. There were footsteps outside, moving slowly, scraping against the dirt and gravel.

Jake switched out his half-empty pistol magazine for the full spare he kept on his belt and watched the alley through a thin cotton curtain.

A shadow passed the house.

Jake pushed open the hanging carpet.

"Drop the gun," Jake said in Arabic.

His pistol was trained on the center of the man's back, less than ten feet away. The bullet would destroy his heart if it didn't sever his spinal column.

The man hesitated.

"Live or die," Jake said. His finger slid toward the Glock's trigger, but the man laid the gun on the ground.

Jake ordered him back into the house and slammed him to the floor, face first.

"Who sent you?" Jake said in Arabic.

But before the man could answer, Jake caught sight of Sunglasses outside with a pistol in his hands, heading toward Pickens. A second later the Somali turned around a corner and disappeared from view.

Jake wasn't equipped to take prisoners. He yanked the clothesline from the ceiling, hog-tied the Somali, and stuffed a dish towel in his mouth.

Jake grabbed the man's Kalashnikov, checked the magazine, and stepped onto the street.

He was worried about his partner. Pickens was strong and fast and knew how to handle himself in a street fight, but he didn't have the paramilitary experience Jake did.

Though the two men joked about the difference in their ages, it was their training that set them apart. Most case officers went their whole careers without carrying a weapon, much less getting into a gunfight.

Jake moved quickly but deliberately, his eyes scanning every potential hiding place and his ears listening for any indication that Sunglasses had doubled back to ambush him. Jake reached an intersection of two alleys and followed a set of footprints that looked fresher than the rest.

Up ahead, twenty feet away, Sunglasses was stalking Pickens's position.

Jake raised the AK-47 just as his partner stepped into the alley. Pickens and the Somali were facing each other when Sunglasses started shouting and waving his pistol in the air.

Pickens spotted Jake in his peripheral vision and glanced over.

Sunglasses's eyes followed.

Pickens fired five rounds into his chest from four feet away.

The Somali fell to the ground and Pickens met Jake's eyes.

"Thanks, brother."

FOURTEEN

JAKE AND PICKENS skipped the meet that had brought them to Kitadra and returned to the safe house. That night they split a bottle of twelve-year-old Macallan scotch that Pickens had smuggled into the country and speculated whether the attack in Kitadra had been spontaneous or targeted—but there was no way to know.

Jake awoke early again the next day. He sat at the kitchen table and checked his email, the room lit only by the bluish glow from his laptop screen. There were dozens of overnight cables on developments in Africa and across the globe—several of which Jake read, and an urgent request for a status update from Ted Graves—which Jake deleted.

He was pleased to also find a message from the technical staff at CIA.

They'd come through with his data request.

It was a large amount of information in two distinct files, and Jake heated a teakettle while they downloaded.

Drinking copious amounts of tea was a habit he'd acquired while working in the Middle East. With alcohol forbidden by sharia law, Muslims often served tea at social events, but Jake had taken to it because dysentery, gastroenteritis, and diarrhea commonly afflicted foreigners in the region, and drinking hot tea was an inoffensive way to guarantee the local water had been boiled before consuming it.

The tea was made and drunk before the files were decrypted, but the team at headquarters had come through with everything he'd asked for. His initial attempt to tie Pickens's sources to the pirate attacks through phone records had failed—the men had all been onshore and using their phones at some point during the attacks—but it had also given Jake an idea.

He opened the first file. There were seven wireless companies in Somalia, and NSA computer network exploitation teams had been able to retrieve data from six of them, capturing 94 percent of all mobile phone users in-country.

The file on his computer contained detailed call histories for the dates around the seven pirate attacks.

Jake had been an analyst before joining the operations side of CIA, and he'd asked the technical team back at Langley to format the information so it could be searched based on multiple variables. He wanted to roll up his sleeves and triage the data on his own.

The first vessel to be attacked had been a *Suezmax* tanker owned by a privately owned Greek shipping company. Jake entered the date of its disappearance, set parameters for five days before and five days after the attack, and queried the database. He was searching for negatives, reasoning that anyone not using his phone for ten days straight might have been out of the country, possibly on a business trip, or a vacation.

Or maybe on a ship.

There were over eight thousand hits.

What the hell?

He added the same parameters for the second pirate attack and the results dropped to 2,200 names.

By the time he entered the seventh attack, the list was down to sixty-two individuals. It was still a big number, and his intuition told him he wasn't dealing with a force that large, but that was why he had the second file.

It was INTERPOL's Global Maritime Piracy Database—every person who'd ever been detained or suspected of involvement in the trade. There were thousands of names from all over the globe, with brief summaries of where, when, and why they'd shown up on INTERPOL's radar. Jake cross-referenced the sixty-two names from the mobile phone records search with the INTERPOL list and found eight names in common.

Eight known pirates who hadn't used their phones during seven out of seven pirate attacks.

Now he had a list he could use.

Pickens wandered into the kitchen, still half asleep. "What's got you up so early?"

"I got the records from cyber."

Pickens refilled the teakettle and turned on the heat.

"We've got eight individuals who are in the INTERPOL piracy database and didn't use their mobile phones during seven out of the seven attacks."

"Your very own gang of eight," Pickens said as he pulled out a chair and sat backward on it. "The gang of eight" was the nickname for the congressmen and senators who were responsible for oversight of America's intelligence agencies.

Jake spun the laptop around so Pickens could see the analysis. "Check it out."

Pickens shrugged. "So damned analytical . . . I told you, espionage isn't about numbers, it's about people."

"Maybe back in your day," Jake said with a smile, "but now we fuse multiple streams of intel to find our targets."

Pickens flipped him the finger. "Speaking of your youth and inexperience . . . How'd you end up in Special Activities at such a tender young age?"

Though they were both part of the Agency's Directorate of Operations, the two men were from different divisions. Pickens had taken the traditional route after college, coming up through the clandestine service trainee program before beginning his career in the field as a case officer. His main job was recruiting sources.

But most of Jake's peers in the Special Activities Center were military special operations veterans who had ten to twenty years of experience in the armed forces before joining the Agency. Jake was considerably younger than his contemporaries, and it was impossible not to notice.

And impossible for Jake to answer.

"Look," Jake said. "We have photos, names, and last known addresses for the eight subjects. Now we just need to pay them a visit and figure out who's who in the zoo."

"You and I can't run that kind of operation alone. We'll get made in a heartbeat—especially you."

"Racist . . ." Jake muttered jokingly as he started typing on his laptop again, drafting another request to the cyber services team in CIA's Directorate of Digital Innovation. "I'm asking headquarters to run call chains on our gang of eight and build an association matrix. Maybe if we see who is talking to who, it will lead us to whoever is running this thing."

Pickens nodded and stepped outside to take a call on his mobile phone. He returned to the kitchen twenty minutes later.

"While we're waiting on that"—he gestured to the laptop as if it were toxic—"I got us another meet for this afternoon, and you're going to want to take this one."

FIFTEEN

THE TWO MEN left the safe house in a maroon Toyota Surf SUV.

"Head on a swivel, brother," Pickens said as they approached a car with its hood up on one side of the road and a stopped minibus on the other. There were six inches to spare on each side of the SUV. "Sometimes the locals stage this shit to funnel people into ambushes."

Jake's hand was already resting on the pistol concealed on his waist, but he relaxed when he saw steam rising up from the car's engine compartment and an old man pouring a jug of water into the radiator.

"Have you met this guy before or is this going to be another battle royale?" Jake asked.

Pickens smirked. "Only once, at a local arms dealer's warehouse. This guy isn't a street thug, though. He runs half of the Bakaara Market. I've been trying to get this meet since I learned you were coming."

Jake was watching the side-view mirror. A silver hatch-

back with peeling paint and mirrored windows had followed them through three turns.

"What made him finally agree?" Jake asked, keeping his
eyes on the mirror.

"He was doing his due diligence on me. One nice perk
of my arms redistribution assignment is that it establishes
my bona fides with some serious dudes."

"Some seriously bad dudes."

"They're generally the best sources," said Pickens.

The silver hatchback turned away and a pair of camels
loped down the center of the busy street with numbers
branded into their hindquarters.

"What's with the numbers?" Jake asked.

"The Somalis call them 'license plates.' They're the
owner's mobile phone number."

"Seriously?"

"Those ugly things were worth $3,000 a head before the
drought, maybe $5,000 now. Steal one and you'll get your
hand cut off."

Pickens did a 270-degree turn around the block and
they headed west through the Hawle Wadag district. While
nowhere in Somalia was considered safe, the Hawle Wadag
was a particularly dangerous area. The neighborhood was
littered with burned-out cars, buildings pockmarked from
bullets and artillery, and craters from IEDs. Armed men
loitered on the streets, watching the SUV roll by.

The two Americans drove past a colonial-era church
that was overflowing with displaced Somalis and turned
into an area with even deeper scars: scorched buildings,

downed power lines, shattered windows. Trash littered the roadside. The stench of sewage was suffocating.

"We're here," Pickens said.

He pointed to a dusty lot behind a chain-link fence and enough barbed wire to secure a prison. Empty and abandoned shipping containers littered the foreground. In the back was a one-story warehouse with its garage door raised.

Pickens approached slowly. A man holding an AK-47 was guarding the entrance. He waved the Americans inside and gestured to the back of the warehouse. Pickens crept forward, past a dozen armed men and several vehicles, including a four-door Nissan Navara with dented fenders and a Russian RPD machine gun mounted in its bed.

"One way in and one way out," Jake noted without enthusiasm.

"Look, brother, I've got four kids back in the States, and even though I don't get back there much, I still want to see them again. We can trust this guy."

A new Mercedes-Benz SUV was parked in the rear. Half a dozen gunmen with Kalashnikovs stood alongside.

"I thought you said this guy ran half of the Bakaara Market," Jake said.

"The illegal half," said Pickens. "Just take everything nice and slow."

He stopped their SUV fifty feet from the Mercedes, and he and Jake stepped out with their empty hands in clear view.

A man emerged from the passenger seat of the Mercedes. Tall and wiry, he was dressed in a crimson shirt and yellow pants.

"I am Gadhka Cas," he said. *"As-salaam-alaikum."*

"Wa-alaikum-salaam," said Pickens.

The Somali motioned to three chairs and a serving of tea.

"How did you get your nickname?" Pickens asked.

"You speak Somali?" Gadhka Cas smiled. "My beard turned gray at a young age and it is a tradition here to color such a thing with henna for one's wedding—so the bride does not feel as if she is marrying her grandfather."

The Somali took his seat and laughed. "It looked ridiculous and my friends stuck me with 'Gadhka Cas' forever."

"It means 'red beard,'" Pickens said for Jake's benefit.

"Somali nicknames can be cruel," Jake said.

"Life can be cruel," said the Somali, suddenly serious, "but the nicknames are honest—maybe the most honest thing in Somalia."

The three men sipped their tea.

"So what can I do for you?"

"My associate is interested in investment opportunities in Somalia," said Pickens. "He's looking to generate some 'offshore income.'"

"I understand that some of the pirate syndicates accept outside investors," Jake said. "And I'd like to make a substantial investment."

"There are a few syndicates that would welcome your money," said Gadhka Cas, "but be cautious, very few boardings are successful. The shipping companies and the world's navies have become much smarter."

"John has told me that there may be a new syndicate operating—one that has a much higher success rate, one that has professionalized the business. I'd be willing to accept a lower return for a more consistent payout. Are you familiar with it?"

"Somalis are great fans of legends," said Gadhka Cas, "so I will tell you what I have heard, but I cannot attest to its accuracy . . . There is a story of a young man who was one of the earliest pirates in its earliest days, but he was injured during an attack and could no longer go to sea, so he staffed his organization with professionals and began gathering advance intelligence—not just chasing targets of opportunity with guns and a few qat-chewing boys, like everyone else. The legend goes that he now runs a very large and very effective operation, but that is all I know."

"Do you believe it?" Jake asked.

"There are parts of it that I find credible, but I also find it strange that this legendary figure and I have never crossed paths. Men such as ourselves operate quite openly in Somalia."

Gadhka Cas stood. The meeting was over.

Jake and Pickens stood in the empty lot as the man departed with his security detail.

"Sorry," said Pickens. "I thought he was going to have a name for us. I'll keep trying my other contacts . . . I've asked a couple of the arms dealers, but this 'legend' is probably one of their best customers, so nobody is talking."

Jake watched a barefoot man lead a donkey cart past the warehouse.

"Do you remember when we were in that building in Kitadra?" he said.

"Just before those four guys tried to kill us? Yeah, vaguely . . ."

"On the wall it said something like 'the building is a gift from Allah, a ladder, and a lion.'"

Pickens laughed.

"Seriously," Jake said. "Gadhka Cas said the legend was injured during a boarding. Maybe the ladder broke and he fell into the ocean."

"And was eaten by a lion?"

"Maybe it was a sea lion."

Jake said it as a joke, but Pickens wasn't laughing anymore. "Do you remember when you told me I needed to go back to language training?"

"I don't, but it sounds like something I'd say. You don't really think it was a sea lion, do you?"

"No, but the Somali word for 'lion' is *libaax* and the word for 'shark' is *libaax badeed*," said Pickens. "I told you that there are two warlords locked in a fight for control of Somalia, right?"

"Yeah, the leader of the Darood and the leader of the Hawiye."

"Well the leader of the Hawiye is from Kitadra, and they call him Badeed."

SIXTEEN

T HAT NIGHT OVER dinner, Jake and Pickens decided to return to Kitadra. They needed to learn more about Badeed, but they'd also killed four of the warlord's clansmen—in his hometown. The trip would be dangerous, but it was a risk they needed to take.

They reached the outskirts of town around noon. An old fisherman was picking the morning's catch out of a homemade wheelbarrow and throwing it into a broken refrigerator that had been flipped onto its back and repurposed as a cooler.

"This place is so damned poor," Pickens said as he stared out the window at the old man. "Nothing gets wasted here."

"Except maybe us," said Jake. He was looking out the windshield at a Toyota pickup with flared fenders and chromed roll bars, parked on the side of the road. Three men with rifles were standing next to it in the shade of a palm tree.

A checkpoint.

Somalia was full of them, run by militias, clans, or civilians in uniform—basically anyone who thought he could make a buck and not get killed in the process. It was all about intimidation.

The pickup lurched into the road and blocked traffic. Jake tried to swerve around it, but he was boxed in with a heavy truck on his rear bumper and traffic in the oncoming lane. He slammed on his brakes and skidded to a stop, denting the pickup's fender in the last instant.

"That's not good," Jake said.

"Just be cool," said Pickens. "They usually just want a few shillings."

No sooner had the words left Pickens's mouth than the gunmen raised their weapons and started shouting for the two men to open their doors. Jake hesitated for an instant and the butt of a rifle stock shattered the glass. Two men yanked him from the car and threw him to the pavement. Pickens met the same fate. Both were quickly relieved of their guns, knives, and identification before having their hands bound and hoods thrown over their heads.

Jake had been hopeful Pickens might be right about it only being a shakedown until the hoods came out. It wasn't the sort of thing most people kept in their vehicles.

The gunmen threw the two Americans into the truck bed and the creaky liftgate slammed closed. Jake tried to free his hands, but they'd been tied professionally—whoever had grabbed them had done it before.

Pickens cursed when he heard a long burst of gunfire.

"Pick?" Jake said.

"Yeah?"

"Do you trust me?"

"Yeah."

"Hang tough. We're not going to die today, brother."

SEVENTEEN

ONE OF THE thugs smashed his rifle stock into Jake's side.

"No talking," he said in English.

The blow had nearly cracked a rib, but it felt like a baby's kiss compared to a beating he'd taken in Iran two years ago. He'd survive.

The pickup's tires squealed as it did an abrupt U-turn and accelerated. The two Americans slid around the truck bed as it swerved through the streets. There had been so many twists and turns and roundabouts that Jake had lost track of their direction. They could be heading north, south, east, or west.

All were bad options.

The pickup skidded to a halt on a patch of dirt.

The gunmen rousted Jake and Pickens and led them, still bound and hooded, into a building. Pickens said something in Somali and received a blow that knocked him to the floor.

"On your knees," said a man in English.

Someone removed the hoods. They were back inside

the Exchange. A man in his fifties with a cane was limping around the interior, inspecting chips in the walls where bullets had struck the concrete.

"You did this?" he asked.

"Those bullets were fired at us," said Pickens.

"And yet those men are dead and you are alive." The man bent over and picked up a lacquered steel shell casing. "Why were you here?"

"We're aid workers," Jake said.

"I thought aid workers were supposed to help people, not kill them."

"It was self-defense."

"You were well armed for aid workers."

"Somalia can be a dangerous place," said Jake, glancing at the men holding them at gunpoint.

The man smirked. "So why were you in my building?" He gestured to the walls around them.

Silence.

The man stepped closer. "Are you familiar with the Somali custom of *diya*?" he said.

"Blood money," said Pickens.

"That is the Western translation, but diya is paid in livestock, not currency. However, given that you are foreigners, I will permit your debt to be paid in cash. Ten thousand U.S. dollars per dead man, forty thousand in total, to be distributed to the surviving family members two weeks from today."

"Forty thousand is a lot—"

"Your employer will understand. Diya is often used to settle debts."

Jake and Pickens were untied and led outside. One of the gunmen had driven their car up from the checkpoint. He put the Americans' weapons in the trunk and closed it.

"You have two weeks," said the man with the cane. He held up the men's identification and put them in his pocket. "Do not make me look for you again."

"How will we find you?" Jake asked.

The man smiled.

"You can ask anyone in Kitadra. My name is Badeed."

EIGHTEEN

JAKE HAD COLLECTED $50,000 from the local CIA station when he'd first arrived in Mogadishu. It was supposed to be used for developing sources, facilitation payments, and unexpected events—like paying off warlords so they wouldn't kill you. The cash was locked inside the gun safe in Pickens's basement, but the two men had decided on the drive home from Kitadra that they weren't going to pay Badeed. It was increasingly apparent that he was the target of their operation, and why give $40,000 to a dead man?

It gave them two weeks to confirm that Badeed was the pirate leader and bring the proof to Ted Graves.

Jake opened his laptop once they were back inside the safe house. The SIGINT analytics team at headquarters had run the queries he'd requested before their trip to Kitadra. He'd asked the team to search for voice intercepts that had been flagged based on the callers' numbers, keywords, or voiceprints. Additionally, he'd requested that the team review the entire universe of Somali mobile phone records a second time, but select for aggregate behaviors such as common times, telephone numbers, or locations that might lead to the identification of the rest of the pirates and hopefully tie them to Badeed.

The results were waiting in Jake's inbox.

The pirate gang of eight had made dozens of calls to common numbers, but further analysis showed them to be prepaid mobile numbers: burner phones with no ownership information, and most had gone quiet after a few weeks of use. The intercepts were nonproductive as well, with no positive voice recognition and only ambiguous, coded texts.

Dead ends.

"The technology failed us," said Pickens. "I guess we're going to have to do this the old-fashioned way."

"Round up a posse and ride at dawn?"

"First of all, fuck off," said Pickens. "Now let's find one of these degenerates that we can develop."

The two men returned their attention to the files on the eight pirates. If Jake and Pickens could find a few candidates for surveillance or interrogation, they could start to build out the pirate network and identify the rest of the players. Jake suspected that the eight men were not part of the tier-one boarding team that was driving the operations, but more likely support staff, given that they'd been involved in piracy during its first iteration and not off training with a foreign military.

The number of potential targets dropped quickly as Jake and Pickens scrolled through the INTERPOL dossiers. Two men didn't have photos on file, and four of them lived in sparsely populated areas far outside Mogadishu, where the two Americans would quickly be spotted as they had been in Kitadra.

The remaining two pirates had each been accused of kidnapping and murder at sea. They'd been apprehended by international naval forces, but the high burden of proof in maritime law had resulted in their release after brief detentions.

Jake studied a high-resolution satellite image of the first man's home. On the outskirts of Mogadishu, it was at the end of a long dirt road with only one way in and one way out. It offered a great deal of privacy for what the Americans had in mind, but it would be a death trap if the operation went sideways.

Pickens was looking at the profile of the last man.

His name was Mahad.

His file said that the pirates he'd been running with had boarded a container ship in the Gulf of Aden in 2013, only to discover that most of the crew had sealed themselves inside the ship's citadel to wait out the attack in safety.

The crew had followed standard procedure by sending a distress call over the radio, sounding the general alarm, and shutting down the ship's engine. They'd huddled inside the steel-walled room for over an hour, watching CCTV feeds from the ship and listening to the pirates strike the watertight door with fire axes and pry bars. When that didn't work, the pirates lit a fire and piled a rubber life raft on top of it, trying to smoke the crew out, but the citadel had been designed with an independent air source and the smoke-out was unsuccessful.

When the assault suddenly stopped, the crew assumed that their distress call had been heard and a friendly naval force had rousted the pirates.

But reality was far worse.

A lone crewman had been working in a noisy mechanical area of the ship's hold and had not heard the general alarm. By the time he finally ran for the citadel, it was too late. He was a hundred yards from the safe room when he saw the pirates climb onto the deck and fire their weapons into the air. The seaman knew the ship better than almost anyone, and he slid down a ladder back into the hold and ran along a catwalk until he found a good hiding place.

But the devil was in the details.

Two pirates were searching the hold, walking the catwalks, when a burst of static came over the crewman's radio. The two Somalis found him inside ninety seconds and escorted him to the citadel—at gunpoint.

Which was where Mahad had distinguished himself.

He stripped the seaman of his clothes and hog-tied him with thick ropes. The pirate then grabbed the man's hair, held his face up to the CCTV camera mounted outside the citadel's watertight door, and began to flay him alive.

The screams echoed through the metal companionway. In less than thirty seconds the rest of the crew voted to open the door. Seventeen of them were held for ransom and released within a year, three died in captivity, and the crewman who'd been partially skinned alive was tossed overboard and into the salt water before sunset.

The survivors had each identified Mahad by name and photograph upon their release.

"Forget about working with this sonofabitch," said Pickens. "I've dealt with this kind of animal before and they only understand one thing: force."

Jake closed his laptop.

"Then force it will be."

NINETEEN

J AKE WAS BEHIND the wheel of the maroon SUV, rolling fast through the narrow streets of Mogadishu with its turbo-diesel motor humming and the hot night air blowing through the open windows.

"Let's not overthink this," he said.

"Never been a problem for me," said Pickens. He jacked the cocking handle on the short-barrel M249 machine gun in his lap. It had a collapsible buttstock and a box magazine holding two hundred rounds. He had two more magazines at his feet.

"Let's not kill him either," Jake suggested.

"That's his call. I'm going home tonight either way."

Jake whipped around a corner and sped down an alley. He and Pickens had cased the area twice earlier in the day. Mahad had done well for himself, with a gated home in a quiet residential area.

"On target in sixty," Jake said.

On the SUV's console was a compact electronic device

known as an IMSI catcher. Among other things, it could trick Mahad's mobile phone into revealing its location.

"Pinging him now," Pickens said. "He's home."

"Thirty seconds," said Jake. He swerved around a few men loitering on the side of the road and turned down a narrow street. "Hit it."

Pickens pressed another button on the device and Mahad's mobile phone started to ring. The IMSI catcher spoofed the phone's caller ID into displaying a number from one of the other pirates.

Pickens killed the transmission the instant Mahad answered.

Dropped calls weren't unusual in Mogadishu's buildings. The concrete walls often interfered with cell reception.

"Hitting him again now," said Pickens.

Mahad's phone rang again as Jake reached the end of the street.

They were three hundred feet from the pirate's house. As it had been both times earlier in the day, the gate was open. The pirate had grown complacent living in Somalia, where there were no consequences for the life he'd chosen.

But that was about to change.

"He's on the ground floor," Pickens said. The IMSI catcher also had direction-finding capability, indicating the azimuth and elevation of the signal it had locked onto.

"Bring him out," said Jake.

Pickens initiated a call using another pirate's caller ID and dropped it as soon as Mahad picked up. Now he was probably wondering what was happening.

"Hitting him with the third number now," Pickens said.

They were a hundred feet from Mahad's gate when Pickens spoke into the phone in Somali. "I'm outside. We have to—" he said before dropping the call again.

Jake turned into the driveway and stopped fifteen feet from the front door just as it opened. The pirate shielded his eyes as the SUV's high beams blinded him.

"What's going on, Badu?" the pirate said. "Jave is calling me too."

Jake stepped out and fired a Taser into Mahad's chest. The two metal prongs blasted the pirate's pain receptors with fifty thousand volts of electricity. Jake cut the power a second after Mahad hit the ground.

Pickens slapped a piece of duct tape over his mouth, cinched flex-ties around his wrists and ankles, and frisked him for weapons before putting a hood over his head and tossing him into the back of the SUV.

Jake backed out of the driveway and the men were back on the street twenty-eight seconds after they'd pulled in. They'd practiced the takedown half a dozen times that afternoon in an abandoned lot in Mogadishu.

Pickens had the butt of the machine gun resting on his hip, the barrel angled up through the open window. Though there was no indication that they'd been seen, good tradecraft dictated that they take precautions. They spent two hours running a surveillance detection route that took them outside the city and back in, through high-security neighborhoods and ones with none at all. By the time they pulled into their central Mogadishu safe house, they were confident that they weren't being followed.

Jake parked close to the building and killed the vehicle's interior lights. The two Agency operatives manhandled their prisoner directly through the basement's exterior doors and into an area they'd isolated with sheets hung from the ceiling. Pickens secured Mahad to a chair with more zip-ties, then stood behind him and removed the hood.

Jake slapped him across the face, hard.

He and Pickens were dressed in dusty camo fatigues and jungle boots. Each had a black *shemagh* wrapped around his head that revealed nothing but his eyes.

Mahad squinted at the halogen work lights that shone in his face, but he was able to see the video camera mounted on a tripod in front of him and the huge serrated knife that was resting on the wooden stool next to Jake. As a man who'd done horrible things to others, it didn't take long for his imagination to leap to a worst-case scenario.

"*Salaam-alaikum,*" said Jake. He had spent some time in Yemen the prior year and mimicked its distinctive accent.

The prisoner had been sweating so heavily that the duct tape fell from his face when he tried to speak.

"*Wa—*"

Jake slapped him again. Harder.

"*Wa . . . alaikum . . . salaam.*"

Mahad flinched as he spoke each word, wary of being hit again, but his apprehension was soon replaced by a much greater, and far more legitimate fear. Jake lifted the sixteen-inch knife from the stool and rotated the blade a few times, ensuring that the spotlights glinted off its polished steel blade.

"We have a problem, brother," Jake said. Though most

Somalis switched effortlessly between Somali and Arabic, the Americans stuck to Arabic to stay in character.

Jake thrust the knife an inch deep into the wooden stool.

The two Americans were pretending to be al-Shabaab militants. The terrorist group had once been the youth wing of the Islamic Courts Union and, upon its rebirth, it invaded the void created by the absence of a central Somali government, attempting to assert authority over every aspect of daily life. It was infamous for committing frequent and arbitrary executions. Espionage, collaboration, adultery, and apostasy were the most common charges, but the radicals saw nothing outside their purview and, like others who'd corrupted their faith, the rules didn't apply to them.

Jake and Pickens spent the next ninety minutes unloading an elaborate fiction onto Mahad. They accused the pirate of cooperating with the Somali National Intelligence and Security Agency in the killing of six of their fighters. Jake kept calling him "Ali" and ignored Mahad's protests that they had the wrong man. Pickens slapped the prisoner around—hard enough to ensure that his survival was not a foregone conclusion. The man was tough, but all resistance ended the instant Jake turned on the video camera and yanked the enormous knife from the stool.

Taped beheadings were a specialty of radicalized Islamists.

Jake shouted a dozen rapid-fire questions as he approached

with the knife. Halfway through the list, Jake asked the Somali who he worked for.

There was no hesitation, no bumbling, no searching for a plausible lie.

The answer came instantaneously.

Yaxaas.

TWENTY

I T PLUNGED THE whole operation into chaos.

Jake and Pickens had expected their captive to confirm that Badeed was the pirate leader, but Mahad's identification of Yaxaas forced the Americans to review the logic behind their theory, including their determination that the pirate gang of eight was behind the attacks. They went through every assumption and conclusion step-by-step, but neither man found any flaws in the reasoning.

Jake was confident that Mahad had been telling the truth. He had clearly been afraid for his life during the initial interrogation and answered the questions without hesitation. During subsequent rounds of questioning, Mahad had asserted that he worked merely as a deckhand on the pirate ship, but he became guarded as the questioning focused less on the killing of the six al-Shabaab militants and more on Yaxaas.

Pickens knew of Yaxaas and, while he was a powerful warlord, the CIA officer never knew him to be involved in piracy. They needed more information. They pulled everything CIA had on Badeed and Yaxaas: photos, known business interests and associates, financial networks. Badeed had a long history with piracy and Yaxaas had none, but Yaxaas's criminal enterprises had grown dramatically in the past decade while Badeed had diversified into many legitimate businesses. The Agency had also requested voice and communications intercepts, but those would take time—assuming the warlords still used electronic devices. Many criminals and terror networks in the post-Snowden era had reverted to sending messages via couriers on motorcycles.

There was nothing to break the tie, and CIA didn't have the luxury of time while men and money were disappearing from the high seas. They had to be proactive.

The only other member of the gang of eight they could possibly approach was Saahid. The dangerous dead-end road leading to his home had put him at the bottom of their list—discreet surveillance would be difficult, and limited options for ingress and egress presented a real danger if things went kinetic—but they needed to do it soon, before Mahad's disappearance became widely known and Saahid was spooked.

One of Pickens's regular sources requested to meet with him on an urgent but unrelated matter that afternoon, which meant Jake would have to perform the initial drive-by on his own. The two men would snatch Saahid that night if it looked doable.

Pickens hit the basement for his daily workout while Jake pored over his laptop, examining satellite images and piecing together several different routes he could use for surveillance, for surveillance detection, or to bail out if the situation went to hell.

He was still working on his computer when Pickens left.

"Wave off if it doesn't feel right," Pickens said. "We can always do it tomorrow."

"We'll do a couple of dry runs when you're back."

PICKENS HAD BEEN gone for a couple of hours by the time Jake started the old Toyota Corolla. The car's white paint had absorbed so much sunshine over the years that it had blistered and cracked, but it blended in seamlessly with the fabric of Mogadishu.

He had the IMSI catcher on the passenger seat next to him.

Saahid's house was on the northwestern edge of the city, close to the Dayniile district, and Jake noticed two vehicles that seemed to take an unusual interest in him during the forty-minute drive, but he carefully followed a surveillance detection route that he and Pickens had established. The silver pickup truck that had followed him for several blocks turned away after Jake drove around a traffic circle, and the man on the motorcycle continued on when Jake made a U-turn at an intersection. It was a sparsely populated area and, after he passed a beige hatchback heading in the opposite direction, he was alone on the road.

Jake had spent countless hours poring over imagery during his time as an analyst—searching for clues in photographs taken from air, land, sea, and space. For years, he'd used cutting-edge technologies such as spectral imaging, ground penetrating radar, and persistent wide-area aerial surveillance to evaluate potential threats from half a world away.

But there was no substitute for being on the ground.

The tree cover in the pirate's neighborhood was denser than when the satellite images had been taken and the road was narrower and in worse condition. Trash covered the roadside where shadows mottled the ground. He could manage no more than ten miles per hour in the low-slung Toyota as he bounced over the rutted dirt road.

Jake began to have doubts. With the only access road in such poor condition, it would be risky to snatch the pirate from his home—and that assumed he was home; the IMSI catcher hadn't yet registered a signal.

Cellular coverage was spotty in the area, and it was possible that Saahid didn't use the phone at home, or maybe he was simply out for a few hours, but the alarm in the back of Jake's mind that had kept him alive in some of the worst places on earth was starting to ring.

He checked his rearview mirror.

There were no one else in sight.

He'd just returned his eyes to the road when he spotted a tree that had fallen across half the road. He swerved onto the shoulder and the sun glinted off a discarded paint can, stuck in a pile of trash.

Jake's mind was already racing, but the tree and the paint can kicked it into high gear. Something wasn't right. The can was perfectly vertical, and the debris around it wasn't moving despite the breeze.

Jake slammed on the brakes and threw the transmission into reverse.

He'd barely released the clutch when his world went black.

TWENTY-ONE

JAKE REGAINED CONSCIOUSNESS in the Corolla's driver's seat.

The windows were shattered and his ears were ringing.

Fragments of glass were in his hair.

Jake wiped blood from his face and inhaled a mouthful of dust and chemicals.

He stumbled from the car, coughing repeatedly, and drew his pistol. Unsteady on his feet, he swept the area with his weapon, but he was alone inside a giant cloud of dust.

He shuffled to the side of the road.

There was a crater where the pile of trash had been.

He'd been hit by an IED.

The entire passenger side of the car was imploded, its frame showing through the sheet metal like the ribs of a starving animal. The tires were shredded and the engine had stopped. Gasoline leaked from the tank.

Jake returned to the driver's seat, punched in the cigarette lighter, and waited. By the time it was hot, there was a puddle of fuel under the car.

Jake tossed the lighter into the gas and it flared instantly. Flames engulfed the car from all four sides.

He staggered to the main road and waved down a Bajaj motorcycle-taxi. The three-wheeled rickshaws were everywhere in Somalia. He switched taxis two more times before heading to the safe house. He unlocked the door and walked inside.

Pickens had an M-4 rifle against his shoulder, pointed at Jake's chest.

"What the hell happened to you?" Pickens said. "I heard the gate open but I didn't see the Toyota."

He lowered the rifle as Jake explained the IED and how he'd torched the car to eliminate his fingerprints and destroy the IMSI catcher.

"You think you were targeted?"

"Maybe Badeed wants his diya."

"Or maybe it was a warning."

Jake went to his bedroom and tossed his shirt and pants into a corner. They were covered with blood, fragments of glass, and explosive residue. Though his ears were still ringing and he had a titanic headache, he looked halfway normal after a shower and a change of clothes. He found Pickens in the kitchen.

"We need to talk to Graves."

"An hour ago you were almost a cloud of dust. Why don't you lay down for a few minutes?"

"I'll feel better once we've made some progress. I'm calling Ted. Do you want in or not?"

The two men videoconferenced Graves from Jake's secure laptop.

"You have a name for me?" Graves asked in lieu of a greeting.

"We're getting conflicting intel," said Jake.

"I'll take that as a 'no.'"

"Ted, we've tried buying people off, we've tried threatening them, and we've tried appealing to their consciences, but the people of Somalia don't see anything wrong with piracy, so we're not getting much cooperation."

"Children romanticize pirates, Keller," Graves said. "This is a national security issue. Ninety-five percent of the world's manufactured goods travel by sea."

"That's exactly what the Somalis are saying. They literally see the world economy passing them by and they want a piece of it. They feel as if foreign powers have taken advantage of Somalia for years and piracy is their right."

"I'm not interested in an imperialist apology tour. I need actionable intel."

"I'm just giving you background, Ted. We've narrowed it down to two warlords. Badeed is a Hawiye clan leader and a founding father of the Somali pirate community. He and his crew were behind a lot of the hostage-taking a decade ago. We zeroed in on him initially, but a new and highly credible source has implicated Yaxaas, a Darood warlord."

"Maybe they're working together," said Graves.

"Not likely," said Pickens. "These two have been at each other's throats for years."

"Then you need to develop some new sources."

"We could liaise with the Somali National Intelligence and Security Agency," Jake said.

"They're no better than the warlords," said Graves.

"Then we're stuck," said Pickens, "and we're starting to feel some blowback from our investigation. Jake's car got IED'd a few hours ago. If we keep working the streets, we're both going to end up dead."

"And I still won't know who's running the show . . ." Graves sat back in his chair. "Do either of you know of Giánnis Romanos?"

"Never heard of him," Jake said. Pickens shook his head.

"He's a Greek shipowner. Two of his tankers vanished in the Indian Ocean six months ago. The crews and ships were never heard from again and he contacted the U.S. Department of State."

"Weren't the ships insured?" Pickens asked.

"For more than they were worth," Graves said, "but Romanos lost more than a couple of ships. His son was captain of the first one."

"The disappearances fit the m.o. of our pirates," Jake said, "but I don't see how he can help us."

"The pirates killed his only son. Men like Mr. Romanos don't just move on. He wants this avenged."

"And you didn't mention this before, because . . ."

"Because I wanted to minimize outside involvement in the operation, but it sounds as if you two aren't very good at your jobs, so we need to risk it. The Agency currently has two aircraft hangared in Mogadishu. I'll authorize one to take you to Greece."

"I'm not so sure that's a great idea," said Pickens. "Most of the players down here know who those aircraft belong to."

Graves stared at the camera for a few seconds.

"Good," he said eventually. "Maybe it'll flush out our boy."

The screen went dark.

TWENTY-TWO

P ICKENS HAD THE machine gun on his lap again.

Dawn was still two hours away as Jake drove to the outskirts of Mogadishu. It was a dangerous neighborhood for two foreigners, made even more so by the nature of their work. A new IMSI catcher was on the center console, acting like radar to locate anyone around them who was using a cell phone. Jake killed the lights and turned off the pavement. The closest user was a quarter mile away.

The two CIA officers drove a hundred yards down a long dirt road and stopped. Jake opened the SUV's trunk and he and Pickens hauled a mildly sedated Mahad fifty feet off the road into a flat area filled with nothing but scrub brush and litter. With Pickens holding the machine gun, Jake loosened the hood, removed the leg restraints, and told their prisoner that there had been a mix-up—that he wasn't the man they were looking for.

Then they let him go.

While the Americans held no affinity for Mahad, detaining him too long would raise questions in the pirate community and potentially put the mission at risk. They needed to move on.

Pickens took the wheel. He'd spent his entire career as an Africa Center officer and eight years working the Somalia account—intentionally skipping rotations to other posts to build an absolutely airtight legend. Though his cover would degrade naturally over time—he couldn't recruit sources if he didn't occasionally risk exposure—he'd decided not to go to Greece. Being associated with a private jet widely believed to belong to American intelligence would be an unnecessary risk for a long-shot lead.

He drove Jake to the rear entrance of a nearby hotel, where he passed through the lobby and caught a cab to the general aviation section of the airport. Aden Adde International was the most heavily defended space in all of Mogadishu. Hundreds of federal and foreign troops guarded the terminal and the entire eleven-thousand-foot runway with armored vehicles, machine gun towers, and serpentine concrete barriers meant to prevent vehicle-borne IED attacks.

They succeeded about 50 percent of the time.

Jake walked across the sandstone-colored ramp, already warm from the sun. He passed an old MD-88 from the United Nations and a newer Airbus 321 operated by Daallo Airlines. The Airbus had a hole blown in its skin where a laptop computer packed with homemade explosives had been detonated by a suicide bomber intent on bringing down the plane.

Fortunately, the suicide was the only successful part of the operation.

Farther down the tarmac was a gray McDonnell-Douglas 520 helicopter that was being rinsed with fresh water. The man working the pressure washer stopped what he was doing and watched as Jake approached the white Gulfstream G550.

Jake exchanged pre-arranged recognition phrases with the two Agency pilots and boarded the aircraft. Fifteen minutes later, they were airborne and on their way to Athens.

JAKE STUDIED THE shipowner's biography as the plane flew northwest over the Red Sea: In his eighties now, the shipping magnate had started his career as a ship broker, mainly arranging shipments of crude and occasionally the sale of the ships themselves. He bought his first tanker from a bank that had foreclosed on it and was so eager to get it off their books that they provided him with the financing to buy it.

The deal happened at the lows of a shipping cycle and the value of the ship quickly appreciated. In eight months, Romanos had built enough equity to buy two more ships. He sold all three at the peak of the next cycle and cashed out for eighteen months until the market corrected again. He repeated the trade several times, perfectly timing his acquisitions and dispositions, until people were afraid to buy ships when Romanos was selling. He started moving them through intermediaries and shell corporations, always spotting the clouds gathering on the horizon before everyone else.

Buying ships at the bottom of the cycle was easier—he was the only one who had any money.

And he had a lot of it.

CIA estimated his net worth to be between five and ten billion U.S. dollars. The exact number was impossible to know because Greece was a notoriously difficult place to track wealth. Shipowners were exempt from most taxation, and men as skilled in international commerce as Giánnis Romanos tended to spread their assets around to preserve them in case of little things like civil unrest or the election of a leftist government. He didn't want to give away his fortune on someone else's terms.

But he had given a lot away.

At least a couple billion.

His late wife had handled most of the philanthropy. Together they'd endowed hospitals and schools, supported the Greek Orthodox Church, and provided lifelines to hundreds of charities around the country. In the absence of a capable federal government, Romanos had stepped in to take care of his fellow man.

THE G550 DESCENDED through light turbulence as it turned onto final approach at Athens International Airport, but the Agency pilots hardly noticed the rough air. After flying spiral approaches into Baghdad at night and under fire for almost a decade, and using unprepared runways across Africa for the last three years, it took more than a bumpy ride on a cool November day to get them excited.

Jake had never spoken directly with Romanos, but his assistant had been cordial and immediately scheduled the appointment when Jake had called. He'd also insisted on sending a car to the airport. It was a midsize BMW sedan, just like thousands of taxis across Europe. The courtesy car prevented Jake from running a surveillance detection route, but he'd just flown in on a private jet from Somalia. A tail was . . . unlikely.

Jake and the driver headed southwest across the Attic peninsula toward the shipping company's headquarters in the affluent Athens suburb of Glyfada—and drove right past it.

Jake caught the driver's eye in the rearview mirror.

"I've been instructed to take you to the residence," he said.

The highway turned into a two-lane road that wound between the foothills of Mount Hymettus on one side and the seaside cliffs off the Saronic Gulf on the other. They soon reached the coastal enclave of Vouliagmeni, where towering palm trees and manicured parks lined the main boulevard.

The driver turned onto a narrow spit of land and entered the Romanos estate, following a crushed-stone driveway through an orchard of olive trees whose gnarled trunks looked as if they'd been twisted by giants. At the end was a sprawling, modern home with glass walls, metal railings, and a flat roof. Its elevation varied with the terrain, masking its true size.

The driver stopped at the front door and Jake stepped out. The air smelled of pine trees, wild chamomile, and the breeze blowing in off the sea. The contrast with Mogadishu was almost unfathomable.

ROMANOS'S ASSISTANT WAS waiting at the door in a light gray suit and a tie.

"It's good of you to come," he said. "Mr. Romanos is on the terrace. Please follow me."

The assistant led Jake through the house, past simple, modern furniture and a few pieces of original art. It was a minimalist style of decorating that suited the home perfectly—anything more elaborate would have been a waste—because nothing could compete with the view. The twenty-three-acre estate had a 270-degree vista of the rocky cliffs and the sea.

A sliding glass wall was open to the terrace. Romanos was alone outside, sitting in a lounge chair wearing a warm jacket with a blanket over his legs. The assistant pointed to a chair next to him.

"I'm sure he'll be delighted to see you. He doesn't get many visitors anymore."

Jake was about to ask the assistant to elaborate, but he'd already returned to the interior of the house.

Jake introduced himself. "I appreciate you seeing me on such short notice, Mr. Romanos."

The silver-haired shipowner nodded behind a pair of dark sunglasses but said nothing.

Jake expressed condolences for the loss of his son and the ships' crews and gratitude for Romanos's offer to help combat the threat. Jake broadly laid out what he'd learned about the highly sophisticated pirate operation and his search for the man who ran it all.

"Who is he?" asked the shipowner.

"We don't know. The United States is hopeful that you might help us identify him."

"Who?"

"The man atop the whole enterprise."

Romanos said nothing.

"We'd like to assemble a list of who knew about the *Lindos*'s and the *Rhodos*'s routes before—"

Jake heard rapid footsteps behind him and turned to see a woman a few years older than himself. She was wearing a black silk blouse over white linen pants and her dark hair was pulled back tight.

She was stunning.

And she was furious.

"Who are you?" she snapped.

Jake stood to introduce himself, but the shipowner's assistant was already there. She started firing off more questions before anyone could answer.

"Who is this?" she said. "What does he want?"

"Forgive me," said the assistant. "He is from the U.S. State Department."

"I'm with the Maritime Security Division," Jake said. "Mr. Romanos contacted us several months ago and offered to assist with an investigation we're conducting."

"And you just let him in?" she said to the assistant.

"I thought it would be good for him—" The assistant glanced at Romanos.

"Let me see your identification."

Jake handed over his State Department credentials. The cover story had been thoroughly backstopped and the information would be corroborated by State Department headquarters if anyone checked.

And she checked.

She pulled out a mobile phone and searched the internet for the State Department's main number—not willing to trust the number printed on Jake's ID. A ten-carat canary yellow diamond engagement ring sparkled in the sunlight as she held the phone to her ear and verified Jake's employment.

"Come with me," she said to Jake once she'd finished.

It was an order, not an invitation.

She led him back through the house to a home office.

Jake began to apologize. "I'm sorry if—"

"I am Athena Romanos. My father had a stroke four months ago and suffers from advanced vascular dementia. He is a kind and generous man, and many people have tried to take advantage of him since his stroke."

"I'm sorry, Ms. Romanos," Jake said. "I didn't know."

"You should have known. What do you want?"

"Your father called—"

"I know about the call. I was the one who insisted he make it after my brother disappeared."

"We were hoping your father could help with the investigation."

"So the authorities are asking the victim to solve the crime?"

Jake didn't appreciate the confrontational attitude.

"I'm sorry about your brother," he said, "but those two

ships were overinsured by almost forty million dollars, so let's not overplay the victim card. Each of—"

"How dare you—"

"Each of the missing ships had a very similar profile in terms of tonnage, cargo, and routes, which means that these hijackings were not targets of opportunity. These were intelligence-led operations, led by a very capable and very dangerous organization. Someone knew the ships' routes, cargo, and timing—probably someone on the inside."

She sat down behind the desk.

"First of all," she said, "the excess insurance proceeds were closer to thirty-three million, and you obviously have no idea what happened to that money."

She typed something on the computer keyboard in front of her and turned the monitor to face Jake.

"Excluding my brother, forty-one crewmen did not return home. Their families each received a million dollars—all of the excess proceeds, plus eight million from the company, which is one hundred percent owned by my family."

Jake examined the spreadsheet. It was the names of the forty-one sailors, their beneficiaries, addresses, bank routing numbers, local currencies, and dates of payment. It could have been fake, but she hadn't even known he was coming.

Athena stood and walked him to the front door. "We didn't call you because we lost a couple of ships," she said. The edge in her voice could have split a block of marble.

"Good-bye."

TWENTY-THREE

JAKE WASN'T GIVING up just yet. The more he analyzed the data, the more convinced he became that the pirates had someone on the inside—someone who was feeding them advance intel on the targets.

And the two Romanos ships were the first to fall.

He spent the night at the Westin Astir Palace in Vouliagmeni and called Athena's office the next morning to schedule an appointment. She acquiesced after his sixth attempt and agreed to see him for ten minutes at the end of the day.

The company's offices occupied the top three floors of a five-story glass-and-steel building in Glyfada. Jake arrived ten minutes early and was escorted into a conference room with seating for thirty and a spectacular view of the Saronic Gulf. The island of Aegina, twelve miles off the coast, looked as if he could reach out and touch it. Lining the conference room walls were models of ships and dozens of deal mementos called "tombstones," eight-inch-high acrylic blocks with the details of various ship purchases and cargo deals encased in the heavy plastic. Jake found the tombstone for the *Lindos*, the first ship taken by the pirates, and took it down from the shelf to read the details.

"That was my brother's ship," said Athena. She was wearing a fitted black suit and a printed silk scarf. Her dark wavy hair was pulled back tight.

She took the tombstone, replaced it on the shelf, and remained standing. It was not going to be a long meeting.

"The pirates aren't striking at random," Jake said. "These are intelligence-led operations, and something caused them to select your ships."

"Do you think we'll be attacked again?"

Jake nodded.

"There's a very real possibility that someone in your organization is feeding information to the pirates."

"I'm not naïve, but I find it difficult to believe that one of our staff would sell information, knowing that it would result in the deaths of their colleagues."

"I'm not accusing anyone, but someone is providing that intel. We need to follow the flow of information and see where it leads us. Roughly half of the tankers that disappeared were loaded with refined products from the Indian coast, mostly Mumbai, Mangaluru, and Kochi. We looked at India as the common element, but other targets were carrying crude and had no connection to India, which is why I'm asking for your help."

"A common destination, perhaps?"

"Some were headed for the Mediterranean, some for Africa, and some for Asia."

"I seem to recall something similar happening a few

years ago," Athena said, suddenly intrigued. "Several tankers vanished in the western Pacific. Do you think it's related?"

"Those ships all reappeared after a few months with new names, counterfeit manifests, and phony flags. It turns out they were smuggling oil into sanctioned countries and trying to hide their tracks."

Athena looked out the window. "How can I help?"

"Tell me about your ships. Who would have enough advance knowledge of their routes to plan an attack?"

"How much time would they need?"

"At least a week before the tanker sailed, probably two."

"Outside our company, only the brokers and the shipping agents would have the details that early."

"Did the same men work the *Lindos* and the *Rhodos*?"

Athena pulled a laptop from a cabinet and her fingers flew over the keyboard—despite the enormous diamond that was weighing one of them down. She had an answer in under two minutes.

"They were different brokers," she said as her eyes rose to meet Jake's, "but the same agent."

TWENTY-FOUR

A THENA MUTTERED SOMETHING in Greek.
Jake didn't speak a word of the language, but he could tell from the tone that she wasn't pleased. She reached for the telephone.

"Who are you calling?" Jake said.

"The police," she said.

"Please don't."

"Why shouldn't I?"

"Well, to start with, you don't have any evidence, only suspicion."

"Then I'll confront him and force him to admit it."

"You can't do that."

"He killed my brother."

"My point exactly. These are dangerous criminals."

"Fine," she said. She lifted up the phone and started dialing.

"Who are you calling now?"

"My operations room. We have another ship at sea with this agent. I'm bringing it back to port."

Jake put his hand on the phone and gently hung it up.

Athena eyes widened in disbelief. She looked as if she might kill him.

"If that ship turns around," Jake said, "the agent will know we're on to him. We have to let it play out."

"I won't let you use my men as bait."

"Then more men will die." He stood from his seat and looked out the window. "Not your men, but men will die, and they'll keep dying until we identify the pirate leader."

"You can't blame me for those deaths . . ."

"No, but the pirates need to be stopped, and right now the agent is our only lead."

Athena stood from her seat and joined Jake, staring out over the Saronic Gulf of the western Aegean Sea.

"How much time do you need?" she said.

"Give me a week."

"The ship will be in the Arabian Sea in five days. You have four."

Jake nodded. "I'll be right back."

He left the building and made several calls on his secure mobile phone as he walked in the park next to Athena's office—using the overhead cover of the palm trees and the noise from the fountains to avoid surveillance. Athena was waiting for him when he returned to the building an hour later.

"You need to visit the agent," he said as he closed her office door.

"I suggested that an hour ago . . ."

"But you can't confront him and go to the police. This

agent is the only lead we have. If you spook him, our investigation is over and your brother's killer gets away."

"So what would you have me do, pay him a social call?"

"Exactly. Tell him you happened to be in the area and stopped by to say hello."

"You must be joking."

"Have a look around his office . . . a detailed look. I want to know the type of phone, the make of his computer, any remote controls, the kind of light fixtures, desktop decorations, furniture."

"What am I searching for?"

"Details," Jake said. "We won't know what's important until you've finished. I can get you a concealed camera if you'd like."

"That won't be necessary. I don't forget anything," she said as she fidgeted with her ring, "unfortunately."

"Ms. Romanos, I want to make sure you understand the risk here. If we're right about this agent, and he gets suspicious, you could be in physical danger. These probably aren't the sort of people you normally associate with."

"You have no idea what kind of people I associate with."

"I didn't mean to—"

"My family has a long history with the Greek mafia."

Jake was shocked that it wasn't in the Agency dossier—it was the kind of information that CIA generally uncovered—even if it was only speculation. He couldn't help but show his surprise.

"We aren't criminals." Athena smirked. "Quite the opposite. Greece is a waypoint and a destination for the Eastern European and African sex trades. My mother started several shelters in Athens two decades ago so the girls would have a place to stay if they were able to escape the traffickers. It gave the girls hope and safety, but my family has lived with death threats, and an occasional attack, from the organized crime syndicates ever since. So thank you for your concern, but I think I can handle the agent."

TWENTY-FIVE

JAKE WORE A black suit and tie as he drove Athena's silver Jaguar sedan along the congested Akti Miaouli boulevard. He stopped outside a five-story office building in the port city of Piraeus and opened the rear door.

Athena stepped out wearing a silk Armani suit with a leather Hermès bag on her arm and took the elevator to the top floor. It was half past six, and most of the employees had already departed for the evening, but the receptionist greeted Athena and escorted her to the agent's office. It was furnished like a British bank from the 1800s, with dark wood paneling and tufted leather furniture.

"Miss Romanos, you honor me with your presence," said the agent. He was in his midforties and wore a gray sharkskin suit, a shiny gold chain around his neck, and matching cuff links.

"Please, call me Athena," she said with a smile. While she would have liked to break his outstretched hand, she took it and gave it a polite squeeze.

He held on for several seconds.

Athena liberated herself and walked to the windows behind his desk. The city was built on a gently sloping hill and the office overlooked the port. Before her were half a dozen large ships, bathed in the port's work lights. It was an imposing view, but Athena thought only of her dead brother.

Until she noticed the agent checking out her ass.

She turned around. She had no desire, and no need, to use her looks to get what she came for.

"How is your father?" asked the agent.

"His memory ebbs and flows, but his brilliant mind is still there."

"Which you've obviously inherited."

Athena tuned out the agent as he droned on about how his business had grown and how he could give her guidance as her father continued to fade. She ignored her burning desire to cut out his tongue and started her mission— strolling around the office and mentally cataloging everything in sight.

In ten minutes, she was ready to leave. The agent armed the alarm system and locked the door as they passed by the night cleaning crew on their way to the elevator.

"Dinner?" asked the agent on the ride down.

Athena's gut tightened, but she kept her composure and smiled.

"That's very kind of you, but I already have plans."

The agent wrote his mobile number on the back of a business card.

"Then maybe a drink later," he said as he grasped her elbow with one hand and gave her his card with the other.

The elevator doors opened.

Jake was standing there—all six feet, two inches of him, tanned and fit—his hands tented in front of him, almost as if he were praying. But he wasn't. The stance would save a few fractions of a second if he had to strike someone in the head or throat.

Like the agent.

Athena's cell phone was transmitting audio to an earpiece Jake was wearing, and he was feeling protective of the woman who'd put herself at risk to help him.

Jake's eyes bored into the man.

The agent released Athena's elbow and bid her good night.

"That wasn't very subtle," she said as Jake followed her to the car.

"I want him to know that someone is watching your back."

"Oh, he already took care of that . . ."

JAKE SPENT TWENTY minutes running a surveillance detection route through the narrow streets of Piraeus.

"Where are we going?" Athena asked after the fifth seemingly random turn.

"We're meeting someone."

Jake stopped in front of a roadside café. A petite woman about Jake's age opened the door and sat in the rear seat next to Athena. Jake pulled away.

"You can call me Thanya," the woman said to Athena. "Thank you for your help. Do you have the device Jake gave you?"

Athena pulled a dog-eared paperback book from her purse and handed it over.

"Thank you. Now can you describe everything you saw from the time you got out of the car until the time you were back in it?"

Athena closed her eyes and recalled the agent's office as if she were still inside the building: the exterior, the lobby, the layout of the office suite, the manufacturer of his telephone and laptop, and the decorations in his private office.

"That's impressive," said the woman from CIA's Office of Technical Services.

"I can draw you a map," Athena said without a hint of self-importance.

Thanya handed her a pad and a pencil and Athena made good on her offer.

"You said he had a collection of tombstones," Jake said. "Were any of them from deals he'd done with your company?"

Athena stopped drawing and stared out the window.

"He had the one from the *Lindos*," she said with ice in her voice.

Jake made eye contact with Thanya in the rearview mirror. She'd also been listening to the conversation inside the office.

She looked at Athena. "So, about that drink tonight . . ."

TWENTY-SIX

I T WAS TWO and a half hours later when Athena's regular driver dropped her off at the Varoulko Seaside restaurant in Piraeus. It was a Friday night and dozens of heads turned as she walked through the crowded bar. She was a beautiful woman, but it was more than her looks that generated all the attention. Shipping was big business in Greece, and she was the head of one of the largest lines in the country.

The front of the restaurant was well-lit and open to a scenic harbor where nearly a hundred pleasure craft were docked—but the agent was in a darkened booth in the back. He popped the cork on a bottle of Cristal as soon as he caught Athena's eye.

THANYA WAS LAUGHING out loud as they walked down the sidewalk. She was wearing a short skirt and a wide hat and had her arm tucked inside Jake's. He wore a fashionable pair of sunglasses and a jacket. Except for the nearly translucent latex gloves they were wearing, they looked like a couple having a night out on the town. They stopped in front of the agent's building and Jake smiled at something Thanya had said as he held his wallet against the keycard reader that controlled after-hours access.

Earlier in the day, when Athena had walked through the same building, she'd been carrying a device in her purse that had queried every keycard within a three-foot radius and stolen its radio frequency identification data. She'd been especially diligent about passing within range of the cleaning crew and the agent, who would have the access the CIA team needed.

Thanya had taken the device from Athena and created a duplicate keycard for Jake.

The door beeped, the magnetic lock released, and they were in. There was a closed-circuit surveillance camera at the end of the lobby, positioned exactly where Athena said it would be, and Jake stared into the lens as they walked to the elevators. Invisible infrared LED lights in the frame of his sunglasses and sewn into the band of Thanya's hat blinded the camera until they boarded the elevator. There was another camera in the elevator's ceiling, but the two CIA officers stared at the floor for the entire ride.

THE SHIPPING AGENT poured the champagne into a pair of crystal flutes and handed one to Athena. He proposed a toast to her father. It was a gratuitous move, and the agent's ceaseless attempts to bed her stoked her temper, but they each had their secrets, and Athena decided that it was worth playing along to avenge her brother's death.

She raised her glass, then settled down and got into character.

THE ELEVATOR OPENED onto the top floor. Jake and Thanya did a quick tour of the floor to ensure that the cleaning crew was gone and check for anyone who might be working late, but the area was deserted. There were two more CCTV cameras mounted in the corners, but Athena had spotted them both, and the infrared LEDs rendered them blind.

They paused outside the agent's office suite. Athena had noted an alarm sensor on the other side of the door and, from the description, Thanya was 90 percent sure that it was a wireless model.

"Black bag jobs," as they were known in the trade, were usually planned days or weeks in advance, but another pirate attack could happen at any moment and Jake had decided to compress the planning phase for tonight's operation into just a few hours. With more time and different equipment, Thanya could have learned the model of the alarm system and fooled it into thinking that all of its sensors were functioning normally even when they weren't, but she had confidence in Athena's recall, and defeating a wireless model was much easier and faster.

It was a calculated risk.

Thanya switched on a device she'd pulled from her purse and nodded to Jake. He pressed his keycard against the reader and opened the door.

The device started flashing red—never a good sign—as

the door sensor began transmitting to its base station that the door had been opened.

But the red light went out a second later and began to flash yellow. The device had discovered the alarm sensor's frequency and instantly jammed it using a higher power signal on the same frequency. The original signal had made it to the base station for only a fraction of a second and had failed to trigger the alarm.

The two CIA officers entered the agent's suite and closed the door behind them. Thanya located the alarm panel, plugged the jammer into a wall outlet to boost its power, and placed it next to the panel to block the signals from any other sensors they might trip while they were working.

She and Jake entered the agent's inner office at the end of the hallway. Their cover story was that they were friends of Athena's who were supposed to pick her up after her meeting with the agent but were running late. It was the thinnest of covers. Neither was armed, and they had good identification, but their only real chance in an encounter with the police would be Athena's word and the hope that the agent wouldn't press charges against his largest client.

They entered the agent's personal office and found it exactly as Athena had described. Thanya inserted a flash drive into his laptop and stole his password in forty-two seconds, then uploaded a piece of software that would transmit copies of every document stored on the hard drive to an untraceable NSA server somewhere in Germany.

Also in Thanya's purse was the acrylic tombstone Jake had noticed in Athena's office. It was identical to the one owned by the agent—a souvenir from the *Lindos* ship transaction—except Thanya had converted it into an electronic surveillance device by drilling a hole into its base and installing a miniature camera, microphone, battery, and transmitter, before resealing the hole.

ATHENA SIPPED HER glass of champagne while the agent drank the rest of the bottle. Several times he placed his hand upon hers, ignoring the engagement ring, as he told another tale of his acumen in business or on the soccer field. Athena sat with a pleasant smile on her face and pretended to enjoy the childish stories—until eleven fifteen.

He'd just brushed his leg against hers when she stood up and patted her jacket pockets.

"I'm sorry," she said. "I just remembered that I need to make a call and I've forgotten my phone. I need to go to my car."

The agent didn't like that idea at all.

"Please," he said. "Use mine."

Athena took the phone and dialed her office, but the loud restaurant made it impossible to hear. She excused herself and walked outside, along the waterfront, where all the sailboats were docked.

JAKE WAS ABOUT to replace the agent's tombstone with the bugged one when Thanya signaled him to freeze. She tapped the Bluetooth headset she was wearing.

"Yes?" she said in Greek. She listened for a moment and

gave Jake a thumbs-up to replace the tombstone and put the old one in her bag.

She pulled out her mobile phone. "I just texted you an executable file," she said. "Open it."

Athena did as she was told and Thanya confirmed that the software had been installed on the agent's phone. It was an XCell Stealth, a high-security phone that was resistant to remote penetration, so the team had decided to breach it via physical access. Twenty seconds after the software began running, it had already transmitted all of his contacts and his call history. Once the agent's phone was hooked up to a charger and idle for an hour, the software would steal his emails and his photos as well.

"We're in," Thanya said to Athena. "Now do three things: Delete this call from his call history, call your office for a few minutes so the record is there if he checks, and delete the text message I sent you."

Thanya ended the call and looked at Jake. "We have control of his device. Let's go."

ATHENA WAS STANDING on the dock, facing the sailboats in the harbor. She'd just deleted the phone call to Thanya and was speaking to her office voice mail account about a fictitious deal with an American oil company when she felt a tug at her elbow.

It was the agent.

TWENTY-SEVEN

JAKE ARRIVED AT the Romanos estate around ten the next morning.

It was the weekend and Athena met him at the front door, wearing a tailored pantsuit with low heels and her hair pulled back. Jake was wearing the same clothes he'd had on the night before and his wavy brown hair was completely disheveled.

She gave him a quick once-over and frowned.

"Busy night with Thanya?"

"Yes."

"She's cute."

"She's good at her job."

They walked to the glass-walled living room where Athena could keep an eye on her father. He was on the terrace, huddled comfortably under a blanket, watching a sailboat heeling under a gusty, gray sky.

"I didn't realize the U.S. State Department broke into people's offices and hacked their phones," she said.

"We discovered a link to Somalia in the agent's contacts late last night . . . while we were working."

"Is it the man you've been searching for?"

"Probably just an intermediary. It's a Swiss national who has regular contact with a banker in Mogadishu."

"So the banker is the pirate leader?"

"No—just another cutout. He doesn't fit the profile of the man we're looking for."

"Which means you don't want me to bring the *Symi* back to port . . ."

Jake shook his head. "Not until we've found the man calling the shots."

Athena stood. "Then I won't keep you, because you obviously have a lot of work to do in the next three days."

"You're still planning to turn your ship around before it reaches the Arabian Gulf?"

"My crews won't sail there as long as the pirate is free."

JAKE WAS WHEELS-DOWN in Mogadishu just after midnight. Given the late hour, the G550's aircrew had radioed ahead to request that a Somali customs agent be available to clear them into the country. The officer walked out to the plane wearing a Kevlar vest and a sidearm over his uniform.

Most of the Somali underworld, and nearly everyone who worked at the airport, knew that U.S. intelligence was running a detention center on the premises. The big Gulfstream often arrived and departed in the middle of the night with no flight plan and no manifest, but those were joint operations with Somali intelligence and not subject to customs oversight.

This was the first time the customs officer had been aboard the big jet.

The Agency pilot pulled out his wallet.

It was always a tricky decision, deciding how much to bribe someone. Too little and he might be insulted, but too much could make him wonder what you were hiding.

"What's the 'fee'?" the pilot asked.

Sometimes it was better to let him set the price.

"Sixty thousand shillings," said the agent—about a hundred U.S. dollars.

Not good, thought the pilot. *Way too low for a guy who wants to play ball.*

"Nothing extra for the late hour?" the pilot asked, holding out two hundred thousand.

The agent took sixty and wrote out a receipt. He was either the only honest cop in Somalia or already on someone else's payroll.

Jake handed over a false passport, often called a "shoe" in the intelligence community. The agent pulled out a handheld scanner and interrogated the RFID chip inside the passport's cover to corroborate the information printed between its covers.

But the shoe fit and the agent continued his inspection, checking the aft baggage compartment and looking under the seats with a flashlight. He opened all the luggage and examined the lavatory. He examined the cockpit and especially the communications gear. Apparently, whoever he was working for wanted a detailed report on the U.S. jet.

"What is the nature of your visit?" the officer asked.

"I'm looking for investment opportunities," Jake said. He still had to play the game.

"Where are you staying?"

"The Jazeera Palace Hotel."

The officer wrote it down and handed Jake the receipt.

Jake entered the glass-walled terminal. It was nearly deserted, with only AMISOM troops, Somali soldiers, and bomb-sniffing dogs inside. He caught a taxi to the Jazeera Palace, adjacent to the airport, where he ordered breakfast. He went to the lavatory before it arrived, changed his clothes, and slipped out the back of the hotel, where he took a second cab to another hotel.

Pickens was waiting down the block in the Toyota SUV.

"How did it go?" he asked.

"A shipping agent fed the pirates targeting data for the two Romanos ships."

As was Pickens's custom, the surveillance detection route took them through a particularly rough area of town where armed men loitered about and the few cars on the road were easy to spot.

Jake had a cable from headquarters waiting for him back at the safe house. The Agency had created a dossier on the Somali banker, with everything from his phone contacts and known associates to email traffic and internet browsing history. He'd been active in Mogadishu for decades, initially as a facilitator for the pirate syndicates, helping them collect ransom money and hide it from the international authorities.

But as the era of open-ocean kidnapping drew to a close,

the man's reputation as a money-laundering expert gave him entrée to the arms dealers and the warlords who kept the country at war. Jake pored over the dossier, looking for commonalities and building an association matrix—cross-referencing his phone records with shared contacts, dates, and events. The deeper Jake dug, the more links he found with one specific arms dealer, Cawar, and one specific warlord:

Yaxaas.

TWENTY-EIGHT

DESPITE THE EVER-INCREASING amount of circumstantial evidence that pointed to Yaxaas, CIA still had only a single piece of human-source intelligence indicating that the warlord was leading the pirates. And though the Agency didn't need a witness who could stand up in court, they needed more than an accusation coerced from a man who'd thought he was going to be beheaded.

Jake needed to speak with the banker.

Pickens chose to skip the meeting, concerned that he'd crossed paths with the banker at some point during his weapons purchases. It was a legitimate concern, but Jake had wanted him along. Human-source contact operations were an art, and not Jake's specialty. Slowly cultivating the banker over weeks or months wasn't going to work when he had only two days left until Athena's deadline to turn her ship around.

Jake needed the information now.

He started his reconnaissance at noon, driving past the

banker's office several times, using different cars and different disguises. It was a lot of time in chaotic traffic, and tempers were short on the already dangerous streets of Mogadishu. He saw a pickup truck driver ram a Bajaj that had cut him off and a fender-bender escalate into a gunfight, but he also developed a good mental map of the bank, noting security cameras and routes of ingress and egress, and, with another IMSI catcher on the seat next to him, he'd tracked the man's mobile phone number and verified his presence inside the building.

Jake returned home, switched to the Toyota Surf SUV that he hadn't used all day, and returned to the bank's parking lot just before closing time. The banker emerged twenty minutes later.

Jake eased the SUV between the banker and his car. Though Jake was still wearing a fake beard and sunglasses, he was careful to shield his face from the surveillance cameras.

"Mr. Zakaria!" he said in English.

The banker turned and smiled politely. He didn't recognize the man, but he didn't feel threatened by him either.

"The bank hasn't closed for the evening, has it?" Jake asked.

"I'm afraid it has."

"A shame. My flight was delayed leaving Zurich."

The banker's ears perked up. He'd laundered a lot of money through Switzerland.

"Have we met before?" he said.

"We have not, but Mr. Kengeter is a mutual acquaintance."

He was the Swiss intermediary who'd been taking the targeting information from Athena's shipping agent and passing it to the banker.

"I have a business proposition for you," Jake said as he opened the passenger door. "Please, join me."

Zakaria looked around, debating his course of action. He and Kengeter had gone to great lengths to not be seen in person together and now this "mutual acquaintance" had arrived completely unannounced?

"I'm sorry," said the banker, "I have a prior—"

Jake's pleasant tone and fake German accent disappeared.

"I know who you are, I know what you do, and I know who you do it for. If you cooperate, it remains our secret. If you don't, the local press will run a story that U.S. authorities have had great success working with a local banker in a yearlong investigation into money laundering for the warlords of Somalia."

Jake held up his cell phone and took a picture of the man's face.

"They'll even run a picture of you," Jake said. "You have five seconds to decide."

Zakaria climbed into the SUV, clearly displeased with the turn of events since he'd finished at the bank.

Jake pulled into traffic.

"Who are you?" Zakaria asked.

"Explain the money trail," Jake said. It was the thing he cared about least, but he was trying to bluff the banker into thinking that he knew everything else—as if they were simply two men chatting about a topic of mutual interest.

Zakaria exhaled deeply. "I get a wire transfer after the cargo is sold—usually from Mauritius or the Isle of Man. I split it up and layer it through a series of accounts and intermediaries in the Cayman Islands and Switzerland until it's integrated into the financial system. It usually takes a few months."

"Then what does he do with it?"

"Some he keeps locally in gold and precious stones, but once it's laundered, the bulk of it stays offshore in foreign currencies, mostly dollars and euros."

"He's a careful man."

"And dangerous," said the banker. "There is no one is Somalia more feared than Yaxaas."

Yaxaas, Jake thought. He'd found what he was looking for. "Tell me about the takedowns."

"I don't know the specifics." The banker looked over his shoulder again as Jake turned down an empty side street.

"Then tell me what you know."

Zakaria scowled. There was no winning in his current situation—only degrees of losing—but it was a situation of his own making. Partnering with the pirates had always been fraught with risk—but mainly from the pirates. Ironically, their success was the source of this new trouble.

"There's a mothership," he said. The banker fidgeted as he explained what he knew about intercepting and taking control of the tankers.

Jake asked more questions about the fate of the crews, how and where the oil was sold, and where the ships went when they were empty. Jake kept pressing and the banker knew more than he'd let on. The two men spent another half hour discussing specifics until Jake stopped the car a block from the bank and motioned for Zakaria to get out.

"We're done for now," Jake said.

The banker looked as if he were turning something over in his mind as he stepped out of the SUV.

"I wouldn't tell anyone about this conversation," Jake said. "Yaxaas won't look kindly on someone sharing his entire operation with a foreign intelligence service."

TWENTY-NINE

T'S YAXAAS," JAKE said upon returning to the safe house.

"The banker confirmed it?" Pickens said.

Jake nodded.

"What about Badeed?"

"Not involved," Jake said. He pulled out a small notebook and dropped it on the kitchen table. He had an excellent memory, but he'd recorded the entire exchange with Zakaria and summarized it in the notebook after the two men had parted.

Pickens was reading it intently when Jake's laptop began to trill.

"That's probably Graves," Jake said. "I left him a message."

Jake opened the secure videoconferencing software on his computer.

"What do you have?" said Graves. He was in a nondescript office building in suburban Virginia.

"We've validated the target." Jake said. "It's Yaxaas."

"Confidence level?"

"Ninety-five percent," Jake said. He typed on the computer as he spoke. "I just sent you our files. We've got communications intel and now multiple-source human intel confirming it."

Graves scratched his chin.

"What's your assessment of this banker?"

"Highly credible. It was a cold approach we developed through the Romanos family—there's no way he invented those details on the spot and under pressure."

"All right," Graves said. He spent a few seconds staring at the monitor before he spoke again. "I've got a few special-mission teams deployed in-country. I'll reassign one to you. They should be in Mogadishu in a couple of days. You're going to need some support for the next phase of the operation."

For years, the Central Intelligence Agency had been funding and training Somali intelligence operatives, intent on helping the country develop its own counterterrorism capability against al-Shabaab, al-Qaeda, and Daesh. The Agency also conducted joint, direct-action raids with U.S. and African military forces, and CIA's manpower contribution was from a paramilitary organization within the Special Activities Center known as Ground Branch. The special-mission team that Graves was sending to Mogadishu was composed of hardened combat veterans, hand-picked from elite military special-operations units.

Trigger-pullers.

"What's the plan for Yaxaas?"

Graves sat back in his seat and crossed his thick forearms in front of his chest. Then he smiled.

Jake knew Ted's body language, and while he didn't know what was coming next, he knew he wasn't going to like it.

"What's the plan for Yaxaas, Ted?"

"I want you to talk to him," Graves said. "Convince him to work for us."

"You want him to work for the government of the United States?"

"He's not going on the payroll, Jake."

"He tried to kill me with an IED."

"Fortunately we don't need him for his bomb-making skills."

"Is this about al-Shabaab?"

"Anybody can fight al-Shabaab. We need Yaxaas to keep doing what he's doing."

Though the two men held enormous respect for each other's professional abilities, Jake believed firmly in the concepts of right and wrong while Graves's beliefs were more nuanced.

Significantly more nuanced.

"Which is what, exactly?" Jake asked.

"Making ships disappear without a trace."

"How does that help the United States?"

"We pick the ships."

"That sonofabitch has killed a hundred fifty innocent sailors plus who knows how many on land. I'm not working with him, Ted."

"Watch yourself, Keller. You know that insubordination is cause for termination."

Termination.

It was Agency-speak for firing someone. Foreign assets were terminated, employees and contractors were terminated. Their relationships with CIA ended, but their hearts kept beating.

It was widely suspected that Ted Graves had a different definition of the word.

The Special Activities Center had always had the highest rate of officers killed in the line of duty—it was the nature of the paramilitary mission—but three of Graves's men had met unfortunate ends soon after known confrontations with their boss. Two had been killed by foreign intelligence services and the other had simply disappeared. Their stars had been etched into the Memorial Wall and their names inscribed in the Book of Honor. No accusations had been leveled, no connections had been found, but suspicions lingered.

Jake and Ted maintained an effective working relationship, but venom flew in both directions when Jake voiced any reservations about his boss's questionable intelligence activities.

Unspoken threats lingered below the surface.

"The end always justifies the means, doesn't it, Ted?"

"Well, look who took a philosophy course in college. Why don't you ruminate on this: You've been chained to a ceiling, hooked up to a car battery, and seen your teammates die in front of you. You've seen what the other side is capable of, Jake, and you know that protecting this nation is bare-knuckles brawling, 24/7. So you can either stick your head in the sand and pretend it isn't happening or get into the fight and do something about it."

Jake wasn't naïve about the evil in the world. He had indeed experienced it firsthand, but he didn't like the idea of working with a warlord. There would have to be a damn good reason to partner with a man who viewed human life as a commodity.

"What do you have in mind?" Jake said.

"I'm glad you asked," said Graves. The anger disappeared from his voice as quickly as it had come. Jake wondered if there was anything genuine about the man at all—anything Ted didn't alter to suit his most immediate need.

"Africa is the world's largest home of radical Islam: al-Shabaab, al-Qaeda, Daesh, and half a dozen other extremist organizations are recruiting, training, and terrorizing the second most populous continent on earth. In another decade, the two billion people living in the failed states of Africa are going to present a catastrophic threat to world stability. The continent has been a nexus for smugglers and arms traffickers for five hundred years, and now Iran, North Korea, Russia, and a dozen others are operating outside the law and bleeding it dry. With the United States pulling out of the region, the continent is going to implode. Tens or maybe hundreds of millions of people will die."

Jake didn't dispute a word that Graves had said. Fueled by corruption and illicit weapons, Africa was on a downward spiral into anarchy.

"Black Flag is about developing a covert instrument of national power," Ted continued. "China is already playing the long game. They're mining raw materials there now, but they'll use that as justification to 'stabilize' the region when their investments are threatened by political collapse. Do you think a China that dominates Asia and Africa might possibly present a threat to U.S. security?"

"All valid points, but we could address the maritime threat with naval patrols."

"The oceans are too vast for denial forces, Jake. Hell, the Arabian Sea and Indian Ocean are almost thirty million square miles. We might need Yaxaas once a year or once a month, but with our intel and his capabilities, we'll be able to prevent a lawless Africa from knocking the world off its axis."

"You're going to use Yaxaas as a CIA navy?"

"We're going to use a local solution to a local problem."

Jake wasn't happy with the idea of working with the warlord, but the logic behind it wasn't as hollow as he'd first thought.

"It does give us deniability," he conceded.

"Better than deniability," said Graves. "Our involvement won't even be suspected. Some of these shipments may not be illegal, but they're unquestionably not in the best interests of the people of Africa or the United States."

"Do you think you can trust Yaxaas?"

"Not even close, but you and the Ground Branch team are going to make him understand that there will be severe consequences if he deviates from our agreement."

Jake kept pressing, but Graves had an answer for every

question. The man was unconventional, but that was part of his brilliance. Few people thought as radically as Ted Graves.

"I think I convinced Athena Romanos not to go to IN-TERPOL," Jake said, "but their next ship will be in the Arabian Gulf in two days, and she's going to turn it around the second she finds out we haven't rolled up the pirate ring."

Graves scowled. "You're covered as State Department, right?"

Jake nodded.

"Then I suggest that you get your ass back to Greece and practice some diplomacy. If Yaxaas spooks before we make contact, this whole operation will go up in smoke."

"ARE YOU CRAZY or do you have some kind of death wish?" said Pickens.

He'd been off-camera during the videoconference, sitting at the kitchen table.

"I'm not afraid of Graves," Jake said. "I just don't like the idea of partnering with a warlord."

"Look, Jake, I respect your idealism, but this is Somalia. The whole goddamn place is corrupt. Everybody is on the take. Hell, the new president was sitting in a cubicle in Buffalo, New York, working for the state department of transportation before the warlords bought the election for him. You've got to get your head around the fact that until somebody better comes along, the warlords make the rules."

"That doesn't mean we have to perpetuate the system."

"This isn't the West, Jake. Hell, the average Somali thinks the warlords have supernatural powers, and it's all about power down here. So unless you've got some way to enforce your values on the entire population, you've got to work within 'the system.'"

Jake was pacing around the small kitchen.

"What do you think Graves does if we tell him we're not going to do it?" Pickens said.

"He'll replace us with someone who will."

"Exactly. It's a lawful order. Our job is to follow it."

Jake stopped pacing.

"It still sucks," he said.

"Brother, I don't like Yaxaas any more than you do, but let's talk to the man."

"All right," Jake said.

"All right," said Pickens, "but first you've got to go to Greece and buy us some time."

THIRTY

I
T WAS RAINING in Athens when the Agency Gulfstream touched down.

Jake declined an umbrella from the aircrew and walked slowly across the tarmac, savoring each cool drop as it hit his face. Having grown up on the east coast of the United States, where rain was largely considered an inconvenience, he'd come to take it for granted, like light or air, but living amid the famine that was killing man and beast in the Horn of Africa made Jake appreciate its life-giving power like never before.

He picked up a rental car at the general aviation terminal and slogged through the tail end of the morning rush hour as he drove to the Romanos offices in Glyfada. Jake was looking out the window of Athena's conference room, searching through the gray mist for the island of Aegina, when she walked in.

She was holding the acrylic tombstone they'd swapped out of the agent's office.

"Did it work?" she asked.

"It did," Jake said. "We've made a preliminary identification of the man we were looking for."

"Preliminary? Are you telling me he still hasn't been arrested?"

"Arrangements are being made."

"But I can fire the agent?"

"Ms. Romanos—"

"You only call me that when you're about to tell me something I won't like."

Jake's expression acknowledged the point.

"We need more time. We have to let this play out."

Athena pulled a sheet of paper from her jacket and unfolded it on the table.

"This is the crew list for the *Symi*. Twenty-three men: sixteen Filipinos, four Eastern Europeans, and three Greeks."

She read each name aloud and gave the paper to Jake.

"I will not send them to their deaths."

She walked out of the conference room.

JAKE WAITED IN the reception area. Athena passed by half an hour later, surprised to see him.

"There's nothing to discuss," she said.

"There is."

She kept walking.

Jake kept waiting.

An hour later, the receptionist picked up her phone, looked up at Jake, and said something in Greek into the phone.

Athena stepped out of her office.

"I have a lunch meeting," she said to Jake. "Walk me downstairs."

When they were alone in the elevator, she said, "Just so it's one hundred percent clear, the *Symi* left Kuwait two days ago. In two more days, it will be in the Arabian Sea. You have until tomorrow to arrest the pirates, otherwise I'm turning the ship around."

Two men entered the elevator on the third floor, and the rest of the trip passed in silence.

Athena strode through the lobby to her reserved parking space and left in the silver Jaguar.

Jake was waiting in the reception area again when she returned.

She shook her head and walked past him.

It was six thirty p.m. when she finished work.

Jake was still waiting.

"I need five minutes," he said.

"I'm late."

"I'll wait."

She cursed at him in Greek. At least he thought it was a curse. He'd been cursed at before, and though the language was different, the tone and the facial expression seemed consistent.

"I have dinner plans," she said.

"I'll wait."

"Fine!" she said, exasperated. "Five minutes, eight o'clock, at the house."

Jake was ten minutes early when he turned onto the gravel driveway. He wasn't sure what he expected to see—

maybe the fiancé, maybe a whole dinner party—but the parking area was empty and the house looked the same.

Maybe they had an underground garage.

One of the household staff escorted him inside, and Jake saw Athena sitting alone at the dining room table with her back to him. The room was bathed in candlelight, and the table set intimately for two. Across from her was a napkin on the table and a half-finished glass of red wine.

Jake turned and nearly collided with Giánnis.

The older man greeted Jake warmly and invited him into the dining room.

Athena turned and glared.

"He and I are meeting after dinner, Father. He can wait in the living room."

"Can't he have a glass of wine first?"

Giánnis was seated at the head of the table, with Athena on his left. He pulled out a chair for Jake on his right—directly across from Athena.

The glaring intensified.

One of the staff brought a glass for Jake and filled it with a French Bordeaux that was at least a decade older than he was.

"You've been here before," said Giánnis. He remembered Jake's face, but the dementia had erased the details. "Are you Athena's fiancé?"

Athena put her face in her hands.

"No, Father. He's here for work."

"Are you in shipping?"

"I work for the U.S. Department of State, Mr. Romanos."

"And what brings you here?"

"I'm part of a counterpiracy task force."

Giánnis nodded slowly. "My son is a ship captain."

Athena stood, took a deep breath, and placed her napkin on the table.

"Father, would you mind if we finished dinner so I could meet with this man from America?"

Giánnis stood. "Of course."

One of the staff led him to his room.

"I need some air," said Athena. "There's a Land Rover parked around the corner. Would you bring it around? The keys are in it, but I can't walk across the driveway in these heels."

Jake nodded. It was a steel-gray Defender with a Bimini top and the doors removed. He pulled to the side of the house and picked her up. She'd put on a jacket and pointed to a road on the edge of the property. It ended at a private beach. He parked facing the water.

The rain had stopped, but it was barely fifty degrees Fahrenheit, and Jake left the engine running and turned up the heat. They stayed in the car.

"Sometimes my father asks me when my brother is coming home," said Athena. "He thinks he's still on a ship somewhere."

A tear slid down her cheek. She didn't wipe it away.

"Have you ever lost anyone close to you?" she asked.

Jake hesitated for a minute. His life as Zac Miller was top secret, code-word classified, but he understood the pain she felt.

"I lost both my parents when I was fourteen," he said.

Athena didn't know what answer she'd been hoping for, but it certainly wasn't that.

"I'm sorry. That must have been awful."

"It was. I went to live with an aunt and uncle, but they had their own issues. It wasn't a happy childhood."

She turned to face him.

"Yet you still think I should send the *Symi* into the Gulf. That I should risk the lives of all those men and potentially leave their children with that same lifetime of loss?"

"You're in a terrible position," Jake said. "If I had never come to Greece you wouldn't know that your men might be in danger, but now you do."

"Don't flatter yourself. I figured out the danger had returned after my brother disappeared."

"Of course, what I meant—"

"I know what you meant, but it doesn't change the fact that he's gone and I can protect these men by turning that ship around."

"But you know that turning the ship around will make the pirates suspicious, and they'll talk to the banker in Mogadishu, and he'll call the intermediary in Switzerland, and he'll phone your shipping agent, who will say that, coincidentally enough, Athena Romanos was just in his office for the first time ever . . . Then the pirate leader will go to ground and we'll spend five years searching for him while he escapes justice."

"I could alter the *Symi*'s course. I could divert it a hundred miles west of the route they're expecting."

"I have no idea if the pirates are targeting the *Symi*, but

I don't want you to delude yourself that altering course would stop them. They've been tracking their targets using the automatic identification system. They're going to find whatever ship they're looking for."

Athena put her hands in her face again, displeased with all of her options.

"When will you arrest him?"

"As soon as we get approval from Washington."

"What could they be waiting for?"

"It's a bureaucracy," Jake said. "I'm sorry."

"I should call INTERPOL. They would arrest him immediately."

"INTERPOL doesn't have an enforcement arm. They'll just pass the information to the Somalis and the pirates have sources inside the government. There's a one hundred percent chance that he'll get a heads-up and maybe a five percent chance that the authorities will even look for him. It will only make him harder to catch."

Athena looked out over the sea again. Moonlight was breaking through the clouds.

"We don't know that they're targeting the *Symi*," Jake repeated.

"They are."

Jake hesitated. "It's possible, but they could be working with other agents too. There could be dozens of potential targets."

"And yet you're convinced that turning one ship around will ruin your whole plan? 'Either your men die or many more will.' Isn't that what you said the first time we met?"

"I only meant that—"

"I'm sorry. I know you're trying to help."

The two of them sat in silence for a few minutes.

"Does the *Symi* have a citadel?" Jake said.

"All of our ships do. We installed them after my brother died."

"Then remind the crew to follow procedures and get everyone into the citadel at the first sign of trouble. They'll be safe there."

THIRTY-ONE

THE GENERAL ALARM was wailing throughout the ship.

The crew had been alerted to something—probably all of their electronics turning to mush at the same time.

Shit happens, thought the pirate commander.

Eight of his assaulters stacked up outside the bridge. The second man tried the handle on the metal door, but it was locked. He stepped back and signaled for the team's breacher—a man trained to gain entry where others hoped to keep them out. He did a two-second evaluation of the door, the lock, and the door frame before lighting a hand-held cutting torch. Though it looked like a road flare, the Breachpen burned at 4,500 degrees Fahrenheit, hot enough to cut through the door and the stainless steel deadbolt in twenty seconds.

The breacher stepped back and the next man in the stack kicked open the door. The eight pirates streamed inside and fanned out against the walls, rifles up and ready for action, but the bridge was empty. They'd met no resistance from a vessel protection detachment, and a quick search of the accommodations area revealed no crewmen—which left one inescapable conclusion.

The crew had retreated to a citadel.

It took four and a half minutes for the assault team to locate it.

But with half-inch-thick steel walls and a waterproof hatch, another Breachpen wasn't going to get them inside. One of the pirates fried the two exterior CCTV cameras with a high-powered laser while the breacher unloaded his backpack.

The team had encountered citadels before.

He removed a four-foot nylon circle with an adhesive backing and slapped it against the wall, then attached nine pounds of explosives and braced it with what looked like a pair of tent poles.

The team retreated behind cover as the breacher unspooled fifty feet of detonating cord and tucked in safely around a corner. After a quick check of the system, he pulled the trigger on the firing mechanism.

The explosion was deafening.

The wall looked as if a four-foot-wide bullet had been fired through it. Two assaulters approached from the sides and lobbed hand grenades into the opposite corners of the room, left/low, right/high, in a well-rehearsed routine to eliminate any chance that they might collide in the air, before juking back behind the steel walls.

Metal fragments ricocheted inside the citadel as the grenades exploded.

Four pirates climbed through the hole and dead-checked the downed sailors with 5.45mm bullets to the chest, more a function of training than necessity—the breaching charge and the fragmentation grenades had already done most of the killing.

A small drone operated by the pirates continued orbiting the ship, its thermal sensors scanning the deck for signs of life while the assault team searched the interior. One man was found in the pump room, two others in the engine control room, and they died where they stood, for there could be no survivors. The pirates would be out of business if the outside world ever learned of their tactics.

Back on the bridge, the boarding team leader shut off the ship's position-reporting system and turned the tanker southeast, toward Indonesia, where the cargo would be unloaded at an unscrupulous tank farm and blended with other crudes to obscure its origin. In a few weeks the oil would be sold to legitimate buyers in Asia with falsified bills of lading.

One of the pirates lowered the ship's Greek flag and tossed it overboard.

The *Symi* had been off the grid for less than fifteen minutes.

THIRTY-TWO

JAKE SPENT THE night at the Westin and took off from Athens International Airport just after ten in the morning. He was nearly to Mogadishu when the flight crew told him he had an incoming call on the Gulfstream's encrypted communications set.

It was Ted Graves.

"Another tanker is missing."

"What was its last known position?" Jake said.

"Gulf of Oman—around two hundred fifty miles past the Strait of Hormuz."

Jake did some quick math in his head.

"It was the *Symi*, wasn't it?"

He knew the ship's route and timing.

Graves was silent.

"You sacrificed the one ship that hurts us the most."

"Don't be melodramatic," said Graves. "We needed to validate the intelligence."

"Melodramatic? You had me fly here to persuade Athena Romanos for more time, and then you used that time to send twenty-three of her men to their graves. You betrayed her trust and mine."

"We're not here to make friends, Keller. We're here to protect the interests of the United States of America. And don't worry about Romanos—today is the day she was going to turn the ship around. It would have been too late anyway."

"She would have turned it around four days ago if I hadn't begged her not to."

"You were doing your job. She'll understand that. People don't become billionaires by playing nice all the time."

"Ted, I want to make sure you understand that there is a very real chance that she's going to go to INTERPOL, either because she thinks we're incompetent or she realizes that we've been lying to her. If she does that, they'll alert the Somalis, and Yaxaas will vanish. The mission will be over."

Graves leaned back in his chair and cracked his knuckles.

"Where are you now?"

"We just passed Djibouti," Jake said. "We'll be wheels-down in Mogadishu in an hour."

"Make a U-turn."

"What?"

Graves spoke slowly, as if speaking to a child.

"Ask the nice men in the front of the airplane to turn it around . . . The Ground Branch team got hung up battling a group of insurgents and won't be able to get to Mogadishu for a few more days, which means we won't be able to get to Yaxaas, which means you need to head back to Greece and convince Ms. Romanos to stay away from INTERPOL, because if those idiots go to the Somali authorities and Yaxaas learns about it, he's gone, and that absolutely, positively, cannot fucking happen."

THIRTY-THREE

I T WAS JUST after five p.m. when the Gulfstream touched down in Athens. Jake had called ahead for another rental car, and he floored it as he left the airport. Graves might have rationalized the deaths of the twenty-three innocent crewmen to himself, but Jake knew CIA could have stopped it, and he saw it as his responsibility to tell Athena about the *Symi* face-to-face. By the time he reached her office building in Glyfada, most of the lights were off, but the silver Jaguar was still in its parking space.

He stopped in front of the main entrance and was headed for the security desk when Athena emerged from the elevator.

"You lied to me!" she yelled across the lobby.

The armed security guard stepped in front of her protectively. He had his hand on his holstered weapon.

She said something in Greek and the man stepped aside, but he kept his hand on his gun and glared at Jake.

Athena brushed by Jake and stormed out the front door without saying another word.

"Athena!" he said, once they were both on the street.

She stopped and turned around with fury in her eyes.

"We stopped getting position updates from the *Symi* six hours ago," she said. "I deluded myself that they were just having communications issues, or maybe they were busy with bad weather, but then you showed up, and I knew."

"I didn't—"

"I trusted you. I believed the citadel would protect my men, but they're all dead now, aren't they? You sent them to their graves."

She looked at her watch.

"Damn it!" She opened her car door. "I need to get home."

"We need to talk."

"There's nothing to talk about. You've wasted the lives of my crew. I'm calling INTERPOL and ending this lunacy."

"Please let me explain."

"Fine!" It was easier for her to say "yes" than to keep arguing, and she needed to take care of Giánnis.

She gunned the engine and chirped the tires as she turned south onto Poseidonos Avenue, the coastal road between Glyfada and Vouliagmeni. By the time Jake reached his rental car, the silver Jaguar was long gone, and he sped under the streetlights for several minutes without so much as catching a glimpse of the car.

The deserted road snaked along a wooded park as he took the turn for Vouliagmeni. He came around a sharp corner and nearly slammed into a gray Volkswagen that was parked halfway across his lane. Two men stepped out. One had a shaved head and was easily two hundred fifty pounds. The other was almost as big and was wearing a leather jacket. Jake hadn't seen them before, but he recognized the type: thick necks, barrel chests—hard men.

They motioned for Jake to keep driving, but he spotted skid marks on the pavement and pulled to the side of the road.

Caught in the glare of his headlights, nose-down in a ditch, with its hood crumpled and windshield shattered, was Athena's car.

The men walked menacingly toward Jake as he stepped out of the car. They were thick all around—street brawlers with the scars to prove it. The one with the shaved head shouted something in Greek and motioned for Jake to drive away.

Jake took a step back.

Shaved Head walked up to him and pushed him in the shoulder.

Jake staggered backward a few steps, and Leather Jacket once again motioned for him to leave.

"That person needs help," Jake said in English.

The two goons exchanged a look.

"You go. We help," said Shaved Head in thickly accented English. It wasn't a Greek accent, though, something Eastern European.

The goon reached for Jake's arm, and he flinched and took another step back.

The man sensed weakness and came at Jake again.

But instead of retreating, Jake stepped forward and quickly closed the distance.

It was during his first field mission for the Agency that he developed the core principle that would allow him to survive in some of the most dangerous places on earth: It was better to be the aggressor, to set the circumstances of a confrontation, than be forced to react to someone else's plan.

Shaved Head was barely an arm's length away when Jake pushed off his back foot and attacked the other man—unexpectedly launching a palm strike that shattered his nose.

It caught both of the ruffians by surprise.

The thug staggered backward and Jake attacked again, chopping the side of the goon's thick neck—but it had no discernible effect. The man regained his balance and came at Jake with his hands up, trying to grapple with him.

It was a situation Jake wanted no part of. The thickset man looked as if he wrestled grizzly bears for fun. If he got Jake on the ground, it would be the end—for Jake and for Athena.

Jake kept moving sideways, keeping the thugs one behind the other to prevent them from attacking him simultaneously. He kept buying time until the one in the leather jacket pivoted toward Jake with most of his weight on his right leg.

It was an opportunity Jake couldn't pass up.

He rotated his hips and kicked the man in the kneecap, driving his heel through the joint until the knee shattered and the goon went down, screaming in pain.

Leather Jacket was out of the fight, but the cat was out of the bag too. Jake wasn't the easy target he'd pretended to be. Shaved Head looked at his friend lying on the ground in agony and decided that it was a condition he'd prefer to avoid, so he reached under his untucked shirt, came up with a snub nose revolver, put his finger on the trigger, and pointed it at Jake.

THIRTY-FOUR

JAKE HAD BEEN on the wrong side of guns before, and he knew there was a short window to act before the other side used the weapon to take control of the situation. He leapt forward, grabbed the man's gun hand, and pushed it to the side.

But the thug was a thick block of muscle, with at least fifty pounds on Jake, and the snub nose revolver felt like it was clamped in a vise. The goon pulled the trigger, but the shot went into the woods. Jake used his other arm to launch three elbow strikes to the man's temple.

The gunman staggered but held on to the weapon. He pulled the trigger a second time and the bullet ricocheted off the pavement.

The goon clamped his other hand over Jake's and began to pry it away. There was no way Jake could hold on. The man was simply too strong.

Jake delivered a throat strike to the man's Adam's apple. It wasn't a killing blow—but it was close. The man's eyes went wide as he lurched forward, but the oxygen he needed to function wouldn't come. Jake drove his knee up into the man's groin several times until he dropped the weapon. A second later he collapsed on the ground, wheezing for air and writhing in pain.

Jake picked up the pistol and turned toward the ditch, looking for Athena.

But she was already out of the car and staring at the scene in the headlights of Jake's car: him, the gun, and the two large men he'd so violently dispatched.

Her knees went weak and she collapsed.

Tires squealed as the two goons fled the scene.

Jake ran to her and gently lifted her head from the ground. A trickle of blood ran down her face.

"We need to leave now," Jake said.

They drove to Athena's home in his rental car. Again seizing the offensive, Jake persuaded her to call the police before the wreck was discovered. He was waiting out of sight on the terrace when two officers arrived twenty minutes later. Athena explained how she'd swerved to avoid a dog in the road and crashed the Jaguar. She didn't have her phone, felt dizzy, and a passing motorist had offered her a ride, so she'd left the scene. She apologized and volunteered to take a sobriety test, but it was clear that she hadn't been drinking, so the officers left without issuing a citation.

Athena washed the blood from her face and went to find Giánnis. He was watching television in the living room and she kissed him on the forehead. She smiled sadly, mourning the men who'd died aboard their ships and longing for the seemingly unlimited source of strength

her father had once been. She sat next to him on the sofa
and they held hands while they spoke.

She joined Jake on the terrace twenty minutes later.

"We need to talk," he said.

"Not here. There's too much sadness here already," she
said. "Can you get the Land Rover? I'm sorry. I'm wearing these stupid heels again."

The gravel driveway crunched underfoot as Jake
walked to the truck and brought it around. They drove in
silence to the beach and Jake again parked facing the water.
Athena pulled a wool blanket from the back seat and snugged
it up to her neck as if to shield herself from further harm.

"You're not with the State Department, are you?" she
said quietly.

Jake stared out to sea.

"I saw what you did to those men."

"I don't think that was an accident," Jake said.

"It wasn't," she said. An edge crept into her voice.
"They were Albanian mafia—the same hoodlums who've
been threatening my family for years. I've never seen those
two before, but I know the type. They obviously haven't
given up."

"You should hire professional security. Those men were
dangerous."

"My fiancé used to say that I always attracted the worst
kind of men."

"Does that include him?"

"Especially him," she said with a smile, but it faded
quickly, "but he died in a car racing accident two months
before the wedding—the same week my brother disap-

peared. Four weeks later my mother's cancer relapsed, and three months after that, my father had his stroke. In six months, I went from being on top of the world to being crushed under its weight."

"I'm sorry."

"And now all those families from the *Symi*," she said. "Shattered."

Athena left her shoes in the truck and rolled her pants up to her calves. She waded ankle deep into the surf with the blanket wrapped around her shoulders. Jake followed. The water was warmer than the air, and it felt good as it swirled over their feet. Neither made eye contact, choosing instead to watch the stars flicker between the clouds blowing overhead.

"I still can't believe that I sent twenty-three husbands, fathers, and sons to their deaths," she said after several minutes.

She walked back to the truck and sat in the passenger seat with her feet on the dashboard and her legs clutched to her chest.

Jake sat in the driver's seat but didn't start the motor.

They sat in silence, staring out over the Gulf. It was twenty minutes before she spoke again, barely above a whisper.

"All day, I had our operations team radio the ship about the most trivial things—minor weather updates, service issues—anything I could think of."

She sighed.

"I deluded myself when they stopped answering," she continued. "I kept saying that they were only having communication problems, but in my heart I knew."

She sighed again.

"I must be cursed," she said. "So much death."

They sat listening to the gentle surf. A warm breeze blew in from the sea.

"Sometimes I think I know more about death than I do about life," Jake said.

She started to say something, but stopped.

"I watched my best friend die last year," Jake said. "He was ten feet in front of me and there was nothing I could do."

She shook her head. "How do you deal with it?"

"I try not to think about it, but sometimes it's all I can think about . . . I don't know if anyone ever gets over that kind of loss, but I try to focus on the positives—what my parents meant to me, what my friend and I accomplished."

She looked back out to sea. "Life is hard."

"It isn't all bad. Humans are just wired to focus on the negative. It's our survival instinct."

The two of them stared into the night sky, looking for light among all the blackness.

"I feel as if I'm in some nightmarish fairy tale," she said, "living this life of ridiculous luxury while I send honorable men to their deaths."

"It's not your fault," Jake said. "I pushed."

Athena looked at him.

"That's kind of you to say, but I have a mind of my own."

"The choices in front of you were terrible."

"'The greater good' is wonderful in theory, but not when you're the wives and children of men who will never come home."

"It's an imperfect world, and we're often forced to use violence to stop violence, but I sleep well at night knowing that I'm fighting for people who can't help themselves. It's what we live *for* that defines us."

Athena tucked her arm inside his.

"Can you do me a favor?"

Jake nodded.

"You know who's responsible for my brother's death, don't you?"

He nodded again.

"Good." She rested her head on his shoulder. "Kill him for me."

THIRTY-FIVE

JAKE FLEW THROUGH the night and touched down in Mogadishu at daybreak. The Ground Branch team arrived a few hours later in three vehicles. The six men, all combat veterans, were independent contractors who'd been working in a CIA Counterterrorism Center team, planning and executing operations with U.S. and African military forces. They'd been in the field for several weeks and looked it, sporting shaggy hair, scruffy beards, and heavy loadout bags filled with survival gear, surveillance equipment, clothing, and weapons.

Lots of weapons.

Though Jake was also part of the Special Activities Center, he didn't know any of the men in the CTC pursuit team or follow normal reporting channels. More accurately, Graves didn't follow normal reporting channels. He routinely circumvented the branch chiefs underneath him and used Jake as a singleton, out on his own, working covert missions where the risk was enormous and no trace could be left behind.

Pickens set the team up in the safe house's family room, with sleeping bags on the floor, and Jake briefed everyone on what the Agency had learned about Yaxaas's background, his piracy business, and his other operations in Somalia.

"You men have been in-country longer than I have," Jake said, "so you know that most of these warlords travel with militiamen who are untrained, undisciplined, and quick on the trigger. Yaxaas isn't going to like what we're telling him, so don't be surprised if it goes kinetic."

The team leader was a five-foot, seven-inch coiled spring who went by the nickname "Clap." Jake was skilled in the martial arts, having studied jiujitsu in college and Krav Maga while at the Agency, and he immediately recognized Clap as someone who knew how to handle himself. Every step, every movement he made, was designed for maximum tactical advantage. He was leaning against a wall, with his arms folded across his chest and a baseball cap pulled down over his tight Afro.

"Frankly," Jake said, "the warlord's death would not be an adverse outcome."

"Ted said you might feel that way," Clap said as he pushed off the wall and took a step forward, "but we're here to make sure that doesn't happen."

The two men stared at each other for a few seconds until Jake laid a marked-up map of the city on the kitchen table.

"Yaxaas's compound is heavily guarded. We'll need to begin pattern-of-life surveillance to locate a spot outside the area where we can make contact, but—"

"He eats lunch a couple of times a week at the Liido

Seafood restaurant," Clap said. He tapped a spot on the map. "We'll set up there in the morning."

THE FIRST TWO Ground Branch men left just before sunrise, when most of Mogadishu was still asleep, and they made it to Liido Beach in under twenty minutes.

The restaurant was directly on the beach, open on three sides with only a thatched roof overhead and a kitchen in the rear. The beautiful white sand beach would have been filled with families before war and famine had devastated the country.

Today it was empty.

The Ground Branch men parked their unfortunately named Toyota Isis minivan on a side street and headed out on foot in opposite directions. Both were African American and trained to remain inconspicuous. They checked in over their communication sets from discreet observation posts flanking the restaurant, casually conducting countersurveillance sweeps on each other every half hour or so. There was little activity on the waterfront aside from the ever-present fishermen who were dragging their nets ashore and the feral cats that were scavenging through them.

The team had no idea if Yaxaas would visit the restaurant today, but at the very minimum it would be an opportunity to set up surveillance, assess security, determine ingress and egress routes, and note any CCTV cameras, private security, or government forces that could potentially interfere with their mission.

An hour later, two different Ground Branch officers

rolled up in a tiny Toyota Starlet to a curbside fruit and vegetable stand. They purchased a pineapple and a few bananas while the original two rotated back to the safe house. And so it went for the next five hours, with the men constantly changing vehicles, disguises, clothing, and locations so that no one in the area would realize the intense surveillance that was being conducted.

It was nearly two p.m. when Jake got the call. Yaxaas's armored Range Rover had just arrived, along with two pickup trucks filled with gunmen. Jake, Pickens, and the rest of the Ground Branch team loaded into the remaining vehicles and executed a plan they'd devised based on the lax posture of Yaxaas's security, who seemed to be relying on their sheer presence to deter any threat as opposed to any tactical deployment. Most were hanging around their pickups with their weapons slung, with only two guards inside the restaurant with the principal.

The Ground Branch men converged on the location from three directions and, in a matter of seconds, had surrounded the restaurant—unnoticed by Yaxaas's goons.

But that was about to change.

THIRTY-SIX

ONE OF THE Ground Branch men jammed all of the wireless communications in the area as Pickens's SUV screeched to a halt in front of the restaurant. The team entered in full tactical gear with weapons in hand. By the time the warlord's bodyguards even noticed, the Agency team had him surrounded and the restaurant sealed.

Yaxaas had survived as long as he had not only because he was ruthless but because he was able to make expeditious and judicious assessments of his opposition. He noted the position, posture, and equipment of the Americans—and they were unmistakably American; with their sleeves rolled up and wearing baseball caps, they could be nothing else—and decided that a firefight was not in his best interests.

He told his men to lower their weapons.

Jake stepped out of the SUV and entered the restaurant.

The pirate leader was sitting across from a younger man, slightly taller and more muscular than the warlord, and Clap identified him over the tactical radio net as the warlord's son, Nacay. While Jake appreciated the intel, he wondered how the Ground Branch team already knew so much about the objective—and what else they might be keeping to themselves, but that conversation would have to wait, because there was a large semiautomatic pistol pointing through Nacay's untucked shirt.

"Lose the gun," Jake said. He barely trusted the Ground Branch team; he certainly wasn't going to let Yaxaas's son keep a weapon.

But Nacay had not inherited his father's calm demeanor. He leapt from his seat, but Jake was too fast for him. He caught the back of Nacay's head, kicked his legs out from under him, and slammed his head into the table and held it there. With his other hand, Jake lifted the pistol from Nacay's holster and pressed it against his neck.

All the guns came up again.

The warlord's guards were shouting and swinging their weapons wildly across the restaurant as they tried to cover the better-placed Americans.

Jake had at least two AK-47s pointed at him.

The CIA team had had a prearranged signal to take the Somalis out, but Clap had made it clear that Ted Graves was calling the shots, and the friction between Jake and Graves had escalated to the point that Jake didn't want to press his luck.

Yaxaas's life might be more valuable than his.

He lowered the pistol and released the warlord's son.

Nacay seethed, but Yaxaas once again motioned his men to stand down. The warlord lit a cigarette and pulled out a chair, as if he'd been expecting Jake for lunch. Jake sat down and motioned for Nacay to leave the two of them alone. The son walked to the other side of the restaurant, but the Ground Branch men blocked him from leaving.

Yaxaas scrutinized the man sitting opposite him. He was young, Caucasian, and spoke excellent Arabic. He possessed a steely calmness despite all the guns and the tension.

"At last we meet," said the warlord.

Jake reached across the table and took a piece of pita bread off Yaxaas's plate. "Do you know why I'm here?"

The warlord poured two glasses of tea and waited for Jake to continue.

"I represent the government of the United States."

"And what brings you to Mogadishu?" said the warlord. He exhaled a cloud of smoke into the air.

"I'm here to solve a problem," Jake said.

"Many people come to me with their problems."

"This isn't my problem. This is your problem."

"Your country doesn't make the rules in Somalia."

"There are no rules in Somalia."

"Ah, but there are. The customs of Xeer have been passed down through the noble clans of Somalia for over a thousand years."

"And who enforces Xeer?"

"I do," said Yaxaas.

"Why you?"

Yaxaas was not an educated man, but he was a smart man. He knew that his authority did not come from a popular vote or even heredity. He ruled because he had the power to impose his will—and the Americans' brash display was meant to show him that a more powerful force had entered the equation.

He stubbed out his cigarette.

"From time to time," Jake said, "we will require you to intercept certain vessels at sea."

Yaxaas raised an eyebrow. "I am a simple businessman. I know nothing of the sea."

Jake took a sip of the sugary tea.

"Those eight tankers didn't disappear by accident."

The warlord lit another of his Turkish cigarettes. "What is to become of these vessels?"

"That will be decided on a case-by-case basis. You'll be given enough time to plan accordingly."

"I expect to be well compensated. Mounting such operations is costly."

Jake shook his head. "Consider it the cost of staying alive. Somalia can be a dangerous place."

"Indeed," said Yaxaas. "Especially for foreigners."

Jake rose from his seat and dropped a cell phone on the table. "We'll be in touch."

"CIA?" the warlord asked in English.

"GFY," Jake corrected.

Yaxaas knew many of the U.S. military units and intelligence agencies that operated in his country, but his puzzled look indicated that he'd never heard of this one.

"You'll figure it out."

THIRTY-SEVEN

NACAY MADE A call on his mobile phone the moment the Americans left.

Yaxaas took a long pull of his cigarette and waved his son back to the table.

"Are we out of business?"

The warlord exhaled.

"Quite the opposite. They want us to intercept ships for them."

Nacay cocked his head. "I hadn't expected that . . . Is it one of their intelligence services or their military?"

"The line has blurred between the two," said the warlord, "but their military has a navy, so it must be an intelligence agency."

Yaxaas picked at his red snapper, but he'd lost his appetite.

Nacay's phone pinged. He held it up and showed two photos to his father.

"These were taken several days ago at Aden Adde."

The first picture was of Jake walking across the tarmac. The second image of was of him climbing into the CIA jet.

"That's him," Yaxaas said. "What of the plane?"

"A Gulfstream. I have someone looking into it."

The men speculated about the Americans' intent for several minutes until Nacay's phone rang. He asked a few questions but mostly listened before hanging up.

"The jet is owned by a holding company and the man entered the country on a nonofficial American passport. It's probably a false identity."

Yaxaas shooed the flies away from his cold fish.

"Send that picture to our Albanian friends and find out if it's the same man they encountered in Athens."

"I could get a bomb aboard the plane and stop this nonsense before it gets out of hand."

Yaxaas turned to face the sea. Except for a few light clouds on the eastern horizon, the sun was continuing its relentless attack on Somalia.

"No," said the warlord. "We cannot afford another enemy right now."

"So what do we do?"

"We wait. The United States has never understood Africa. It is only a matter of time until they make a strategic mistake, and once they do, we will use them to finish off Badeed once and for all."

THIRTY-EIGHT

"YOU'VE GOT YOUR first mission," said Graves via videoconference. It had been just two days since Jake's meeting with Yaxaas. "There's a Saudi tanker leaving for North Korea that needs to disappear."

"Why is the Agency handling this? This is as black and white as it gets."

"Jake, you're a talented operative, but you still have a lot to learn about politics. Relations with Saudi are still tense after the drone strike on Mecca."

"I thought I resolved that."

"At the end of the day, it was still an American aircraft. Now the Saudis are testing us, seeing how much slack we'll cut them because of any latent guilt we might have."

"Sinking their ship should clear that up."

"That's why we're using Yaxaas. If the U.S. Navy stopped the ship, the Saudis would say that it wasn't going to North Korea and the ship would turn around. They'd sell the oil somewhere else and blame us for not trusting them."

"It's like dealing with a manipulative child."

Graves nodded. "Welcome to international relations."

"So we sink the ship, the Saudis never know exactly what happened, and they lose twenty million dollars' worth of oil."

"Now you're catching on," said Graves.

"Except a Somali warlord gets the twenty million and the entire crew has to die—all because the president doesn't want to call the Saudi king and tell him to knock it off?"

"There's that, but this also sows distrust between the Saudis and the North Koreans. Both parties will think twice before trying something like this again."

"I still don't agree with it," Jake said, "but I get it. What do you need me to do?"

THIRTY-NINE

A FEW WISPY CLOUDS hung in the sky over Mogadishu, glowing pink in the late-day light.

The dusty lot was surrounded by a mangled fence, its rusty chain links and broken gate providing more than enough security for the litter and empty shipping containers that had been dumped there over the years. Lying on the ground were a few homeless boys, half-stoned and half-dead from sniffing glue they'd poured into discarded plastic water bottles.

It was a run-down area, in a run-down city, in a run-down country.

Jake and Pickens pulled inside and parked facing the road, with the engine idling.

A pickup truck filled with half a dozen gunmen in back pulled around the corner ten minutes later, followed by Yaxaas's black Range Rover. The warlord's SUV drove through the open gate and stopped next to Jake and Pickens, passenger side to passenger side. The warlord lowered his window. Jake's was already down.

"We have a mission for you," Jake said.

"When?" said Yaxaas.

"Two weeks."

"Impossible. We depart tomorrow for another job."

"I'm not asking."

"It will cost me millions."

"Not necessarily," Jake said. "It's a tanker."

The warlord raised an eyebrow.

"It's right out of your playbook," Jake continued. "The ship is called the *Amjad*. It's owned by Bahri, the Saudi national carrier. You'll pick it up in the Indian Ocean and send it to the bottom."

Yaxaas nodded.

The warlord took notes as Jake gave him the details he'd need to identify and intercept the sanction-evading vessel.

"And the crew?"

Jake shook his head.

FORTY

NTERCEPTING THE *AMJAD* and sending it to the bottom would take Yaxaas's team only a few hours, but the warlord would need a full week to prep the crew and get them into position. It presented Jake with his first downtime since arriving in Africa, and he decided to use it to visit Greece. He told Graves that he was worried Athena Romanos might change her mind and go to INTERPOL, but the truth was, Jake wasn't completely sure why he was going.

The Agency Gulfstream landed uneventfully in Athens and Jake retrieved a rental car. While he'd once considered Greece out of the pirates' reach, he was more vigilant since Athena had been run off the road and nearly killed. Jake knew that men like the warlord could never be trusted. The international criminal network that he was a part of was more accustomed to violence than to rolling over and playing nicely.

Jake drove an extensive surveillance detection run as he headed southwest. Athena was at her office in Glyfada but had asked him to meet her at the family home in Vouliag-meni. He took the highway and local roads, he made cover stops at a gas station and a convenience store, and as he pulled through the open gates of the Romanos estate and drove into the olive grove, he knew that he hadn't been followed.

It was an unseasonably warm day in Greece and Giánnis was lounging on the sunlit terrace. The shipowner was at-tired in his typical casual elegance, white pants and a thick cashmere sweater. Jake was still wearing the frayed khakis and untucked shirt that had become his de facto uniform in Mogadishu, but Giánnis greeted him warmly and asked one of the household staff to open a bottle of Malagousia wine. Neither man was particularly hungry, but the staff whipped up a spread of souvlaki and spanakopita to politely obscure the fact that it wasn't much past ten thirty in the morning.

With some prompting from Jake and the wine, Giánnis began to regale the younger man with tales of his past. Though the shipowner often struggled to recall minor de-tails from his short-term memory, he could recount stories from fifty years earlier as if they were happening right in front of him. He spoke of a deal where he'd made a fortune buying eight half-finished tankers from a shipyard that had gone bankrupt at the bottom of a cycle, and he told of the time he'd purchased a pair of cutting-edge deepwater drillships at the absolute peak of the market. He lost half a billion dollars on the two ships by the time he finally found a buyer to take them off his hands, but Giánnis told both stories with equal enthusiasm, grateful to have been in the game and lived to fight another day.

Jake had many stories of his own, but most were classified and he still had to maintain cover. Officials from the State Department's Maritime Security Division didn't evade Iranian assassination teams and prosecute drone strikes in Yemen, so Jake revealed the loss of his parents at a young age and told how it had troubled him until he'd found camaraderie and a sense of belonging in college. He spoke of pouring himself into his friendships and his career, until he'd once again lost everything that was important to him—Jake couldn't reveal that his change of identity drove the seclusion that troubled him—but he could see in the shipowner's eyes that the older man's dementia was isolating him in much the same way. Though the two men had led very different paths, they had much in common and had built a natural rapport during Jake's visits to the family compound.

They'd already uncorked a second bottle of wine and were sitting in a pair of lounge chairs, overlooking the sea, when Athena returned home midafternoon.

Giánnis spoke in a stage whisper.

"Shhhh," he said with a conspiratorial grin. "The boss is home."

Athena beamed as the two men rose to greet her. She had changed from her work clothes into a lavender sarong and a white silk blouse that she'd tied at the waist. Her hair was down and there was no grimace on her face, no phone in her hand, and no shoes on her feet. She had a firm hug for her father and soft kisses on both cheeks for Jake.

For the first time since Jake had met her, she looked at peace.

A complicated wave of emotions washed over him. He felt truly at home with Giánnis and he and Athena had opened up to each other in a way he hadn't done in years. The joy that Jake had been missing in his life had finally returned, displacing the loneliness and despair that gnawed at him when he wasn't on the job. It was as if he were part of a family.

And it tore him apart, knowing that he had to lie to them.

Athena took him by the arm.

"Is he dead?" she said.

"Soon," Jake said.

"I hope you don't think I'm being morbid, but we should celebrate."

"You need to keep those gates closed outside," Jake said.

"You worry too much," she said. "I've moved our business away from the agent, but I'm stringing him along—promising him more business down the road. He doesn't suspect anything."

She led Jake to the dining room. The table was set for three, with a white tablecloth, silver flatware, and a champagne bucket. Giánnis caught sight of his daughter, animated and grinning as she led Jake to the seat across from hers. The old man smiled. It had been a long time since he'd seen her so happy. Everyday life might have been slipping past the shipping magnate, but he was still processing things that were important to him.

"You have him?" Giánnis asked.

Athena tightened her grip on Jake's arm, although the older man had been referring to the pirate.

"We have a plan," Jake said.

He felt profoundly guilty. These kind and generous people trusted him, they'd helped him in the pursuit of a greater good, and it turned his stomach knowing that he was working with the man who'd killed their son and brother.

Athena popped the champagne cork and handed Jake a glass. She wasn't wearing the engagement ring. He looked up and met her eyes. She smiled. It was a smile of contentment, of closure.

"Yamas," Athena called out. "To our health."

They sipped their champagne. It was vintage Dom Perignon, but it burned like acid as it slid down Jake's throat. Athena picked up on his body language and cocked her head a few degrees, subtly inquiring about his mood.

"Just tired," Jake said, compounding his lies.

He was miserable, but Athena's enthusiasm was unyielding, relentlessly prodding Jake until the mood in the room turned lively and even humorous, with the three of them exchanging playful barbs. Jake teased her about the overinsured tankers and even Giánnis piled on, chastising his daughter for not insuring the ships for even more. Athena would have none of it and put both men in their places by pointing out that it had taken a woman to figure out the agent's treachery when none of them could.

By the end of the meal, Jake was grinning, making jokes, and feeling more at home than he had in years. It was the closest he'd felt to a family since he'd lost his parents.

They'd just finished dessert when Giánnis spoke up.

"It's a warm night," he said. "It would be a lovely evening for a walk on the beach."

"We'd be happy to take you, Mr. Romanos," said Jake.

"I would like nothing better," he said, pausing for effect, "than to go to bed."

"Then Jake and I will go," said Athena. "I'll walk you to your room, Father."

She took his arm and looked at Jake. "Maybe you could bring the car around again?"

Jake squinted at her. He was still feeling playful.

"You don't know how to drive a stick, do you?"

She scowled at him. "I can't walk on the driveway in bare feet."

"Or find a pair of shoes, apparently . . ."

Jake departed for the gravel driveway with a grin. Athena was waiting for him by the time he returned with the Land Rover. With the olive grove behind her, and silhouetted by the landscape lighting, she looked like an angel. He walked to the passenger side and held her door.

She brushed by him so close that he could smell her.

A warm breeze was blowing in off the night sea, and Jake left his jacket in the truck and rolled up his sleeves when they reached the beach. Athena wrapped her arm inside his and placed her other hand upon his bare forearm as they walked over the sand. The surf broke gently on shore.

"I don't know if you noticed it," she said softly, "but you frightened me when we first met."

"You must be joking," Jake said. "Is that why you threw me out of the house?"

"I suppose I've learned to attack before I get hurt."

"I've been known to do that myself on occasion," Jake said, although he wasn't talking about his emotions.

"It was your eyes. I felt as if you were looking into my soul."

"I suppose I was."

"What did you see?"

"I saw someone strong, and kind, and generous."

Athena smiled and they walked in silence for a few minutes.

"Would you like to join us for Christmas," she said, "or are you going back to America?"

Though he loved his country and loved what it stood for, there was no one for Jake back in the United States.

"I'd like that very much."

They stood in the sand as the breeze blew her hair across her face.

"When do you think you'll get him?" she asked.

"The pirate?"

She brushed her hair back into place and nodded.

"As soon as I get the order."

"How do you deal with all the treachery, all the duplicity?"

She'd meant a career in espionage, but Jake's guilt from working with Yaxaas rose quickly to the surface.

"I believe in what I'm doing—protecting those who can't protect themselves—but it comes at a cost. Sometimes I miss normal life."

They walked to the water and stood with their feet in the surf.

"You should be thinking about your future."

He looked at her in the moonlight, with the breeze ruffling her hair and the surf washing rhythmically over their feet.

"I should be getting back."

FORTY-ONE

THE SUN WAS high in the Somali sky, with only a few cottony clouds floating in the upper atmosphere, when the four SUVs turned off the cracked pavement and onto a dirt road. Barely more than a pair of tire tracks, the path wound through steep hills for almost a mile until it reached a rural camp about the size of a football field. It was set in the middle of a valley with a winding river on its western edge and the narrow road was the only way in or out.

The two-year drought had parched the life from the countryside. The grasses in the hills and lining the riverbank were withered and brittle and the river was nearly dry except for the few feet of muddy water that snaked down the middle of its wide banks. The skeletal remains of several animals littered the dry riverbed, picked clean by scavengers and bleached white by the sun.

The camp's gate slid open and a tall man, wearing a sleeveless shirt and bandoliers of machine gun ammunition draped across his chest, met the four vehicles in the center of camp. Camp workers unloaded the trucks while the man with the bandoliers led the newly arrived men into one of the camp's crude buildings.

Yaxaas was waiting inside.

Though the warlord had no formal education, he was a student of history.

The earliest Somali pirates had been men with no schooling and no hope, men like Badeed who'd had taken to the sea in small skiffs, targeting ships that were anchored or sailing close to shore. They would threaten the crews with guns, steal their possessions, and maybe score some portable electronics if they were lucky.

Glorified muggers.

But the ships adapted quickly and sailed farther offshore— out of range of the little fishing boats and their smoky outboard engines.

But the Somalis adapted too. They used larger fishing boats, often seventy feet long, to tow the skiffs offshore where they could wait for targets of opportunity in the shipping lanes. Once a ship was spotted, the skiffs would race after it, firing automatic weapons and sometimes RPGs at the bridge until the ship's master stopped the vessel.

The strategy worked for a few more years, with minor evolutions in tactics on both sides—the most significant of which was when the Somalis started kidnapping crews for ransom. Some of the hostages were held on the ships, some on land. Some were released within days and some were held for years. Some died in captivity.

The rising tide of violence eventually led to defensive measures that worked: armed vessel protection detachments, razor wire, water cannons, and increased involvement from the world's navies.

By 2015, the age of the Somali pirates had come to an end.

But Yaxaas knew there was still money to be made.

The country's strategic location on the Horn of Africa hadn't changed. It was only the pirates' rudimentary tactics and equipment that had been outmatched. He'd studied the world's top special operations forces and concluded that if the pirates could devise new tactics and keep them secret, they could be victorious once again.

He started by recruiting from the competition.

It wasn't difficult. The twenty-first century's global surge in special operations forces had invariably left a few men out in the cold, men who'd felt they weren't adequately appreciated or appropriately compensated by their governments. Others were just out for a thrill—after years of combat and intense training, they didn't want the adrenaline rush to subside, ever.

The result was the same. They were for sale.

Yaxaas didn't look at contractors from established firms. He wanted independent operators: mercenaries who'd accumulated a black mark or two over the years—sailors and marines who had tier-one skills but lacked the moral compulsion to use them the way in which they'd been trained. He wanted men who cared more about the tactical situation than the strategic one.

The warlord had laid out two rules: First, there would be no Americans and no Russians. Though it was for different reasons, the warlord trusted neither. Second, with the exception of his fellow Somalis, no more than two men could come from the same country. Yaxaas had a keen understanding of human nature and he knew that he was hiring renegades. He didn't want any factions developing within the team that might challenge his authority.

The Norwegian had been the first to join. Trained to be one of his nation's elite Marinejegerkommandoen, he was six feet two inches of lean muscle, with piercing blue eyes that were constantly in motion and analyzing everything he saw. But while he could look at any man and instantly assess the threat he presented, the Norwegian had no such ability with the fairer sex. After a string of weddings, affairs, and divorces, he found himself deep in debt, so he started pulling private security jobs in combat zones, where the pay was five times higher than he'd been earning working for his country. Yaxaas promised him double that.

The second hire was the Pole. He'd spent eight years as a member of the Polish Jednostka Wojskowa Formoza, serving four tours in Afghanistan, where he'd earned a reputation for being highly accurate with a rifle but too quick on the trigger. He'd once nearly started an international incident when he killed several noncombatants in pursuit of a high-value target. The JWF had discharged him for it, but he was exactly the type of man Yaxaas was looking for.

The rest of the warlord's men had similar stories and were hired from the Kenyan Special Boat Unit, the Turkish Maroon Berets, the Italian Gruppo Operativo Incursori, and the South African 4 Special Forces Regiment. Yaxaas added several Somalis as well, men who'd proven themselves in the early years of piracy and could learn from, and support, the foreigners.

But there could be no learning on the job if the warlord's plan was going to work. As always, secrecy was paramount. There could be no outside knowledge of the team, much less its tactics. The men trained for months before their first mission. Selection was conducted. Men who washed out of the top-tier boarding teams were recycled into boat crews or shore teams. Those who still couldn't find a home simply disappeared.

Forever.

But manpower was only half the battle. To succeed, the next generation of pirates had needed modern training and weapons. And while most of the objects of their desire were available on the black market, in other cases they'd simply adapted the military tactics they'd learned to dual-use civilian equipment. The goal had never been to match the world's navies but merely to leapfrog the shipping industry's security measures—to hit the ships so hard and so fast that the world would never learn how the pirates had done it. The world's navies couldn't respond to a threat they didn't understand.

NACAY UNROLLED A waterproof map and a paper schematic of the ship atop a large folding table, scrounging rocks from the camp building's dirt floor to hold down the corners.

Obtaining the plans for the Saudi tanker had not been difficult.

It was one of a series from a South Korean shipyard, and Nacay had asked a contact in the shipping industry to acquire the drawings for one of the sister ships under the pretext of potentially purchasing it. The ship broker had initially demurred, until two days later, when he'd received a dozen photographs of his eight-year-old daughter in the mail. The pictures had been taken at her school while she'd been studying, outside her home while she'd been playing, and from the foot of her bed while she'd been sleeping.

They received the plans the next day.

"Why are we hitting this piece of junk?" the Turk said as he examined the plans. The Saudi ship was about twice the age and half the size of their recent prizes.

Nacay glared at the Turk, and there was no further discussion of the topic.

"The target will be exiting the Persian Gulf in six days," Nacay continued. "We'll head east while it heads south, and the intercept point will be here, around 13 north latitude and 72 east longitude, on the core route from the Strait of Hormuz to the Strait of Malacca."

Nacay drew a red circle on the surface of a map.

"Will we be tracking her on AIS?" asked the Kenyan.

"I doubt she'll be transmitting," said Nacay.

A ship's automatic identification system was meant to improve safety at sea by transmitting a vessel's name, type, and location to everyone monitoring the system, but participation was voluntary and, not surprisingly, smugglers and pirates were not heavy users. It was another data point that told the men this wouldn't be a normal takedown.

"We'll set a picket line across the shipping lane here." Nacay marked an area just north of the 13th parallel. "The mothership will set up in the middle, Team One will be three miles to the east, and Team Two will be three miles to the west. We'll move south at three to five knots, each varying speed so it doesn't look as if we're traveling together, and wait for the target to pass."

Yaxaas handed a printout of the ship's plans to the man with the bandoliers. "Set it up."

He left the building and began directing the camp workers. Men paced off distances and marked lines in the sand. They placed movable walls around the interior—some no more than bedsheets on wooden frames, while others were plywood panels with makeshift hatches and doors, but they were all placed precisely according to the ship's plans, so the boarding team would know exactly what to expect from the moment they hauled themselves over the sides of the *Amjad* and onto her deck.

When the deck level was complete, the workers moved to another section of camp and set up the superstructure, the engine room, and the ship's control rooms, where the oil was pumped and monitored.

Other support personnel set up the assaulters' gear inside the camp mess hall. Each man used the same core kit, in the same configuration, to ensure interoperability. The rifles were short-barreled AKS-74Us, the pistols were Glock 17s, and the body armor was made from Dyneema, a synthetic fabric that could stop bullets and was buoyant enough to act as a life preserver.

The boarding team suited up in the mess hall once Nacay had finished his briefing and, half an hour later, they were back outside under the relentless sun and brilliant blue sky. The boat captain and assaulters from Team One were on the port side of the mockup while their counterparts from Team Two were on the starboard side.

Nacay stood atop a platform on the camp's northern wall, from which he could see the entire exercise. He opened his laptop, ran through a quick radio check, and gave the order to begin.

The clock started ticking.

The boarding team simulated the climb up the ship's sides and stepped over the lines drawn in the dirt. They were on deck. Nacay had stationed camp staff throughout the mockup, acting as the ship's officers, crew, and security personnel. All of the weapons were loaded with blank cartridges, but the sound of gunfire and the sight of a dozen highly trained naval commandos wielding rifles was real enough to get everyone's adrenaline pumping. Nacay started calling out random equipment malfunctions and other surprises—heavy seas on the port side, a jammed rifle, a locked door—but the team kept pushing. They pushed through the failures, they pushed through the choke points, they pushed through the opposition.

The assault team performed well, completing their first run-through in seventeen minutes and thirty-one seconds, with two assaulters suffering simulated non-life-threatening injuries. Nacay moved the "defenders" to different parts of the model, and ran it again.

By the fifteenth repetition, the pirates flowed through the target in thirteen minutes and forty-seven seconds and not a single defender got off a shot.

The assault team was ready.

FORTY-TWO

THE HELICOPTER LIFTED into the air over Mogadishu as the pilot pulled back on the collective.

Kenyan by birth, he had been trained by his country's Defence Forces to fly Russian Mi-17 transport helicopters. The twin-turbine Mi-17 was large and capable, but frequently down for maintenance due to a shortage of spare parts. With a low mission capability rate, the pilot's flying time suffered, and he put in a request to transition to the smaller Hughes OH-6.

It felt like a sports car compared to the lumbering Mi-17.

And the pilot treated it like one—routinely flying between trees at high speed, occasionally doing aerial loops, and once, just for fun, landing on the bed of an unsuspecting flatbed truck as it drove down a highway at fifty miles per hour.

It was the last stunt that had gotten him discharged—the Kenyan military was not awash in excess funding and the pilot's superior officer didn't want to have to one day tell his commander that they'd lost a precious rotorcraft while one of his men had been hotdogging.

But the skill and the audacity of the stunt had also gotten the pilot his current job.

The MD 520 he flew for Yaxaas was almost identical to the OH-6, except the new helicopter lacked a tail rotor, instead using high-velocity air to control its heading. Several manufacturers had experimented with the unusual design, but it added weight and maintenance expense and had remained a niche segment of the market. But it was an important niche that had one significant advantage over its tail-rotor-equipped brethren. It was quieter.

Much quieter.

WITH THE HELICOPTER'S doors removed and its main rotor spinning overhead, the air blowing through its cabin was a welcome change on the ninety-seven-degree day. The pilot flew northeast along the sandy coastline for fifteen miles until they reached a deserted stretch of land and abruptly turned out to sea.

Nacay was in his usual seat to the pilot's left, and he entered a set of coordinates into the GPS as the helo accelerated to 125 knots. The ocean blurred beneath them as the helicopter flew just fifty feet above the surface. The pilot climbed to three hundred feet once they were ten miles offshore and out of sight of land.

Forty minutes later, he backed off the cyclic and slowed the aircraft.

"Mothership in sight," he said over the intercom.

It was an unremarkable general cargo vessel, one hundred thirty feet long, with a white pilothouse above her stern and a crane mounted amidships. She could make fourteen knots when she left the shipyard twenty years earlier, but Yaxaas had repowered her when he'd bought her. With a new engine, a new shaft, and a new propeller, she could now do twenty-one knots—a significant advantage when closing on unsuspecting adversaries.

She was named the *Triomphe* and flew the flag of France; except when she was called the *Bonassola*, out of Genoa, Italy; or known as the *Miro*, registered in the Marshall Islands. Even the color of her hull changed frequently, often after every mission. Sometimes she berthed in the Port of Mogadishu but was just as often tied up farther south in Kismaayo. There were usually three forty-foot containers on her deck, except when there were six.

The thirty-two men on board had boarded solo or in pairs, staggered over a period of five hours to mask their number. The mothership itself required only a crew of six, but each of the two semisubmersibles carried six assaulters and a boat crew of four, plus two ground crew and four snipers for the helicopter. Another container in the hold had been fashioned into a bunkhouse. It wasn't luxurious, but it had lights and air conditioning, and most importantly, it could be sealed and locked if the ship was ever boarded and inspected by naval forces.

The Turk and the Italian were on deck at the bow, smoking cigarettes and watching a pod of dolphins swim alongside when the helicopter landed.

Ten minutes after the helo powered down, the ground crew had folded its rotors and wheeled the entire bird inside one of the containers on deck—to hide it from prying eyes, and to prepare it for attack.

They had four days.

FORTY-THREE

T WAS NEARLY time.

Boat-1 had been motoring south for almost four hours. For most of its time afloat, the thirty-eight-foot assault craft looked like a go-fast Cigarette boat, but it was actually a semisubmersible, a relatively new class of vessel that was capable of sealing itself up tight, filling ballast tanks with seawater, and moving slowly through the ocean with no more than eighteen inches—just enough for the windshield and a few instruments—riding above the waves.

She was invisible to the human eye and to radar.

Boat-1 was running at three knots with its navigation lights off and its ballast tanks full when the former Polish commando spoke up. It was just past 02:00 hours and he was inside the sealed hull, looking through a small periscope.

"This could be our boy—starboard quarter, bearing 165 degrees."

The boat commander looked with his own gyro-stabilized scope.

"That's him. Call the boss."

The boat's communications man sent a message to Nacay over the encrypted radio. Thirty seconds later, a siren wailed over the mothership's public address system. The entire ship was on alert-three status, meaning that every man had to be at his battle station within three minutes of the siren—but most were ready in one.

Four crewmen rolled the helicopter out of its container and began unfolding its rotors while two others launched a small commercial drone off the bow. The eight-engine drone had originally been designed for the movie industry and was capable of flying at sixty miles per hour, carrying a heavy camera, and an hour's worth of flight time—all while remaining too small to be detected by a ship's radar.

"Drone is up, good feed," said the drone pilot over the radio. *"Objective coming into view."*

Nacay watched on his laptop as an image of the ship emerged from the darkness. It was roughly seven hundred feet long and a hundred feet wide, a "coastal" tanker, small by tanker standards but perfect for smuggling oil into a sanctioned country. Though it was the type of ship they'd been told to expect, and where they'd been told to expect it, the route between the Strait of Hormuz and the Strait of Malacca was the prime oil shipping route to Asia, and there were hundreds of similar ships afloat.

They had to be sure they had the right one.

"Drone, show me the stern," Nacay said over the radio.

The target ship was moving at a steady fifteen knots as he read its name using the drone's night vision camera.

Amjad.

"*Target confirmed,*" he said. "*Drone, switch to thermal and fly a low orbit.*"

The matte black drone descended to a hundred feet above the surface and flew a racetrack pattern around the tanker from a quarter mile away. The lower altitude and heat-sensing thermal camera would reveal any crewmembers who'd been obscured from overhead surveillance by a roof or other structure.

"*We've got a single lookout on the bow, one on starboard quarter and one on port quarter,*" said the drone pilot. "*No sign of weapons.*"

"*Concur, three personnel on deck,*" said Nacay. "*Boat-1, the forward lookout is yours. Air-1, you have two targets, one on port quarter and one on starboard quarter.*"

"*Boat-1 has the forward lookout,*" confirmed the team leader.

"*Air-1, two targets, roger,*" confirmed the pilot. He was already in his seat with the rotors turning and the Allison turboshaft engine warming up. Nacay was strapped in next to him as they waited on deck.

They let the tanker pass.

"*All teams, stand by for launch orders,*" said Nacay once the tanker was two miles in front of them. He entered positions, headings, and speeds for the target and the other vessels into a worksheet on his laptop.

"*Air-1, launch on my mark . . . Boat-1, launch nine-one seconds from my mark . . . Boat-2, launch three-five seconds from my mark . . . 3-2-1, MARK.*"

The helo lifted from the deck with its lights off and

dove for the wavetops to avoid being silhouetted against the moon and stars as it flew toward the tanker. The *Amjad* was making fourteen knots. On its radar, moving at twenty-five knots on a parallel course, the helo would appear to be just another ship.

"Activating EW," said the helicopter pilot.

Mounted under the aircraft's fuselage was a Russian electronic-warfare pod that had been purchased from Cawar the arms dealer sixteen months earlier for ninety thousand euros. It immediately jammed the tanker's radios, GPS, and satellite communications, cutting it off from the outside world. The pirates' radios operated on a short-range, high-frequency band that was outside the jammer's capabilities.

The helicopter tilted its rotor forward and accelerated to one hundred knots.

The high-capacity pumps aboard the two semisubmersibles began emptying their ballast tanks, raising them out of the water and turning them into speedboats. Boat-2 accelerated on schedule and was soon planing over the sea at forty knots, her pilot using an inertial navigation system and a gimballed thermal camera to guide her onto the target.

Fifty-six seconds later, Boat-2's pilot hit the throttles and closed in from the opposite side.

Between the tanker's enormous engine, the sea churning along the hull, and the noise of the wind, the deck of the ship was a noisy place, but the sound of an approaching helicopter, even the quiet MD 520, was impossible to conceal.

As the first faint image of the port-quarter lookout appeared in the snipers' sights, they could see the man searching for the source of the noise, scanning the sea with binoculars, or possibly a night scope of his own.

But it didn't matter.

Each of the airborne marksmen was equipped with a Polish SKW semiautomatic sniper rifle and FLIR thermal weapon sight.

It was an incredibly difficult shot, shooting from one moving platform to another, and the right-side snipers acquired their target and adjusted for shifts in trajectory and drag inherent in firing from a moving helicopter. They also adjusted their aim down slightly, to compensate for the fact that the clockwise-spinning bullets would generate additional lift as the airflow from the moving helicopter hit them from the left.

They fired at the same time and the sentry went down with two rounds in his chest.

The helo flew in an arc behind the ship's stern until the other lookout came into view. This time the left-side snipers fired, aiming slightly higher to compensate for the clockwise spinning bullets' tendency to bite into the air and pull themselves down.

One of the shooters missed.

But the second sniper caught the sailor in the edge of his hip. The round had knocked the man to his knees, but he staggered to his feet behind the ship's railing.

Both marksmen fired a second time.

Two hits, and the crewman didn't get up.

From first to final shot, the entire engagement had taken eleven seconds. The helo turned away and took up station half a mile behind the tanker, where the *Amjad*'s crew was less likely to notice it, but its electronic-warfare equipment would still isolate the ship.

The semisubmersibles converged on opposite sides of the tanker. On board Boat-1, the Turk shouldered a pneumatic cannon and fired a grappling hook over the ship's gunwale. Standing next to him, the Italian was already in a climbing harness and hooked into the line. He used an electrically powered ascender to haul him up the sixty-foot side of the tanker in just five seconds. He attached two webbed climbing ladders to the railing and dropped them into Boat-1 so the rest of the team could climb aboard.

The first two men over the rail linked up and went forward.

It was four hundred feet to the bow. The pirates advanced steadily, their rifles up, their rubber-soled boots silent as they stayed in the shadows of the thick cargo pipes that ran the length of the ship.

The remaining lookout was on the starboard bow, about twenty feet back from the front of the ship. It was a warm night, and he was leaning against the railing, with his arms folded over the side. With the ship's bow wake churning steadily below him, he hadn't heard the helicopter or the suppressed gunshots.

The first pirate aimed for the center of the man's back, but his teammate waved him off. He was concerned the body might tumble forward and fall overboard, and the pirate didn't want to risk that a dead crewman with bullet holes in his back might be spotted floating in a busy shipping lane.

The steady churn of the ship slicing through the ocean grew louder as the second pirate slung his rifle behind his back and silently approached the bow. With his left hand, he reached around the sentry and grabbed the man's chin. With his right hand, the pirate drew a nine-inch knife across the man's throat and hauled him backward onto the deck.

Ten and a half minutes later, the last living member of the *Amjad*'s crew took his final breath, and the bodies were transferred to the ship's walk-in freezer. Once the oil was offloaded, the ship would be scuttled and the crew would undertake their final voyage—to the bottom of the Java Trench, twenty-four thousand feet deep in the waters off Indonesia.

FORTY-FOUR

IVE DAYS HAD passed since the *Amjad* disappeared.
Jake and Pickens drove the beige Daihatsu through
the Hamar Weyne district of Mogadishu. Pickens was
behind the wheel, navigating down a dusty street where children in ragged clothes lived in the ruins of crumbling buildings. Plastic water bottles lined with yellow glue littered the
ground. With no food, the homeless kids sniffed the glue to
get high, to sleep at night, and to escape the hell their lives
had become. Fights among the street children were common, with even minor injuries occasionally leading to fatal-
ities because of severely compromised immune systems and
a lack of medical care.

The Port of Mogadishu came into view as Pickens
turned west on London Road. A pair of rusty tramp
freighters and a small container ship were tied up at the
quay and a few puffy cumulus clouds floated out over the
ocean—but they were too light and too distant to bring
the life-giving rain the country so desperately needed.

Jake opened the glove compartment and spotted the

Glock 19 he'd stashed there when he'd arrived in-country. As they stopped in front of a building with a distinctive, red-tiled roof, Jake removed the pistol and held it low at his side, down between the seats.

Clap and the Ground Branch team pulled in behind them. A blue SUV with tinted windows was waiting across the street.

A man exited the car holding a package of some sort. He crossed the road and held out a brown paper envelope.

"Open it," Jake said. He visualized putting two quick rounds between the man's eyes.

The man gave a toothy grin full of perfect white teeth and tore off the top.

"No bomb," he said.

Inside were a few papers and maybe twenty photographs.

THEY VIDEOCONFERENCED GRAVES once they were back at the safe house.

"The *Amjad* is no more," Jake said.

"Where is it now?" asked Graves.

Jake held a photograph up to his laptop's camera. It was taken at night, with a time and date stamp, showing a ship called the *Al Marzoqah* sinking beneath the waves.

"They changed the name and scuttled it," said Jake.

"Judging by the date, it looks as if they waited a few days," Graves said.

"I'm sure they offloaded the oil before they sank it."

"Excellent," said Graves.

Jake was about to point out that they'd also sent twenty men to their deaths and put millions of dollars in a warlord's pocket, but his position on the issue was already well known.

As if reading his mind, Graves said, "Better Yaxaas than the North Koreans. Maybe it will keep him docile for a while—the next mission isn't going to be so lucrative."

"What next?" said Jake.

"We're monitoring a commercial fishing boat, allegedly working the Gulf of Aden and the Red Sea, but in reality, it's headed for Sudan to supply the government with Iranian weapons."

"I thought the new government had stopped supporting these corrupt regimes," said Pickens.

"They have, John, and that's why we need a guy like Yaxaas. When the new president and PM took over, they had the support of the people and the regular army, but not the Revolutionary Guards. The IRGC under General Shirizani is still just as corrupt and as insidious as it ever was."

"And just about the only source of hard currency they have is smuggling weapons," Jake added, seeing Graves's plan.

"That transfer is in direct contravention of at least two UN sanctions," said Ted. "I'm sure half a dozen nations would leap at the chance to stop that ship, but that would embarrass the new leaders of Iran, who we want to succeed. Our issue is with the IRGC, not the civilian government."

"It's just like the Saudi oil," said Jake. "We're trying to force a rift between Iran and Sudan."

"Exactly," said Graves. "When those weapons don't arrive, the Sudanese are going to be pissed because they've already promised them to the Janjaweed militia, who needs them to slaughter more non-Arabs in western Sudan, but the IRGC is going to say that the ship left on time and should be there. Maybe the Sudanese security services will believe the Iranians, but it's more likely they won't. The IRGC is going to expect Sudan to pay for a second shipment while the Sudanese are thinking they've been ripped off once and aren't going to fall for it a second time. There aren't too many countries that can supply what Sudan wants, and if we can sabotage their relationship with the IRGC, we'll save thousands of lives."

"I get realpolitik," said Jake, "and I'm all for stopping that ship. I just think there has to be a better option than Yaxaas."

"Jake, there have been alliances of necessity since there were three cavemen. Do you think Roosevelt and Churchill linked up with Stalin thinking they were taking the moral high road? How about your work with the Saudis last year? Do you keep in touch with the king—maybe get together around the holidays and behead a few dissidents? Of course not, but you did it because it prevented a war. Sinking this ship is going to fracture the relationship between two bad actors and put a shipment of weapons at the bottom of the sea. Allowing Yaxaas to steal a few tankers full of oil might save a hundred thousand lives in Darfur."

"We could sink it with an aircraft."

"We could, but then we wouldn't know if we actually eliminated the weapons. Yaxaas's men need to photograph the ship and the cargo before they send it to the bottom—just like the *Amjad*."

"Look, Ted, using Yaxaas to stop a shipload of oil is one thing, but a cargo of weapons is a different story. We can't trust this man."

"The IRGC is trying to destabilize a continent, evade UN sanctions, and smuggle weapons to the government that committed the largest genocide of the twenty-first century. Working with Yaxaas may not be a great option, but it's the best one we've got."

FORTY-FIVE

A WAKE OF DUST followed the small convoy as it sped through the cramped streets of Mogadishu. Two pickup trucks of gunmen were escorting Yaxaas's armored Range Rover, and a man in the back of the lead pickup fired a long burst into the air from his AK-47 as the three vehicles approached a busy intersection.

The other traffic yielded.

The warlord's motorcade continued on for several more blocks before turning onto a quiet side street and stopping at the end of the dead-end road. Yaxaas's gunmen had dismounted their pickups and were patrolling the area on foot when Jake approached in the maroon Toyota Surf. Clap and the Ground Branch team were a car length behind him.

The sun was overhead as Jake stopped alongside the Range Rover and lowered his window. There were a few clouds offshore and a light breeze blowing in from the sea.

"We have another assignment for you," he said.

"This time you pay me. I could have made twice as much on my original job."

"Maybe you'd like to trade places with the crew," said Jake. "It could be arranged."

"I'm not like you, American. I do not fear death."

"No one is Somalia is afraid of death because people like you have made it a living hell," Jake said. "Besides, death would be the easy way out for you. We prefer to grab you out of your bed in the middle of the night and lock you in a six-by-six-foot room where the walls are concrete, the ceiling is concrete, and the floors are concrete. There's no day, no night, no sound, and certainly no human contact. Think about that. You'd never see another living thing as long as you live—not even a fucking plant. Most people start to lose their minds after a few days or maybe weeks, but if you cross us, you'll have your whole life to enjoy it."

"The same thing could happen to you," said the warlord.

"Except ten more will be right behind me, and a hundred more behind them, and they will never, ever give up."

The warlord scowled.

"What is this next job?" he said.

"Two days from today," said Jake, "a commercial fishing boat will pass through the Strait of Hormuz on its way to Sudan."

Jake handed over a manila envelope. Inside were several photographs of the ship and a detailed route map. All were completely untraceable.

"It's called the *Saviz*," Jake said, "and it can't make port."

The warlord thumbed through the package, doing

some arithmetic in his head. He would need to get his crew assembled, practice a few dry runs on land, and put the mothership to sea in four days to intercept the fishing boat before it entered the heavily patrolled Gulf of Aden. It could be done.

He nodded once.

"It needs to disappear without a trace," Jake said. "No distress call, no survivors, no sign of the cargo—just like the tanker."

The warlord's face was an expressionless mask. Disappearing a ship and its crew he could handle.

"What is it carrying?"

"Not important," Jake said. "It's the ship itself that needs to be taken out."

Jake raised his window and the Americans pulled away.

THE WARLORD SAT in the armored Range Rover for a few more seconds while his gunmen climbed back into their pickups. It didn't require a great feat of reason to conclude that the American was lying, and Yaxaas didn't know precisely what his men would find aboard the fishing boat, but he knew it wouldn't be fish.

The warlord smiled as the Range Rover pulled away from the curb. He'd finally figured out how the Americans were going to help him defeat Badeed.

FORTY-SIX

THE MOTHERSHIP WAS two hundred miles off the coast of Oman, chugging east at six knots. It was on a reciprocal course for the fishing boat and had deployed its drone countless times over the past seven hours to investigate every westbound radar contact within a ten-mile radius. The drone operators were routinely swapping out battery packs and even had a spare aircraft ready to launch in case of an equipment failure or if the need arose to investigate two targets simultaneously.

The plan was to intercept the Iranian vessel before it entered the Gulf of Aden, where the coasts of Africa and Asia compressed the shipping traffic heading toward the Suez Canal into a narrow space. While the Gulf had been the traditional haunt of the Somali pirates, who preyed on targets of opportunity, the increased density of ships would work against Yaxaas's team, who valued secrecy above all else.

They wanted to intercept the *Saviz* while it was off on its own.

Separated from the pack.

Lagging the herd.

IT WAS JUST past 17:00 hours when the drone operator radioed the bridge.

"Positive contact, bearing 343 degrees, range eight point seven miles."

Nacay glanced at a live video feed from the drone, which was being broadcast on a twenty-four-inch video monitor on the mothership's bridge. The ship's profile and coloring matched the photos he'd been given.

"Show me the stern," he said.

The drone pilot flew a thousand meters behind the fishing vessel and used a high-magnification daylight camera to zoom in on the ship's name.

Saviz.

Written in English and Farsi.

They had their target.

But the *Saviz* was ahead of schedule, and the pirates operated only at night. They would have to bide their time until the attack window opened—sunset would occur that evening at 17:32 hours and twilight would persist for seventy-five minutes after that. It gave the pirates a five-hour window to hit the ship, establish control, turn for the open ocean, and send it to the bottom before the moon rose half an hour past midnight.

They could do that in their sleep.

Nacay entered the variables into a spreadsheet on his laptop and came up with the plan. They'd let the *Saviz* pass by in the opposite direction until the mothership was out of radar range, then turn 180 degrees and lay on the speed, appearing to the *Saviz* to be a new contact approaching from astern.

The mothership would then pass far enough in front of the *Saviz* to drop off her radar again before launching the semisubmersibles once night had fallen. The two speedboats would lie in wait on either side of their target's projected course—just like a World War II submarine wolfpack.

THE DRONE WAS running nonstop, alternating between low light and thermal modes as it orbited the target ship, gathering intelligence and informing the assault.

The ship was roughly 120 feet long, with a sharply raked bow and a two-story deckhouse in the stern. The waters off Oman were popular fishing grounds for sailfish, tuna, and dorado, and the *Saviz* was running longlines from her outriggers to keep up appearances.

Nacay updated on his laptop the positions and speeds for the target and the other vessels. They were close, there were more ships around than they would have liked, and it was going to be fast.

"*Air-1, launch on my mark . . . Boat-1, launch one-one seconds from my mark . . . Boat-2, launch one-five seconds from my mark . . . 3-2-1, MARK.*"

It was 19:42:03 hours when the helo lifted from the deck. They were two miles behind the *Saviz*, which was one mile behind the picket line formed by the two semisubmersibles.

The helicopter approached at wavetop level until the

semisubmersibles had emptied their ballast tanks. The pilot activated the electronic-warfare pod, and the fishing boat's radios, GPS, and satellite communications immediately turned to static. If the Iranians had put a military crew aboard, they'd know they were being jammed.

The semisubmersibles were alongside the *Saviz* thirty seconds later. The Norwegian on Boat-1 and the Italian on Boat-2 used bolt cutters to sever the longlines while the rest of the team threw grappling hooks and web ladders over the rails.

The gunfire started a minute later.

While the assault team had expected the smaller fishing boat to be an easier target than a thousand-foot tanker, the *Saviz*'s small size also made the approach of the two semisubmersibles impossible to conceal, and the Iranian Revolutionary Guard sailors fired down from the deckhouse at the men climbing over her sides, barely forty feet away. Two pirates received light wounds before the team was able to move to cover and return fire. They raked the bridge with automatic weapons fire, shattering glass and sending bullets through its thin metal skin.

The Norwegian took four men and advanced to the deckhouse. The door was locked, and he called the breacher forward. They hadn't brought the fancy explosives for the small fishing boat, and the muscular man took a full swing at the lock with a sledgehammer. It broke halfway, with the bolt still holding the door closed, and he wound up for a second try just as a burst of gunfire came through the door. Two of the rounds were stopped by his Dyneema vest and its bulletproof ceramic, but the third round caught him in his left eye and he fell to the deck, dead.

Standing off to the side, the Norwegian picked up the sledgehammer and finished the job as the Iranian gunman continued to fire. The door crashed open, and the Kenyan tossed a grenade inside, primed to explode almost instantaneously.

The blast killed the Iranian defender, and the three pirates stormed in. It was a small room, no more than an entryway and, except for the smoke in the air, the blood on the walls, and the body on the ground, it was empty. There were two doors on either side of a stairway that led up and down.

The Norwegian tried the first door.

It was unlocked.

The three pirates stacked up outside. The third man opened the door while the first two stepped inside. The room was tiny, a small cabin with a single berth and a grimy porthole. It smelled like mildew and it was empty.

The pirates checked the second door. It too was unlocked, but when they opened it they found a crewman inside, hiding under a table.

Two pirates fired at once and the room was cleared.

Outside, the helicopter had closed with the ship and the snipers were firing at the bridge with their semiautomatic sniper rifles, blowing out the windows so their thermal sights could acquire targets. The heavy rifle rounds killed one of the ship's officers and drove the others from the glassed-in bridge.

"At least two crew squirting from the bridge," said one of the snipers over the assault frequency.

The Norwegian motioned to his team.

They ascended the first few stairs, with weapons pointed up the staircase, but he raised a closed fist in the air when he heard footsteps racing toward them.

The two remaining Iranian naval officers raced down the stairway—straight into the pirates' sights, barely three feet away.

The noise was deafening as each pirate fired twice, sending half a dozen rounds flying through the cramped space in the span of a second.

The Norwegian stepped over the dead Iranians and keyed his radio.

"Air-1, Boat-1, squirters down, friendlies approaching the bridge."

The heliborne sniper fire ceased immediately and the Norwegian radioed Nacay that the assault team had taken command of the bridge.

Back on deck, the former Polish commando led the rest of Team-2 down a set of steel-grate steps into the hold. A commercial fishing boat of this size would have at least six more crew.

The accommodations level was one level down. It looked like a budget motel, with linoleum floor tiles and crude carpentry. There were four doors, two on each side. All were closed. The Pole signaled for the team to split up, with two men holding the hall, while two teams of shooters stacked up outside the first two doors. All the gunfire had eliminated any element of surprise and the assaulters immediately kicked open the doors. Both rooms were empty, but an Iranian crewman stepped into the hall from another room and opened fire with an AK-47.

A member of his country's elite Sepah Navy Special Force, the IRGC marine had known it would be a suicide mission before he fired the first shot, but he'd heard his countrymen killed like animals and decided that going down quietly was not his destiny. He tucked the weapon into his shoulder and held down the trigger, spraying rounds throughout the cramped hallway. Three pirates were hit. The first was protected by his body armor, the second caught a round in the shoulder, and the third had his femoral artery obliterated when a bullet caught him in the thigh.

The Iranian absorbed nine rounds in the chest and four in the head before he fell to the deck.

A collage of blood and spent shell casings littered the hallway.

The Pole cleared the remaining rooms with two of his men, swiftly dispatching two more unarmed crew members while the other assaulters tended to their wounded colleagues.

The shoulder injury was non-life-threatening, but the Italian who'd suffered the leg wound was laid flat on the ground while a teammate cut away the tiger stripe camouflage pants he was wearing. Another teammate applied two tourniquets and cranked them tight before locking them off, but the location of the wound high up on the thigh prevented the lifesaving devices from stopping the blood flow. The Italian's breathing grew shallow and desperate, and five minutes later, his eyes blinked for the last time.

The Pole returned to the main deck and radioed Nacay that the target was secure. The jamming stopped and the helicopter returned to the mothership just as the deck crane finished hauling aboard the second semisubmersible. Two and a half minutes later the helo landed amidships on the unmarked helipad and shut down its engine. The ground crew began folding its rotors the instant they stopped turning.

Thirty-one minutes after the first semisubmersible returned to the mothership, all of the equipment and weapons were secured in their containers. The ship could withstand a physical inspection from a naval boarding team.

Aboard the *Saviz*, the Pole took two men below. The hold was dark and cold and smelled of rotten fish. The men had quickly searched it earlier, but now they were opening the massive freezer cases.

They hit pay dirt with the second case. Inside were dozens of olive-drab wooden crates. The pirates hauled the nearest one out by its rope handles and popped the metal latches.

Packed inside were a dozen Iranian-made AK-47s. Other crates held machine guns, RPGs, and nearly a hundred 107mm rockets for a Chinese multiple launch rocket system. The Pole radioed Nacay about what he'd found.

"Photograph everything, then set the charges," replied Nacay. *"We'll be alongside in ten minutes."*

FORTY-SEVEN

A RED BAJAJ SLAMMED on its brakes and pulled to the side of the road. The three-wheeled taxi had a cracked windshield, a greasy fringe dangling from the ceiling, and a driver who was missing several teeth.

Pickens got in.

"Olympic Hotel," he said in Somali.

"The Nasa-Hablod is better," said the driver.

"What about the Sahafi?"

The recognition sequence complete, the driver nodded and pulled away from the curb. It had been four days since the attack on the *Saviz*, and the pirate mothership had returned to Somalia the prior morning.

The Bajaj wound its way down the main road and passed through the K5 intersection, where al-Shabaab militants had detonated an enormous truck bomb a few months earlier. More than two hundred people had died and hundreds more were wounded. The area still bore deep scars from the attack, and Pickens was staring at the wreckage when the driver passed him a manila envelope.

The CIA officer stepped out of the cab at the next intersection and waited with the envelope in his hand.

He scratched his right ear.

Clap pulled to the side of the road. He and Jake had been following the taxi at a distance, running protective surveillance for the meeting. Pickens climbed into the back seat and Jake glanced at the envelope.

"You look at it yet?"

Pickens shook his head and tore the top off. Inside were two dozen photographs from the *Saviz*. There were several shots of open crates filled with grenade launchers, rockets, and more rifles and machine guns than they could count. More pictures showed the interior and exterior layout of the ship, including the name painted on the stern, and finally, there was a series of overhead thermal images showing the ship listing to one side and ultimately sinking beneath the waves.

"Graves certainly is unorthodox," Pickens said, "but maybe that's his genius."

Clap glanced at Jake. Unlike Pickens, he also worked for Ted Graves.

And "genius" wasn't the word either of them would have chosen.

Pickens passed the photos to Jake in the front seat. There were several dozen wooden crates in the massive refrigerator cases, which would have held the fishing boat's catch until it returned to land. Yaxaas's men had opened a few of them, and Jake counted the Kalashnikov rifles (twelve to a crate) and Iranian-made RPG-7 rocket launchers (eight to a crate), plus hundreds of warheads and several PKM machine guns. Jake finally reached the pictures of the ship going down.

He was going through the photos a second time when something caught his attention.

One of the machine gun crates was painted the same drab green as the others, and it had the same rope handles and metal latches, but it had glistened when the camera's flash hit it, as if it were wet.

Jake checked the other photos to see if the crate had been opened. It hadn't, but it had been captured in another picture from another angle, and Jake saw the same phenomenon—moisture on its surface while similar crates around it were dry.

He put the photo back in the stack and looked out the window.

It was probably nothing.

FORTY-EIGHT

THE WHOLE TEAM was in the safe house living room when Jake called Ted Graves.

"I'll call you back in five," Graves said. He was breathing heavily. Well into his forties, the Special Activities chief often exercised for two hours a day, in addition to spending fourteen hours in the office, and Jake had caught him on the treadmill.

Jake killed the connection and paced around the room. Taped on the wall next to Clap's gear was a picture of a woman in running clothes crossing a finish line somewhere.

"Who's that?" Jake said.

"Wife," said Clap.

"Attractive."

"Yeah."

"What was she running?"

"Potomac River Marathon."

"Amazing."

"That she could run twenty-six miles?"

"Nah. That her Seeing Eye dog could."

Clap punched Jake in the shoulder.

Graves called back a few minutes later. Even though he was speaking on a secure encrypted phone, and everyone in the Agency gym had at least a top secret security clearance—including the guy handing out the towels—Graves still had to be discreet.

"What's the latest?" he asked.

"The *Saviz* is in the Arabian Basin, under ten thousand feet of water."

"You have confirmation?"

"Pickens picked up the photographs today."

"What about the cargo?"

"The crates were all labeled and Yaxaas's men did spot checks. It was small arms: rifles, machine guns, and grenade launchers—plus some unguided rockets."

"Perfect. The source who tipped us off just earned himself a ten-thousand-dollar bonus."

"Ted . . . Was there anything else on that ship we should be looking for?" said Jake.

"Like what?"

"I'm not sure, just a hunch. There's nothing we should be worried about?"

"Well, if there was something else, you don't need to worry about it, because as you just pointed out, it's all under ten thousand feet of water."

FORTY-NINE

S TEVE, THE ARMY Special Forces major, arrived at the safe house and spread several surveillance photos across the kitchen table. He was giving Pickens context on the images and hoping the veteran CIA officer could help him identify some of the men.

"I've seen this guy before," Pickens said. "He's a weapons smuggler based somewhere outside Mogadishu, but I don't know his name."

"Any issues with us rolling him up and asking him some questions?" Steve asked.

"Have at it," Pickens said. "Somalia has enough arms dealers."

Jake and Clap joined the conversation and the four men chatted for a few minutes about the challenges faced by the various parties who were trying to stop the civil war. So many people were getting rich from the bloodshed that there was little desire from the entrenched interests in seeing peace take hold.

"The problem," said Steve, "is that the border is just

too damn porous to stop the flow of weapons. Just yesterday, we intercepted a shipment of small arms coming out of the Port of Kismaayo."

The CIA men didn't react visibly, because Steve wasn't read-in on their operation, but they all had the same thought.

"What were they moving?" Clap asked.

"Iranian AKs and RPGs—garden variety stuff."

"Anything else?" Jake asked. "Anything unusual?"

Steve hadn't mentioned the rockets or the machine guns, and the crate with the condensation was still on Jake's mind.

"No," said Steve, "but there was other vehicle traffic that night, so I suppose they could have snuck something out before we established cordon."

"Any idea who was moving the guns?" Jake said.

"No. Cawar is the biggest dealer around, and we're questioning the drivers, but I don't expect much to come from it. In this fucking country, it could literally be anyone."

After Steve had left, the CIA team reconvened in the living room.

"So Yaxaas stole the weapons from the *Saviz* before he sank it," said Clap.

"I should have pushed Ted harder to find another way," Jake said.

"Don't put this on yourself," said Clap. "You told him we couldn't trust Yaxaas."

"Besides, there's nothing we can do about it now," said Pickens.

"Do you think any of your sources might know who bought them?" Jake asked.

"The guns are gone, Jake. Don't waste time chasing ghosts."

"It's not the guns and rockets that I'm worried about," Jake said. "There was something else on that ship."

"Something worse than guns and rockets?" asked Clap.

Jake nodded.

"This is like a bad dream," said Pickens.

"If that ship was carrying what I think it was," Jake said, "then it's about to turn into a nightmare."

FIFTY

ASIDE FROM THE buzz of the insects and songs of the birds, the only sound in the picturesque valley was the hum of a diesel generator. It reverberated softly through the hills, muffled by the grasses and trees of southern Somalia. Down on the valley floor, next to a bend in the Jubba River, clusters of work lights illuminated a fortified camp.

Inside the thick stockade walls were rough-hewn buildings and even rougher men—irregular fighters with rifles slung across their chests and over their shoulders. Several of them were clustered around three off-road trucks that had parked under a canopy of camouflage netting.

Half a dozen men were unloading the trucks, using rope handles to lower heavy wooden crates down from the truck beds and into the waiting hands of their comrades, who then carried them inside the largest of the buildings. Other men opened the crates and unpacked them, stacking the stolen rockets and machine guns against the wall.

But it was in a smaller structure on the other side of camp that Yaxaas and his son sat in hardwood chairs, smoking cigarettes and drinking a blend of cardamom and cinnamon teas. The camp was just a few miles north of the equator and far inland from the coast. The smoke hung in the hot and stuffy air.

"Badeed has stung us hard," said Nacay.

"A few more defeats and inertia will overtake us," Yaxaas said. "I've wondered more than once if we don't have a leak inside our organization."

Nacay nodded. "He has been unusually well informed. I hesitate to say it, but—"

The warlord stared at his son, encouraging him to continue.

"Do you think your old friend Cawar might be playing the Hawiye and the Darood against each other?" Nacay said eventually. "Alternately favoring one side, then the other, to drive his sales?"

Yaxaas laughed.

"He's been doing it for years. Peace would put him out of business."

"Then why do you let him manipulate us?"

"Because like every skilled liar, he adds enough truth to the lies to make them believable. Ignoring him completely could put *us* out of business."

"But he doesn't know about the weapons we've liberated from the Americans."

The warlord threw his cigarette on the dirt floor.

"No, but a few rifles and rockets will not change the course of the war."

The man with the bandoliers entered the room and stood in the doorway.

He did not look pleased.

"You should see this," he said.

FATHER AND SON followed him outside. The scene in camp had changed dramatically in the twenty minutes they'd been talking. The fearsome Darood militiamen were now huddled in the most distant corner of camp, speaking of black magic and the devil, and fearfully watching the trucks they'd been unloading just minutes earlier.

The man in the bandoliers swore at them as he walked across the camp. Behind the nearest truck was a crate like the others—except for the cloud of dense fog that rose from within it and billowed slowly over the sides before settling to the ground.

The man with bandoliers stopped ten feet away and gestured for Yaxaas to have a look. Bent nails protruded from the lid lying next to it on the ground.

"It was nailed shut?" said the warlord.

The man nodded.

Yaxaas spotted two crowbars under the rolling fog.

They had been dropped in haste.

Nacay joined his father and the two men peered into the wooden crate. Inside, surrounded by blocks of dry ice, was a heavy-duty plastic container with an airtight seal and half a dozen latches securing its lid.

The warlord was not an educated man, much less a scientist, but he had learned much in his fifty years on earth—especially in the field of weaponry.

"Rifles and rockets may not change the course of the war," he said to Nacay, "but this will."

FIFTY-ONE

JAKE LAID OUT a photo the pirates had taken aboard the *Saviz* before they'd scuttled her.

"We're missing something," he said. He was in the safe house kitchen with Pickens and Clap.

"Missing something, as in we don't understand what we're looking at, or missing something, as in we can't find it?" Clap asked.

"Both."

Clap and Pickens studied the photograph. A few of the crates had been opened. Most were still shut. To their untrained eyes, the containers all looked the same, but Jake's years as a CIA analyst showed him something else.

"What are we looking at?" said Clap.

Jake pointed at the suspect crate.

Pickens squinted. "I got nothing."

"Same," said Clap.

"Do you see how the lid on this one is nailed down?"

There were a dozen faint pinpricks in the photograph, ringing the top of the lid.

"Vaguely," said Clap.

"Well, it is," said Jake, "to prevent it from being opened out of curiosity. You'd need to pry it open."

"And?" said Clap.

"And it's the only one that was nailed shut—plus you've got condensation all over the exterior."

Pickens and Clap looked at each other.

"It's in the bottom of a ship," said Pickens.

"But it's the only one," Jake said.

"If the condensation is such a dead giveaway," said Clap, "why didn't whoever packed it do something to prevent it?"

"Because these crates were packed in Iran, probably somewhere in the desert, where the humidity is next to zero. No one anticipated the condensation that would occur once the ship reached the open ocean."

"But why just the one crate?" said Pickens. "They all came from Iran."

"Because that one is being cooled from the inside."

Clap looked up. "Do you know what's in there?"

"I know what isn't," Jake said. "Chemical weapons don't need to be refrigerated, high explosives won't ignite until around four hundred degrees Fahrenheit, and nuclear weapons can survive the heat of re-entry through the atmosphere."

The three CIA officers stood silently for a moment.

"The only thing that makes sense," Jake said, "is a biological weapon."

* * *

JAKE VIDEOCONFERENCED TED Graves. He was in his office, wearing a suit and tie. Though he'd been a member of the senior intelligence service for years, he still looked uncomfortable in the traditional uniform of an executive. His sleeves were rolled up and the top button of his shirt was open to accommodate the poorly knotted tie around his neck.

"This is your third call in as many days," said Graves. "You're supposed to be a fire-and-forget weapon."

Jake explained his conclusion about the biological agent.

"So let me get this straight," said Graves. "You think the Iranians were shipping a weapon of mass destruction to Sudan because you saw a photo of a wooden crate, with water on it, on a ship? There's a lot of water on ships, Jake."

"The water is on the outside, Ted. That's how ships work. And this was condensation on a single crate, not a splash of seawater across the hold."

"What do your teammates think?"

"My teammates don't know what to look for."

Graves was one of a handful of people at CIA who knew Jake from his prior life. He'd been a strategic weapons analyst before moving into the field and, while Graves was smart, he knew he didn't have Jake's technical skills.

"We were expecting small arms and rockets," said Graves.

"And we found them, but we also have this. You mentioned paying our source a bonus, so I assume it was HUMINT?"

Human intelligence. A living person.

"It was," said Graves.

"Did we get a manifest?"

Graves shook his head. "Just a heads-up about the transfer."

"We've got a problem, Ted."

"I think you need to take a deep breath, Jake. Even the IRGC wouldn't give Sudan a biological weapon."

"This isn't about arming Sudan. Iran is hiding evidence. U.S. sanctions have bitten to the point that Iran has been forced to let UN weapons inspectors back into the country to keep their economy from imploding. The inspectors started making site visits a few months ago and snap inspections a few weeks ago. I'm guessing the *Saviz* shoved off from Bandar Abbas just as the inspectors arrived."

"What kind of biological agent?"

"There's no way to tell without testing it."

Graves sat back in his chair.

"Well, it may be a sanctions violation, but it's a moot point. It's at the bottom of the ocean now."

"I don't think it is."

Graves leaned forward again and braced his thick forearms on his desk. His face filled the screen of Jake's laptop.

"You told me you saw the photos of the ship sinking. You told me it's at the bottom of the ocean."

"The ship is at the bottom of the ocean, but Yaxaas stole the cargo before he sank it."

"Is this another one of your hunches?"

"SOCOM intercepted a convoy leaving Kismaayo yesterday. It was carrying weapons from the *Saviz*."

"Fucking warlords," said Graves. "I'm not surprised.

Let me make a phone call and figure out the best way to get that crate transported and tested."

"The crate wasn't in the trucks, Ted. A few trucks made it out of the port before U.S. forces arrived."

Graves stared at the screen.

"Yaxaas has the bioweapon, Ted."

"We don't know that it's a bioweapon, Jake. It could be nothing."

"It's a bioweapon."

"You're going to have to ignore it for now," said Graves. "We still need Yaxaas."

Jake shook his head.

"Jake, for your own sake, forget about it. All you have is a picture of a wet crate and a razor-thin theory. I can't go to the Seventh Floor with this and say we've got a loose Iranian weapon of mass destruction. It'd be Iraq Two all over again."

"Ted, Iran has had a biowarfare program for forty years. It's a biotechnology leader in the developing world. Ten years ago they were sanctioned for buying pathological instruments, spray driers, and other now dual-use technologies from the Chinese, and Somalia is in the middle of its third famine in twenty years. A biological epidemic here would send the country back to the Stone Age."

"I'm not disputing any of that, Jake, but what are you going to do about it? Ask Yaxaas if he has it and to kindly return it? Then he'll know there's a loose weapon of mass destruction out there, or at least that we think there is. At that point, even if he doesn't have it he can claim that he does, then blackmail us."

"Sometimes you have to poke the bear."

"Move on, Keller."

"I'm trying to save a country, Ted."

"So am I," Graves snapped. "The United States of America. Stay away from Yaxaas."

FIFTY-TWO

THE NURSE'S BLUE hijab and brilliant smile were like beacons of hope to those inside the clinic.

She was on her knees, showing a weary mother how to feed her malnourished child with a peanut-based paste that would give him desperately needed calories. Without access to clean drinking water, and already weakened by hunger, the boy had succumbed to a parasitic infection. His bulging eyes blinked slowly and he was close to death, but he still had a fighting chance, thanks to the clinic.

It had been founded two years earlier, after the nurse had approached her clan elders and demanded that something be done to save the tens of thousands of Hawiye who died in Mogadishu each year from the effects of war and famine.

She was summarily dismissed. Unmarried women did not demand things of any man in Somalia, much less the rulers of the clan.

But Farida was undeterred.

She'd pulled a laptop from her shoulder bag and laid out a spreadsheet showing how much the clinic would cost to build, staff, and operate. She identified an abandoned building in the Wardhiigley district that had been damaged in a mortar attack but could easily be repaired, then proceeded to explain how even the most rudimentary care could save thousands of lives, and finished by telling the elders that their inaction would be inexcusable in the eyes of God.

She'd nearly been thrown from the room and beaten.

But the young woman's preparation and tenacity had impressed the most powerful of the Hawiye clan elders, and Badeed agreed to personally fund the clinic on one condition—that she would join as its director.

THE CLINIC WAS technically a stabilization center—meant to prevent at-risk patients from deteriorating past the point of no return—and in a country where 15 percent of the children did not live to celebrate their fifth birthday, the director's time was in high demand. Farida passed the peanut paste to the boy's mother and moved to the next area.

The building was long and narrow, like a railroad car, and she entered a room where several adults stricken with tuberculosis were lying prostrate on mats on the floor and wearing surgical masks to protect those around them. One of the men had also lost a foot in an IED attack, and gangrene had infected the stump. The risk of potentially fatal sepsis was high because of his weakened condition and old age.

An old man in Somalia was in his fifties, maybe sixty if Allah was really punishing him.

The director looked at the old man. Sitting on the floor next to him was Badeed. The warlord saw the director approach but continued massaging the old man's bony foot until he drifted off to sleep.

"Miss Hassan," Badeed said as he raised himself up with his cane.

"We need more medicines," she said as they walked to another room. "Our shipment from the Red Crescent was stolen outside the city. The workers were killed and the medicines stolen."

"I heard," said the warlord. "It was Masaska."

The nickname meant "snake" and the man had gotten it after being bitten by a highly venomous puff-adder. Subsequent necrosis of the face had left him with a ragged hole where his right cheek had been. He was one of Yaxaas's men, angry at the world, and notoriously violent.

"Please." Farida put her hand on the warlord's arm. "Just help us get more medicine."

"But he will do this again . . . and he is Darood."

"Please," she implored.

Badeed nodded.

Though the warlord was eager to avenge the killings and the theft, he had chosen the administrator of his clinic well.

FIFTY-THREE

THE MAN WITH the bandoliers was a descendant of the Masai warriors of Kenya. Intense and driven, he'd needed only two days to acquire all of the items on Yaxaas's list—a remarkable feat given that most of them, including the doctor, had to be brought down from Mogadishu.

Only the test subjects had been sourced locally.

Everything was ready by sunrise on the third day. Yaxaas and Nacay were in camp, the equipment had been unpacked and tested, and all non-essential personnel had been dismissed. Three holding pens had been constructed fifty meters outside the western fence line. With corrugated metal roofs and chain-link walls, they resembled primitive jail cells, which would have been accurate—had they not been something infinitely worse.

The twelve test subjects were moved at gunpoint under blue skies and scattered clouds until each pen was filled with a juvenile and an adult of each gender. Obtaining a perfect distribution of age and sex had been easy—Yaxaas's men had simply kidnapped who they'd needed off the streets of a neighboring town.

The warlord had recognized the biohazard symbol—three sets of pincers arrayed around a circle—when he'd first seen the plastic container packed in dry ice, but neither he nor anyone else in camp, including the doctor, knew precisely what they were dealing with. Everyone assumed it was a weapon because it had been found among weapons, but they had assembled today to test whatever it was inside the thirty-six sealed glass vials.

The doctor had come to Dujuma more or less willingly—one did not say no to an invitation from Yaxaas—but he did not know why he'd been summoned until he'd arrived in camp. Upon learning that his duties would likely result in the deaths of many, he hid his displeasure in order to minimize further loss of life.

Specifically, his.

He inspected the safety gear that Yaxaas's men had procured: Soviet-era gas masks, a scuba tank and regulator, latex examination gloves, spray bottles, and several other well-intentioned but wholly inadequate items for handling a potentially weaponized pathogen.

But as it was with the rest of his assignment, the doctor did not have a choice. He donned a pair of gloves and a gas mask with an expired canister and slowly removed the first vial from the container's foam padding.

The test subjects had been divided into three sets based on the method of transmission. It was a small sample size, but the doctor suspected he already knew the outcome of the tests and had chosen to waste as few lives as possible.

First up were The Breathers. Using an eyedropper, the doctor transferred a single drop of the virus to a plastic spray bottle and mixed it with several milliliters of water. He approached each individual and misted them in the face. The captives were not naïve. None of them saw the holding pens, gas masks, and armed guards as good omens, but when faced with a spray bottle or an AK-47, the decision at the time seemed obvious.

In time, it would seem much less so.

The next group were The Touchers. The doctor used a cotton swab to apply a small amount of the virus to the skin of the test subjects. Cutaneous transmission was less common for bacterial infections, but not unheard of, and Yaxaas had insisted upon exploring the possibility.

Last were The Drinkers. Each was given a bottle of water mixed with a drop of the virus. The older man in the pen took his bottle from the doctor and threw it back at him without taking a sip.

The man with the bandoliers was standing outside. He didn't have gloves or a gas mask, but he did have a Browning Hi-Power pistol strapped to his hip. He approached the man who'd refused to drink, shot him once in the gut, and left him in the dirt, howling in pain.

The others finished their water.

THE SUBJECTS WERE given food and clean water to drink—probably more than they'd had in a week outside the camp—but despite Muslim rules of modesty, bodily functions were taken care of inside the pens for all to see.

While still displeased with his task, the doctor attempted to be scientific about the results. He observed when the subjects became symptomatic and noted that there was little difference attributable to age or gender.

Six hours from contact, most of The Touchers had developed visible rashes. For whatever reason the young women displayed symptoms more quickly than the others, but the difference would prove tragically insignificant before the day was out.

Twelve hours after inhaling the virus, each of The Breathers had developed a cough. Short and raspy at first, the coughs rapidly evolved into painful and persistent deep-chest spasms that contained blood and other, less easily identified bodily fluids. The older man fell to the ground and curled into the fetal position.

Slowest to react were The Drinkers. Most took twenty-four hours before they began to display symptoms. What began as severe abdominal pain soon gave way to vomiting, diarrhea, and intestinal bleeding, leading the physician to suspect some sort of hybridized hemorrhagic fever, but he never had a chance to confirm his suspicions in a lab, because within forty-eight hours, all of the subjects were dead, including the doctor.

But while the test subjects had died from the effects of the biological weapon, the physician had succumbed to a more immediate fate—a bullet to the back of his head.

FIFTY-FOUR

TWO HUNDRED MILES to the east, the town of Afgooye was situated in the Shebelle River basin. For centuries, the fertile land had attracted the farmers and herders that were the backbone of the nation's economy. More recently, Afgooye had also become a refuge for those who'd lost their homes, families, or livelihoods because of famine or the civil war. While Somalia had traditionally been a large recipient of foreign assistance, donors tightened their purse strings over the years as they watched most of the aid be siphoned off by a combination of warlords, corrupt politicians, and al-Shabaab. Maybe 10 percent of it actually made it to the people in need.

Tens of thousands of these internally displaced persons were forced to travel, often on foot, along the lonely road west from Mogadishu, in search of a place where they could live in peace and escape the ravages of war.

Makeshift tents, made from plastic tarps and cotton blankets and anything else that might block the sun, had sprung up in fields, along dirt roads, and wherever else the refugees thought they might be able to grow some food. Men with sunken chests and distended bellies hobbled through the Afgooye camp. Women whose depleted bodies had no milk to give cradled their infant children in their arms, watching them suffer, feeling them die, and enduring pain only a mother can know.

Other children, clad in dusty clothes, ambled barefoot through the camp, begging for food from people who had none. A man with hollow cheeks and ribs that nearly burst through his skin lay in a wooden wheelbarrow, waiting to die.

In the eastern section of camp was a well.

It was the main source of drinking water for a quarter of the camp's sixteen thousand inhabitants. Though it was pumped by hand and of questionable purity, after two years of drought the residents were grateful for anything that might sustain life for just one more day. Nearly a hundred men, women, and children stood in line, buckets in hand, awaiting their turn at the well.

But dehydration and starvation were not the only dangers faced by the camp's inhabitants.

Ninety-five percent of Somalia's population belonged to one of the country's six noble clans, and Afgooye had been Hawiye clan territory since the time of Samaale's sons, so no one expected anything good to happen when two olive-drab pickup trucks filled with Darood gunmen arrived at midday. They were seated on plywood benches with their legs hanging over the sides and rifles held across their chests.

Mixing between most clans was strongly discouraged and intermarriage was absolutely forbidden, with conservative elements often bestowing beatings or death upon newlyweds in lieu of gifts.

Still, one of the men in the Hawiye camp had taken a Darood bride when they were living in Mogadishu, where anonymity came more easily and clan ties were easier to obscure, but the bride's eldest brother, a disfigured Darood enforcer named Masaska, had always suspected that something was amiss with her new husband. When the building housing their ground-floor shop and second-story apartment was destroyed a few months earlier by an al-Shabaab truck bomb, their newfound poverty forced husband and wife to relocate to a camp.

The Hawiye camp.

Masaska and his Darood militiamen jumped down from their pickups, stripped the well's two security officers of their weapons, and tore the facility apart—wrecking the shanties and terrorizing the refugees until they found his sister and her husband, cowering in their tent.

Made from bamboo stalks that had been lashed together, then covered with blankets and a tarp, the tent was little more than a sun shade. The brother knocked it down in less than a minute.

With his own sister begging for mercy at gunpoint, he forced the offending couple to lie in the wreckage of the tent. The gunmen wrapped them in the tarp and blankets and carried them on their shoulders, like a rolled-up carpet, toward the pickup trucks.

But the Darood did not go to the vehicles. They stopped at the well, and the brother fired a long burst from his rifle over the heads of those queued up for water.

The crowd scattered.

The henchman advanced toward the well with the screaming couple still wrapped in the blankets. A man ran to them and fell to his knees, pleading for mercy.

Masaska shot him in the face, as casually as he might check the time on a wristwatch, then pointed to the well.

The Darood goons dumped the couple into the well.

They fell thirty feet to the bottom, screaming as they tumbled against its rock walls.

The brother looked down the shaft and saw movement at the bottom—the couple thrashing in the waist-high water. His sister yelled to him in tears, begging for mercy.

He pointed his AK-47 down the well and squeezed the trigger. The rifle jerked wildly in his hands as he emptied the magazine.

The yelling stopped.

The brother and his henchmen returned to their trucks and sped from the camp, laughing as they struck and killed a pedestrian who'd been too weak and slow to get out of the way.

FIFTY-FIVE

Y AXAAS RETURNED TO his compound in Mogadishu
as soon as the tests were completed. Badeed's intelligence operation had eyes and ears everywhere,
and the Hawiye warlord had used past absences as opportunities to stir up trouble.

He didn't realize that the balance of power was about
to change.

"We could kill hundreds of Hawiye," Nacay said,
"maybe thousands."

Father and son were in Yaxaas's office with the French
doors open to the courtyard. Below them, Little Yaxaas
was resting motionless on the banks of the pond with his
enormous mouth open to cool his body. Though towering
cumulus clouds had blown in from the sea over the past
few days, no rain had come.

"Killing Badeed will be a technical challenge," said
Yaxaas. "He is a wise fool."

"So we target their leadership," said Nacay, "then start
a rumor of a mystical Sufi curse brought on by Badeed's

evil actions. Once the people closest to him start dying mysteriously, the rest of the Hawiye will seal him in one of his own barrels and throw him into the sea."

"'The Shark Plague,'" mused Yaxaas. Victory was close. He could feel it. He needed only to develop the delivery system he envisioned.

He'd just begun to explain it when his mobile phone rang.

"It's the American."

JAKE ENDED THE call. "He won't discuss it over the phone."

"Meeting in person is a bad idea," said Pickens. The big man had been pacing around the safe house since Jake had come up with his plan.

"Concur," said Clap. "It could be an ambush."

"And it could be that Yaxaas has no idea what he has," said Jake. "If we can buy the weapon crates back from him before they're opened, he might play ball."

"He sure as hell won't give them up if he learns he's got a weapon of mass destruction in there," said Pickens.

"Ignoring the danger isn't going to make it go away," Jake said. "Bioweapons are engineered to be highly contagious and resistant to treatment. If enough people are infected before they become symptomatic, it could kill half of Mogadishu inside a few months—call it a million people. In a year it could decimate the entire Horn of Africa. It has to be destroyed."

"We'll support you—whatever you decide," said Clap,

"but let us put together a tactical plan that makes sense. We choose the time. We choose the place."

The Ground Branch team members were mostly special-ops combat veterans in their forties and had all been working with unsavory types a lot longer than Jake.

"Listen, brother," said Pickens, "you've got to trust me on this. Yaxaas is not going to negotiate. He's going to kill you."

"Not if we kill him first," said Jake.

"Graves won't like that," said Pickens.

"Fuck Graves," said Clap. "He's lost sight of why we're here."

"But he's still our lawful authority," Pickens said.

"Is Black Flag lawful?" said Clap.

"Probably," said Jake. "We're not directly involved with piracy."

"But we're perpetuating it," said one of the other Ground Branch men. "What was Dante's line? 'The darkest places in hell are reserved for those who maintain neutrality in times of moral crisis.'"

"Look, if it's not Yaxaas, it'll be somebody else," said Pickens. The discussion was getting heated and he was pacing around the room again.

"Are we going along with Graves because it's the right thing to do or because it's the path of least resistance?" Jake said.

There wasn't a man in the room who thought Graves was doing the right thing.

"OK," said Pickens, "but what can we do about it? Yaxaas has the entire clan militia behind him."

"I don't think there are many problems that the men in this room can't solve with a little cunning and a lot of force," Jake said.

Heads nodded.

"This is outside our orders," Clap said, "so I can't speak for the men on my team, but I'm in."

The other Ground Branch men nodded without hesitation.

"All right," said Pickens. "I'm in too."

It was unanimous.

Jake looked around the room. He was a solo operator, and a damn good one, but it felt good to be part of a team again.

"So what's the plan?" said Pickens.

"We snatch him and force him to trade the weapon for his life."

"Or call our bluff," said Pickens.

"He's a megalomaniac, not a martyr."

"Agreed," said Clap. "Saving his own ass will always be his primary objective."

The tension left the room as everyone coalesced around the new plan. Jake looked over at Clap.

"There's one thing I've been meaning to ask you . . . What kind of name is 'Clap'? Is it short for something? A nickname? What's the story?"

Clap rolled his eyes. The rest of the guys on his team snickered.

"It's a nickname—a gift from the cadre at my operator training course. My initials are V.D."

Pickens broke into a wide grin.

"You could be Somali with a nickname like that," said Jake.

"So . . . about Yaxaas," Clap said, eager to steer the conversation elsewhere.

"Right. I'd like you to plan the operation," Jake said. "We'll probably be outmanned and your team has ten times the experience I do."

Clap nodded. The real number was probably closer to a thousand times, but at least Jake knew what he didn't know. That awareness would improve their odds of coming out of this thing alive.

"Well," said Clap, "the first thing we'll need to do is get him out in the open."

FIFTY-SIX

THE BAKAARA MARKET looked like an enormous maze that had been packed with people. Men in long pants and dress shirts and women in brightly colored hijabs walked haphazardly across the dusty ground and between the densely packed collection of outdoor stalls. Nearly everything that was for sale in Mogadishu was available within its borders, and all of it would be taken home in the back of a three-wheeled Bajaj.

Many stalls were little more than an umbrella, a man in a plastic chair, and a few ceramic pots or maybe a box of vegetables that had escaped the drought. The more established storefronts had sun-bleached tarps strung across wooden frames. One vendor served nothing but clay bowls filled with rice while the butcher next to him left rare and expensive slabs of raw beef hanging from a tree branch in the afternoon heat and swarming with flies.

Yaxaas had agreed to meet at the market, but only in the Abdalla Shideeye section. It was a black market within the Bakaara—a place to acquire counterfeit items such as identity cards and passports, or stolen items, such as rifles and RPGs.

Clap and the rest of the Ground Branch team arrived early to conduct pre-mission reconnaissance and run a communications check. Everyone including Jake was wearing a covert microphone and earpiece. The team had two vehicles parked nearby and all the gear they'd need for the snatch: a fast-acting sedative, weapons, flash-bangs, restraints, and even a disguise for Yaxaas if it became necessary to get him through a checkpoint.

The Bakaara Market was a central fixture of Mogadishu life and had attracted several IED attacks over the years. Bombs had been hidden in everything from fire extinguishers, toolboxes, and flashlights to cars and trucks. The Ground Branch team quickly identified several men as potential threats, but it was impossible to know if they were terrorists, undercover guards employed by the market, or Yaxaas's goons.

It was midday, and the heat was oppressive in the congested bazaar. A pregnant woman walked by, sweating profusely under her hijab and dragging her purchases behind her in a canvas sack. A skinny old man passed by in the opposite direction, leading an even skinnier mule to what could only be its grave.

Jake pretended to browse the stalls while he waited for the warlord. Clap and half the team were positioned across the small square, about a hundred feet away, with compact submachine guns hidden inside their loose shirts and their vehicle parked behind a nearby shop. The rest of the team was parked a block away and shadowing Jake in a loose formation. The dense crowd complicated everything.

Jake passed a stall selling canvas bags and approached a row of shops selling fabrics. He spoke into the microphone hidden in his shirt collar as Yaxaas emerged from one of the shops, surrounded by half a dozen armed men.

"Look alive, ladies," said Jake.

"Eyes on target," Clap responded.

The other Ground Branch operatives checked in as well, but direct lines of sight to the warlord were broken up by the throngs of people, and Yaxaas's own security would make the job more challenging.

"You were supposed to sink the ship and its cargo," said Jake.

"Two of my men died and four more were injured. Consider it compensation."

"Those weren't the terms of our deal."

"Deal?" Yaxaas scoffed. "We had no deal. There is give-and-take in a deal. You have given me nothing, so I have taken my due."

"I didn't realize you were so desperate for a few rifles and RPGs," said Jake.

"Desperate? No," said Yaxaas, "but what I found on that ship is going to change Somalia forever."

It was the confirmation Jake had been after. The warlord wasn't talking about rifles and RPGs. He'd found the bioweapon from Iran.

"Go home, American, and don't worry about Somalia. It's none of your business."

"*We'll be in touch,*" Jake said.

It was the code phrase for the Ground Branch team to move in.

Just as Clap and the others emerged from the shadows, the pregnant woman wailed and fell to the ground, clutching her stomach. Clap was a warrior, but he was also a husband, a son, and a father. His inherent compassion caused him to reach for her.

But the instant she looked up and met his eyes, he knew he'd made a terrible mistake.

FIFTY-SEVEN

T HE WOMAN TREMBLED as she raised her hijab.

She wasn't pregnant.

The only thing she was carrying was an explosive belt, and detonating it in the crowded market would kill half the Ground Branch team and at least twenty civilians.

"Abort, abort," Clap said into the radio. *"Suicide bomber, contact range."*

The frightened woman looked as if she had been forced to be an unwilling accomplice, but the presence of the bomb had neutralized the Ground Branch team and dashed any hope they'd had of capturing Yaxaas.

Clap and his men would be lucky to escape with their lives.

"I've got a visual on the actuator," Jake said over the comms net.

Yaxaas was holding a cheap mobile phone. He smiled as his thumb hovered over the send button.

"It's cellular," Jake added.

"Confirm cellular," said Clap. *"Can you get clear?"*

One the warlord's goons jammed the muzzle of a rifle under Jake's chin and took his pistol.

"*Yes,*" Jake said stiffly.

"*Banger coming your way on three,*" said Clap. "*One, two . . .*"

Jake saw the flash-bang flying through the air and closed his eyes.

"*Three!*"

It was a perfect throw. The bright flash and concussive blast hit just as it flew past Yaxaas's head.

Jake pushed the rifle to the left and stepped to the right. The gunman pulled the trigger and emptied his entire magazine into the sky as the two men wrestled for control of the weapon. Jake planted his right leg behind the man and threw him to the ground.

The flash-bang had temporarily blinded and stunned Yaxaas, but he still had the wherewithal to press the phone's keypad.

Nothing happened.

One of the Ground Branch team had activated the same multifrequency jammer they'd used before to block the signal to the explosive belt.

The flash-bang and the gunfire had triggered chaos inside the market. People were screaming and rushing from what they assumed was another terrorist attack. Jake lost sight of the Ground Branch team as people ran in every direction.

Two of Yaxaas's thugs rushed him and sent him tumbling backward into a stack of woven baskets. Jake scrambled to his feet and took off through the crowded market, shoving some people out of his way, jumping over others, and sprinting to one of the team's prearranged rendezvous points.

"Heading for alternate exfil alpha," he shouted into his radio.

But he turned a corner and found more gunmen blocking the exit. Jake didn't know if they were Yaxaas's thugs, but he had two men following him from behind and was about to be trapped in the middle. He ducked into an abandoned shop and pressed himself against a wall.

Outside, the men who'd been following him began shouting, and Jake heard someone in the crowd respond. The entire exchange had been in Somali, but Jake didn't need to understand the language to know that he'd been given up.

Yaxaas's soldiers entered the shop, AK-47s against their hips, fingers on the triggers. The first man was the one who'd taken Jake's pistol. He relaxed when he saw that the American was still unarmed. The gunman slung his weapon and took out a length of coarse rope to tie Jake's hands.

Jake doubled over and looked as if he might throw up.

The two men were nearly on him when he straightened up.

Neither man saw it until it was too late. Jake pulled the karambit from the sheath under his shirt and raked the knife up the first man's leg, diagonally slicing at least six inches of his femoral artery. At the top of the arc, Jake rotated the curved blade and brought the knife down hard along the second man's neck, slashing his carotid artery. The man dropped the gun before he could get off a shot.

The entire attack had taken less than two seconds.

Both men would bleed out in less than two minutes.

But Jake didn't have that long to watch them die. It was pandemonium outside as more of Yaxaas's men closed in.

Jake burst through the shop's rear door and into an alley. It was a part of the market he'd never seen before, but it opened onto a busy street, and for the first time since he'd come to Somalia, the streets of Mogadishu looked like the safest place around.

Jake sheathed the knife and ran.

There were a few cars and trucks, several Bajaj taxis, and a man on a dirt bike stuck in traffic. Jake tackled the man on the motorcycle and took the bike.

"On a moto, heading west," Jake said into the radio. He'd figure out where he was and where to go later. Right now he just needed to get clear of the market and open up some distance between him and his pursuers.

He put the bike in gear, gunned the engine, and aimed the bike toward a gap between two cars heading in the opposite direction.

He was nearly home free when a black SUV rammed him head-on.

The impact smashed the motorcycle's front fork and sent Jake flying backward through the air. He crashed to the ground ten feet away with the wind knocked out of him and his radio mic and earpiece missing. By the time he raised himself up to his hands and knees, three men with Kalashnikovs were standing over him. A fourth man emerged from the SUV's passenger seat.

Nacay.

The warlord's son walked to Jake and stomped him in the back, sending him sprawling on the ground once again. Nacay kicked him a second time, then a third, each time driving the toe of his heavy boots into Jake's ribs.

Two of the gunmen hauled Jake to his feet. He was bloodied and wheezing and no longer a threat to anyone, but Nacay wound up and threw a haymaker punch at his face, drawing more blood and sending Jake to the dirt a third time.

The goons stripped Jake of his knife, bound his hands, and threw him in the back seat of the SUV. The rest of the team mounted up and the man sitting on Jake's right fired a dozen rounds into the air through the truck's open window.

The SUV sped from the scene and disappeared down a side street.

FIFTY-EIGHT

THE LINE OUTSIDE the clinic was moving slowly, and the infant children in their mothers' arms were restless, but the women did not leave, for it was the only clinic in Mogadishu that was open to the Hawiye, and the doctor came but once a week.

And for once, the mothers did not have to stand in the glare of the sun. The cottony clouds that had been building over Mogadishu during the past week had turned thick and dark, ushered in by a strong, gusty breeze, and they cast wide shadows across the street. Though their hopes had been dashed countless times before, enthusiasm was building across the country about the possibility of rain.

It was late afternoon when a Toyota Land Cruiser pulled up outside. Badeed's bodyguards paid no mind to the man who exited the white SUV. His name was Robleh, and eight years earlier, he had acquired the rights to distribute the popular Caafi brand of bottled water throughout the Hawiye clan territories in northeastern Somalia. It was a massive franchise in a country plagued by polluted groundwater, and it had made him a rich man.

He passed the guards and found Badeed inside the clinic, holding an emaciated boy whose eyes and ribs bulged from a body that should have been twice as heavy. Badeed held the boy on his lap, patiently feeding him sips of sugar water, trying any way he could to get calories into his dangerously malnourished system. The warlord spotted Robleh and nodded, but continued to feed the boy until he'd finished the eyedropper full of sugar water.

Badeed picked up his cane and gestured for his friend to follow him to an empty room. Both men were Hawiye clan elders and had known each other since childhood. Robleh was also Badeed's cousin, although this was of lesser importance, as everyone in the clan was, by definition, related to everyone else.

The two men skipped pleasantries and quickly got to the reason for Robleh's visit. Badeed considered the clinic his refuge, and visiting him there to talk business was not recommended for anyone but his closest friends and advisers.

"I received a phone call yesterday," said Robleh, "from a government official in Afgooye. You know of the displacement camp there?"

Badeed nodded solemnly. "Last I heard, it was ten thousand people . . ."

"Sixteen thousand now," said Robleh, "and someone fouled one of their wells."

Badeed shook his head. He thought of himself as ruthless, but just. Depriving a refugee camp of drinking water made him ponder the existence of humanity.

"And they asked you for bottled water?"

Robleh nodded.

"I will help with the cost," Badeed said.

"Thank you, but that is not why I am here. I will provide the water until the well is cleaned, but I do not have the resources to do what needs to be done next."

Badeed realized at last why Robleh had come. It was a security matter.

"Who did it?" he said.

"I assumed it was al-Shabaab, but then I went to the camp this morning and started asking around."

Robleh explained the history of the couple who'd married outside their clans and the actions of the bride's brother.

"Spilling blood in the well was excessive," said Badeed, "but they deserved to be punished. I am not certain that this concerns us."

"It was Masaska," said Robleh.

It was the same man who'd stolen the medicines bound for the very clinic they were standing in.

Badeed looked at his friend.

"Then I'm afraid the time for diya has passed."

FIFTY-NINE

IT WAS LATE afternoon in the Yaaqshiid district of eastern Mogadishu and maybe a dozen people were on the street—a few men chewing qat and a handful of homeless children looking for scraps of food among the dust and litter that blew across the road.

The auto shop in the middle of the block was little more than a rollup garage door and a single repair bay. Inside was a pickup truck that had started making noise after striking something the prior day.

It was a Darood neighborhood, and the garage's owner, mechanic, and sole employee was Darood, but he wasn't the reason the truck filled with Hawiye gunmen had stopped at the end of the block.

They were there for the other man, the driver of the pickup. They'd been searching for him since Badeed had put the word on the street that the attack on the Hawiye refugee camp in Afgooye would be avenged. A few hours later an enterprising Bajaj driver had spotted the olive drab pickup with the dented front fender and reported its location to his cousin, a fighter in the Hawiye militia. The cousin had told his commander and the commander had called Badeed.

The gunmen jumped down from their truck. They asked no questions. They entertained no pleas.

They opened fire.

The Hawiye raked the garage with bullets, killing its owner and the owner of the pickup truck. The gunmen kept firing with their automatic weapons until the fuel leaking from the pickup's tank ignited.

Filled with greasy rags, a barrel of motor oil, and several cans of gasoline and diesel fuel, the garage erupted in flames. Fire leapt from the open door, rising into the air above the building. The flames ignited a rats' nest of power lines that were strung overhead and sparks flew and lines crackled as they fell to the street. Thick black smoke filled the air.

Their mission complete, the Hawiye were returning to their vehicles when four teenage boys ran onto the street. They were part of the neighborhood Darood militia, paid by Yaxaas in drugs and food but mostly threats. They were outnumbered and outmatched, but they had their orders, and those orders were to repel the Hawiye.

Bullets flew in both directions, sprayed aimlessly down the street. Neither side cared that the locals who were caught outside took more fire than the enemy. Innocent men, women, and children fell where they stood.

Bodies lay strewn about the block. The neighborhood children, numb from years of war and hungry from years of famine, quickly stripped the dead of anything of value:

sandals, weapons, and whatever else they could scrounge. By the time the fighting was over, the road was lined with shattered windows, pockmarked walls, and puddles of blood.

More bystanders were killed than enemy combatants and, in a place where human life had no value, both sides considered it a victory.

SIXTY

H OT AIR BLEW through the SUV's interior as the passengers rode with their gun barrels sticking out the open windows. Nacay was in the front passenger seat and regularly checking his side-view mirror while the driver hurtled down side streets and up alleyways. One of the gunmen riding in back had put a hood over Jake's head and the SUV made dozens of turns until the men inside were sure they weren't being followed.

Two men slid open the fifteen-foot-high doors to a warehouse as the black SUV approached. It sped inside and stopped in the back. Nacay took Jake and three henchmen and climbed into a white sedan with heavily tinted windows. Less than a minute later, the white sedan and two decoys drove out of the warehouse and fanned out in different directions to confuse any aerial surveillance the Americans might have deployed.

Jake was sandwiched in the back between two Darood gunmen while Nacay rode shotgun. The sedan's driver had undergone a remarkable transformation—waiting patiently while a Bajaj in front of him blocked traffic to discharge a passenger, then slowly pulling around and driving down a side street. In stark contrast to his time behind the wheel of the black SUV, the driver was doing everything possible to avoid drawing attention to the sedan.

Probably 80 percent of the cars in Somalia were white sedans or hatchbacks, and as they headed northwest through the city, the vehicle with Jake inside had effectively disappeared. They were making no more than thirty miles per hour, simply going with the flow of the traffic around them—when the Toyota minivan in front of them slammed on its brakes.

Clap and two of his men stepped out of the van and raised their weapons. A second later, a gray SUV holding the rest of the Ground Branch team skidded to a halt behind the sedan and pressed hard against its rear bumper.

Though Jake had lost his earpiece, he still had the radio transceiver unit strapped to his waist. Clap and the Ground Branch team had been tracking him using a system known as ATAK, which, among other things, overlaid his position onto a moving map on their mobile phones.

Nacay's driver revved his engine and shifted into reverse.

The Ground Branch team opened fire.

Clap fired half a dozen rounds into the Nissan's engine compartment. The CIA contractor on his right shot out the sedan's two left tires while the man on his left fired three rounds at the driver's chest. The rest of the team targeted the right-side tires and rushed the back seat doors, where Jake was being held.

But the Nissan's driver mashed the gas pedal to the floor. The white sedan shot backward, pushing the SUV back a few feet and sending the Ground Branch men scrambling for cover. Clap fired off another five rounds, but the unobtrusive sedan was armored all around, from the engine compartment to the windows, including run-flat tires. Nothing seemed to affect it. The driver shifted back into first gear and clipped the minivan as he sped away.

Clap ordered the CIA men back to their vehicles. The minivan was heavy and slow, so the gray SUV took the lead spot in the pursuit, ramming the sedan twice and trying to spin it out of control.

But Nacay's wheelman knew his car and he knew the roads. He quickly opened up the distance with his pursuers and floored it down a bumpy alleyway before disappearing down another side street. The Agency vehicles followed.

The road was a single lane wide, with two-story buildings on each side and strings of power lines up above. The Agency SUV had closed to within a few car lengths of the white sedan when it made a sharp right turn and stopped.

Blocking the intersection ahead was a technical, a pickup truck with a light machine gun mounted in its bed. The improvised guntruck had become a staple of the Somali civil war, and the site of the ambush had been chosen well. The tight quarters made it nearly impossible for the Americans to reverse to safety.

The gunner opened fire with long bursts from the machine gun. Its heavy 7.62mm rounds tore through the Americans' passenger compartments.

Clap took a round to the shoulder, and the man next to him was hit twice in the chest. The Agency SUV was peppered with bullet holes and shattered glass. The Ground Branch contractor in the front seat was killed instantly when a round tore out his throat.

Another operative leaned out his window and smoked the technical's gunner with three quick rounds to the face.

It bought the two CIA vehicles enough time to back out of the alley, but Jake was gone.

SIXTY-ONE

THE WHITE SEDAN swerved around a corner and accelerated. Pocked with bullet holes, it made close to seventy miles per hour through the narrow streets as it sped across two intersections and turned into a junkyard. Workers unloading bags of trash from a garbage truck pretended not to notice Nacay and the two gunmen who stepped out of the back seat.

It was safer not to notice a lot of things that happened in Mogadishu.

The Darood thugs yanked Jake from the car and threw him to the ground.

"He has a tracking device," screamed the warlord's son. "Find it!"

The goons stripped Jake to his underwear and found the radio transceiver.

Nacay drew his pistol and pointed it at Jake's head, but he lowered the weapon when he heard a car engine being pushed to its redline and closing in fast.

"We'll finish this later," Nacay said to Jake. "I promise you."

The men threw Jake back into the sedan and the car did a U-turn in the sandy lot. Nacay lowered his window as they approached the exit and, with the skill of an NBA all-star, lobbed the radio beacon into the garbage truck's hopper.

Ten minutes later, the white sedan pulled back inside the Darood warehouse. The black SUV was gone, the doors slid shut, and the sunlight vanished. Overhead fluorescent lights struggled to light the cavernous room. All around, the high walls were lined with metal racks filled with boxes of ammunition, crates of weapons, and sundry items acquired by Yaxaas's men from around the Horn of Africa.

The goons hauled Jake from the back seat, threw him to the floor, and struck him roughly.

A man with a disfigured face approached from a dark corner.

"What do we do with this one?" he said.

"Soften him up," said Nacay.

"How soft?"

"Liquefied."

Nacay and his men left in the white Nissan, wholly unconcerned about driving around Mogadishu in a car scarred with dozens of bullet holes.

The man wasted no time carrying out his instructions.

Two of his cohorts manhandled Jake to the back of the warehouse and tied him spread-eagle to one of the metal racks. They were thugs, wholly untrained in the art of extracting information through pain, but information wasn't their objective. Their goal was pain itself.

And at that they excelled.

THE BUILDING WAS a hive of activity when Jake regained consciousness. Two white pickup trucks were parked in the center of the warehouse floor. Behind them, four men were busy sliding rectangular plywood benches into the beds—it gave the passengers the option of riding with their legs inside or dangling them over the fenders. More men stood throughout the warehouse, speaking a mixture of Arabic and Somali and loading their chest rigs with AK-47 magazines and hand grenades. Whatever they were suiting up for was going to be bloody, and Jake hoped it wasn't going be another assault on the Ground Branch team. He'd seen the technical open fire on his friends and knew they'd taken casualties. In their current condition, there was no way they could survive a second assault by a force this size.

Jake spotted the man with the disfigured cheek walking toward him in the dim light. He had a pistol in his hand.

Jake closed his eyes and played dead. He knew he couldn't take much more. But the man had a great deal of experience with torturing people, and he grabbed Jake's crotch and twisted his testicles as if he were trying to wring out a wet towel.

Jake would have screamed, but his pain needle was already pegged on 10 and his body had only one response left.

He passed out again.

SIXTY-TWO

IT WAS MIDMORNING, the clinic's busiest time of day, but it looked like dusk on the streets of Mogadishu. Days of strong winds had blown towering dark clouds over the eastern horizon, blocking the sun's relentless rays and heightening anticipation of the rains to come.

The mood on the streets, even among the line of patients waiting outside the clinic, was one of yearning. Hopes had been dashed before, but after two unrelenting years of drought, cholera, and famine, even dreams had to be seized.

A woman in a tan hijab was next in line when the clinic's director walked outside past the two security guards to do a preliminary evaluation. The director was kneeling, with a clipboard in her hand, when two white pickup trucks stopped out front.

Ten gunmen jumped out.

The director leapt to her feet and yelled for everyone to scatter, but the patients were sick and slow to move. One of the gunmen saw the director yelling and spotted the clipboard in her hands and identified her as an authority figure.

He raised his rifle.

But the clinic guards were unconstrained by cumbersome rules of engagement—or any rules of engagement, for that matter; it was Mogadishu after all, and ten men with rifles did not portend good news. The guards fired simultaneously into the cluster of gunmen. Neither man had any real training, but they did have automatic weapons, so the law of averages worked in their favor and they managed to hit a few of the attackers—including the man who'd been aiming at the director.

It bought her enough time to grab the woman in the tan hijab and push her inside the clinic, but it was the last of many selfless acts the director would perform in her lifetime. The gunmen counterattacked, and she was hit several times in her hip, back, and arm as she attempted to save the next person in line. She fell to the ground, just a few feet from the clinic that had saved so many but could not save her.

The gunmen continued firing into the crowd until everyone who'd been waiting had either escaped or been killed. The body count was already approaching twenty by the time the head gunman stepped over the director's body and entered Badeed's clinic.

It was Masaska.

Yaxaas's orders has been explicit—the attack on the Darood garage had to be punished, and punished severely.

Masaska had neglected to mention to his boss that the attack on the garage was likely retribution for the attack on the refugee camp in Afgooye, but it would not have mattered.

The woman in the tan hijab saw the man with the mutilated face enter the clinic and fled deeper into the building. She'd just made it through the small lobby when Masaska pulled the pin on a hand grenade and lobbed it inside. The explosion blew out the room's windows, sending shards of glass hurtling outward through the steel bars that had once seemed to provide so much security.

The clinic was long and narrow, and Masaska and his men flooded through it. Most patients were barely able to move, and the attackers walked calmly through the building, firing blindly down hallways and finishing off the wounded with knives and machetes.

One of the invaders, who possessed a live fragmentation grenade and a poor understanding of chemistry, tossed it into a room filled with oxygen bottles. The ensuing explosion destroyed the concrete wall he was hiding behind— and the three rooms around it—killing him and another attacker and narrowly missing the woman in the tan hijab, who was staggering toward the clinic's exit.

The Darood hit team reached the far end of the clinic and discovered that more Hawiye security guards had arrived. A second gun battle erupted on the street until Masaska grabbed the woman in the tan hijab around the throat and used her as a human shield until he and his remaining men were safely to their vehicles.

By the time the second pickup truck sped away, forty-eight Hawiye patients, workers, and innocent bystanders had been slaughtered.

Such was the endless cycle of violence among the warlords of Somalia.

SIXTY-THREE

SUNRISE WAS STILL a few hours away when twenty heavily armed men climbed into their vehicles.

Badeed hadn't sat down, much less slept, since the attack on the clinic. He felt an unfamiliar and distinctly unpleasant emotion, somewhere between guilt at not having killed Masaska when he'd first wanted to and fury toward the animal who'd attacked a refugee camp and a clinic in the same week.

The warlord preferred an informal leadership style, but his vast business holdings, his immense wealth, and the constant and evolving friction with the other parties to the civil war necessitated a disciplined command structure, one with a cadre of senior staff running everything from operations and finance to communications and intelligence.

Each branch was efficient and professional, but it was Badeed's intelligence arm that lifted his organization above its rivals. Led by a fellow Hawiye clan elder, who was also the number three official at the Somali National Intelligence and Security Agency, the warlord's intel shop had government-quality resources throughout the country.

And every one of them had been searching for Masaska.

The tip ultimately came from a paid informant inside the Darood organization. The target was in a warehouse across town.

"WE CAN HANDLE this," said Badeed's chief of operations. Badeed was strapping on an assault vest, and there was no reason for the big boss to risk his life on such a mission.

The warlord put a hand on the man's shoulder and looked him in the eyes.

"Some things a man must do himself . . . for his soul."

He climbed into the lead pickup truck and signaled the small convoy to move out. The operations chief had put a man with binoculars down the block from the warehouse twenty minutes after the tip came in, just before midnight.

Three of the pickup trucks stopped a hundred meters away. Badeed's men exited their vehicles and advanced on foot, hoping to catch the enemy asleep.

Two of Badeed's men went behind the warehouse. Most power lines in Mogadishu hung in low bunches across roads and sagged diagonally across streets. Sometimes fifty separate wires would be mounted on a single pole, and it took one of Badeed's men ten minutes to isolate the line into the warehouse.

The other men surrounded the building with Kalashnikov rifles, Norinco machine guns, and a pair of rocket-propelled grenades while the fourth pickup crept forward silently, barely above idle speed, until it was thirty feet from the entrance. Two men ran chains from the truck's frame and hooked them to the warehouse's sliding doors.

The driver gunned the engine.

The six-thousand-pound pickup had already accelerated through twenty miles per hour by the time the chains went taut.

JAKE HAD DRIFTED in and out of consciousness many times since the torture had begun in earnest. It was his body's way of conserving all of its available energy to save itself.

But this time when he opened his eyes, he saw nothing. His world was black. He had no idea where he was or what was happening . . . until he felt the pain.

And it all came back.

Nacay had returned and hooked Jake up to a truck battery with a pair of jumper cables. The warlord's son had taken an almost deviant pleasure in watching Jake's muscles and nerves seize up and spasm as the current coursed through his body. A few times, Jake thought his heart or his eyes might explode, but his body had somehow survived. Then had come the burns, and the stress positions that had nearly dislocated both of his shoulders.

A faint glow spilled in through a skylight in the building's roof. A moment later, Jake heard muffled snores coming from a distant room and realized that he was still in the warehouse, still tied to the rack. The coarse ropes tied around his ankles, wrists, and throat were supporting most of his body weight.

He was still assessing his situation when the warehouse's sliding doors were ripped from their tracks.

Fifteen feet high and fifteen feet wide, the two metal doors screeched as they buckled and tumbled into the parking lot. A dozen tactical lights swept across the warehouse like miniature searchlights.

A beam illuminated the Darood militiaman who'd been snoring on a cot twenty feet from Jake. He sat up when he heard the noise and saw the lights—and instinctively reached for his rifle, but a burst of gunfire changed his mind.

Into a bloody pulp.

Six more Darood who'd been sleeping elsewhere scrambled to the front of the warehouse but raised their hands in surrender when they saw the superior firepower arrayed against them.

Badeed's men disarmed them and held them at gunpoint on the ground, their faces pressed against the dusty warehouse floor. There was shouting from outside, and two of the warlord's men manhandled another Darood thug into the warehouse.

"We caught him out back, trying to escape."

Badeed shined a flashlight in the prisoner's face and nodded once.

A soldier kicked the prisoner in the back of the legs and forced him to kneel. Another soldier tied his hands.

"You are Masaska?" said the warlord, but it was a rhetorical question. The hole in his face left by the snake venom was unmistakable. "You destroyed my clinic?"

"I—"

Badeed pulled the top off his cane, revealing a nine-inch stiletto. He grabbed Masaska's hair and plunged the blade into his chest, where it skewered the diaphragm that allowed him to breathe.

It wasn't a fatal wound, but it was a painful one.

Excruciatingly painful.

Masaska tumbled to the floor, struggling for breath while surrounded by more air than he could breathe in a lifetime.

Badeed signaled his men with a flick of his chin.

It was time for the next phase of the plan.

The Hawiye goons rolled large barrels into the warehouse. Jake could smell the diesel fuel as they poured it across the warehouse floor. It puddled around the Darood prisoners who'd been tied up in the middle.

"Boss!" said one of Badeed's men.

He'd found Jake, far in the back, tied to the rack.

The warlord approached and his henchman shined a flashlight in Jake's face.

Badeed recognized him from their encounter in Kitadra.

"Trouble follows you like a shadow," said the warlord.

"Yaxaas doesn't like me very much."

Badeed raised the stiletto and pressed the tip against Jake's throat. The blade was still warm and wet from Masaska's blood.

"And why is that?" said Badeed.

"I tried to kill him."

The warlord jerked the blade up and back, slicing the rope around Jake's neck. Badeed cut the ties from his ankles and wrists and two of the warlord's men dragged Jake outside.

Once all the Hawiye were outside, Badeed nodded to one of his men. The man shouldered his weapon, lined up on one of the empty barrels of diesel fuel, and pulled the trigger.

The rocket-propelled grenade leapt from the launch tube at almost a thousand feet per second, and its 105mm thermobaric warhead exploded as soon as it hit the ground, dispersing oxygen-starved explosives into the air. They detonated a fraction of a second later, igniting the diesel fuel and triggering an explosive pressure wave that even the Hawiye, back at their vehicles one hundred meters away, felt violently in their chests.

Jake was sitting on the liftgate of one of the pickup trucks, dressed in secondhand clothes someone had given him and drinking a bottle of water, when Badeed limped over. He'd cleaned the stiletto and replaced it atop his cane.

"Thank you," said Jake. The two men spoke for a minute.

Small explosions punctuated the night air as stores of ammunition cooked off inside the warehouse.

Badeed walked Jake to a Bajaj taxi that one of his men had hailed.

"You have heard the expression 'The enemy of my enemy is my friend'?"

Jake nodded.

"Your diya is forgiven, and may Allah shower his blessings upon you."

SIXTY-FOUR

JAKE REACHED THE safe house just before dawn, stumbling the last four blocks on his own because he didn't trust the Bajaj driver.

He buzzed at the gate and Pickens came out. He'd seen Jake on the video feed on his phone.

"Dude . . ."

Jake was a mess: bruised, bloodied, and wearing the clothes Badeed's men had stripped from a corpse in the warehouse—complete with bullet holes and bloodstains.

"How are Clap and the team?"

Pickens shook his head. The Ground Branch team was out of the fight. Two were dead, and another had been airlifted to a U.S. military hospital in Ramstein, Germany.

"Ramstein might not be a bad option for you," said Pickens.

"I'm going to take an ice bath. I'll be fine."

Jake explained how he'd been captured by Yaxaas and liberated by Badeed.

"Badeed forgave the diya."

"You know that's not a gift," said Pickens. "You owe him now. It might be time to get out of Somalia before the two warlords who run the place both decide to kill you."

"I'll figure it out."

Pickens shrugged. "OK, but you'd better call Graves. He's been calling every few hours for an update. He sounds worried."

"I'm sure he is worried," said Jake, "but not about me."

Jake swallowed four acetaminophen tablets and four ibuprofen pills while Pickens ran the water and dumped all of their ice in the tub.

Jake lowered himself into the bath. The water turned brown as the dried blood washed from his body. The cold and the drugs soon numbed the pain and he closed his eyes.

Terrible thoughts raced through his mind: Clap and his men being ambushed, the Bakaara Market, Masaska, the torture Jake had endured inside the warehouse and then the horror that had taken place when it was set ablaze—but more than all of that, more than anything, the thought of a bioweapon in the hands of men like the warlords convinced Jake that they had to be stopped.

He tried to clear his head. Too many random thoughts were jamming him up, preventing him from thinking straight. He focused on his breathing, inhaling as deeply as his bruised ribs would allow, and relaxing all of his muscles as he exhaled. Inhale, exhale, relax. After thirty or so repetitions, he drifted off to sleep.

"Yo."

"Yo!" Pickens repeated, his baritone reverberating

through the small tiled bathroom. "Your pasty-white skin is turning blue. Get the hell out of there before you die for real."

Jake had been shivering in his sleep.

Aside from a cut under his eye and a few small burns from Masaska's cigarettes, Jake almost looked normal after he'd dressed in clothes without bullet holes in them. His bruises were hidden by the long sleeves and long pants.

"I'm calling Graves," Jake said. "Do you want in on this?"

Pickens fled the room.

"Great work," Graves said over the video link. "You really showed Yaxaas who's in charge. Now the U.S. has lost its credibility and this guy thinks he can do whatever he wants."

"He's got the weapon, Ted."

"You saw it?"

"No, but his men saw it. They held me in a warehouse and I overheard some of them talking about it. They told some of the others that they ran into a river to wash away the evil spirits."

"These aren't educated people, Jake. Did they say what it was?"

"They called it 'the Devil's Box.'"

"That could be a television set."

"It's the weapon. They also said there was 'smoke' coming off it, which would be consistent with dry ice evaporating, which would have caused the condensation I saw in the photos. We're one bad decision away from a catastrophe."

"The only bad decision I'm concerned with is you ignoring my order to keep your distance from him."

"Ted, Yaxaas has no idea what that weapon will do. Maybe he thinks it'll kill a few people or maybe a few hundred, but a state-manufactured biowarfare agent could decimate the population of Africa. With healthcare, famine, and living conditions what they are down here, it could kill a million people in Mogadishu alone. He needs to be stopped."

"Listen to me, Jake. We get reports of stray weapons of mass destruction two or three times a week. If you had proof that this bioweapon existed, or even if you'd seen it yourself, I'd have a counter-WMD team there in twenty-four hours, but all you've got is a wet box and some Darood militiamen talking about black magic."

"You're wrong about this, Ted. Put your ego aside and weigh the risks."

"Ego? I'm not worried about my reputation, Keller. I just don't want more bodies piling up while you pursue this fantasy, so stand down while I try to unfuck your mess and keep Black Flag from imploding. Take some personal time and think about your future—think long and hard about whether or not you can be a part of this team."

SIXTY-FIVE

CLAP WAS IN the next room with his arm in a sling. He had lost teammates before and he would probably lose more. It was the nature of the work, but it never got easier, especially when he saw a friend's final moments pass by just a few feet in front of him and Clap had given the order that got him killed. He could keep doing hits on bad guys and helping good guys, but his downtime mostly consisted of hard drinking and thrill-seeking to keep the adrenaline pumping and the bad memories from returning. Though he still loved his wife, his marriage was on the rocks because he rarely went back to the States anymore. It felt too foreign to him, too detached from his reality.

When he was still in the army, he'd once spent a week with a charitable organization in Montana that helped active-duty special operators get their heads straight. It had been like hitting a reset button on his entire life, allowing him to return to duty but also reconnect with family and friends and once again feel joy. The experience had been cathartic, and he'd donated to the group every year since he'd left the army, but a lot of years had passed since he'd gone through the program at Big Sky Bravery. It might be time to call the team and see if they could take him in for a tune-up.

"I'm sorry about your men," Jake said. The guilt was visible on his face.

"I've never seen anybody talk to Ted Graves that way," was all Clap could say.

"Probably not the smartest thing I've ever done."

"It couldn't hurt to get a remote starter for your car."

Jake looked at him curiously.

"I've wired a lot of ignition systems for Ted over the years. It's one of his favorites."

The two men locked eyes for several seconds until Clap grinned.

"I'm just breaking balls. We're good."

Pickens looked at the two men and decided that all was indeed well between them. Whatever had happened was part of the job, and they respected each other.

"I'm sorry the operation went sideways," Jake said, "and I'm sorry that good men died, but that's all the more reason why Yaxaas has to be next."

His look and his tone told the others that he was serious.

"I'm going to kill him."

Pickens looked distressed. He'd heard Ted explicitly or-der Jake to stand down. Putting more men and the Agen-cy's reputation further at risk was going to infuriate Graves.

But not Clap. He sat down on the living room sofa with a confession of his own.

"There was this bomb-maker in Iraq back when I was in the army—all his devices had a real distinct signature—and we figured he'd killed thirty-three of our guys and at least five hundred Iraqi civilians. We put on a full-court press to find him and after a couple of months we finally dialed in his location, but it was in a residential neighborhood in western Mosul, in the middle of an insurgent stronghold. There was no place to land helos and he would have seen a ground force coming from a mile away, so my teammate and I snuck into the area disguised as civilians and set up in an apartment that was four hundred fifty-two meters from his building.

"We were there for a week. It hit 115 degrees every day, maybe 125 once or twice. I was stiff, my back hurt, and I had a headache like someone had stuck a drill in my brain, but I wanted that sonofabitch dead so bad that I couldn't think of anything else, so we stayed put. Sometimes when it gets that hot the locals head up to the roof to sleep, where it's cooler, and I was on the gun one night when he came onto the roof. They had sheets hung up for conceal-ment, but there was a little breeze and I caught a glimpse of the bomb-maker when the sheets flapped in the wind. He couldn't have been outside for more than three sec-onds when I pulled the trigger. The first round went low/right and smacked into a short concrete wall around the roof. He heard the impact, but I'd already sent the second shot by the time he figured out what it was. That .308 Winchester caught him in the side, and he was done.

"Look, Jake," Clap continued. "Killing that bomb-maker was one of the most satisfying moments in my life. My teammate and I probably saved a couple hundred lives—so don't feel guilty about wanting Yaxaas dead. Your reasons are just."

Jake was sitting at the kitchen table and staring at the floor. He wasn't an assassin, and he'd be violating orders if he dropped the hammer on Yaxaas.

But he'd be doing the world a favor.

He looked up at Clap. "You want to lend me that rifle?"

Clap grinned again and the two men bumped fists.

"You really think a bioweapon could kill a million people?" said Pickens.

Jake nodded. "I don't know why Ted is being such a hardass. He's dead wrong about this one."

"We could go over his head," said Pickens.

Clap scowled.

"Look, I'm going to Germany tomorrow to check on my guy, but you better have your case air-fucking-tight before you go over Ted's head. He may be a sonofabitch, but he's a smart sonofabitch, and he plays for keeps. If those orders are coming from the Seventh Floor, or they haul Ted before the Inspector General and it doesn't stick, we three are finished."

"I have someone back at headquarters I can talk to," Jake said.

"Be careful, brother," said Clap. "Ted's got a lot of loyal soldiers in the Directorate of Operations."

"My guy isn't in operations."

Jake did indeed have a very senior contact inside CIA.

The relationship was especially useful because no more than a handful of people knew of it. Peter Clements had been chief of station in London and Jake's boss when he'd made his first foray into the field. Jake was still known as Zac Miller then, and he'd volunteered for a milk run that had turned into a nightmare. When it was over, he'd needed a new face and a new identity, and the cover story had cost Peter Clements his job.

But just as Zac Miller had been resurrected as Jake Keller, Peter Clements had quietly returned as the number two executive in charge of the Directorate of Analysis, an enormously influential job with wide-ranging access and authority.

Peter would be able to give Jake a read on the atmospherics back at Langley.

JAKE RETIRED TO his bedroom and videoconferenced his old boss, candidly explaining his concerns about the bioweapon and his concerns about using Yaxaas as a tool of U.S. policy. Jake didn't need to explain his concerns about Graves—Ted had been the one who'd forced Clements out of the chief of station job, then taken it for himself.

Clements knew Ted was a sonofabitch.

He called back two hours later.

"The order to establish a covert interdiction capability in the region came from the Seventh Floor," said Clements.

Peter was an associate deputy director. The Seventh Floor generally meant his level or above—someone very senior.

"Director Feinman?" asked Jake. He'd met the CIA director once the year before, after a pair of rogue government officials had nearly started a war between the U.S. and China.

Clements said nothing. Though he trusted Jake, Peter was still a senior CIA executive. He would bend the rules to help his protégé, but he wouldn't break them by revealing the exact source of the order.

"It's a legal order," said Clements, "and Ted documented it so the 'how' and 'with whom' has been delegated to the men in the field."

"Me and Pickens . . ."

"And a special operations team. There's nothing in the case file about piracy or biological weapons."

"Our initial orders were to find out who was running the pirate ring."

"Not to develop an interdiction capability?" asked Clements.

"No."

"Then I suspect Ted knew who it was all along, and he left you a trail of bread crumbs to find this warlord."

"So it looks as if I recruited Yaxaas on my own . . ."

"And if a bioweapon is in play—"

"It's because I recruited a warlord to do the work," Jake said. "The goal of Black Flag was to covertly neutralize ships acting against U.S. interests."

"Just like Ted said. He's a grand master at this game. By careful omission, he's given you enough rope to hang yourself."

"And if we go over his head?"

"Then he'll kick the stool out from under you."

"Understood. Thanks, Peter."

Jake was about to sign off, but Clements wasn't finished.

"I know Ted can be ruthless and self-serving, but a lot of people on the Seventh Floor are afraid that Congress wants to turn back the clock on CIA. They want to refocus the Agency on intel gathering and analysis and give most of our operational authority to the Department of Defense. But no one at the Agency wants that, so the brass are probably willing to give Ted a lot of leeway right now to accomplish his mission. Don't let your history with him cloud your judgment."

"Understood," said Jake.

"Ted was right about one thing," said Clements. "You should take some time off and think about your future. It's a tricky time at the Agency."

SIXTY-SIX

JAKE HESITATED WHEN the CIA pilots contacted him and told him that the aircraft was fueled up and ready to go. Graves might have told him to take some time off to think about his future, but he didn't expect Ted to authorize further use of the jet. The more Jake thought about it, the more concerned he became. The big Gulfstream's crew mostly handled renditions. They were experienced at taking unwilling passengers to places they would never know, and never leave.

Jake couldn't help but wonder if he was next.

A strong breeze blew in from the sea as he walked across the tarmac. Far out over the ocean, a bolt of lightning flashed among the dark clouds that now blanketed the sky.

The copilot was leaning against the main entrance door with his arms folded across his chest and he motioned for Jake to board. Jake searched for any telltale signs that a Graves-organized ambush was afoot, but the flight officer exuded the same professional calm he always had.

In ten minutes, they were airborne and headed north,

but Jake was glued to the moving map display for every second of the trip. There was an Agency black site in Romania, and one word from Graves and a few degrees' deviation from the flight plan could mean the difference between Jake spending a couple of days with Athena or the rest of his life in a cell, pumped full of drugs and, for all practical purposes, vanished from the face of the earth.

The relief was palpable when the pilots started their descent over the Aegean Sea and landed uneventfully in Athens.

The staff at the general aviation terminal brought over the unremarkable Fiat sedan Jake had reserved, and he took the rental car southwest along the Attiki Odos toll road toward Vouliagmeni. He'd been driving for twenty minutes when he noticed a white Škoda hatchback shadowing him a hundred yards back.

For an intelligence officer, losing a tail was easy. The hard part was doing it covertly. Emergency-brake turns and driving the wrong way through traffic could be effective, but such drastic maneuvers also confirmed that you were a person of interest. Jake wanted his pursuers to believe that they'd lost contact not because of his skill, but through their own carelessness.

He exited the highway onto a long, divided boulevard and pulled into a busy gas station. He spent a few minutes in the convenience store making a cover stop—a plausible detour his tail wouldn't alert to—while he discreetly watched for the Škoda, another surveillance vehicle that might have taken its place, or any other sign that he'd been made.

But he didn't see anything out of the ordinary. He appeared to be clean.

Jake returned to the Fiat and drove onto the boulevard, glancing down side streets as he passed. A full block down, parked on the side of the road and facing the boulevard, was the Škoda. He kept driving normally until the little Czech sedan was out of sight.

Then he floored the accelerator.

The entrance ramp to the highway was maybe two hundred yards away, and Jake aimed the Fiat right toward it as he climbed through the gears. He was nearly at the ramp when he checked his rearview mirror. There was still no sign of the Škoda. At the last second, he veered away and made a quick right into a dense commercial area bordering the highway. He glanced at the car's GPS as he made turn after turn, ensuring that he never wound up on a long straightaway, bottled up in a dead-end, or visible from the highway. The GPS dutifully recalculated his route with each turn until Jake was confident that he'd lost the tail. He took side roads the rest of the way to Vouliagmeni.

The gates to the Romanos estate were open, and Jake followed the winding driveway through the olive orchard and parked the car directly in front of the house.

Giánnis was in the dining room overlooking the sea, eating dinner with another man about his age. Jake headed out to the terrace. Athena was lying on a lounge chair, reading a novel under the outdoor lights. It was a warm night and she was dressed in a bright blue sundress and casual shoes. She looked as relaxed as he'd ever seen her. He sat on the chair next to her and their knees touched.

"I'm glad you're back," she said, "but maybe you should tell me why you came."

"Do you remember when you told me that I should be thinking about my future?"

Of course she remembered. It had been during their last visit, standing side-by-side on the beach on another warm night, and she'd been disappointed and hurt after Jake had walled himself off emotionally and returned to Africa, but she'd buried her feelings down deep, in the pit of her heart where she kept all the other tragedies of her life. It was a coping mechanism that got her through the long days and the lonely nights.

"Vaguely," she said.

She could play defense too, if that was what it took to avoid getting hurt again.

"Well, I wasn't ready to get into it then, but I am now."

He couldn't ignore it when Clements, Graves, and Athena all told Jake that he should be thinking about his future. His unusual career had forced a number of issues to the surface, and he needed to deal with them. He hadn't joined CIA to empower warlords. The plan had been to stop men like Yaxaas from acquiring weapons of mass destruction, not enable them.

Jake set down his duffel bag and took her hand. It was cool and soft, but it felt like a bolt of lightning.

"On one condition," she said as she closed her book. "Regardless of what you decide, promise that you'll still be here for Christmas."

"I'll be here by the twenty-fourth," he promised.

"Good." She stood. "Now let's eat something. I'm starving."

The two of them stood in the kitchen for half an hour, picking through leftovers and sharing a bottle of wine.

"So what inspired your change of heart?" said Athena.

"Disillusionment, I suppose. There are some parts of my career that I've come to despise."

Athena finished the bite of cold moussaka she'd been chewing.

"Everyone hates some part of what they do. The hours and the stress get to all of us."

Though Athena undoubtedly suspected who Jake worked for, he still couldn't tell her what he did. "My boss and I often differ on the best way to accomplish our goals."

"Like the *Symi*?"

Jake nodded. The death toll from the *Symi* might end up being a rounding error if Yaxaas dispersed the bioweapon into the general population.

"Have you thought about doing something else?" she asked.

"Protecting my country is what drives me forward."

"Could you do it somewhere else, maybe work for a different group?"

Jake stood there in the kitchen, watching Athena eat leftovers with her fingers, and realized that she'd zeroed in on exactly what was bothering him.

"No," Jake said. "I need to be exactly where I am to counterbalance my boss. It's where I can do the most good."

"Then you're in the right place. You have the first half of your answer."

Jake nodded again. It was as if a weight had been lifted from his shoulders.

"What's the second half?" he said.

"Can you do this job and have a personal life?"

Jake walked to Athena and took her hands in his. "I can if I work harder at it."

She kissed him gently on the mouth. "Let's go for a walk on the beach."

Jake smiled. "I'll get the Land Rover."

"Not tonight." Athena pointed to her casual shoes. "Go say hello to my father while I bring the car around."

JAKE WATCHED HER walk up the driveway, with her footsteps crunching on the gravel and her silhouette framed by the soft exterior lighting. Athena looked over her shoulder and saw him. They both smiled as she walked out of sight. It was a warm night for December, with clear skies and a single songbird chirping in the trees. For the first time in a long time, Jake felt at peace.

But it all changed in an instant.

SIXTY-SEVEN

THE SKY FLASHED orange and the ground shook, followed by a deafening roar a fraction of a second later.

Jake sprinted up the driveway toward a column of smoke that was billowing into the night sky. Broken glass and debris littered the ground: The Land Rover wasn't much more than a collection of twisted metal and charred plastic. Tendrils of flame rose from its frame.

Jake climbed into the wreckage, shielding his face from the heat, until he reached Athena in the driver's seat. He lifted her out and laid her gently on the grass.

He checked her neck for a pulse. It was fast but weak. She'd already lost a lot of blood and her heart was pumping furiously to circulate what was left.

"Athena!"

Her eyes flickered.

"Stay with me," Jake said. She was tiptoeing along a precipice. If he left her now, she might tumble away from him forever.

Her breathing was fast and shallow.

"Stay here, Athena!"

Her breathing stopped.

Jake started CPR, pressing down hard and fast, but the trauma was extensive.

Giánnis walked out of the house a minute later and stared at the burning wreck.

Jake wiped the blood from his hands and went to him.

"I'm sorry," Jake said as a distant siren began to wail. "This was meant for me."

The old man stared at the wreckage, hypnotized by the flames.

He still didn't understand.

Jake took him by the hands and looked him in the eyes.

"Athena is dead."

SIXTY-EIGHT

THE SIRENS GREW louder.

Jake's recent appearance in Athena's life, his light cover story, and the private jet with the impenetrable ownership structure would immediately make him a prime suspect. The Hellenic police would detain him while they conducted their investigation and, with Jake out of the picture, there would be no one to stop Yaxaas.

A million people might die.

Jake sanitized the house, removing all traces of his presence. He grabbed his duffel bag, wiped away his fingerprints, and deleted his calls and contact information from Athena's phone. He drove the speed limit as he left the estate and passed an ambulance and two police cars headed in the opposite direction. He glanced down at his clothes. His shirt was singed by fire and stained with Athena's blood. He was innocent, but he was acting guilty and he looked guilty—and he had to expect the police to treat him as such if he was caught. He stopped at a gas station once he was clear of Vouliagmeni, tore the shirt off, and held it to his face. It was his last connection to Athena, but it was also a ticket to jail if the police found it. He balled it up and buried it in the trash.

THE AGENCY PILOTS were used to abrupt changes of schedule.

Jake had called them from the road, and the Gulfstream was idling on the tarmac by the time he arrived. They took off under visual flight rules, a rarity for a high-performance corporate jet, especially at night, but it allowed them an immediate departure from Greek soil. Once they were airborne, they filed a flight plan to Djibouti. They refiled for Mogadishu a few hours later.

The flight to Somalia was like torture. Jake wanted to run, to scream, to find some way to vent his rage—his guilt. Instead, he sat in his seat and stared blankly out the window, clenching and unclenching his fists, his mind stuck in an endless loop that constantly replayed the last few hours of Athena's life: the car that had followed him from the airport, the clarity that had followed their conversation in the kitchen, and the joy he'd felt watching her walk to the Land Rover.

The truck he'd driven every single time they'd gone to the beach.

Except this time.

Someone had learned their routine and wired a bomb to the ignition circuit—expecting to kill Jake, but ending Athena's life instead.

THE MOGADISHU AIRPORT was right next to the ocean, and the winds were gusting over thirty miles per hour as the

Gulfstream touched down. Thick clouds muted the sunrise.

The copilot said something to Jake as he walked down the plane's stairs, but Jake wasn't listening. A few raindrops landed on his face as he walked past the United Nations jet, past the mechanic working on the gray helicopter, past other things that had once seemed to matter.

He texted Pickens and hailed a cab to a local hotel as part of his regular security routine.

It all seemed so pointless.

Pickens was waiting at the hotel in the beige Daihatsu.

"Didn't expect to see you back so soon," he said.

"Lots to do."

It was the morning rush hour and the Makka al-Mukarra boulevard was clogged with cars, bicycles, Bajajs, and a smattering of pedestrians. Traffic was forced to stop completely for a few minutes when a pickup truck drove the wrong way down the divided road just so it wouldn't have to make a U-turn at the next intersection.

"You just missed Clap," said Pickens. "He took off for Germany to check on his guy."

"He left you a present," Pickens continued, but Jake was silent, staring out the window.

"You all right?" asked Pickens.

"Just tired," Jake said.

Pickens took a harder look and decided he wasn't buying it.

"Lady trouble?"

"You could say that."

"Sorry, brother."

Pickens turned onto the main boulevard, following one of his regular surveillance detection routes. They drove around a traffic circle and passed a pair of AMISOM armored vehicles that were parked outside the soccer stadium, then turned onto a residential side street.

It was as if rush hour had ended in an instant.

The traffic disappeared: the Bajajs that were angling for the same section of road, the pedestrians who were meandering across the streets, the trucks that stopped in the middle of the boulevard to unload their cargoes.

They were all gone.

Jake instinctively went into high gear.

He reached into the glove compartment and grabbed the 9mm Glock pistol he kept there. He pointed it at the floor and press-checked it, moving the slide forward a quarter inch to confirm that a round was in the chamber.

"This doesn't feel right," he said as he surveyed the street.

No sooner had the words left his mouth than a white pickup truck with dented sheet metal and off-road tires appeared from a side street and skidded to a stop a hundred feet in front of them, blocking the intersection.

Pickens stopped the car.

Three men with rifles jumped down from the bed and started walking toward the Americans.

Jake checked his side mirror. A van with more gunmen had stopped behind them.

Jake glanced at his partner. The big man still had his pistol holstered.

"It's game time, Pickens. Get that weapon out."

"It's just a shakedown," Pickens said. "Let's not do anything that's going to get us killed."

But Jake had been through private checkpoints before. Rarely were they inside the city limits, and they never targeted a single vehicle.

"Somebody tried to kill me in Greece and they're trying again now."

Pickens was frozen. The gunmen were halfway to them.

"Athena is dead," Jake said.

Pickens was speechless.

The gunmen split up. One stayed in front and one walked to each side of the car.

Pickens looked back and forth between Jake and the approaching men.

"I'm not going to let them take me," Jake said. "I'm going to fight this one out."

"We're outgunned, brother. Let's just pay them and be gone."

"Money isn't going to make this problem go away. We're going to have to resolve this."

Jake checked his mirror again.

"On three," he said. "One, two, *three!*"

Jake raised the Glock and fired three times, dropping the gunman on his side of the car, but Pickens was still frozen with his hands on the wheel. His sidearm was still on his hip.

Jake swung his weapon to the left and fired three more rounds just a few inches from Pickens's face, shattering the driver's-side window and striking the gunman in the gut. The man dropped his rifle and slid down the side of the car, his face pressed against the bloody glass.

"John! Engage!" Jake yelled, but Pickens was sitting motionless behind the wheel, his foot still on the brake.

Jake jumped out and ran between two buildings as the gunmen sprayed the car with automatic weapons. He caught a glimpse of the group's leader, standing behind one of the vehicles and screaming at his men.

It was Nacay.

Jake braced himself against the house on his right and raised his weapon. Rounds snapped past his head and ricocheted off the nearby buildings as half a dozen men fired at him, but Jake lined up his sights and pulled the trigger.

The round caught Nacay in the side of the head, just behind his eye.

He crumpled to the ground instantly, as if his entire skeleton had suddenly been removed. Jake fired more rounds at the shooters, trying to draw their fire from Pickens, but the volume of incoming fire soon forced him behind cover.

Jake took a deep breath, dropped to one knee, and popped out from the wall. He skipped a few bullets under the truck, hoping a ricochet would neutralize some of the gunmen and maybe save Pickens, but they kept firing. The staccato reports of the AK-47s echoed through the narrow street as they raked the car with gunfire.

Lead chunked into the sheet metal.

Bullets shattered the glass.

Rounds smashed through the seats.

And that's when Jake saw the windshield . . .

Covered in Pickens's blood.

SIXTY-NINE

JAKE YELLED TO his partner, but there was no reaction.

Pickens's head was slumped forward, his chin resting on his chest. The windshield was covered with blood. He looked as if he'd taken a round to the back of his skull, straight through the brain. Not even former outside linebacker John Pickens, built like a tank and nearly as tough, could have survived it.

Nacay's men directed their fire toward Jake.

Jake shot back and quickly wounded one of the gunmen, but he had only a single magazine and his attackers had enough ammunition to fight a war. The volume of incoming fire quickly pushed him back behind cover.

With his back against a nearby house and the gunmen closing in, Jake dropped his magazine and checked how many rounds he had left. He'd been serious when he'd said they weren't going to take him alive.

He was down to his last bullet.

He saved that one for himself.

Instinct drew him to Pickens. Abandoning Athena moments after she'd died had blown a crater in Jake's heart, and he knew that leaving his fallen partner would be almost as bad, but there was nothing he could do. Getting killed while trying to stop a biological attack was one thing, but sacrificing his life for a man that was already dead was just a waste.

Jake darted between the houses while voices shouted, engines revved, and tires chirped in the street behind him. But the surrounding streets were dense with traffic, and Jake was light and fast and driven. He lost the shooters in just a few blocks and was able to hail a passing Bajaj.

It was a thirty-minute taxi ride back to the safe house and three years since Jake had felt a real connection to a woman. And watching the last threads of life drain from Athena's body while he cradled her on the ground had been excruciating.

Pickens had sensed it. The two friends had survived more close calls together than Jake could count, from muggings by street hoods to ambushes by Somali warlords. They had been threatened, kidnapped, and shot at, but the one constant through all of it was that they'd had each other's back.

And now Pickens was gone too.

Jake stared out the open side of the Bajaj, completely skipping any sort of surveillance detection route, and took it directly to the safe house and walked inside. It was a reckless move after being the target of two assassination attempts in the past twenty-four hours, but Jake had reached a point where he just didn't care anymore.

Not about himself.

Not about Yaxaas.

Not about anything.

Everything Jake had ever valued had been stripped from him. From his parents, to the life he'd rebuilt, to the friends he'd made working for the Agency, and ultimately, the women he'd loved.

They were all gone.

Death followed him everywhere.

Jake sat in the kitchen, staring at the Glock in front of him on the table.

It had a single round in it.

It would be enough.

The people closest to him always suffered the most. It didn't seem fair that he should live when they were dead.

Jake stacked guilt on top of anger until their combined weight nearly suffocated him. He second-guessed every decision he'd made since coming to Africa, from meeting Yaxaas at the Bakaara Market, to involving Athena in his war with the pirates, to ignoring Pickens's advice about engaging the men at the checkpoint.

And now Jake was alone once again. It was a crossroads he'd visited before, and each time he'd dug deep and fought the temptation to quit when it would have been the easiest thing in the world to do. Most people thought of evil as an abstract concept—the opposite of good. But true evil was more destructive, and Jake had seen it manifested more than once. Allowing Yaxaas to use the Iranian bio-weapon would make Jake no better than the warlords.

And that was unacceptable.

Despite the pain, despite the frustration, it wasn't what Jake stood for.

It wasn't what the United States stood for.

It just wasn't right.

He had been so focused on what he'd lost that he'd lost sight of what he still had.

Though both had been tested severely in the past few weeks, he still had his faith in God and country. Jake understood that he was not the center of the universe, but when pain was piled upon loss, it was easy to lose sight of the beliefs and ideals that put his existence in context.

And while he was struggling mightily with survivor's guilt, that very survival obligated him not to waste the rest of his life feeling sorry for himself or blaming others. Jake had always distinguished himself by his ability to maintain a level head and keep pushing forward when the world around him was crumbling, and it was time to do it again. The forces of good needed him back in the fight.

He would have to be his best when he felt his worst.

It was time not only to accept that death followed him but to embrace it. If the Ground Branch men, Athena, and Pickens had to die, then so would Yaxaas and the other sons of bitches who'd made Somalia a living hell. Jake would use that energy to once again drive him forward.

All the pain. All the suffering. All the death.

It was like sharpening the sword.

SEVENTY

J AKE TOOK THE Glock off the table.

It was time to get to work.

Jake had never let hatred guide his actions. Hate was too emotional, too unfocused—more a product of internal strife than external forces. And Jake did not take lightly the act of ending another man's life. He'd done it many times since joining CIA, but killing had never been the primary goal—it had simply been necessary to accomplish the mission.

But not this time.

He'd decided days ago that Yaxaas had to die, but that had been business—just a tactic to achieve a objective.

Now Jake wanted to see the life drain from the warlord's face as the man took his last breath.

Graves called several times, but Jake ignored the calls. More than once it crossed his mind that Ted might have been responsible for the blast that had killed Athena. As Clap had said, car bombs were one of Ted's specialties. But for the immediate future it almost didn't matter whether

Jake had been disavowed and targeted for elimination or the explosion was merely a coincidence. With two dead on the Ground Branch team, and now Pickens, Graves was going to shut Jake down one way or another—leaving Yaxaas free to unleash a biological weapon on the citizens of Somalia.

Jake couldn't let that happen.

He was going to have to stop it by himself.

But first he would have to find it.

He knew Yaxaas was storing the weapon in a camp outside the city, but Somalia was a rural country, with thousands of dirt roads and too many buildings to count. Yet, like a good analyst, Jake broke the job down into manageable pieces and got to work. He began searching online satellite maps using the only other data point he had—according to the men he'd overheard while being held in the warehouse, the location was within walking distance of a river.

An hour later, he pushed back from the computer and cursed.

Somalia had a lot of rivers.

There were two main ones, the Shebelle and the Jubba, and like the Tigris and the Euphrates in Mesopotamia, the basin between the two rivers was the most fertile land around and where most of the population had settled.

The Shebelle was closer to Mogadishu, but for most of its length it ran through territory that had belonged to the Hawiye for centuries—an unlikely spot for a Darood warlord to build a camp.

So Jake focused on the Jubba.

It meandered south from Ethiopia to the Indian Ocean . . . for 550 miles.

Two hours later, he pushed back from the computer and cursed again.

There were seventy-one facilities that had the potential to be armed training camps, so Jake eliminated anything that was in a city or town, along a main road, or in the populated areas along the coastline—they would all be too conspicuous.

Which left thirty-six possible locations.

Thirty-six places to hide a deadly biological agent.

Thirty-six possible targets, Jake thought.

He started ranking them but stopped a third of the way through. It was pointless with the satellite images he'd found online. Jake had been a strategic weapons analyst in his prior life at CIA and had been an acknowledged expert at analyzing overhead imagery, but the low-resolution images he was now using simply didn't have enough detail to differentiate between them, even for him.

What he needed was a Predator or some other surveillance aircraft to overfly the sites. Their sophisticated sensors could search for radio-frequency emissions and perform multispectral analysis—searching for heat signatures and other signs of recent human inhabitation, then further explore areas of interest with high-resolution imaging equipment. In different circumstances, Jake could have passed the coordinates over to JSOC or CIA's aviation wing and have the data collected on all thirty-six sites in a matter of hours.

It would have been an easy ask if he weren't persona non grata back at the Agency.

He was mindlessly staring at the computer screen when it hit him.

Someone had already done it.

Jake went to the basement, triple-checking that he'd disabled the self-destruct system before he opened the hatch—just about the only way his day could get any worse was if a dozen blocks of plastic explosive detonated underneath his feet at twenty-six thousand feet per second.

He wandered through the stacks of weapons, still amazed and dismayed by the firepower Pickens had been able to acquire on the black market. With Pickens dead, Jake would at some point have to contact his superiors at CIA and notify them about the arms cache. He certainly wasn't going to call Cawar and sell the weapons back to the largest illicit arms trafficker in Africa.

Back against the far wall was the large gun safe where Pickens had stored sensitive electronics, classified materials, and even batteries. Jake had given his partner a hard time for leaving millions of dollars of weapons loose in the basement and locking up twenty dollars' worth of batteries, but the big man had protested with his big laugh that he liked to keep them with the electronics for convenience.

Pickens's eight years in IED-ravaged Somalia had made him an expert in security, and in explosives. Using detonating cord, a blasting cap, and a thermate grenade, he'd wired a self-destruct system to the safe's electronic lock. While the grenade wouldn't explode violently, it would burn at over four thousand degrees Fahrenheit, ensuring that nothing in the safe, or anyone near the safe, would survive if he entered the wrong combination.

Jake wiped his sweaty hands on his pants and began slowly punching in the code.

Like most Special Activities officers, Jake had been taught the basics of identifying, building, and defeating various explosive devices by members of the Agency's Explosive Ordnance Disposal team. He knew that thermate had low sensitivity to external impulses, but he also knew that some of the third-world blasting caps used to ignite the grenades did not, and he didn't want a drop of sweat or a spark of static electricity to trigger it by accident.

The safe beeped twice and the lock clicked open. Inside were bricks of U.S. dollars and euros, shelves filled with batteries and electronic gadgets, and two boxes of manila folders.

Jake found what he was looking for in the second box— a folder containing the overhead reconnaissance images Major Steve had shared at their first meeting. They'd been taken when an Air Force U-28 turboprop and a pair of RQ-1 Predators had searched the region looking for the three trucks with fake Kenya Defence Forces markings.

Analysts from SOCOM had reviewed the take from the aircraft, including the multispectral and ultra-hi-res images Jake didn't have access to, and instead of thirty-six facilities, they'd narrowed the list down to two.

Jake glanced at the two photos and immediately agreed with Pickens's earlier assessment of the facility outside Jilib. It was a disused commercial farm, dried up and probably abandoned sometime during the drought.

Jake examined the second image. His partner had dismissed it as an empty livestock farm, based on its stockade walls and location bordering a river near rural Dujuma, but Jake gave it a hard look, and his trained eyes spotted features inconsistent with a cattle ranch that hadn't been used in years: The fences were solid, high, and in good repair. The dirt roads were well worn in an area otherwise overrun with vegetation. Though it was near a river, there was no pasture or grazing area. It was located in a hilly region, ill-suited to raising cattle.

As Jake ticked off the list of inconsistencies in his head, he came to the inescapable conclusion that it wasn't a cattle ranch.

It was a training camp.

SEVENTY-ONE

JAKE SLEPT SOUNDLY that night. For the first time since he'd arrived in Africa, he knew exactly what he needed to do. It was a dangerous plan—somewhere between reckless and suicidal—but he wasn't living for himself anymore. He was living for Athena and Pickens and the men from the Ground Branch team.

He was living for the people of Somalia.

Jake went to Pickens's bedroom and rummaged through his friend's personal effects. The top drawer of his dresser was filled with "pocket litter"—generic receipts, business cards, and other miscellany that supported his cover identity. The second drawer contained more pocket litter, but for Pickens's alternate cover as an arms dealer—a fake passport, rolls of cash held together with rubber bands, and several cell phones—with their passwords written on a sheet of note paper that was taped to the bottom of the drawer.

CIA security would not be impressed.

But it was inside a hand-carved wooden box that Jake

found what he was looking for: a picture of Pickens with his ex-wife and their four kids, taken several years ago during happier times back in the States.

Jake found a pen and wrote a letter to Pickens's children, telling them of their father's death. He told them how brave John had been, how he had served his country nobly, and how much he had loved them. The distance, the uncertainty, and the loss were burdens born by the families of intelligence officers and military personnel everywhere. The people at home could never know precisely what their loved ones had been working on or how the final moments of their lives had played out, but Jake wanted Pickens's family to know that they were always on their father's mind and in his heart.

Jake sealed the envelope and sat back from the table.

He should write a death letter of his own.

But he had no one to send it to.

HE RETURNED TO his bedroom closet to find a set of camo fatigues. Stacked against the wall was a sniper rifle, more precisely, Clap's sniper rifle—a semiautomatic Delta Level Defense CT-M110 that could put a .308-caliber round into a man's eye socket at two hundred yards. It was the same gun Clap had used to take out the bomb-maker in Iraq, and there was a note taped to the massive Nightforce scope that sat atop it.

With you in spirit.

Jake sat on his bed and held the rifle for a few minutes while he thought about the risks Clap had taken and the hell he'd gone through to take out that bomb-maker. Going after Yaxaas wouldn't be any easier.

Jake donned the fatigues, folded a boonie hat into his pocket, and loaded up a beige Toyota pickup with everything he thought he might need to accomplish his mission. There were so many guesses and estimates in his planning, so many variables in the composition of his adversary, that he needed a lot of options. He needed to be able to change his plans on the fly when something inevitably went wrong.

He covered all the gear in the truck bed with a canvas tarp and tied it down. Even in war-torn Somalia, the pickup truck's cargo would raise a few eyebrows. Jake, fully dressed, caught a few hours of shut-eye and was on the road before dawn. He passed swiftly through the deserted streets of Mogadishu, stopping briefly at the British embassy to mail the letter to Pickens's children, before turning southwest on the coastal road to Dujuma. The entire trip would take eight to ten hours.

The sunrise was muted by thick cloud cover as Jake drove along the ocean road. A strong easterly wind had been blowing for days, building heavy seas and an endless procession of whitecaps that kept even the ubiquitous small fishing boats onshore—no mean feat in a nation rocked by famine.

He reviewed his plan as he drove, constantly refining it and planning for contingencies, but there were more unknowns than knowns, and the permutations were endless.

Jake didn't fear death, but he did fear failure. He'd used that fear in the past to drive him forward, to elevate himself to the task in front of him, but letting fear be his motivator and not his master was a tricky balance to maintain.

He was six hours into the drive when he turned onto a road that paralleled the Jubba River. Flowing south from Ethiopia, the twisting waterway was a critical vein of life through Somalia's barren interior. For hundreds of years, its fertile floodplains had provided for the farmers who'd settled along its banks and the herders whose livestock had once been the backbone of the region's economy.

The tiny village of Dujuma was one such settlement. Situated on a wide bend in the Jubba, it had a few dirt roads and maybe thirty buildings, the most luxurious of which had cinder-block walls, glassless windows, and a solitary goat lying in the shade of its corrugated tin roof.

Past the village, another dirt road disappeared into the hills. According to the overhead reconnaissance photo that Jake was now using as a map, the road led to Yaxaas's camp. Jake wanted a closer look, but he drove past without slowing. He didn't want to draw attention to himself in case the warlord had scouts in the village.

Jake drove until sunset before turning around and returning to a desolate plain two miles from the village. He doused his headlights, eased the pickup off the road, and parked it under an acacia tree. The wind howled through the tall grasses as Jake stepped into the darkness. Distant peals of thunder and an occasional animal call were the only other sounds. There wasn't another man-made object in sight.

A drop of rain splattered against his face.

It was time.

He topped off the truck's fuel tank with a pair of twenty-liter gas cans he'd brought from Mogadishu and started unpacking his gear. Ten minutes after he'd started, there was only one thing left to unload.

He leaned a wooden plank against the pickup's liftgate and rolled a 450cc dirt bike down from the bed. He'd camouflaged the motorcycle with a few cans of matte tan and green spray paint, using the overhead images taken a few weeks ago as his guide. He tossed a camouflage net over the truck and gave the starter a swift kick. The two-stroke motor came to life. Jake shouldered his pack, flipped on his night vision goggles, and set off for camp, stopping frequently to look and listen as he followed a series of game trails toward the river. While the trails were preferable to hacking through thickets of thorn bushes and stands of sharp grasses with a machete, the fact that the trails been made by large animals did not escape him. In addition to several species of antelope, Cape buffalo, and cheetahs, crocodiles and the occasional prides of lions also roamed the area.

He passed the skeleton of what he guessed was a zebra, with flies buzzing through its empty eye sockets, and rode south along the grassy riverbank for half a mile until the trail disappeared into the muddy river. It was the kind of place where a lion or a crocodile might lie in wait for animals looking for a drink in the cooler temperatures that followed sunset, but Jake had to dump the bike and cross the river, and he soon accepted that he would be both predator and prey for the duration of the mission.

He shut off the bike and hid it in the tall grass, marking the location on the GPS receiver on his wrist. He would infiltrate the rest of the way on foot.

Like everything else in Somalia, the drought had taken its toll on the Jubba, and the once mighty river had been reduced to little more than a stream meandering through the mostly dry riverbed. Jake slung his rifle in front of his body and waded into the warm water up to his knees. The current was so slow as to be nearly imperceptible, trickling softly as it passed over the occasional rock or stump. He spied a few animals drinking along the water's edge—antelope mostly—but no crocs, no lions, and most importantly, no humans.

He reached the opposite bank in less than a minute.

Jake surveyed the low hills through his magnified rifle scope and hiked to a hilltop he'd marked on his map. In the shallow valley on the other side was a sprawling camp the size of a football field. Shielded by the valley walls, it was invisible from the surrounding area. It had stockade walls and a metal gate topped with barbed wire. Inside were several buildings, maybe a dozen goats in a small pen, and a few armed men—including one with bandoliers of rifle ammunition slung dramatically across his chest.

But there was no sign of Yaxaas or the bioweapon.

Jake had hunted in his youth and was skilled with a gun, but he wasn't a trained sniper. Even with the precision rifle Clap had left him, Jake wouldn't be killing Yaxaas with a thousand-yard high-angle shot through a valley swirling with thermals and crosswinds.

He needed to be closer.

He hiked down the ridge, ensconced in darkness and searched the area for sentries, until he spotted movement on another hilltop and froze. He clipped a night vision device in front of his rifle scope, and spied two men who had a commanding view of the approach road and the camp—and a mounted machine gun.

The machine gun nest wasn't on the reconnaissance photo. Jake zoomed in further. The AN/PVS-27 night vision device's catadioptric lens illuminated the scene crisply, and he spotted one of the opposition staring out over the valley behind a belt-fed PKM machine gun.

There were many challenges ahead: Jake was still three hundred yards from camp, vastly outnumbered, and facing a crew-served weapon that could cover the entire valley. But the machine gun nest was new, and several PKMs had been stolen from the *Saviz*.

Jake lowered himself into the tall grass, released the straps on his rucksack, and grunted with relief as the eighty-pound pack slid to the ground.

He'd found the right camp.

SEVENTY-TWO

THE RAIN MOVED in.

At first it was just a few drops splattering on Jake's boonie hat as he lay behind the rifle, but by midnight it had turned into a steady drizzle. The camp workers went about their business under the lights of a portable generator, until that too was shut down a few hours later.

It was a darkness unlike any Jake had experienced. The light wasn't muted. It wasn't dim. It was simply gone—as if someone had extinguished the sun and stolen the stars. Nothing penetrated the thick clouds. Even with his night vision goggles, Jake could barely see around him. The goggles couldn't amplify what didn't exist.

The rain intensified throughout the night, blown into the valley by strong winds and even stronger gusts. By morning, the east wind had brought a downpour. The dense, gray clouds had finally released the moisture they'd accumulated over weeks at sea.

At first, the men in camp stood in the courtyard and

marveled at the falling rain like a group of children. But like children, the wonder wore off quickly, and the man with the bandoliers soon came out and prodded them to get back to work.

The rain intensified as the day passed.

Jake sat motionless in his post, observing the camp, watching the men, looking for anything out of the ordinary, but the camp workers simply went about their duties, performing routine maintenance and repairs—and already cursing the wind and rain that had turned easy tasks into muddy projects.

Jake spent twelve hours taking everything in through the magnified optics. He saw animals come and go by the river, guards patrolling the camp's perimeter, and crews switching duty on the mounted machine gun up on the hilltop. He might have found Yaxaas's camp, but Jake was wet and cold and he still had no idea where the biowarfare agent was being stored—if it was even there. There was no biohazard sign on a door, no extra security around one of the camp's huts, and no sign of Yaxaas or a potential delivery mechanism.

Doubt crept into his mind.

Jake had based his entire plan on a few clues he'd overheard while being tortured by Yaxaas's goons at the warehouse. He'd heard some of them speak fearfully about "the Devil's Box," and some of the men in camp seemed to detour around a specific building every time they passed it, but he had no hard evidence. And even if he was lucky and the weapon was there, he would have only a single chance to neutralize it before the element of surprise was lost and an overwhelming force descended on him to extinguish his life.

Jake had brought several options for destroying the bioweapon, but access, the weather, and a half dozen other factors would determine what he'd be able to use. The only way to guarantee its destruction was to be right on top of it. Everything else was a fallback plan, with the odds of success dropping off like a cliff.

Jake needed to get close.

He needed to get inside the camp.

SEVENTY-THREE

JAKE LAY IN the thick grass and waited. Darkness came early that night, ushered into the valley by dense clouds and heavy rain. By ten p.m., the men in camp doused the work lights and retired for the night, leaving only those on guard duty outside. There were two men in the machine gun nest, four patrolling the outside walls, and four walking the interior.

The generator was finally shut down a little after midnight.

Jake assembled a small pack of gear and crawled down the muddy ridge through waist-high grass until he was a hundred feet from camp. The remaining distance to the wall was bare—conspicuously so—as if it had been clear-cut and burned out.

Like a minefield.

Jake was far from an expert on land mines. In fact, he knew a single salient fact about them—and it was that they could maim him horribly. It was enough. He lowered himself to the ground and waited. The guards came and went, patrolling the exterior fence line but never venturing into the clear-cut zone.

It was nearly an hour later when a greater kudu wandered into view.

The five-hundred-pound antelope was alert, walking with its head up and its ears twitching in the rain as it followed a rivulet of water past the camp and down to the riverbank. Jake marveled at its muscular body, long legs, and sharp horns that spiraled into the sky.

It was a magnificent beast.

But more importantly, it wasn't a gooey mess, blown to pieces by a land mine.

The kudu jumped down to the riverbed. The heavy rains had begun to refill it and what was a trickling stream just two days ago was now ten feet wide and flowing steadily. The kudu bounded across in a single leap.

The jumping antelope provoked no reaction from the guards. Whether they'd grown to ignore such crossings or simply hadn't seen it, Jake couldn't know, but the strong winds and the first rain in two years were providing plenty of distractions in the valley. Depressions flooded, trees toppled over, and mudslides crashed through the hills. The hard, dusty ground simply couldn't absorb all the moisture.

Distant thunder rumbled in the valley as Jake switched on his night vision goggles. The four exterior guards were each pacing up and down one side of the rectangular camp, carrying rifles under their plastic ponchos. The interior sentries had been doing the same when Jake had last seen them from the hills. Carefully timing his moves to avoid them, he waded into the river and followed it to the camp's long northern wall.

The north-side guard was two hundred feet away and closing when Jake scrambled up the riverbed and began crawling through the mud with his rifle in his arms. As soon the guard made his turn at the corner, Jake went to the wall and threw a knotted rope into a crook atop the stockade fence. He pulled himself up the side of the fence, his muddy hands and feet slipping several times as they struggled for purchase.

Jake reached the top and looked for the nearest guard. He was fifty yards away and closing quickly.

Jake dropped into camp.

He flicked the rope off the fence, stuffed it into the exterior webbing of his pack, and crouch-walked to the nearest darkened building. Its glassless windows were covered with canvas tarps, flapping in the wind and heavy rain.

Covered in mud and sitting on the ground under a wooden eave, Jake was effectively invisible. He raised his rifle and tracked the nearest guard as the man passed and made his turn at the northwest corner. Thunder cracked nearby as the guard passed by a second time and began the long slog back across the northern side of camp. The western guard passed by a moment later.

With his right hand holding the rifle firmly against his shoulder, Jake used his left hand to pull one of the tarps back a few inches and look inside the building. Through his night vision goggles he saw knives, hatchets, and Zulu and Masai spears along the walls, plus two bunks and a table and chairs—but no people and no sign of the bio-weapon.

Jake suspected it was being stored in a building fifty yards to the east. No one had entered or exited that single building since he'd arrived in Dujuma, and many of the men in camp seemed to give it a wide berth as they went about their duties.

Jake checked the positions of the four interior guards, lowered himself to the ground, and started crawling again. The mud was thick and the puddles deep. By the time he was halfway to the next building, mud had made its way into his clothes, his hair, and his boots.

A bolt of lightning struck somewhere in the southern part of the valley, illuminating the entire camp as if the sun had come out for a split second. Colors came to life, details became crisp, and the impenetrable curtain of the heavy rain was lifted. Jake saw the buildings along the north wall that he believed to be the barracks and the latrine. He saw the structure in front of him that he suspected of housing the weapon.

And he saw the guards pacing along the north and south walls.

Which meant that they could see him.

Jake froze.

He was flat on the ground, practically inhaling mud, but he still had a pack and a rifle—distinctive shapes that didn't blend in with the land.

A crack of thunder rolled through the valley several seconds later. Jake had been timing the lightning and the thunder and knew that the worst of the storm was still approaching. Another flash of lightning lit the camp. This time, the southern guard was closer and the northern guard was farther away. Jake couldn't see the other two. The lightning was turning his mission into Russian roulette. It might not be the next flash, or the one after it, but eventually one of the guards would spot Jake and sound an alarm. He might be able to kill one of the guards, or maybe two, but he'd never reach the weapon.

He would have to find another way.

SEVENTY-FOUR

JAKE SNUCK OUT of camp and climbed back to his observation post in the hills. He had a direct line of sight into camp and to the machine gun nest—but lines of sight worked both ways. With the lightning flashing and dawn not too far away, he needed to find some concealment, to find a place where his every move wouldn't put his life at risk.

But where to go? His entire body of knowledge on scout/sniper operations consisted of a documentary he'd watched and a few war stories from the ex–Delta Force operators he'd trained with upon joining Special Activities. It wasn't much, but he knew that if he was going to observe the camp in daylight, he needed to camouflage himself and have routes of ingress and egress that wouldn't leave him exposed.

He crawled farther up the hill and tucked in behind a ridge, away from game trails and thickets of thorn bushes, where he could still see most of the camp but was invisible to the men in the machine gun nest. He was using his knife to cut some nearby twigs and grasses—then stuffing them into his hat, on his clothing, and on his rifle to break up his outline—when another bolt of lightning struck nearby, temporarily blinding him. The thunder was instantaneous and so loud that he felt it in his chest and in his bones.

Jake lay prone on the ground, pointed the rifle toward camp, and parted the thick grass with the tip of his suppressor.

He took a few deep breaths and settled in for the day.

It was Christmas Eve.

JAKE LAY THERE for hours.

Occasionally he turned on the night vision sight for a detailed scan of the camp, but for the most part, the routine was the same. The workers did their chores and the guards did their patrols—all of them slogging through the mud and looking miserable.

The rain was incessant.

The hills channeled most of it into the valley where it ran into the rapidly expanding Jubba, but in other places, the heavy, water-soaked earth could no longer support itself and came crashing down the side of the hills. Most of the mudslides were small, yet Jake had seen a few with enough force to bury him alive, but he was undeterred.

Instead of celebrating the holiday in Greece with Athena, he was spending it alone in the hills of Africa, waiting to kill one man before he could kill a million.

The first sign of unusual activity came just as the first

hint of morning twilight glowed faintly through the clouds.

Several men trudged past the goat pen and across the camp's muddy courtyard, led by the man with the bandoliers. He wore no hat or poncho to protect him from the rain, just a few hundred rounds of machine gun ammunition to protect him from everything else.

He pointed into the hills, not far from where Jake was holed up, and two armed patrols departed through the main gate. Fortunately for Jake, they mostly ignored their orders and instead followed the game trails on the valley floor, where the ground was level and the risk of mudslides was lower. Jake spotted them intermittently over the next few hours as they crisscrossed the countryside. Several times they walked to within a hundred yards of his position. Good siting and good luck kept him safely hidden in the tall grasses, but luck was a fickle thing, and Jake didn't like relying on it when so much was at stake.

Despite the weather, the animals came out again at sunset. Several antelope wandered toward the river and a small jungle cat prowled the fence outside camp, but there was still no sign of Yaxaas or the weapon. The only human activity was the constant patrols. Yet Jake took perverse comfort from the men combing the hillside, rationalizing that they would only guard something of value.

The mission was taking much longer than he'd planned. He'd run out of food and his body was stiff and sore from lying nearly motionless twenty-four hours a day. The constant rain and lack of sunlight had soaked his clothes and robbed his body of heat. His senses were dull.

But Jake waited into the night, with the rifle to his shoulder and his eye to the glass. He was watching the patrols' flashlights move slowly across the far hillside when something rustled the grass to his right.

It wasn't the wind.

As slowly as he could, Jake rotated his head a few degrees. There were two men, ten yards from his position, carrying Kalashnikov rifles.

And one was pointing a flashlight at Jake.

SEVENTY-FIVE

THE TELEVISION DOCUMENTARY Jake had watched on sniper training had made it look sexy—small teams of elite soldiers who stalked enemy positions using expert camouflage and precision weapons. It was about using art and science to conduct reconnaissance and eliminate distant targets without ever being seen.

Now, shivering from days of cold rain, out of food, short on drinking water, and worrying that something as trivial as the reflection of a flashlight against the whites of his eyes might betray his presence to an armed patrol, it didn't seem quite as sexy.

In fact, it sucked.

Jake was tempted to kill the two men, to eliminate the threat. He could roll onto his side, swing his weapon around, and pump two rifle rounds into each of the men before they even realized what was happening.

But instead of solving his problems, killing the guards would more likely set in motion a chain of events that would quickly spiral out of control. The guards' absence would be noted and more of Yaxaas's men would pour into the hillsides. Jake knew that this mission would likely kill him, that infiltrating the camp undetected, destroying the weapon at close range, and killing Yaxaas would probably cost Jake his life, and he was prepared for it, but he did not want to die before it was done.

No less than the fate of the nation of Somalia hinged on the guards' decision in the next few seconds. If they raised a weapon or walked in his direction, Jake would be forced to kill them and hope for the best.

He lay motionless, hoping that his camouflage and the darkness would give him another option.

After a few more seconds, the flashlight moved on and the armed patrol continued down the hill.

Jake exhaled and glanced at his watch.

It was just past midnight.

Christmas Day.

SEVENTY-SIX

THE RAIN ENDED before daybreak. Mist rose from the grasslands as three days of downpours evaporated back into the sky from which they had fallen. The air was sweet with the fragrance of balsam and cedar trees and a dozen different spice plants. The runoff from the hillsides subsided and the muddy ground began to dry. Across the valley, monkeys screeched and birds chirped in anticipation of the food that would soon come.

With sunrise came the insects. Swarming in clouds, they soon discovered Jake hidden among the tall grasses. They flew up his pant legs and down his shirt. They crawled inside his nose and burrowed into his ears.

But insect repellent still didn't make his Christmas list.

He was cold and wet. He hadn't eaten in thirty-six hours and the only water he'd drunk in the past twelve was what he'd been able to collect in his upside-down hat. Cramps had seized his legs and his head pounded. But more than food, more than water or a comfortable bed, what Jake wanted was confirmation—some sort of evidence that the weapon was in camp and he wasn't wasting time in Dujuma while Yaxaas was preparing to use it somewhere else.

Six hours later, Jake got his present.

Four men slid open the camp's main gate and the warlord's armored Range Rover pulled in, followed by a refrigerated delivery truck. Both vehicles were caked with mud. From the windshields, where the wipers had cleared just enough area for the drivers to see, to the doors and fenders, which looked as if they'd been dunked in quicksand, there wasn't a speck of paint or glass showing. Jake realized that, in a land that had gone years without more than an inch of rain, the downpours of the last few days had washed out the roads. The rural camp had been cut off from the rest of Somalia.

Which was great news for the rest of Somalia.

The man with the bandoliers walked across camp to greet the warlord. Yaxaas stepped out wearing a pair of crocodile-skin cowboy boots.

Jake moved no faster than a caterpillar as he reached over the rifle and increased the scope's magnification. Tucked into his shoulder and resting on a bipod, the rifle was as stable as a rock. The wind was calm and his hold-over at this distance would be negligible. The .308 Winchester would do its job as long as he did his. He visualized the bullet leaving the rifle, its vapor trail arcing down toward Yaxaas, and the warlord collapsing on the ground with a terminal chest wound.

But it wasn't time.

The bioweapon had to be destroyed first.

The Range Rover's rear doors opened and two men with AK-47s stepped out, followed by a third man who'd been pinned in the back seat. He moved slowly, with a bandage covering most of his head. One of the gunmen motioned toward the western edge of camp and the three of them began walking with the prisoner in the middle.

The wounded man looked into the hills as he walked and Jake caught a glimpse of his face through the high-power rifle scope.

It was Pickens.

SEVENTY-SEVEN

THE THREE MEN disappeared from sight, blocked from Jake's view by the hills, but a wide grin crept across his face as he raised his head from the scope. Pickens was alive.

It was the first good news he'd had in days.

But it wrecked his plan.

Ever since he'd left Mogadishu, Jake had been focused on eliminating the weapon and killing Yaxaas. He knew that assaulting a larger and better armed force would be dangerous, and if he didn't destroy the bioweapon on his first attempt, he might become its first victim. But Jake was disillusioned with Graves and the Agency and had devised his plan just after losing Athena and Pickens. He was willing to sacrifice his own life to save the people of Somalia. Surviving the mission had never been part of the plan.

But Pickens wasn't dead.

And it was time for a new plan.

Jake valued nothing more than loyalty, and Athena's death had unleashed in him a flood of emotions. The sense of loss and the void in his future were brutal, but what had nearly suffocated him was the self-loathing he'd felt about abandoning her and Giánnis so abruptly after causing her death. Leaving Pickens had been almost as hard. Jake had replayed the scene in his mind too many times to count— standing on the roadside, powerless to stop the shooting as his partner slumped forward in the seat, his blood splattered across the windshield—dead and abandoned on the streets of a foreign country.

Or so Jake thought.

He'd been given a second chance to get his partner back alive.

Whatever it took, Jake was going to make it right.

A one-man hostage rescue was just about the most difficult thing Jake could imagine. Surveillance, intelligence gathering, and operational planning were usually handled by teams of men with deep experience, extensive training, and nearly unlimited resources. The actual raid was usually carried out by a nation's top special operations force—groups such as America's Delta Force or SEAL Team Six, Israel's Sayeret Matkal, or the pioneering British SAS.

And Jake was on his own.

As usual.

But it was pressure that had forged him into the weapon he'd become. He just needed a way into camp. The lightning had stopped, but so had the clouds and the heavy rains that had provided him with cover. Now with patrols scouring the hills and the machine gun nest covering the valley, crossing the clear-cut area around camp would be nearly impossible.

He needed a way in that no one would expect.

Something impossible.

Maybe something crazy.

He lay motionless, scanning the banks of the Jubba. The thirsty animals once again started to appear at dusk. At first there was only a small serval cat and a few dik-dik, cautiously approaching to take a drink, but more animals arrived as night fell, including a lesser kudu that appeared from the plains and bounded into the river.

The current was flowing swiftly from all of the runoff, and the antelope made slow progress as it tried to cross to the near side.

Jake peered through the night vision scope atop his rifle.

Unlike the greater kudu he'd seen before, the lesser species was maybe 150 pounds and three feet tall at the shoulder, with stripes on its hide and patches on its neck to camouflage it from predators.

It was perfect.

Jake snugged the rifle stock into his shoulder as the antelope approached the near bank. The shot would be heard by everyone in the area as the bullet broke the sound barrier, but Jake had learned many years earlier that pinpointing the source of a single gunshot was exceedingly difficult—especially with a suppressor—but a follow-up shot would give his position away.

Success would depend on a single cold-bore shot, from a rifle he'd never fired, that had been sitting in the rain for days.

Jake pressed his cheek against the stock, exhaled, and disengaged the safety.

The kudu shifted its weight to its rear legs as it prepared to leap out of the water.

Jake fired.

The round caught the antelope just behind the ear. It fell back into the water and disappeared below the river-bank.

The nearest patrol stirred briefly but soon returned to their routine in the absence of any further noise or commotion.

Jake lifted himself onto his elbows, moved forward a few inches, and remained motionless for several seconds. There was no sign that he'd been seen by Yaxaas's men, and he crawled a few more inches toward his objective. Even in the darkness, it took nearly an hour to cover the one hundred yards to the banks of the Jubba, where a wide bend in the river protected the camp's western edge like a moat.

The dead kudu was fifty yards downstream, caught in the riverbend.

Jake hauled the downed animal onshore and into a stand of reeds. He pulled the karambit from his vest and skinned the antelope from stern to stem, removing its legs and dumping the innards into the fast-moving water. After rinsing the head and hide, he lashed it to his back and wore it like a helmet and a cape.

Then, with the machine gun nest above him, the camp's guards in front of him, and the patrols in the hills all around him, Jake started crawling on his hands and knees.

A sharp-eyed lookout with a night scope would have spotted the ruse in a second, but Jake had seen dozens of antelope since arriving in Dujuma and Yaxaas's men had undoubtedly seen thousands. He was counting on the guards seeing the kudu's distinctive spiral horns and dismissing it out of habit.

Otherwise, he'd be dead.

Jake moved across the clear-cut zone, briefly lowering his head to mimic nibbling on some grass, and stopped behind the stockade fence, where he was shielded from view.

With the karambit on his vest and a suppressed .45-caliber H&K pistol in a drop-leg holster, he ditched the kudu hide and scaled the fence using the same knotted line he'd used before. From atop the fence he could see that most of Yaxaas's men were working under the lights in the center of camp, rinsing the warlord's SUV and the delivery van with buckets of water. The building holding Pickens was twenty yards away, so close that Jake could almost touch it.

He dropped into camp, drew the pistol, and heard a strange noise behind him.

At first he thought it was thunder, once again echoing through the hills, but the skies were clear and the sound was too steady and too rhythmic to be thunder. An uneasy feeling overtook him as it grew louder and louder until it was deafening. Jake pressed himself to the ground and looked up, just in time to see a helicopter roar by a hundred feet overhead.

SEVENTY-EIGHT

JAKE SWITCHED ON his night vision goggles as the helicopter skimmed the nearby hilltops. It was the MD-520 he'd seen at Mogadishu airport, but with benches mounted to its sides. Strapped onto the benches were men with helmets, goggles, and sniper rifles.

The helo flew a wide orbit around the valley while the snipers scanned the ground below. Jake realized that it was the same helicopter Yaxaas used to seize the tankers, and the men on the benches were the highly trained ex-military marksmen that he'd heard about.

Jake crawled back to the wall as more of the warlord's men poured into the courtyard.

A gunshot echoed through the hills as the helicopter flew another loop around the valley. One of the snipers had fired his weapon. Out of the corner of his eye, Jake noticed one of the goats tumble through the air and land on its side, dead.

It was a spectacular shot—from a moving aircraft, against a small target, at night, and at least fifty of Yaxaas's militiamen surrounded the helicopter as it landed in the center of camp. A few of the men fired their rifles into the air once the helo was on the ground.

Jake wouldn't be rescuing Pickens tonight.

He'd be lucky to make it out alive.

He looked around carefully, making a detailed mental map of the camp, and climbed over the wall before dropping down outside. Jake tied the kudu hide on his back and crawled back across the kill zone toward the hills. He moved slowly—painfully so for a man on whom so much depended—until he was back at his original observation post.

Jake put the rifle to his shoulder and scanned the camp. Dozens of armed men were circulating inside the walls. The helicopter crew was folding its rotors while another group of men finished rinsing the warlord's car and the delivery van.

The delivery van . . .

Emblazoned on its side was the name and logo of the popular Caafi brand of bottled water. It was one of the largest suppliers in Mogadishu—and it was owned by a Hawiye businessman. Even a few cases tainted with a weaponized virus had the potential to spread it throughout the entire country.

Strapped to Jake's pack was a rocket-propelled grenade launcher and two warheads. He'd originally set up one hundred yards from camp, but the patrols and the terrain had forced him back another three hundred yards. It was technically within range for the RPG-7, but Jake had never fired one, and anything less than a direct hit on the bioagent would simply disperse it into the atmosphere, leaving the men in camp, including Pickens, to become the first victims in a cycle of infection that would spread throughout the country once they'd returned to the capital city of Mogadishu.

Using the RPG from four hundred yards was off the table. He needed to be closer.

IT WAS NEARLY three a.m. by the time he reached the dirt bike.

The motorcycle started after a few kicks. Jake rode under night vision goggles, with the rifle strapped to the bike, his pack on his back, and the pistol strapped to his thigh. High grasses brushed against his legs and rodents scurried from his path as he navigated a series of game trails to the paved road on the outskirts of Dujuma.

Jake stopped to check his map and cross-check his wrist-mounted GPS. The dirt road to Yaxaas's compound was a mile north of his position. He sat for a moment, caught a whiff of the motorcycle's two-stroke engine idling beneath him, and visualized the plan he'd devised. It was a plan born of increasing desperation, one that would depend on skill, determination, and a tremendous amount of luck.

He set off, riding no faster than fifteen miles per hour to minimize the noise. While the grassy hills would absorb much of the sound, Jake was going on the offensive, and that necessitated complete tactical surprise. He needed to hit his enemy when they felt safest, when their guard would be lowest, and to have any chance of success, he would have to achieve his objective before Yaxaas's superior forces could organize and react.

Jake stopped at the entrance to the camp's access road. The main gate was a mile in, at the end of a twisting single-lane road that had been cut through the valley. The road was a death trap, with steep sides and the machine gun nest covering the final approach to camp.

Jake turned off the road, dropped a satchel in the tall grass, and headed into the hills, riding up increasingly steep slopes. Several times he threaded his way through narrow ravines or cut switchbacks across the hills until he'd reached his destination. He shut down the bike and hiked the last hundred yards to a location he'd noted on the map.

He crawled up the side of the hill with his rifle laid across his forearms. The land smelled of dirt and grass and wildflowers that were already blooming from the rains.

Still prone at the summit, Jake raised the rifle, switched on the night scope, and scanned the area. Off to the left, hidden behind a hill, lay the machine gun nest and the camp. To his right, obstructed by other hills, lay Dujuma.

But Jake hadn't come for the view.

What he wanted was right in front of him.

He took his pack and climbed down the hillside. Dawn was two hours away—and he had work to do.

SEVENTY-NINE

THE SUN HAD just risen above the horizon when Jake climbed back to the hilltop. His work in the valley had been productive but taken longer than expected. He applied fresh camo to his face, tucked fresh grass into his hat, and settled in behind the gun. The road was sixty feet beneath him and shaped like a giant letter V. To his left was a straightaway, directly under him was a sharp corner, and to his right was another straightaway.

There wasn't much left for him to do, but wait.

With the rainstorm gone and the skies clear, the temperature soared quickly into the high nineties, along with the humidity. Jake lay prone in the grass under a majestic old leadwood tree, whose barren branches would break up his form on the ground. Aside from the buzzing of insects and the occasional screech of a distant monkey, the scene was quiet.

Nearly twenty-four hours later, it was just as quiet.

It was just before daybreak when a familiar sound woke

him from a catnap. It was the helicopter's turbine engine spooling up.

A shot of adrenaline coursed through Jake's veins and he was instantly hyper-alert. As before, the success of the mission would hinge on the events of the next few minutes—it was the nature of being a solo operator. There was no second line of defense if Jake were to die. The helicopter was the single greatest threat he faced and he had no control over it.

Not directly, anyway.

He switched on his NVGs and watched the helo lift into the air above camp. It flew slowly, making no more than five or ten knots. It meant that Yaxaas wasn't moving the biowarfare agent by air—otherwise the helicopter would have flown directly to Mogadishu—which was good news.

But it also meant that the helicopter was flying convoy protection for whatever ground vehicle was moving the virus, which meant the snipers would be scanning every inch of the area looking for someone like Jake, which was not so good news.

He watched the aircraft come closer until he could clearly make out the snipers with their legs dangling over the skids and their rifles slung over their shoulders. Three sets of headlights came around the corner to his left, bouncing slowly over the rutted dirt road. In front was Yaxaas's Range Rover, followed by the delivery truck and a pickup filled with gunmen.

The helo had closed to within a hundred yards. In another fifty yards, the helicopter's rotor wash would flatten the tall grass and the snipers would spot him.

The fate of the goat in camp left little doubt as to what would happen next.

Jake flexed his hand as the helicopter loomed closer—forcing himself to be patient. He could clearly see the snipers with their weapons up, sweeping the ground, searching for targets.

It was nearly overhead when he squeezed the remote firing device. Half a mile away, where the camp road met the paved road, the coded radio signal was received and an electrical impulse triggered a pair of blasting caps—each about the size of a cigarette—which in turn detonated the four blocks of British PE8 plastic explosives that Jake had left in the satchel. The explosion sent a tower of flames and a column of smoke rising into the air.

The helicopter roared past to investigate.

But the sound of the departing helo was quickly replaced by the throaty growl of the Range Rover's supercharged V8 engine.

Jake grabbed a second actuator and paced the SUV's approach.

Three, two, one . . .

He pulled the trigger.

A fraction of a second later, another ten blocks of PE8 exploded in a brilliant flash, a violent pressure wave, and a deafening blast.

A cloud of dust rose into the air where the Range Rover had been.

The SUV was literally blown off the road at thirty miles per hour. It fishtailed wildly and nearly slammed into the hillside, but the warlord's wheelman knew his trade. He let off the gas, turned into the slide, and got his vehicle back under control. The supercharged V8 snarled once again, the run-flat tires bit into the ground, and the big SUV launched itself back onto the dirt road. Jake looked into the distance, watched the taillights disappear around the corner, and muttered to himself.

Motherfucker.

EIGHTY

BUT THERE WAS no time for mourning.

The delivery van had been right behind the SUV. It was inching through the shallow crater made by the IED and was already halfway up the opposite side. The pickup truck filled with gunmen was right on its bumper, laying on the horn and practically pushing it down the road.

Jake got to his feet, lifted the RPG out of the grass, and fired.

The pickup disappeared. Dead men flew through the night like chunks of lava from an erupting volcano.

Jake reloaded the RPG.

He was thirty yards from the delivery truck—a can't-miss shot, even for a novice—but he didn't know for sure if the warhead would burn hot enough to destroy the weaponized bioagent or if the explosion would simply disperse the virus into the air, infecting him and anyone else who visited the site.

There was only one way to destroy it for sure.

He shifted his aim to a spot ten feet in front of the delivery truck and fired again.

A crater exploded in the dirt. The front of the truck was shredded, its windshield shattered and blown in. Smoke rose from the engine compartment.

Jake ran to the dirt bike. He had a minute, maybe two, to finish the job before the helicopter returned—call it a hundred seconds. He kicked the bike to life and sped down to the road at top speed, skidding to a halt in front of the delivery van. There were two men in the front seat wearing the sky blue uniforms of the bottled water company. They were dazed, and their faces were peppered with fragments of glass, but they were conscious. Jake recognized them as one of the patrols he'd seen guarding the hills around camp.

Jake drew the pistol from his leg holster and punched two pairs of .45-caliber holes through the windshield to ensure the men would never make their intended delivery.

He leaned the bike against the van. For all the violence that had occurred, the scene was strangely quiet. The smoldering pickup truck and the dead gunmen were silent. Only the soft idle of the dirt bike and the distant thrum of the helicopter penetrated the dawn air.

The van's rear doors hung at odd angles, partially blown from their hinges by the force of the RPG. Jake pried them open and hauled himself inside. Easily five hundred cases of bottled water were stacked in front of him, shredded by shrapnel. Water was everywhere—in the air, on his hands, running across the floor, and dripping from the ceiling.

Jake had been inoculated against anthrax and everything else the U.S. government had vaccines for, but a weaponized virus was a different animal altogether. His chances of survival would be next to zero if it had already been mixed into the bottles.

But Jake didn't have time to ponder his own fate. He heard the pitch of the helicopter's rotor change as it turned around. At most he had sixty seconds before it was on him.

He knocked over several cases of water and found what he was looking for tied down in the center of the refrigerated van.

It was a large black case with heavy-duty latches, airtight seals, and a biohazard logo.

Jake had known that the black market for arms in Africa was robust ever since he'd joined the Agency, but still he'd been stunned when Pickens had shown him the weapons he'd accumulated in the safe house basement. Jake was on board with the mission—supporting CIA's African partners and getting dangerous arms out of the hands of terrorists and warlords—but it was still disturbing to know that anyone with the means to pay for it could acquire such a wide range of destructive devices . . . until Jake had learned of the bioweapon.

And then, like everything in life, Pickens's arms cache became a matter of perspective. A weaponized virus could survive heat, air, and sunlight far better than the natural version. It wasn't just dangerous, it was evil, just like Yaxaas.

And evil did not die from exposure, or time, or hope.

Evil had to be killed.

EIGHTY-ONE

J AKE REACHED INTO his pack and took out three thermate grenades.

Known officially as AN-M14 incendiary hand grenades, each was about the size of a can of beer. Made from aluminum powder, iron oxide, and barium nitrate, the first one Jake had seen had been in Pickens's safe. The big man had wired it to the lock, along with an anti-lift switch and enough heavy-load explosive detonating cord to obliterate everything inside. Once ignited, the thermate burned at four thousand degrees Fahrenheit. It even generated its own oxygen so it could work underwater.

Nothing on earth could survive its wrath.

Jake took the grenades, wrapped them twice with detonating cord and a fistful of blasting caps, and duct-taped the assembly to the crate. One grenade probably would have been enough, but Jake wasn't fucking around.

He unspooled another fifty feet of det cord out the back of the truck just as the helicopter roared by overhead. Bullets thudded into the dirt around him as the helo banked steeply and turned back toward the van. The helicopter's high speed and rapidly changing angle had probably saved him, but Jake had seen the snipers in action. It wouldn't take long for them to adjust their aim.

He jumped on the dirt bike and ignited the det cord. Unlike a timed fuse, the explosive cord burned almost instantaneously, detonating the blasting caps and the grenades in a few thousandths of a second. A blinding light radiated from the back of the van as molten slag incinerated the plastic container and began destroying the virus.

The helicopter finished its turn and was zeroing in on his position. Jake twisted the throttle and launched the dirt bike forward. The helo was closing the distance quickly. In another few seconds, the snipers would have his position dialed in. Jake turned the bike ninety degrees and climbed into the hills—toward the oncoming helicopter. The distance closed immediately and the snipers lost sight of Jake as he passed underneath the aircraft.

Jake flipped his night vision goggles into position and accelerated into the hills. The bike spit a wake of dirt and debris as it scaled the soft earth. Behind him, the thermate slag had melted through the van's chassis and ignited its fuel line. A hundred gallons of burning diesel engulfed the truck and sent flames a hundred feet high—illuminating the valley in every direction.

But the aircrew was tenacious. The pilot slewed the helo to the side and the snipers rained down more gunfire. A bullet tore through Jake's backpack and more rounds crashed into the earth around him as he accelerated up the hill.

He crested the ridge with the throttle wide open and

launched the bike into the air—flying forty feet over the ground before landing in a ravine. The helicopter doubled back, but the glare of the burning truck and the ravine's steep sides shielded Jake from view. The helicopter made another tight turn to the east to cut off Jake's access to the main road.

But Jake headed away from the road and away from Mogadishu. He turned northwest and drove through the low hills, shifting into high gear and opening up the distance with his pursuers with every passing second.

He caught sight of the MD 520 crisscrossing the countryside several times over the next twenty minutes until it finally abandoned its search and flew away.

EIGHTY-TWO

JAKE STOWED THE dirt bike in the back of the pickup before starting the drive back to Mogadishu.

He drove the old Toyota like he stole it, speeding recklessly through the darkness and swerving around animals and slower vehicles. Once he was in cell phone range, he placed an anonymous call to AMISOM headquarters about the mysterious explosions near Dujuma.

IEDs were so common that they had become a business. Bomb-builders turned to almost assembly line construction to increase output. They bought supplies in bulk and regularly used the same blasting cap and booster charge combination—usually Russian or Chinese Semtex—to ignite base charges of homemade explosives.

Come daylight, African Union ground troops would arrive. Explosive experts would use spectrographs to analyze the debris and search for the bomb-maker's signature, but the bomb technicians would be in for a worrisome surprise when they saw the results of this site. The presence of the thermate and the biological agents would quickly be shared with U.S. forces in the region and ring alarm bells at the Pentagon and Langley.

Graves would undoubtedly piece the parts together.

Good, Jake thought. *Here's your proof, Ted.*

But Jake wasn't celebrating. Yaxaas still had Pickens, and there was no telling how the old crocodile might vent his rage once they reached Mogadishu.

Jake had been lucky in Dujuma.

He would need a miracle in Mogadishu.

He skidded to a stop outside the safe house and went straight to the basement. He walked among the stacks of weapons and explosives, looking for inspiration, looking for anything that would give him a fighting chance. Thoughts formed and faded, but one man simply couldn't assault a force that was twenty times larger and expect to live.

He spotted the two crates of British PE8 plastic explosives stacked in the corner. Jake had used the blocks in the top crate to hit Yaxaas's Range Rover and to create the diversion that had drawn the helicopter off the delivery van.

He'd need a similar diversion tonight to distract.

Jake moved the empty wooden box to the floor and popped the latches on the second one.

He stared at it for the better part of a minute.

It was nearly empty.

A disturbing idea crept into his head—regardless of how hard he tried to block it out. It was ridiculous, really, and Jake chided himself for wasting time and got back to work, collecting weapons and gear for his assault on Yaxaas's compound.

Jake went to the safe for fresh batteries for his night vision equipment.

He entered the combination and picked through the shelves. Up top were stacks of dollars and euros. He lifted a brick of hundreds and briefly considered trying to buy Pickens's safety, but there were simply too many guards to bribe. A single loyal soldier would ruin everything. Jake kept looking. On the second shelf were the electronics, including more night optics and a device known as an FTIR spectrometer.

Jake looked at the spectrometer. He'd used one briefly during ordnance training back in the States. It was a high-tech gadget but simple to operate. Similar models were in the hands of U.S. soldiers, sailors, and marines through-out the world. It analyzed and identified the type of explo-sives used in an IED to assist in identification of the bomb-maker.

Jake found fresh batteries for his night vision goggles and the laser on his pistol. He was about to close the safe, but his analytical mind was still having trouble reconciling events as they appeared with facts he knew.

He took the spectrometer down from the shelf. It was a little larger than a brick and about half the weight. He pushed the power button, half wishing that it wouldn't turn on, but the display lit up, ready for action.

Jake returned to the bottom crate of PE8 and used his knife to slice open one of the remaining packages. He pointed the spectrometer at the exposed block and in just a few seconds it completed its analysis: 12.5 percent bind-ing agents and 86.5 percent RDX.

No surprise there—those were the plastic and the explosive in plastic explosives.

But the remaining 1 percent was something called a taggant, and it was a highly specific chemical included by manufacturers to allow product identification, like a serial number. In this case it was 1 percent dimethyl-dinitrobutane, and its precise formulation identified the explosive as British PE8.

No surprise there, either.

Jake had pulled it fresh from the crate.

But his legs felt impossibly heavy as he walked upstairs—like a man walking to his own execution. He rummaged through his bedroom until he found the shirt he'd been wearing weeks ago when his own car had been hit by a roadside bomb. He'd thrown it in a corner and forgotten about it. The shirt was still covered with fragments of glass, dried blood, and bomb residue.

He pointed the spectrometer at it.

PE8.

Jake aimed at a different part of the shirt and took a second reading, just to be sure.

PE8.

And for the second time in as many days, Jake looked into the distance and muttered to himself.

Motherfucker.

EIGHTY-THREE

JAKE RETURNED TO the house and removed the cell phones from Pickens's dresser.

He scrolled through the text messages until he found what he was looking for.

Jake sent a message of his own.

If he didn't survive the night, and even if he did, Graves would argue that what Jake was about to do should have been left to others—teams of highly skilled men who operated as a unit and trained constantly, but Jake's head was spinning. He wasn't following orders. He wasn't on CIA business anymore.

He spent the next hour laying out the equipment he'd gathered for the assault: explosives, weapons, and assorted gadgets. It was enough to equip a squad of soldiers, but he wasn't a squad of soldiers. He was a single man, going up against a numerically superior and better armed force. Stealth would be more important than firepower.

He stripped away everything that wasn't absolutely essential, declining even to bring a rifle. Jake was an exceptional pistol shot, and tonight's work was going to be up close and personal. He reloaded the compact Heckler & Koch pistol he'd used in Dujuma. The HK45 was accurate, deadly, and completely reliable. By the time he'd finished paring down his gear, he could carry everything he needed on a tactical vest and a small backpack.

He was standing at the kitchen table, taking one last look at online satellite images of the warlord's neighborhood, when the mobile phone pinged.

He'd gotten a response to his text.

Midnight, Jake sent back.

It was the last piece of the puzzle.

He grabbed the backpack, set the alarm, and rolled from the safe house in a white Suzuki Alto. The online maps he'd been studying were low-resolution and had provided only basic details of the area. Jake needed to get eyes on target while there was still daylight.

He had two hours.

Jake pushed the small car to its limit, racing the wrong direction up one-way roads, careening onto cross streets through oncoming traffic, and dodging pedestrians while speeding down narrow alleys. Maintaining cover was a thing of the past. Jake now cared only about arriving without a tail.

He entered the Yaaqshiid district of eastern Mogadishu and approached Yaxaas's neighborhood from the south. Trash blew across the roads, abandoned buildings outnumbered those that were occupied, and emaciated residents wandered aimlessly through the streets.

The warlord's compound filled an entire block. The satellite images had shown a square building in the middle, with a courtyard and what looked like a pond in its center, but all Jake could see from the street was a high wall. The roads on three sides of the block were wide and exposed, and would be dangerous for Jake to cross, but the street on the western edge was no more than a narrow alley bordered by a cluster of shanties.

Jake turned down the alley. Though there were thousands of similar cars in Mogadishu, the little white Suzuki with the tinted windows attracted hard stares from the warlord's guards. Jake counted four of them stationed outside the compound's walls—all carrying Kalashnikovs and wearing radios strapped to their belts. There were sure to be more men inside.

On his left were the shanties, dozens of palm trees, and the wall to Yaxaas's compound. It was twelve-foot-high poured concrete, topped with barbed wire. Jake drove slowly and studied the layout through the heavily tinted windows. The canopy of palm trees had hidden the alley and the shanties from the satellite images—and given Jake his infiltration point.

He drove out of the district and spent hours winding his way through the city streets, killing time, until it was time to kill.

He returned two hours after dark.

Jake parked four blocks away and infiltrated on foot. The night air was hot and dry, and he wore an open shirt over his tactical vest and a small pack on his back. A gentle breeze rattled the overhead palm fronds while candlelight and the occasional kerosene lamp flickered inside the shanties. Despite the rats' nest of power lines directly above, none of the makeshift homes had electricity.

He moved silently between the shacks, catching snippets of unintelligible conversations and seeing occasional shadows. He paused only once, when a growling dog blocked his path, but Jake knelt on one knee, drew his pistol with his right hand, and slowly extended his other one. The mutt lowered its head, sniffed Jake's hand, and licked it once. Jake scratched the mongrel behind the ears and holstered his weapon.

He continued on to a single palm tree that towered above the others and duct-taped a block of plastic explosives and a radio detonator to its trunk.

Across the alley was Yaxaas's compound, bordered by more trees. The same four guards were patrolling the walls.

Up and back.

Up and back.

Even after the melee in Dujuma, it was a monotonous routine, and Jake crouched in the shadows until the nearest guard passed by, his senses dulled by the endless repetition.

Jake walked silently across the alley and shimmied up one of the larger palm trees until he could see over the wall into the compound. He counted three more guards, all armed, including one barely fifty feet away. The main building was a square mass of cinder blocks and steel doors. Against the far wall were four pickup trucks.

And the battle-scarred Range Rover.

Jake settled in, concealed in darkness, with his feet

propped against the compound wall and his back against the tree. The western guard passed by underneath him at least a dozen times without ever looking up.

It was midnight when the mobile phone vibrated in Jake's pocket. He checked the camera feed from the security system and saw a man standing outside the safe house.

Jake buzzed him in.

Five minutes later, a second man arrived.

But instead of buzzing him in, Jake dialed another number and punched a four-digit code into the phone.

The sky over central Mogadishu turned orange and a rumble like a thousand claps of thunder rolled across the ground.

Yaxaas's men assumed the massive explosion was another al-Shabaab IED targeting Villa Somalia.

But they were wrong.

EIGHTY-FOUR

I T WAS THE CIA safe house.

Jake pressed the radio firing device on his vest, detonating the plastic explosives he'd planted a hundred feet away at the base of the palm tree. The big tree snapped in two and fell to the ground—taking the overhead power lines with it.

The neighborhood plunged into darkness.

Jake moved quickly. The element of surprise was his greatest tactical advantage—and it wouldn't last long. He flipped his night vision goggles into place and activated the infrared laser on his pistol.

Inside the compound, a metal door burst open and four men with flashlights ran from the main building. They started the pickup trucks and sped through the gate to block the intersections around Yaxaas's compound with the vehicles. The guards who'd been patrolling the exterior linked up with the trucks, weapons at the ready, while two more guards slid the gate shut and took up station inside the compound.

The warlord's men were sealing the perimeter—focused on external threats—just as Jake had hoped.

With one hand on his NVGs and one hand holding his weapon, he dropped over the wall and rolled onto his side to absorb the impact. He came up on one knee with the pistol in both hands, scanning the interior of the darkened compound.

Another man ran out of the building with a submachine gun in his hands. Jake recognized him as one of the guards who'd been shadowing Pickens in Dujuma.

Jake blew out his heart with two .45-caliber bullets from close range. Secondary explosions from the safe house drowned out the suppressed gunshots.

Jake skulked along the wall, in the darkest shadows where the moonlight failed to shine, and made his way to the main entrance. The remaining two guards were seventy-five feet away, shouting to each other from either side of the gate. Jake raised the pistol in a two-handed grip, exhaled, and placed the infrared laser dot on the first man's chest. He fired twice, then shifted his aim to the other guard and put two rounds in his back before the man realized what had happened.

Jake jogged over and anchored each of them with a round to the forehead.

He dragged the bodies away from the gate and cleared the rest of the parking area. From the southwest corner of the building, candlelight flickered through a second-floor window.

Yaxaas.

With his weapon in his right hand, Jake shoved the

door open with his left. It struck something halfway. Jake pushed harder—and felt someone push back.

"Al'abalah," Jake yelled. It was Arabic for "idiot."

The man yelled back.

It wasn't Yaxaas or Pickens.

Jake fired two rounds through the door and the resistance stopped. He looked around the door and recognized the man on the other side. It was one of the goons from the Bakaara Market.

Jake stepped inside and moved forward along the right wall. His eyes and the weapon moved as one—swinging in a wide arc and covering every inch of the room. The space was utilitarian, with a metal table in the middle and folding chairs strewn across the floor. A mini-fridge sat silent in a corner.

Jake bolted the exterior door behind him and pushed deeper into the building. The next room was a small warehouse, with crates and pallets stacked along the walls. He sensed movement to his right and brought his weapon around, but it was only two goats in a cage.

At the far end of the warehouse was a set of concrete stairs. Jake climbed slowly, his pistol aimed up the stairway. At the top, a long hallway led to the candlelit room he'd seen from outside.

Someone was speaking.

Jake moved slowly, clearing the rooms on each side of the hallway as he advanced. Most were offices, one was a bathroom.

The voice became louder—a one-sided conversation— the speaker yelling into a phone. Shadows danced on the walls as the candle flickered and the figure paced. The man crossed into the light in front of a large wooden desk.

Yaxaas.

Jake glanced at his watch. It had been three and a half minutes since the CIA safe house had blown. The army and the volunteer ambulance service would be swarming Villa Somalia and soon discover that it wasn't another terrorist attack on the president, but an explosion at a private residence in the Warta Nabada district.

Word would get out.

Yaxaas's guards would return to the building.

Jake would be trapped.

He stood in the darkened hallways and took off his NVGs. There was enough light in the office to do what needed to be done.

Jake glimpsed a gun in the warlord's waistband as Yaxaas ended his call and fished a lighter out of his pocket. He lit a cigarette and stepped through the French doors onto the veranda, staring into the darkened courtyard as he exhaled.

Jake entered the office.

There were a few chairs, a desk, a sofa . . . and maybe a hundred edged weapons hanging on the walls.

There was another door to the right of the veranda.

But no sign of Pickens.

The warlord finished his cigarette and tossed it over the railing.

When he turned around, Jake was ten feet away, with the suppressed pistol pointed at his chest.

EIGHTY-FIVE

A BREEZE RUSTLED THE linen drapes on either side of the warlord. He was still wearing his crocodile-skin cowboy boots.

"So, American . . . Have you solved all of Somalia's problems?"

"I'm about to solve one of them."

Yaxaas scoffed. "Killing me changes nothing."

"You're too modest," Jake said.

The warlord fished out another cigarette and reached for his lighter.

"Slowly," Jake said. Yaxaas did as he was told.

"You think you are protecting my country? You can't even protect those closest to you." The warlord exhaled. "It's a shame, what happened in Greece, but the electrical systems on English cars have always been tricky. At least you can buy another Land Rover."

Jake's finger slipped inside the trigger guard.

"Be careful with that," said Yaxaas, staring down the barrel of Jake's gun. "I have twenty men outside. You'll never—"

"It was more like ten, and they're all dead. I killed every one of them."

"And nothing will change if you kill me. Someone will take my place before sunrise."

"Like Badeed?" Jake asked. "He would have, but he's dead."

"Then Cawar—"

"Also dead. Nacay too. Dead. Dead. Dead. There seems to be something going around."

The warlord inhaled deeply from his cigarette and blew the smoke in the air. "I can make you rich, you know. You—"

"I don't want your money. I just want my partner."

"He's not here," said the warlord. He turned to face the courtyard. "He's in a rural camp, several hours from here, but perhaps—"

Yaxaas spun around with his gun in his hand.

Jake fired first.

The .45-caliber bullet hit the warlord in the chest. Jake squeezed the trigger a second time, but the hammer fell on an empty chamber. The gun was empty.

He dropped the spent magazine and reached for one of the spares on his belt, but they weren't there. They must have fallen out when he'd jumped into the compound.

He was out of ammunition.

A bloodstain blossomed across the warlord's shirt. The hollow-point round had mushroomed inside his chest and nicked his heart. Even a trauma team couldn't save him now.

But he wasn't dead yet.

Yaxaas staggered backward, his strength leaving him rapidly. He grasped at the linen drapes as he fell onto the veranda floor. His gun tumbled into the courtyard.

The two men locked eyes as the life drained from the warlord's body.

The world was a better place.

But Pickens wasn't in Dujuma.

Jake could feel it.

Shadows flickered in the candlelight as his gaze moved from Yaxaas's body on the veranda, to the weapons mounted on the walls, to the door on the side wall.

Jake holstered his pistol and drew his knife. He tested the door handle with his left hand.

It was unlocked.

He leaned forward, tightened his grip on the knife, and opened the door.

It was a bedroom, lit by another candle. To the left was another set of French doors, also open to the courtyard. To the right was a four-poster bed, with a bathroom in the far corner.

In the middle of the room, wearing a sleeveless T-shirt and handcuffed to a chair, was Pickens.

EIGHTY-SIX

PICKENS WAS SLUMPED over, with a bandage wrapped around his head. A strip of duct tape covered his mouth.

Jake ripped it off.

"Sonofa—" Pickens said as he came to. The tape had nearly taken a layer of skin with it.

"They never taught you how to get out of handcuffs in the OSS?" said Jake.

"First thing I learned," Pickens said with a smile. He raised his hands. Dangling from one wrist were the open cuffs. "But I didn't know if it was going to be you or Yaxaas coming through that door."

"I'll bet."

Jake glimpsed the roll of duct tape on the bedside table.

"You here alone?" said Pickens.

Jake glanced back to the office to make sure no one had entered behind him.

Pickens's massive biceps glistened with sweat as he unlocked the other handcuff and rubbed his wrists.

"Lead the way," Pickens said, gesturing toward the door.

He took a step forward.

The two men were an arm's length apart.

Jake stepped back into the warlord's office. Yaxaas's body was just a few feet away.

"I thought you were dead," said Jake.

"They brought me here after you left me at the checkpoint."

"The ambush," Jake said.

Pickens shrugged. "They had us boxed in."

"You knew I'd be unarmed coming from the airport, but you forgot about the gun I kept in the glove compartment."

"Are you all right, man? You know I'm the one who got shot in the head."

"Seriously?" said Pickens. He took another step forward.

Jake moved to the side, putting the corner of the desk between them.

"It was all a big show, wasn't it?" said Jake. "Just like this."

"What about the handcuffs?" Pickens asked.

"I'd be surprised if there weren't handcuffs in Yaxaas's bedroom."

"Jake—"

"How did you get out of the other cuff so quickly, John? And what about the duct tape? It sure was sticky for a guy who's sweating so much. It couldn't have been on there more than a minute."

"I'm not sure where this is coming from, partner, but let's get out of here and talk about it."

Pickens stepped around the desk. The warlord's body was at his feet.

"Badeed's dead too, by the way."

"How did—"

"Remind me . . . Why were all those weapons in the basement?"

"I told you, brother. Those are for the militias to fight Boko Haram. They're—"

Jake shook his head. "I did some research, John. The one militia you were supporting switched sides four years ago. They stopped fighting Boko Haram and pledged allegiance to al-Shabaab."

"It's a gray area."

"It's clear as fucking day. They're terrorists."

"Look, Jake. The administration shut down support for the militia. They didn't care who won—they just didn't want the bodies in the news every day."

"But you didn't shut it down, did you?"

"I thought I could still do some good."

"I found a bag of diamonds hidden in the safe."

"I'm taking a small cut. It's how they do business here."

"It's a slippery slope once you take that first step," Jake said. "Pretty soon you're in bed with arms dealers and warlords."

Pickens shook his head in protest, but Jake kept speaking.

"Speaking of warlords, Badeed and I had a nice chat—before I killed him—obviously. He told me that the four men who tried to kill us in Kitadra were hired by a guy who looks a lot like you, to kill a guy who looks a lot like me. Apparently, you were not a target."

"A lot of guys in Africa look like me."

"That's some racist shit right there, John, but I'm going to let it slide."

"You're going believe a warlord over me? Half the sources we talked to said Badeed was the pirate leader."

Jake smiled. "Only the sources you were running, John."

"Did you really kill him?"

Jake nodded. "I told him Yaxaas had the bioweapon and asked him to meet me at the safe house. Cawar fell for the same ruse."

"Cawar is dead too?"

"I found the phone you used to text him, John. I sent him a message—pretending to be you—and told him we needed to meet. He and Badeed died in the explosion. You may have felt it just before the power went out."

"That was the safe house?"

"Ironic, right? All the weapons you bought from Cawar ended up killing him."

Pickens said nothing.

"Speaking of karma," Jake said as he drew the pistol and pointed it at Pickens's chest. "Turn around and put your hands on top of your head."

"Listen to me, Jake. You've got it wrong, brother." Pickens was speaking quickly, anxiously. "You and I are on the same side of this thing. I spent eight years building my cover here so they would trust me, so they would think I was one of them. It looks like I'm involved because it's supposed to look like I'm involved."

"I believed that, John, I really did, but a funny thing happened in Dujuma. Remember when the Range Rover was hit by that roadside bomb? That was me. I used those British plastic explosives you showed me in the basement. I didn't use all of them, though, just enough to disable the truck so I could rescue you and kill Yaxaas."

Pickens stared at the gun in Jake's hands.

"I needed a few more blocks tonight," Jake said, "to knock out the power. So I opened the second crate, but it was almost empty . . ."

The big man's shoulders sank. He looked down at Yaxaas's body.

"It didn't make any sense, John. And you know how I am, 'so damned analytical.' I just couldn't let it go."

"Don't jump to conclusions, Jake. There's a lot of plastic explosives in Somalia."

"True enough, but you bought all the PE8. 'Every last block in the Horn of Africa,' is what you said. And do you know what I discovered? I discovered that the PE8 in that crate was an exact motherfucking match for the IED that almost killed me."

"I know it looks bad—"

"Only one person had access to those explosives, John."

Pickens raised his hands in surrender—and lunged.

He was strong and fast, but the floor was slick with blood and it gave Jake the fraction of a second he needed to sidestep the attack. Pickens came up short.

Jake still had the gun pointed at his former partner.

"Shoot me!" Pickens yelled as he closed in. "C'mon, Keller. Finish it."

"It doesn't have to end that way, John. Give me the key and put the cuffs back on."

Pickens laughed and faked another charge as Jake circled behind the desk.

"You're not the only 'analytical' one," Pickens said as he came closer. "I was changing my bandage when you showed up, then I heard the shot and a body hit the floor . . . I figured maybe Yaxaas got the drop on you, because badass Jake Keller never fires less than two rounds."

The two men slowly circled the desk, with Pickens in pursuit.

"I know the gun is empty, Jake. Even by one goddamned candlepower I can see there's no magazine in it."

Jake holstered the pistol.

"Why all the games, John? Why didn't you just kill me yourself? You had a hundred chances to do it."

"I was just trying to warn you off, brother. Somalia is a lost cause. Nothing we do here is going to make a damned bit of difference, so why shouldn't I make a little something on the side—maybe fund my retirement and pay for my kids' college?"

"Because you're a traitor. That's the legacy you're going to leave for your kids."

"I didn't have a choice. Once I did that first deal with Cawar, they had me."

Pickens pointed one of his meaty fingers at Jake.

"I got nothing against you personally, Keller. You can still walk away."

Pickens gestured to the door.

"I'm afraid I can't, John." Jake pulled the karambit from his vest.

The big man laughed again and grabbed the three-foot-long Ngulu sword off the wall. It was a cross between an axe and a broadsword and its heavy curved blade was designed to sever a man's neck.

Pickens swung it like a cleanup hitter.

Jake ducked as the edge sliced through the air just inches from his head, then leapt up and elbowed Pickens in the face, shattering his nose.

But it didn't affect the big man. He wielded the sword effortlessly, like a painter with a brush.

Jake shifted sideways, keeping the desk between them, until Pickens attacked again, swinging the sword overhead as if he were splitting firewood. The blade crashed into the desktop, chopping off a foot-thick corner of the hard mahogany.

Pickens stepped around the desk and swung again.

Jake rotated his body out of the way and drove a heel kick to the big man's pelvis. Pickens staggered backward but still managed to slice a gash in Jake's arm.

Jake retreated back behind the desk.

"It's only a matter of time, Keller," said Pickens as he feinted to his left and moved right. His natural athleticism masked his enormous strength.

Jake realized that the desk was keeping Pickens away but also giving him an advantage with the longer weapon.

Jake was never going to win a fight for his life by playing defense.

He stepped into the middle of the room with the knife in his right hand and his wounded left arm held against his chest. There could be no mistakes now. If Pickens connected, Jake would die.

The big man came to the same conclusion.

And smiled.

He came at Jake with a stutter step and then charged. He held the axe low and swung it hard enough to fell a redwood.

The blade nicked the front of Jake's vest as he leapt backward. He counterattacked with a knife strike to Pickens's rib cage as the big man followed through on his swing.

But Pickens still had the situational awareness he'd developed on the football field and the reflexes to match. He tucked his arm in to protect his ribs and received only a deep cut to his biceps. He seemed impervious to the pain as he spun around and once again raised the sword.

The two men were five feet apart, circling each other.

Pickens's arm was bleeding heavily, but he was holding the Ngulu sword over his right shoulder and wagging it from side to side, like a batter waiting for a pitch.

Jake feigned an attack, but Pickens didn't bite. He kept circling, the sword constantly in motion.

Jake was standing in front of the French doors when the big man shifted his hands. Jake recognized the grip as the one Pickens had used for the earlier baseball-swing attack.

Jake was ready for it when it came.

He dove onto the terrace and rolled onto his side.

Pickens tried to check the swing, but he'd already committed. The sword connected with the poured-concrete wall.

The hundred-year-old blade shattered into a dozen pieces. All that was left was a gnarled metal shank at the end of the wooden handle.

Jake lunged with the karambit and raked the blade down Pickens's thigh, severing two of the muscles in his quadriceps.

Pickens screamed in pain and lashed out furiously, whipping the axe handle at Jake and connecting with his forehead.

It was a solid blow, and the knife fell from Jake's hand as he almost lost consciousness.

He was on his back on the terrace, dazed and unarmed, his face covered in blood.

Pickens limped over and moved in for the kill.

"I tried to warn you off." He spoke through gritted teeth as he raised what was left of the sword over his head.

Jake braced his body on the ground and kicked up, using his hips and legs for power. He drove his heel into Pickens's groin with so much force that it lifted the two-hundred-forty-pound man off the ground.

Pickens dropped the sword and clutched his crotch. Practically delirious, he staggered backward onto the terrace, tripped over the warlord's body and crashed into the railing. He tried to prop himself up but his injured leg couldn't support his weight and he tumbled into the courtyard.

Jake heard a thud.

Then a splash.

Then a scream.

He walked to the edge of the balcony and switched on his night vision goggles. In the middle of the compound was the large courtyard he'd seen from the satellite images, complete with ferns, flowers—and a pond.

And in the middle of the pond was a fourteen-foot-long crocodile, pulling Pickens to the bottom.

Little Yaxaas.

EIGHTY-SEVEN

JAKE WAS SEATED alone in a booth at the back of the restaurant, watching a split-screen video feed on his laptop. Not much had changed onscreen since he'd arrived, but the same could not be said for Somalia— the deaths of the two warlords had upended the entire nation's balance of power.

Infighting among the Darood and the Hawiye had weakened the two clans as competing factions struggled to assert control the only way they knew how—the man with the bandoliers and Badeed's chief of intelligence were each assassinated by rivals within twenty-four hours—and their deaths had been only the start of the bloodshed.

Foreign and domestic security services leapt into the mix, leveraging the chaos to sow discord among the other warlords. Disinformation campaigns, false-flag operations, and more assassinations led to a period of intense fighting among the minor clan militias. The violence cost them all dearly in men and in weapons, and with Cawar dead, the largest arms trafficker in Africa was no longer able to re-stock their armories.

Predictably, Islamic terror groups attempted to fill the power vacuum, but AMISOM forces, U.S. special operations personnel, and CIA pursuit teams used the relative peace afforded by the interclan strife to increase operations and kill anyone foolish enough to assume a leadership position.

It had been an inflection point for the nation's citizens as well. Most Somalis were firm believers in *qadar*, the Islamic tenet of predestination, and it was that faith—that they were following God's will—that had allowed them to maintain hope during the humiliation of colonial rule, the bloodshed of civil war, and the hardship of famine. But belief in fate was more than just a salve for adversity. As news spread of the warlords' deaths and the terrorists' set-backs, the population—long fearful of retaliation—sensed an opportunity for lasting change. Many cooperated with the security services, and hundreds of extremists were sub-sequently hunted down and jailed or killed. The Somali people's willingness to collaborate despite persistent threats of retaliation was yet another example of their al-most superhuman resolve to recover from tragedy.

Perhaps, Jake reflected as he took a sip of wine, they'd inherited their resilience from the land. The thunder-storms that had blown through had been the start of a proper rainy season and, within days, grass and wildflower seeds that had lain dormant for years had sprouted and returned life to the barren countryside. Ranchers who'd managed to save a few head of livestock for breeding were once again grazing their animals and restoring the herds that were the bulk of the nation's food supply and the backbone of its economy.

A sliver of normalcy had returned.

Jake had witnessed it on his last day in-country as he'd driven past the Liido Seafood restaurant where he'd first encountered Yaxaas. The wide sand beach had been empty then, but on his way to the airport, Jake had seen maybe a dozen families laughing, smiling, and playing in the surf. It was a little thing, to be sure, but it foretold a brighter future for the people of Somalia.

JAKE'S FUTURE, ON the other hand, was still very much undecided.

He had contemplated it often since the night of Athena's death. She'd given him a glimpse of a normal life—and he'd gotten her killed. It was another ache he'd have to live with on a list that just kept getting longer, but somehow each personal setback made him a little better at his job: a little harder, a little sharper, a little quicker on the draw. More than once he'd considered that maybe he just wasn't cut out for a normal life.

Athena had asked him point-blank how he dealt with all of the treachery and the duplicity. Jake said it was because he felt a burning need to protect others, and it was true, but he now realized that the treachery and duplicity that was eating at him was coming from inside CIA.

It was coming from Graves.

* * *

JAKE TOOK A sip of his Malagousia wine and looked across the crowded Varoulko Seaside restaurant as the shipping agent answered his mobile phone. It was the same phone Athena had compromised on another Friday night exactly two months earlier. The restaurant was noisy, as it had been that first night, and the agent walked outside to take the call—leaving his fashion model dining companion alone at the table.

With tousled hair, a low-cut dress, and sky blue eyes, she attracted the attention of half the restaurant's patrons, including Jake, who scrutinized her as she absentmindedly lifted her date's champagne flute, took a sip, and set it down.

And even though he'd been watching for it, Jake still missed the exact moment she slipped the poison into the agent's glass.

It would take effect in about six hours, when he would be home in bed, alone—disappointed that his flirtatious and enticing date had chosen not to spend the night. There would be no one at his side to call emergency services, no one to inject him with an antidote. The coroner's toxicology report would list the cause of death as an overdose of the drug Ecstasy laced with black-market Chinese fentanyl, and the police would close their investigation upon discovering more of the tainted drug in the agent's medicine chest.

The man who had sent so many others to their deaths would become just another statistic in a spate of synthetic-drug-related deaths over the past few years—including two rough-looking men who'd been gunned down just days earlier at the nightclub where they worked. Though the masked shooters were never located, the victims were reputed to be members of the Albanian mafia, and authorities suspected the attack was carried out by a rival organized crime syndicate over drug distribution territories.

JAKE RETURNED HIS attention to the laptop. There was activity on the left side of the screen.

Sixty thousand feet over the western Indian Ocean, a U.S. Navy MQ-4C surveillance drone was tracking an airborne helicopter. A thermal imaging camera under the drone's fuselage kept the helicopter centered on the screen as it began a wide right turn.

On the right-hand screen was a feed from another navy asset, a P-8 Poseidon maritime patrol aircraft. Essentially a highly modified Boeing 737, the P-8 had the ability to collect intelligence, track objects above and below the surface of the sea, and prosecute targets. It was flying wide orbits thirty-two thousand feet above the sea while it stalked a small freighter steaming east through the Indian Ocean.

Before Jake left Mogadishu, the Somali banker had come to him and complained bitterly that one of the pirates had taken over the operation and was no longer paying the banker. The former Norwegian commando was reputedly splitting the proceeds among the team members, just like the pirates of old.

The two images on Jake's screen converged as the helicopter landed on the deck of the ship.

He activated the encrypted Bluetooth headset he was wearing and cupped his hand over his mouth as he spoke.

"Red Flag is a go. Repeat, Operation Red Flag is a go."

A Harpoon anti-ship missile dropped from the Poseidon aircraft and fell nearly to the surface of the sea before igniting its turbojet motor and skimming over the wavetops toward its target. Jake watched as the five hundred-pound warhead detonated against the side of the pirate mothership, filling both screens with an enormous thermal bloom.

The big Harpoon had been overkill for the small merchant ship and when the explosion died down the screens showed nothing but small fragments, barely a few feet across, slowly sinking below the surface. The rest of the ship, and all of the men aboard, had been vaporized in the explosion.

JAKE WAS STILL staring at the laptop when he sensed someone approaching the booth.

"I can come back if you're busy," the man said.

"Not at all," Jake said as he closed the laptop. He rose to his feet and smiled at Giánnis.

"I was just taking care of some unfinished business."

Keep reading for an excerpt from
David Ricciardi's next Jake Keller Thriller . . .

SHADOW TARGET

Coming soon in hardcover
from Berkley!

I T WAS ALL strangely still, despite the violence.

A breeze blew up from the valley. A raven soared over the treetops. A hot piece of metal ticked as it cooled in the freshly fallen snow.

Jake Keller opened his eyes.

Debris was scattered across the mountainside. A few wisps of smoke rose into air where the snow had been cleared. Jake wiped the blood from his face and lifted himself to one knee. Everything hurt.

The air smelled of charred plastic, burnt jet fuel, and death.

Jake rose to his feet and staggered through the wreckage: past gnarled metal and ripped leather, around bundles of scorched wires, through a graveyard of personal possessions. Off to his left, a piece of the landing gear was sticking out of the snow; a smoldering rubber tire attached to a sheared-off metal strut. To his right, at the base of a thick pine tree, was the lifeless body of the man who'd been sitting by the wing. He'd been launched headfirst from the fuselage when it broke in two.

Jake stumbled to what had been the nose of the aircraft. The pilots had made a commendable effort, guiding them down onto a relatively flat section of the Alps, but they'd been given an impossible task. The crash had driven the engine, and what was left of the bent and broken propeller, back through the cockpit and into the passenger compartment. Both pilots had suffered massive trauma, as had the English couple sitting behind them.

Jake was the only survivor.

He looked to the east, across the Three Valleys. The light was fading quickly, but the warm glow of the setting sun reflected off a moving object on the distant horizon. The faint whir of a helicopter echoed through the mountains, growing louder as it flew toward the crash site.

Jake glanced downhill. He spotted something sticking out of the snow—something manmade. He knew it was significant, but not why. Jake looked at the helicopter, looked at the object, and knew that he would never reach it before the helo arrived. He headed uphill instead, driven by instinct into the woods, using a downed evergreen bough to brush away his footprints. The hasty subterfuge wouldn't survive a close inspection, but time was just another item on the long list of things Jake needed, but didn't have. He crawled into a pit at the base of towering pine tree and hid.

He was a hundred yards from the edge of the crash site when the helicopter arrived. It was a black twin-engine Airbus, large and powerful and well suited to the French

Alps. It created its own blizzard as it orbited the wreckage a hundred feet off the ground, with its side doors locked open and the downwash from its rotor simultaneously blowing snow down from the trees and up from the ground.

The helicopter slowed to a hover over the crash site and a thick rope fell from its open door. Two men slid down swiftly amid the cloud of blowing snow. They wore cold-weather hiking boots and insulated parkas, and each carried a small backpack with snowshoes, climbing ropes, and an ice axe strapped to the outside.

Serious mountain gear.

Twenty seconds after it had arrived, the aircraft flew away.

The site was still once again. The two men made their way to the forward end of the fuselage and worked their way aft, past each of the victims. The plane's tail section had settled on its side and one of the men used a high-intensity flashlight to illuminate the interior—the very place where Jake had been seated. The man spoke into a radio, but was too far away for Jake to hear what was said or even what language had been spoken.

The men switched on red-lensed headlamps and began an organized search as the sun fell below the distant peaks. Starting at the center of the crash site, they walked north, east, south, and west—methodically extending each leg of the pattern by a few paces. They were five minutes into it when one of them squatted in the snow to examine something he'd found.

Footprints.

Jake's footprints.

The man reached inside his jacket and removed a pistol with a long suppressor screwed onto the end. His partner pulled a folding rifle from his pack and put it to his shoulder. The men moved uphill cautiously—their heads swiveling in every direction—like predators tracking dangerous prey.

Which of course, they were.

Jake Keller had been with CIA for seven years and part of its elite Special Activities Center for the last two. He'd traveled the world, fighting America's enemies wherever he was needed. From warmongering theocrats in Iran and rogue politicians across Asia and the Middle East, to sadistic warlords in Africa, the mission to protect his homeland and its citizens had driven Jake to some of the most dangerous places on earth. It had never been quick, it had never been easy, but he was tenacious, tough, and a lethal threat to any and all who wished harm to America.

But today's battle was one he could not win.

Routine passenger screening for the short commercial flight had seen to it that he was unarmed, and he was too battered to run. The best he could hope to do was hide.

The searchers were fifty yards distant, sweeping their headlamps across the increasingly dark mountainside, when Jake used his bare hands to burrow into the snow. The cold stung his skin, but frostbite and hypothermia could be treated—certainly moreso than the alternative.

The men were twenty yards away. Jake piled snow on top of himself, hoping that darkness and a miracle might let him see another sunrise.

But the men kept coming.

The snow crunched underfoot with each step, but darkness and a healthy fear of the unknown slowed their advance. They'd closed to within ten yards when something froze them in their tracks. It was the muted thrum of another helicopter echoing through the winding valley. The men doused their lights and listened. Aircraft were common in the valley, but not after sunset, when the mountainside Altiport closed.

The second helicopter roared over the mountaintop and began a wide, arcing turn back toward the crash site. The two men scattered, running downhill through the deep snow to stay outside the helicopter's xenon searchlight. In just a few seconds, they vanished into the darkness like shadows.

Jake watched the helicopter descend amid the trees until it was hovering a foot over the ground. It was a large aircraft, more powerful than the first, and painted blue with a white stripe. Two men jumped out. The helicopter climbed back into the night sky and began orbiting the crash site—illuminating the mountainside with its searchlight once again.

Jake rose to his feet. He was delirious, stumbling, and shivering, but inexplicably drawn toward the brilliant cone of light. He staggered a few more steps, light-headed and in pain, and searched for the object he'd seen stuck in the snow.

He was in a whiteout when he came to.

The helicopter was a hundred feet overhead and descending steadily, its powerful main rotor slicing through the air seven times a second. A man stared down at Jake from inside the aircraft, apparently unconcerned that the heavy machine would soon crush Jake beneath its skids. It drew closer, whipping snow into the air and stinging Jake's face and eyes. His heart beat furiously and his lungs gasped for air. He tried to run but his legs wouldn't move. His arms were frozen at his sides.

He was paralyzed.

TWO

K ELLER IS ALIVE."

Misha was standing in the steam room, still kitted out in his mountain gear—everything except the boots. While weapons, drugs, and more prostitutes than a man could shake his stick at were routinely kept inside the chalet, shoes were not.

Ever.

Nikolai Kozlov was a man of absolutes.

The room was laid out like an amphitheater, with three rows of seating to accommodate the owner and his frequent guests. The walls were mosaics of smooth stone and glass that had been polished to look as if eons of waves had tumbled over them on some deserted beach in the South Pacific. Purple, green, and yellow LED lights embedded in the walls and ceiling changed colors in tune with the electronic dance music that was piped into every room in the house.

It felt like a cross between a primordial cave and a 1970s discotheque.

"How is this possible?" said Kozlov.

"He survived the crash," said Misha. "We found his footprints, but a rescue helo showed up before we could locate him."

"Were you seen?"

"*Nyet.*"

Kozlov stood, naked, and walked across the teak floor. Fifty-five years of age, he kept himself in peak physical condition, refusing to concede anything to the advancement of time. He opened a stainless steel freezer that was recessed into the wall, removed a bottle of Leon Verres vodka, and took a long pull.

"We cannot allow him to find what he is searching for."

"The only thing he's going to find is a shallow grave," Misha said.

"A second accident will not look like an accident."

"He'll be just as dead."

Kozlov took another drink and sat on his towel. "I need you focused on London."

"I'm focused," said Misha. "The advance team is there now, scouting routes and locations. I'll do preliminary recon as soon as Keller is in the ground and out of the picture."

Kozlov took another long pull of vodka and lay down on the bench. Misha rolled his eyes. It might have been 115 degrees in the steam room, but he'd spent fifteen years in an elite military special operations unit where he'd routinely deployed to either the coldest place on earth or the hottest. Wearing his heavy mountain gear inside the steam room was like a fucking holiday.

"It must look like an accident," said Kozlov as the door to the steam room opened.

Misha turned to see a woman enter wearing a bikini made from what appeared to be a few pieces of string and three postage stamps. The tall Slavic beauty was young enough to be Kozlov's daughter but most certainly wasn't. She was part of a group of "massage therapists" who stayed in a nearby hotel for the month encompassing Orthodox Christmas and Russian New Year.

"Nadia," acknowledged Misha.

She ran her hand inside his jacket and over his equally impressive chest.

"You're hot," she said.

She walked over to Kozlov and lay down with her head in his lap.

Misha took that as his cue to leave.

He took the elevator upstairs. The chalet was twelve thousand square feet of wood beams and locally sourced stone. Kozlov had had it built three years earlier. He'd chosen Courchevel because of the French mountain town's natural beauty, expansive ski terrain, and large Russian expat population. He counted himself among the group, having lived and conducted his business affairs abroad for eleven years, two months, and six days.

It was an easy date to remember, for it was the day the Russian president had taken power.

He and Kozlov had been classmates at the prestigious Moscow State School 57. Both had been star students in math and science and fierce competitors on the school's elite chess team. They'd gone their separate ways during college but upon graduation each had been recruited to GRU, the nation's military intelligence directorate and external security service. The president had joined Second Directorate, focusing on intelligence analysis, while Kozlov had found his calling as an operations planner for the Main Directorate of the General Staff. Though their careers rarely intersected, the two men had rekindled their schoolboy friendship and become close. When the president departed GRU to run for local, and then regional office, Kozlov had been an ardent supporter. Upon his ascension to the Kremlin, the president pulled Kozlov from GRU and put him in charge of a steel mill.

Though Kozlov was a chess grand master and a certified genius, all he knew of the steel industry was that the mill had been seized three months earlier by the Russian tax authorities. Yet, within a year, the once-failing mill became enormously profitable as inflated government contracts flowed in.

Kozlov channeled the initial profits back into the business. Other mills were acquired. More contracts were obtained. Competitors found themselves with legal trouble, labor problems, or supplier disruptions. A monopoly emerged. Kozlov funneled the profits through a Swiss bank with murky rules and ever-murkier ownership. For every ruble that was deposited, 25 percent went to a management company owned by Kozlov, 25 percent went to an investment portfolio owned by Kozlov.

And 50 percent went to the Russian president.

COLLEGE FOR THEIR CHILDREN

A portion of my royalties from each copy of *Black Flag* sold goes directly to Children of Fallen Patriots Foundation, a 501(c)(3) charity whose mission is to provide college scholarships and educational counseling to military children who have lost a parent in the line of duty. The organization is dedicated to serving the families of service members who have died as a result of combat casualties, military training accidents, and other duty-related deaths.

If you have lost a parent in the line of duty, or would like to help those who have, please visit FallenPatriots.org.

David Ricciardi

Ready to find
your next great read?

Let us help.

Visit prh.com/nextread

Penguin
Random
House